W9-BGF-413

THIS GUN FOR HIRE

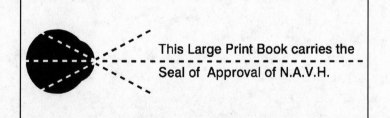

This Large Print Book carries the
Seal of Approval of N.A.V.H.

THIS GUN FOR HIRE

JO GOODMAN

THORNDIKE PRESS
A part of Gale, Cengage Learning

GALE
CENGAGE Learning·

Farmington Hills, Mich • San Francisco • New York • Waterville, Maine
Meriden, Conn • Mason, Ohio • Chicago

GALE
CENGAGE Learning·

LIBRARY OF CONGRESS CATALOGING-IN-PUBLICATION DATA

Goodman, Jo, 1953–
   This gun for hire / Jo Goodman. — Large print edition.
     pages cm. — (Thorndike Press large print romance)
   ISBN 978-1-4104-8119-1 (hardback) — ISBN 1-4104-8119-0 (hardcover)
   1. Large type books. I. Title.
PS3557.O58374T48 2015
813'.54—dc22
                                           2015012020

Published in 2015 by arrangement with The Berkley Publishing Group, an imprint of Penguin Publishing Group, a division of Penguin Random House Company LLC

Printed in Mexico
1 2 3 4 5 6 7 19 18 17 16 15

This one's for you

CHAPTER ONE

August 1888
Falls Hollow, Colorado

He watched her pause at the head of the stairs and survey the room. Her eyes swept over him and did not return. If she noticed that she had his full attention, she gave no indication. Perhaps she considered it no more than her due. Experience must have taught her that it gave a man a savoring sort of pleasure to look at her. Her pause had been deliberate, had it not? She raised one hand in a graceful, measured arc and placed it on the banister. The gesture drew his gaze away from her face. He doubted that he was alone in following it, but he glanced neither right nor left to confirm his suspicion.

She wore no gloves, no rings. Her hands needed no adornment. Her fingers were long and slender, the nails short but buffed. There was a moment, no more than that, when he could have sworn her hand tightened on the railing, gripping it hard enough for her knuckles to appear in stark, bloodless relief. Curious, his eyes lifted to her face to search for corroborating evidence that she was not quite at her ease. Nothing in her expression gave her away, and when he regarded her hand again, her fingers were merely curved over the rail, pink and perfect, and featherlight in their touch.

Quill McKenna wondered at what price she could be bought.

He had money. He had not planned to spend any of it on a whore, true, but experience had taught him that plans could, and should, change when new facts presented themselves. *She* was a new fact, and her presentation damn near took his breath away.

He was not entirely sure why that was so. As a rule, he preferred curves. Round breasts. Rounder bottoms. Soft, warm flesh in the cup of his palms. Also, he was drawn to blondes. Strawberry. Gold. Corn silk. Honey. Ash. Wheat. He liked a woman he could tuck under his chin. There was a certain comfort there, her being just so high that she was tuckable. Blue eyes, of course, liquid, lambent, and promising. He appreciated a woman who made promises, whether or not she intended to honor them. It kept him hopeful.

The woman standing on the lip of the uppermost step had none of the physical features that he typically admired. From face to feet, he counted more angles than curves. High cheekbones and a small pointed chin that was softened by the shadowed hint of a center cleft defined her oval face. Heavily applied lip rouge the color of ripe cherries accented the wide lush line of her mouth. Her eyes were almond shaped. He could not make out their precise color, but he doubted they were blue. Her hair, hanging loose behind her back, evoked the colors of night, not noon. Nothing about this woman was as it should be, and yet he continued to stare, knowing himself to be oddly fascinated.

With the exception of the brothel's madam, who wore an emerald green silk gown and matching green slippers, the whores who worked for her appeared in various states of dress — or undress, as it were. Sleeveless, loose-fitting, white cotton shifts that dipped low at the neckline seemed to be preferred, and fallen straps artfully arranged around plump arms exposed naked shoulders. The women wore the shifts under tightly laced corsets to accentuate hourglass figures. Most of the whores sported ruffled knickers that they tugged above their knees. A few wore black stockings and black ankle boots. Some wore no stockings at all and red or silver kid slippers.

Quill had spent enough time in uniform to recognize one when he saw it. The woman at the top of the stairs wore a variation of the theme. The straps of her shift rested on her shoulders; perhaps because she had not yet resigned herself to the languid, lounging posture of her sisters who occupied overstuffed sofas, wide armchairs, and the laps of contented cowboys and miners.

She apparently had no use for a corset, and the shift hung straight to the middle of her calves. There was no flash of ruffle to indicate that she wore knickers. It was an intriguing notion that she might be naked under the shift, and the notion was supported by the fact that not only was she without stockings, she was also without shoes. Quill had no memory that he had ever found a barefooted woman immediately desirable, and yet . . .

Judging by the stirring in the room as the woman began her descent, he was not alone in his notions.

Quill's gaze returned to her face, and he saw that her eyes — whatever the color —

were no longer surveying the room but had found their target. He tracked the direction to the source and discovered a man of considerable height and heft standing in the brothel's open doorway. It occurred to Quill that he might have mistaken the reason for the earlier stir in the room. It was certainly possible the madam, her girls, and her patrons had more interest in the man crossing the threshold than they had in the barefoot whore.

Out of the corner of his eye, Quill saw the madam step away from her place beside the upright piano, where she had been turning pages for one of the girls. She came into his line of vision as she approached her new guest. Quill recalled that he had been greeted warmly when he entered the house, but not by the madam. She had smiled and nodded at him, acknowledging his presence, but she had not left her post. Instead, one of the girls — whose name he never caught — relieved him of his hat and gun belt and escorted him to his present chair. Except to fetch him a whiskey, she had not left his side.

Clearly the madam had decided this customer deserved her special attention, although whether it was because he was a favorite or because of his considerable size and the potential threat it posed, Quill had no way of knowing. It occurred to him to put the question to the girl at his side, but then he became aware that her fingers were curled like talons around his forearm where they had only been resting lightly moments before. Posing the question seemed unnecessary. This man represented someone worth fearing.

The madam smiled brightly if a shade stiffly. She held out her hand for his hat and gun belt, neither of which he gave her. Her extended arm hung awkwardly before she withdrew it. She took a visible breath and then spoke. "We've been expecting you, Mr. Whitfield. I suppose this means you heard about our new girl, the one I found especially for you." She tilted her head ever so slightly toward the stairs.

Quill thought the gesture was unnecessary. Mr. Whitfield's gaze had been riveted on the woman on the staircase since he entered the brothel. Quill was not convinced that Whitfield had even seen the madam's outstretched arm or been aware that she wanted to relieve him of his gun.

"By God, you did, Mrs. Fry," he said under his breath. "I'll be damned."

"You will get no argument from me."

Quill suppressed a grin at the madam's

cheek. Mrs. Fry had spoken softly, but she was in no danger of being heard even if she had shouted the retort. Whitfield was paying her no mind.

Whitfield lifted his hat, slicked back his hair with the palm of his hand, and then replaced the black Stetson. He sucked in his lips as he took a deep breath. He had the manner of a man calming himself, a man who did not want to appear too eager or at risk for losing control.

Quill's gaze swiveled back to the stairs. The woman was standing on the lip of the bottom step. He could see that she was not as young as she appeared from a distance. He had taken her for eighteen and no more than twenty when she appeared on the landing. He revised that notion now, adding four, maybe five years to his estimate. There was a certain maturity in her level stare, a composure that would not have been carried so easily by someone younger, or someone inexperienced. If the madam had hoped to present a virgin to Mr. Whitfield, she had very much mistaken the matter. It did not seem Mrs. Fry would have made such an obvious error. That could only mean that something else was afoot.

Quill wished he had resisted giving over his Colt. It would have been a comfort just then to have it at his side.

Whitfield's gaze did not shift to the madam when he asked, "What's her name?"

"Katie. Katie Nash."

Whitfield's lips moved as he repeated the name but there was no accompanying sound. He nodded slightly, as though satisfied it suited her, and it struck Quill that there was something inherently reverent in the small gesture.

Mrs. Fry crooked a finger in Katie's direction. "Over here, girl, and make Mr. Whitfield's acquaintance."

Katie took a step forward, smiled.

Whitfield put out his hand, stopping her approach. "You don't have to listen to her," he said. "I'm paying for your time now. You listen to me, Miss Katie Nash, and you and I will do proper acquaintance making upstairs."

Katie Nash stayed precisely where she was.

The madam boldly cocked a painted eyebrow at Whitfield and turned over her hand, showing her empty palm. Quill thought Mrs. Fry demonstrated considerable temerity to demand payment up front from this customer, especially when it appeared she had made some effort to please him by recruiting Katie Nash for her house. Again, he was not alone in his thinking; he

14

was aware that the girl at his side was holding her breath.

Whitfield stared at the madam's hand for several long moments. He had the broad shoulders and barrel chest befitting a man of his height. His chest jumped slightly as quiet laughter rumbled through him. Abruptly, it was over. He laid his large palm over Mrs. Fry's, covering hers completely. "You must be very certain of my satisfaction." When she did not respond, he said, "In good time, Mrs. Fry. Allow me to be the judge of how well you've done." He waited for the madam to withdraw her hand before he lowered his. He smiled, but it did not reach his eyes, and no one in the parlor was comforted by it.

It was Katie Nash who eased the tension. She ignored Whitfield's earlier edict and crossed the room to stand directly in front of him. With no hesitation, she laid her palms against his chest and raised her face. Her smile held all the warmth that his had not. "About that acquaintance making . . ."

As though mesmerized, he blinked slowly.

Katie Nash's dark, unbound hair swung softly as she tilted her head in the direction of the stairs. "I have whiskey in my room. Mrs. Fry told me what you most particularly like."

Quill did not doubt that Miss Nash was speaking to something more than Whitfield's taste in liquor. Whitfield seemed to know it, too. Quill almost laughed as the man nodded dumbly.

Katie's palms slid across Whitfield's chest to his upper arms, and after a moment's pause, glided down to his shirt cuffs. Her long fingers were still not long enough to completely circle his wrists. She held them loosely, lifted them a fraction, and then dropped the left one in favor of taking him by the right hand. "Come with me," she said. And when he did not move, she tugged and turned, and led him, docile as a lamb, toward the staircase.

Quill tracked them as they climbed. They were just more than three-quarters of the way up when he was seized by a sudden impulse to follow. He did not realize that he had in some way communicated that urge until he felt his companion's outstretched arm across his chest. He glanced sideways at her, saw the small shake of her head, and released the breath he had not known he was holding. He leaned back the smallest fraction necessary to encourage her to withdraw her restraining arm. When she did, he settled more deeply in his chair, the picture of self-control and containment

16

while every one of his senses was alert to a danger he could not quite identify.

At the top of the stairs Katie Nash and Whitfield turned left and disappeared from view. The moment they were out of sight, there was a subtle, but unmistakable, shift in the mood of the girls, their patrons, and the madam herself. The whore at the piano began playing again, softly at first, and then more loudly as her confidence grew. Someone tittered. A giggle, pitched nervously north of high C, followed. That elicited a chuckle from one of the cowboys, then some deep-throated laughter from another.

Quill did not join in, although the woman beside him did. Without asking if he wanted another drink, she plucked the empty glass from his hand and went to the sideboard to refill it. She returned quickly, a little swing in her nicely rounded hips as she approached. Standing in front of him, she held out the glass. When he took it, she eased herself onto his lap.

"So what about you?" she asked, sliding one arm around Quill's neck as she fit her warm bottom comfortably against his thighs. "What is it I can do for you, Mr. —" She stopped and made a pouty face. "I do not believe you told me your name. I would remember." She leaned in so her lips were close to his ear. Her warm breath tickled. "I remember names. I am very good at it."

"I can't say the same right now," he said. "I don't recall yours."

She sat up, the pout still defining the shape of her mouth. "Honey. They call me Honey on account of my hair." With this, she tilted her head to one side so a fall of curls cascaded over her shoulder. She fingered the tips. "See? You can touch. It feels like honey. Soft, you know. But thick, too."

"Viscous."

"What? Did you say vicious?"

"Viscous. Thick and sticky."

"Oh." Her pout disappeared in place of an uncertain smile. "I suppose." She withdrew her fingers from her hair. A few strands clung stubbornly until she brushed them away. "I don't figure I would mind having your fingers caught in my hair."

"Hmm." Quill's eyes darted toward the top of the stairs.

Honey touched his chin with her fingertip and turned his attention back to her. "Forget about her. You have no cause to worry. Do you see anyone else here showing a lick of concern?"

He did not. There had been interest when she appeared, but it was Whitfield's arrival that aroused apprehension. What he felt in the room now that Whitfield was gone was collective relief.

"Quill McKenna."

"How's that again?"

"My name. Quill McKenna."

She smiled, tapped him on the mouth with the tip of her index finger. "I see. Finally." She removed her finger. "Quill. It's unusual, isn't it? What sort of name is it?"

"Mine." He remained expressionless as Honey regarded him steadily.

"Not much for words, are you?"

"Not much."

His response gave rise to Honey's husky chuckle. "That's all right by me," she said. "I'm thinking there's other things we could be doing. You want to finish that drink, maybe go upstairs, have a poke at me?"

He should have wanted her, he thought. When she first approached him, he was glad of it. Honey hair, in color and texture. An abundance of curves. Lambent, cornflower blue eyes. A nicely rounded bottom that fit snugly in his lap and breasts that looked as if they would overflow the cup of his palms to the perfect degree. Spillage, but no waste. Before he saw Katie Nash, this woman would have satisfied him.

Quill finished his drink, knocking it back

19

in a single gulp, and placed the glass on the side table. He held Honey's eyes and jerked his chin toward the stairs. She grinned, took him by the hand as she wiggled off his lap, and Quill gave her no reason to think he did not enjoy it. She drew him to his feet, letting him bump against her before she coyly turned and led him to the steps. Giving him an over-the-shoulder glance, she released his hand and began to climb.

Quill followed until she reached the top. She went right; he went left.

"My room's this way," she said when she realized he was no longer behind her. Quill ignored her and she hurried after him, looping her arm through his. She tugged hard enough to pull him up. "The other way."

"Show me where her room is." Gaslight flickered in the narrow hallway. Shadows came and went across Honey's troubled face as she shook her head vigorously. Quill was unmoved. "Show me."

"No. It's nothing but trouble for me if I do. You, too."

"I'll knock on every door." He counted them quickly. "All four."

In response, Honey doubled her efforts to hold him back by circling her other arm around his. She squeezed. "You don't understand. You're a stranger here. Let it be."

Quill looked down at her restraining arms and then at her. "I don't want to hurt you, and I will if I have to shake you off. And I *will* shake you off. Let me go." He was used to being taken at his word, but she was right that he was a stranger, and so he allowed her a few extra moments to make a decision about the nature of his character. He held her gaze until he felt her arms relax, unwind, and then fall back to her sides. "Which room?" he asked quietly.

Honey tilted her head in the direction of the room on her right. "You are hell bent on makin' trouble, aren't you?"

Quill had no answer for that, at least not one that he cared to entertain now, so he merely shrugged. He was not surprised when Honey, clearly disappointed by his lack of response, sighed heavily.

"Go," she said, waving him on. "But don't ever say you weren't —" She stopped abruptly, startled by a thud heavy enough to make the door she had pointed out shudder in its frame. A second thud, only a slightly weaker echo of the first, caused the floor to vibrate.

Quill moved quickly, pushing at the door while it was still juddering. He expected some give in it, but there was none. He looked over at Honey. She had turned toward him, hands raised, palms out, a gesture that was meant to absolve her of all responsibility and remind him he was on his own.

Behind the door, Quill could hear scuffling sounds and labored breathing. He examined the door; saw there was no lock plate, and therefore no key. He raised an eyebrow at Honey. This time she was the one who shrugged.

Quill turned the knob again and threw his shoulder into the door. It moved a fraction, but he could feel resistance on the other side. From below stairs, he heard Mrs. Fry calling for Honey. She did not hesitate to desert him to answer the summons. Once he heard Honey offer assurances to the madam, he paid no more attention to their exchange.

When Quill put his shoulder to the door again, it moved just enough for him to insert his fingers between the door and frame and provide additional leverage.

"Good way to get your knuckles crushed."

Quill recognized the voice immediately, and nothing about it was masculine. He withdrew his fingers.

"Very wise."

Katie Nash did not show herself in the narrow opening, but neither did she close it. Quill did not know what to make of that. "Are you all right?" he asked.

"No one's holding a gun to my head, if that's what you mean."

He wondered if that were true. He heard some more scuffling, a husky moan, and then . . . nothing. He glanced down the hallway and saw that Honey was no longer standing at the top of the stairs. He waited several long beats before he pushed at the door a third time.

The response he got for his effort was, "What do you want?"

"In."

"I am with someone."

"I know."

"I do not entertain two men at one time." A brief pause. "Unless they are brothers. I believe I would make an exception for brothers."

"Winfield *is* my brother."

"His name is Whitfield."

"That's his *last* name. Winfield's his first."

"Uh-huh."

Her dry response raised Quill's smile. He was coming around to the notion that she was just fine, but before he quite got there, he heard her swear softly. This was followed by another thud against the door, this one hard enough to shut it in his face. "Oh, for God's sake," he muttered, and twisted the knob and pushed.

This time he was met with little resistance, which made his entrance ungainly as he more or less fell over himself crossing the threshold. He stumbled clumsily past the woman he meant to save.

"That's one way to do it," she said, not sparing him a glance as she pushed the door closed behind him.

Quill straightened, regaining his equilibrium if not his dignity, and turned. He was glad she did not look up as astonishment had momentarily made him slack-jawed. She was kneeling at Mr. Whitfield's side, testing the ropes that trussed that former tree of a man into something more closely resembling a stump. He lay awkwardly and uncomfortably curled on his side by virtue of the fact that his wrists and ankles were now bound behind him. His sweat-stained neckerchief was wadded in his mouth, secured by a piece of linen that Quill recognized as a strip torn from the hem of Katie Nash's shift.

He watched her place a hand on Whitfield's shoulder, shake him hard enough to rattle his teeth if he had not been gagged and unconscious, and then, apparently satisfied, raise herself so she could rock back on her heels and finally turn narrowed eyes on him.

"Well," he said. "So it's true."

She cocked an eyebrow at him. "What's true?"

"The ropes and gag. My brother's proclivities in the bedroom run to the peculiar." He thought she might smile, but she didn't. She continued to stare at him, more suspicious than curious.

"I was concerned about you," he said.

"Can't think of a reason why that should be so."

"Just now, neither can I." Quill's gaze darted to Whitfield and then to the clothes scattered across the floor. His gun belt hung over the headboard. The man certainly had been eager. She had managed to subdue him while he was still wearing his union suit, but even that was unbuttoned to the navel. Whitfield had a chest of hair like a grizzly. His cock was a small bulge pressing weakly against the front flap of his drawers. It occurred to Quill that stumbling through a door was a lesser indignity than being laid low with a cock curled in on itself like a slug.

When Quill's attention returned to her,

his eyebrows beetled as he scratched lightly behind his right ear. "I admit to being a tad perplexed."

She stood, hands at her sides. "A tad?"

"A touch. A mite. A bit."

"I know what 'a tad' means."

"Good. It's better if I don't have to explain."

"Words I live by." She pointed to Whitfield. "You want to give me a hand, you being here and all? Uninvited, for a fact."

"Depends. Are you going to drop him out the window?"

"A temptation, but no. Help me get him on the bed and then tell Mrs. Fry she can send for Joe Pepper. He's the sheriff."

"All right." He observed that his agreement seemed to make her more suspicious, not less. "Did you expect an argument?"

She said nothing for a moment then her cheeks puffed with an expulsion of air. "Not sure what I expect. You're not a bounty hunter, are you?"

"No, ma'am."

"That's no good," she said, more to herself than to him.

"How's that again?"

"I said it's no good. You would lie about it if you were."

"Lying doesn't come naturally to me. I

have to work real hard at it."

"Are you working hard now?"

"No, ma'am."

"Katie," she said. "Call me Katie."

"I don't think that's your name." If he had not been watching her closely, he would have missed her almost imperceptible start. It pleased him that he had guessed correctly, though he took pains not to show it.

"You were sitting beside Honey downstairs. I saw you. You heard Mrs. Fry tell Whit my name."

"I heard what she said. I am no longer certain I believe it."

"I can't be responsible for what you believe. Call me Katie or nothing at all. Now, you take his shoulders while I get his feet."

It was no easy task hoisting the man she called Whit, so they dragged and carried and dragged some more, and heaved him onto the bed together. Whit made unintelligible guttural sounds but never woke up.

"He's a big one," Quill said. "What did you use to put him down?" When she did not answer, he surveyed the room again, overlooking the scattered clothes and gun belt this time. His eyes fell on the whiskey bottle on the bedside table and the twin tumblers beside it. Only one of the tumblers still had whiskey in it. "Remind me not to drink from that bottle."

"Suit yourself." She picked up the glass that held a generous finger of liquor and knocked it back. Smiling ever so slightly, she replaced the tumbler on the table.

Eyeing the bottle again, Quill said, "I don't suppose he is worth laying a bottle of good whiskey to waste, not when you can drop chloral hydrate into his drink."

She gave him no direct response, pointing to the door instead. "You are supposed to tell Mrs. Fry about getting Joe Pepper."

"Right. The sheriff." His eyes darted briefly to Whitfield. "He's going to come around soon, a big man like that. Will you be —" He did not finish his sentence because she gave him a withering look. "I am going now."

Quill did not have an opportunity to close the door; she closed it for him. He had not yet taken two steps when he heard the telltale sounds of a chair banging against the door and then being fitted securely under the knob. Shaking his head, he went in search of Mrs. Fry and discovered that the twin parlors on the first floor were largely deserted.

Honey, he saw, had found another lap to warm. He meant to give her a wide berth, but she put out a hand to stop him when he would have walked by. "If you're looking for Mrs. Fry, she's gone for the sheriff herself. I warned you not to interfere."

He frowned. "What are you saying? She's not bringing the sheriff here for me."

"You certain about that?"

"He's coming for Whitfield."

Honey shrugged, dropping her hand. "Two birds. One stone."

Quill looked to Honey's companion for confirmation, but the lanky cowboy had his face in the curve of her neck and was rooting like a piglet to his mama's teat. He regarded Honey's guileless expression and wondered what he could believe. After a moment's consideration, he said, "I'll take my chances."

She merely smiled and ruffled her cowboy's hair. "Upstairs, lover. You can nuzzle at your leisure."

Quill stood back as the pair got to their feet. He watched Honey pull her cowboy along just as she had pulled on him. It was as choreographed a move as any he had seen in a Chicago dance hall, and while he could appreciate, even admire, the practice needed to acquire the skill that made such moments appear spontaneous, he had a deeper regard for those moments between a man and a woman that *were* spontaneous.

He turned away before Honey and her new partner reached the stairs. No one was at the piano. The brothel was as quiet as it had been when Whit came calling. He approached a pair of whores drinking beer in a dark corner of the main parlor. Although they looked up when he came upon them, neither gave an indication they welcomed his attention. Just the opposite was true. Their expressions were identically sullen.

"Mrs. Fry," he said. "Where can I find her?" At first, Quill thought they did not mean to answer him, but then they traded glances, shrugged simultaneously, and pointed to the front door.

"She's really gone for Joe Pepper?" he asked.

They nodded, and the one with a drooping green velvet ribbon in her hair was moved to add, "Had to, what with you causin' such a fuss. The menfolk that took off kicked up dust like stampeding cattle. You cost us some earnings there."

The whore who wore a cameo pendant around her neck said, "The ones who stayed skedaddled to the rooms. I expect they're under the beds, not on them."

Quill frowned, but he said, "All right. I suppose you can tell the sheriff that I am

30

waiting for him upstairs."

"As if we wouldn't," said Droopy Ribbon.

It occurred to Quill to retrieve his hat and gun belt, but then he thought better of it. There was no sense in tempting fate, and Whit was no longer armed. That evened things out if he came around, and the Colt was useless against Katie Nash. Quill had never shot a woman, never pointed a gun at one, and if he were going to start now, he figured he would take aim at Miss Droopy Ribbon or her equally bad-tempered companion, Miss Cameo Pendant.

That thought buoyed him all the way to where Mr. Whitfield was being held, and he was still grinning when he politely knocked on the door.

"Is that you, Joe Pepper?"

"No. Not Sheriff Pepper. But he will be here directly if that eases your mind."

"My mind is not uneasy."

"That's good. A clear conscience is a comfortable companion."

"Who said that?"

"I thought I just did. Why? Did it seem profound?" Quill drew back when he heard the chair being moved aside. A moment later the door opened, although she blocked his entrance with a hand placed on either side of the frame.

"It seemed," she said, "like something a badly behaved schoolboy would have to write repetitively. Probably under his teacher's watchful eye."

A small vertical crease appeared between Quill's eyebrows as he gave her observation full consideration. A few strands of sun-licked hair fell across his forehead when he tipped his head sideways. He raked them back absently, still mulling. When he was done, his face cleared and he regarded her with guileless blue-gray eyes.

"No," he said. "I never put chalk to a slate to write something like that. I think it is an original thought."

"Well, damn. When I woke this morning, I did not anticipate standing in the presence of a man with an original thought, and yet here I am, practically basking in his glow. My day is steadily improving, wouldn't you say?"

Quill grinned. "You think I have a glow?" A chuckle stirred at the back of his throat when her eyes narrowed — green eyes, he noticed, not blue, not soft, but remarkably fine in their own way, sharp and sentient, a shade sly, and framed by a sweep of thick, dark lashes. She surprised him by opening the door wider and gesturing him to enter. Afraid she would change her mind, he did not hesitate to accept the invitation.

Whit was still bound and gagged on the bed, though it was clear from the state of the covers and the angle of his body that he had been restless in Quill's absence. "He woke?" asked Quill.

"Briefly."

Quill did not ask how she subdued him a second time. He suspected that a careful inspection of Whit's skull would reveal a lump or two. The man's revolver was no longer in its holster. Instead, the .36 caliber Remington rested on the windowsill, far outside of Whit's reach should he free himself. He did wonder for a moment if Whit was still alive, but then he observed a breath shudder through the big man and had his answer.

"I wasn't sure you would let me in," he said.

She shrugged. "I wasn't sure I could keep you out."

He nodded, looked her over. She was no longer wearing the cotton shift; or rather she was no longer wearing *only* the cotton shift. He supposed it was under her black-and-white-striped sateen dress, along with a tightly laced corset, a chemise, a flounced petticoat, a wire bustle of only moderate size, white or black stockings, suspenders to hold them up, and knickers. Courtesy of the corset and bustle, there was an illusion of curves, but Quill did not think they suited her.

"You dressed," he said.

"Nothing gets past you."

His grin came and went like quicksilver. "The sheriff should be here soon. Mrs. Fry had already gone to get him when I went downstairs. It appears there is some confusion about her mission. Honey seems to think she's bringing Joe Pepper here for me."

"And?"

Quill pointed to the bed. "He's the one roped like a calf for branding."

"He sure is. You, on the other hand, are still free to go. You probably should."

Quill decided not to pursue it. It would require a conversation with Joe Pepper to make sense of what the women were saying. "Mind if I sit?" he asked.

"Suit yourself."

He ignored the room's only chair and sat on the oak chest at the foot of the bed. That put his back to Whitfield, but he was confident that he would feel the man stir. The room was sparsely furnished but cluttered nonetheless. The surface of the vanity was crowded with pots of creams, perfumes, and a pitcher and basin. One door of the wardrobe was ajar, stuck in that open position by a white froth of petticoats spilling out from the bottom. Hanging over the knobs was an array of limp velvet ribbons in a rainbow of colors, all except for green.

"Huh," he said. Aware that she was watching him, he lifted his head and turned to her. "This is not your room."

"Huh," she said.

"The ribbons," he said, although she did not ask for an explanation. "They belong to one of the women still sitting downstairs. This is her room." When she merely shrugged, he asked, "Do you even work here?"

"Today I do."

"Are you a whore?"

"Whit certainly thinks so."

"What am I supposed to think?"

"Whatever you like."

"Huh." His blue-gray eyes made another head-to-toe assessment, which he observed tested the limits of her patience. Although her placid expression remained firmly in place, Quill detected a flutter at the hem of her gown indicative of a rhythmically tapping foot.

"Well?" she asked. "Are you decided?"

"I am."

"And?"

"It doesn't matter."

"I don't understand."

"Whether you're a whore or not. It doesn't matter."

"Oh."

He smiled because her features finally hinted at the confusion she was feeling. Her foot had stopped tapping, and he supposed that was because she needed to regain her balance. She had no idea what to make of what he said, even less idea what to make of him. That was all right. The confusion should not be solely on his side.

"Who are you?" she asked.

"Are you asking for my name or seeking a broader answer to the nature of my existence?"

She retreated to the straight-backed chair he had ignored and, much like a deflated balloon, abruptly sank. A soft whoosh of air accompanied the movement. She blinked. "Jesus, Mary, and Joseph."

"No," he said. "Quill McKenna." The squinty-eyed look she gave him made him steal a glance at the windowsill. The Remington revolver was still there.

"I would not use the Remington." She turned over her right hand, revealing a bulge at her wrist beneath the long sleeve of her gown. "Derringer."

"Ah. Some things do get past me."

"It happens." She settled her hands in her lap, threading her fingers together. "I am not sufficiently provoked to shoot you. Yet."

"Good to know."

"So, Quill McKenna, what matter of business brings you to Falls Hollow?"

"No business. Passing through."

"On your way to . . ."

"Stonechurch. That's near —"

"Leadville. Yes. I know where it is. Stonechurch Mining. You can't pitch a nickel there without hitting something named after the man himself."

"Ramsey Stonechurch."

She snorted softly. "Ramses is more like it. The pharaoh."

"People call him that?"

"Not to his face. Not that I ever heard."

"You know him?"

"I know *of* him."

"Then he has never sought your . . . um, services."

She smiled thinly. "Um, no."

"Have you been to —" Quill stopped, distracted by footfalls on the stairs. "Company." He cocked his head, listened, and held up two fingers.

"Mrs. Fry and the sheriff," she said. "This

is your last chance to leave."

Since the window was his only exit, he shook his head.

Shrugging, she stood, smoothed the front of her gown, and went to greet Joe Pepper and the madam. Her mistake, she reflected immediately, was in not confirming identities before she opened the door. It seemed that Mr. Whitfield had at least two friends, and she was confronting the pair of them across the threshold. She nodded to each in turn, one half a head taller than she, the other at eye level. Black Stetsons shadowed their broad, squared-off faces. The taller of the two had a silver-studded hatband and stubble on his chin. The shorter one's hat sported a sweat-stained leather band. He was clean-shaven. They both carried Remington revolvers, and both guns were still strapped.

"Gentlemen," she said, genial in spite of the fact that they were more interested in looking past her than at her. She might have been insulted if it had not served her purpose.

"He's really here," the taller one said. "Damn me if she wasn't telling the truth."

"I didn't doubt her, not after you knocked her sense in and her teeth out."

"Gentlemen? Who did the knocking? And

who was knocked?"

The shorter one jerked his thumb at his compatriot. "Not me. Him."

"Mrs. Goddamn Fry," the compatriot said. "How about you stepping aside?"

She did not move. Her mind whirled. If this pair had intercepted Mrs. Fry on her way to the sheriff's office, that meant Joe Pepper was not coming, and with so much time having already passed, that seemed the likeliest scenario. She lifted her left hand and placed it on the door frame while she shrugged her right shoulder. The movement was as casual as it was calculated. The derringer slipped comfortably into her palm, unnoticed by either of them. She would have one shot. Her chances of making it count, should it prove necessary, were improved by the fact that the guns of both men were still strapped.

"Step aside," the taller one said again.

This time she did, pivoting out of the way before they hurried past her. It did not surprise her that Quill McKenna was not in sight. Although she primarily worked alone, and entered into partnerships with considerable reluctance, she had not forgotten her guest or the reason for his interference in the first place: *I was concerned about you.* Perhaps it was not a lie. Not only had Mc-

Kenna disappeared, so had Whitfield's gun belt and gun. The chair she had been sitting on was now the resting place for petticoats, shifts, chemises, and a bright scarlet corset.

She did not permit herself to glance at the wardrobe, although she doubted Whit's friends would have noticed. They only had eyes for him.

The short one nudged the bed with his knee so that it shook slightly. Whitfield did not stir. "Is he alive?"

"Would he still be tied if he wasn't? Use your head, Amos." He looked to Katie for an explanation. "Who did this to him?"

So Mrs. Fry had not given her up. "I don't know," she said. "I was told to sit with him until the sheriff came. I did not see what happened."

He watched her closely, looking for the lie. He knuckled his stubble thoughtfully. "This is on account of that whore he tussled with the last time he was in town."

"You must mean Daria. I've only heard things, you understand. Whispered things. I am new to the house and not long for it what with the goings-on tonight."

Amos leaned forward and began tugging on Whit's gag. His fingers were clumsy on the knot, and after several attempts he gave up and yanked the strip of linen down and removed it. Whit snuffled, sucked in a mouthful of air, and began to snore. Sighing heavily, Amos straightened. "I don't see how we're going to get him to his horse. Whit's not a lightweight in any circumstance, Chick, and in this circumstance, he's a deadweight."

Chick ignored his partner and continued to direct his attention elsewhere. "What do you know about that whore's kin? Did you hear a whisper maybe that one of them was around tonight? Plenty of folks knew Whit was coming back today. Could be someone was waiting for him."

"I never heard anyone say that she had kin. Most of us don't, or we have kin that don't claim us."

Chick's dark eyes narrowed as they settled on her mouth. "You haven't taken a notion in your head to protect someone, have you?" He did not wait for a response. "Because I have to tell you, that would be as foolish a notion as there ever was. I got the sense that you're the sort of woman that Whit would want under him. Hair color's right. He likes it dark. And you're on the bony side of thin. You put me a little in mind of his sister, fragile-like." He elbowed Amos to get his attention. "What do you think? Does she put you in mind of Whit's sister?"

"Not sayin' one way or the other. Hell, I'm not even going to think about it. The way Whit talks about her, it ain't right."

Chick shrugged. "Just an observation. It makes me wonder if you were bait, you being new to Mrs. Fry's establishment, her being a businesswoman who doesn't want her girls roughed so they can't work. You have anything to say to that?"

"No," she said. "I don't."

He grunted softly, skeptically, but then turned his back while he helped Amos tear at the knots at Whit's ankles.

"Would it help if you had a knife?" she asked as she looked on with interest.

"Yeah, it'd help," said Chick. "Do you have one?"

"No, but I can get one from the kitchen." She started to turn, but Chick barked at her to stop. She tried another tack. "Perhaps some cold water in his face would bring him around. Then he could walk out on his own."

"Well, do you have *that* here?"

"Behind you, on the vanity. The pitcher's half full."

"All right. Bring it here."

She did, holding it in her left hand so she could grip it properly without interference from the derringer. When she returned to

the bed, she went around to the side opposite Amos and Chick so she was facing
Whitfield. His eyes were still closed. Except
for the occasional snore shuddering through
him, he was quiet. Amos and Chick had
been successful at untying the ropes, and
Chick was unfolding Whitfield's stiff legs
while Amos tried to arrange his arms in
what he imagined was a more comfortable
position.

Comprehending her time for action was
short, she cleared her throat and held up
the pitcher. Amos and Chick looked up in
unison and, confronted by her genial smile,
did not see the shower of water coming at
them until they were wet-faced and sputter-
ing. She threw the pitcher, aiming for
Chick's head, but he sidestepped it, and it
glanced off his shoulder and hit Amos
squarely in the jaw. Amos yelped, palming
the side of his face while Chick momentarily
lost his mind and threw himself across Whit
and the bed to get to her.

She raised her right hand and delivered a
hard blow to the crown of his head with the
derringer still in her palm. He collapsed,
arms and legs splayed, pinning his friend
under him. She entertained the fleeting
thought that she was fortunate the pistol
did not discharge because then she would

have no defense against the revolver Amos was trying to draw. He fumbled with the strap in the same manner he had fumbled with the knots.

"Leave it," she said. "Leave it or I will shoot."

Amos's fingers stopped twitching. He blinked rapidly; water dripped from his eyes like tears. When he could see clearly, he stared at the derringer and put his hands out. "Easy now. Go easy. Just tryin' to do a friend a favor. You mind if I look after Chick? You clobbered him pretty hard."

"He's fine."

"Maybe I could just pull him off Whit."

"You can try."

Amos started to reach for Chick's legs and then stopped abruptly. He straightened.

She smiled. "Uh-huh. I'll shoot."

"You ain't right. In the head, I mean. Even for a whore, you ain't right."

She declined to comment, asking instead, "Where did you and Chick leave Mrs. Fry?"

"Behind Sweeney's. We bumped into her when we was leaving the saloon. Since we was coming here anyway on account of what we heard inside, Chick decided we should escort her around back and hear what she had to say for herself. Chick's the one who knocked her around. I told him to pull his punches. You gotta know, I made him stop. We left her alive on account of that."

"All right," she said, believing about half of what he told her. "Take off your gun belt — carefully — put it on the floor and kick it under the bed."

"Aw, Jeez. Don't make me give it up, I —" He stopped. "I know. You'll shoot if I don't."

"No," she said, surprising him. Her eyes darted to the wardrobe, where Quill Mc-Kenna was finally stepping out. "But I'm fairly certain he will."

Amos turned his neck so sharply that vertebrae cracked. Wide-eyed, he put a hand to his nape and massaged the crick while he stared at the gun aimed squarely at his chest. "That looks like Whit's gun."

"It should," said Quill. "It *is* his gun." He shook off the ruffled petticoat clinging rather comically to his shoulders, caught it before it reached the floor, and tossed it toward the chair. It spread open, fluttering like angel wings, and mostly covered the scarlet corset when it dropped. He intercepted Katie's amused glance and gave her a much less amused one in exchange.

"I have you to thank for smelling like attar of roses," he told her. "Droopy Ribbon must wash everything she owns in the stuff."

"You could have hidden under the bed."

"You could have shown more caution opening the door. You did when I was doing the knocking."

"I had reason to be suspicious then."

"I wasn't carrying."

"I didn't need your help. Still don't."

"And I didn't want to give it just now. Still don't."

"So why . . ."

"Leg cramp."

"Really?"

"Yes." Quill sneezed. "That, and I don't like the smell of roses."

Amos listened to this exchange, eyes darting back and forth, fascinated in spite of himself. He carefully released the gun strap, and his hand curled around the butt of the Remington. He drew the gun out slowly.

The barrel just cleared his tooled leather holster when they both shot him.

CHAPTER TWO

Joe Pepper arrived at Mrs. Fry's establishment soon after he learned shots were fired. He was out of breath when he reached the house, and taking the stairs two at a time further pained him. He had passed his fifty-second year a few months back and soon after he heard creaking in his left knee and spotted gray threads in his dark hair to match the ones sprouting in his mustache. His wife had commented on his thickening waistline and started denying him dessert, and although he complained, he saw the sense in it when the first thing he had to do upon confronting the scene in the bedroom was remove a handkerchief from his vest and mop his sweat-beaded brow.

Crumpling the damp handkerchief in his fist, he asked, "What in the name of all that's holy happened here?" He made a second survey of the scene. When he was done, he had the cause of it all full in his sights and his stare did not waver. "Miss Nash," he said, pleasant but with a slight edge. "I thought we agreed that when you came to Falls Hollow, you would drop by my office. Nothing more than a courtesy call, just to keep me informed."

"Hello, Joe," she said. "Do you really want to fuss about a courtesy call, or can we manage the business at hand first and share tidbits later?"

Sighing heavily, he stuffed the handkerchief back into his vest without folding it. It made a small bulge under his tin star, which he did not bother to correct as he considered anything that raised his profile as sheriff to be a good thing, especially in present company. "Business, then. Mine first." He jerked his chin in the direction of the only other man standing in the room but put his question to Miss Nash. "Who is he?"

Quill started to take a step forward but stopped when Joe Pepper made a move for his gun. Quill fell back into place and showed his hands, palms out.

"That's right," Joe said. "You be real easy about coming at me. There's facts to be established, starting with who you are."

"Careful, Joe," she said. "When I asked him that, he answered all queer-like. Something about the nature of his existence. I

48

wanted to shoot him right there, but I squelched the impulse. I only mention it so you won't hesitate when you are struck by the same urge." She paused, glanced at Quill, then offered Joe her most sincere assurance. "And you will be."

Quill let her smug smile pass. "Quill McKenna." He lowered his hands when the sheriff nodded. "Just passing through."

"Huh. Maybe you do not comprehend the concept. Passing through suggests that you keep on moving."

"I thought exactly the same thing," she said, pointing to herself, then to Joe, and then back to her. "Like minds, Joe. You and me. Did you ever think it could happen?"

"Not in this lifetime," said Joe. "Start explaining. And keep it —" He broke off, turning toward the open door in response to whispering and shuffling in the hallway. He stepped out of the room and looked pointedly at the three whores jockeying for a position where they could hear everything. Even as he stood there blocking their view, they tried craning their necks and standing on tiptoes to see over his shoulders. "Has someone gone to Sweeney's like I said when I came in? Yes? No?" When they all nodded, he said, "Good. Wait downstairs. Mrs. Fry will need tending when she's brought back.

If Doc Maine does not accompany her, fetch him. Otherwise, don't go anywhere, and consider the house closed for the night. Do you understand?" There was grumbling but no mutiny. He watched them until they started down the stairs, and then he backed into the room and closed the door.

Joe was still shaking his head when he turned. His lips curved downward at the corners. He pressed a thumb and forefinger to the bridge of his nose, rubbed it while he closed his eyes. After a moment, he said, "Sweeney stopped me. He found Mrs. Fry out back of his saloon and took her inside. He had already fetched Doc Maine for her, and she was being tended when Sweeney pulled me in. She had trouble talking, what with her jaw being broken and her mouth all swolled up, but between her and Sweeney, I could understand enough to learn it was Chick Tatters and Amos Bennett who laid hands on her."

He pointed to the man lying facedown between Quill and Katie. There was blood on the floor, a small pool near the man's right thigh, and another at his left shoulder. Two wounds, neither of them fatal, although given the man's repetitive and annoying moaning, Joe found himself wishing one of the shots had finished him off.

"Amos?" he asked. "Did you shoot him, Katherine?"

Before she could answer, Quill said, "I knew you were not a Katie. Katherine. That suits."

Joe chuckled. "Like a hair shirt suits. I only call her Katherine or Miss Nash when I want to raise her hackles. Fair is fair since I am sincerely peeved. She prefers Calico." He grinned toothily at her. "Isn't that so . . . Katherine?"

Quill turned sharply toward her. "Calico Nash? You are Calico Nash?"

She gave Joe Pepper a withering look. "See? This is your fault. He said it did not matter if I was a whore, but this seems to matter."

The sheriff shrugged. "He would have come to it sooner or later."

"Calico Nash," Quill repeated under his breath. "I always imagined you would be —"

She grimaced. "A man?"

"No. Taller. Amazon warrior tall."

Calico stared narrow-eyed at Quill while she held out a hand to the sheriff. "Give me your gun. Mine's spent and the urge is back."

Now Joe Pepper laughed outright, and he admitted to himself that it felt good. Still, to be safe, he kept his gun holstered and waved at Calico to put her hand down. "Are you going to tell me what happened?"

"We both shot him," she said. "Shoulder's mine. Mr. McKenna put his bullet in Amos's thigh." Hearing his name, Amos Bennett emitted a pitiful moan. Calico pressed the toe of her shoe close to the wound in his leg. "Will you stop that? It is unbecoming. You are not going to bleed to death." She permitted him a short grunt when she toed him a little harder, but after that he was quiet and she removed her foot. "It was sorely tempting to kill him, Joe, after what he told us happened to Mrs. Fry, but you can see that it was more or less an eye for an eye."

"More or less," Joe said dryly, his eyes swiveling to Quill.

"Is that your story, Mr. McKenna?"

"I was concerned about Mrs. Fry, but I shot him because he was attempting to draw on Miss Nash."

Calico snapped at him. "You want to raise my hackles, too? Call me Miss Nash again and see what happens." Beneath her skirt, her toe started to tap. "Here's how it is, Joe. Mrs. Fry hired me to remove Nick Whitfield as a threat to her girls. He is the one snoring on the bed, but you probably know that. He used his belt to beat Daria Cole within an inch of her life."

"I do know about Nick Whitfield. I know about Miss Cole, too."

"Mrs. Fry said you did. She also said you told her you could not do anything."

Joe Pepper shifted his weight from one foot to the other. "Whit was already gone by the time I got wind of what happened. I could not spare a deputy at the time, and as you might imagine, there were no volunteers among Mrs. Fry's regular customers to go after him."

"Couldn't spare a deputy?" she asked. "What about you? Or didn't you think a whore was worth the effort?"

Joe's chin came up and he gave her an eyeful of admonishment. "Careful, Calico. I still hold the keys to the jail." He took a deep breath and released it slowly. "We were dealing with an outfit of rustlers from over Shelton way, stopping trains by pulling up tracks and taking cattle directly from the cars. But I don't suppose Mrs. Fry mentioned that."

"She did. She thought Daria should be your priority."

"Because Daria Cole makes money for her. Let me tell you something, Calico, the way Mrs. Fry looks at her whores is not so different than a rancher looks at his cattle."

"And ranchers vote."

"Yes, they do. It's just the way things are. Now, if you want to change it, maybe you should carry a placard that reads 'Votes for Women' instead of a gun. Are we done?"

Calico was not mollified in the least, but she agreed to end it with a curt nod.

Joe continued, "I never told Mrs. Fry I wouldn't do anything about what happened to Daria. I told her she would have to be patient." He held up his hand when Calico would have interrupted him. "I will admit that I could have been more diplomatic. I couldn't hear myself think for her screaming at me, the harridan. I stood it as long as I could and then I escorted her to the door. I spoke to Doc Maine later and learned for myself about the extent of Miss Cole's injuries, and then I went to speak to Miss Cole herself. She was against me pursuing Whitfield. She hardly had any flesh on her back, but *she* was the one not in favor of bringing him in."

"She was afraid."

"Yes. Afraid he would blame *her,* come after *her,* beat *her.*"

"Mrs. Fry told me Daria left town."

"That's right. When she was well enough to travel, she took off. I don't think she told anyone where she was going, or if she did, no one's saying, which is just as well to my way of thinking. You see, Calico, Mrs. Fry hired you to remove Nick Whitfield as a threat to her future earnings, not to right the wrong that was done to Daria Cole."

"I know that, Joe. I am not naïve. I also know there is no righting that wrong, but avenging it appealed to me. That is why I took the job."

Joe Pepper was quiet for a long time as he judged Calico's expression against the sincerity of her motives. "All right," he said, satisfied with what he observed. "What's the rest? And don't leave him out." He pointed to Quill in the event Calico had doubts about whom he meant.

Calico touched the side of her head. "Do you mind? I want to take this wig off. It is giving me a headache."

Joe shrugged. "Fine. I figured it was part and parcel of your foray into whoredom."

"Whoredom, Joe? You are reading too many dime novels."

"Probably."

Calico sat down at the vanity and began plucking pins from under the ebony wig. She intercepted Quill McKenna's frozen stare and heard the sheriff's deep chuckle. She caught Joe's eye in the mirror. "I guess he didn't know." She lifted the wig, tossed it on top of the vanity, and removed the thin white cap that held her own hair in place. She shook out her hair, raked it with her fingers, and then pulled it forward over her right shoulder and began to plait it.

"It's red," Quill said. "You're a redhead."

Calico said to Joe, "He and I established earlier that not much gets past him, but I suppose he felt the need to prove it to you."

That made Joe's grin deepen. He almost felt a little sorry for Quill McKenna. The man still had not made a full recovery. "Close your mouth, Mr. McKenna. There's no telling what you'll trap there. Besides, with Calico it's mostly better to go along with what comes along."

Quill nodded slowly. "I suppose." She was a *redhead*. Here was the final proof that she was genuinely outside his usual tastes. The fact that she was carrying a pocket pistol did not set him back on his heels as much as discovering she was a redhead. And not just any shade of red. Not a shade that might be mistaken for auburn, nor one that might highlight a chestnut. No, her hair was Irish red. Bright. Coppery. The flame atop a candle taper.

He watched her open a pot of cream, dip a fingertip inside, and swipe it across the edge of her brow. She used a scrap of linen to remove the black and reveal eyebrows every bit as vivid as her hair. When she batted her eyelashes at his reflection, he knew what was coming. She wiped away the black there also and fluttered them again. A shade darker than her hair, Quill saw, but still unmistakably ginger. She chose a new cloth, dabbed cream on her forehead, cheeks, lips, and chin, and removed the last vestiges of rouge and powder.

"Freckles," he said under his breath. "Of course there would be freckles."

"What's that?" she asked, swiveling on the stool to face him. "You have to speak up."

"Nothing." Out of the corner of his eye, he saw that Joe Pepper was manfully trying to suppress laughter. He gave the sheriff a sour look. "It was nothing."

Joe distracted himself by going over to Amos and hunkering down beside him. "Don't start caterwauling again. I'm going to have a look at your shoulder and leg." He probed both wounds. He was not as gentle as he would have been with an innocent. "Well, you're lucky, Amos. You have hardly more than a graze on your thigh. That bullet's lodged around here somewhere. It's Calico's slug that's buried in your shoulder, but since that came from her peashooter, it didn't do much in the way of damage. Doc might not even want to take it out."

"*I* want it out," Amos whined.

"You're not going to get weepy, are you? I hear some commotion downstairs. That's probably the doctor now with Mrs. Fry. We'll get him up here directly. In the meantime, you are sprawled on the floor like a cheap rug. One of us is bound to trip over you. How about you get yourself to that corner by the window where you will be out of the way?"

"It hurts to move."

"It will hurt worse if Mr. McKenna moves you. I would do it, but my knee aches something fierce and it's making me cranky. There is no telling how badly I would hurt you. Now get."

Amos pushed himself onto all fours, listing heavily to the side of his uninjured shoulder, and half crawled, half dragged himself to the corner. He sat up, drew his good leg toward his chest, and dipped his forehead to his knee.

"Good," said Joe. "Stay there. You have no friends in this room that can help you." Joe put out a hand for Quill to help him to his feet. His knee popped as he rose. "Thank you, Mr. McKenna."

"Quill."

"Thank you, Quill." Joe moved to the opposite side of the bed so he could get a better look at Whit and Chick Tatters. They were a sorry sight. "I am still waiting, Calico."

"Well, Mrs. Fry knew that Whit was partial to a particular kind of girl. Daria told her about a photograph that he showed her. He was real taken with the girl in it — who it turns out might be his sister — and said he wanted Daria to be more like her. Dark hair, shy smile, slim. Daria could not be any of those things, and when he had enough of what she *could* offer, he took his strap to her."

Joe darted a look at the wig. "And you could be all of those things to him."

"After a fashion. Mrs. Fry let it be known she had a new whore and waited for word to reach him."

"So you reeled him in. How long have you been hiding out here waiting for him?"

"A week. No, eight days. You have no idea how glad I was to hear he had arrived and to finally catch sight of him from my window. You also cannot imagine the boredom. They do not even have any books here. And I displaced Marisa Shreve so she had to share a room with Onisha Gilbert, and that did not endear me to either of them, no matter that I was here to help."

"All right," said Joe, striving for patience. "So he came, you brought him up here, and then . . ."

She pointed to the bedside table. "The whiskey's fine if you want a drink. Use the glass on the left. There might be a little chloral hydrate in the other."

"Ah. You drugged him."

"I might have hit him on the head a couple of times."

"A couple of times?"

"Um, let me think. Twice with the butt end of the whiskey bottle to put him out when the drops only knocked him to his knees, and two more times later with the butt of his Remington when he started to thrash around on the bed. See? A couple of times. Twice."

"Interesting 'rithmetic."

She laughed softly, shrugged helplessly.

"And Chick and Amos?" asked Joe.

"Mrs. Fry never told me about them."

"They weren't with Whit the last time he was here, but I knew they ran with him, which I would have shared with you if you had stopped by my office and told me what you were up to."

Calico went on as if he had not spoken,

which she found was a better strategy in dealing with Joe Pepper than entertaining an argument. "They showed up after they heard someone at Sweeney's talking out of turn. That's what I got from what they said. There were a fair number of men here when Whitfield arrived. They did not all stay afterward."

Quill said, "I heard it was a stampede to get out." He shrugged when they both stared at him. "At least that's what one of the girls told me."

Calico gave her attention back to Joe. "I imagine one of the girls said something about what was going on, maybe to calm some nerves, and it was repeated at Sweeney's. Amos and Chick overheard, decided to see for themselves, and bumped into Mrs. Fry when they left the saloon. They obviously have been here before because they knew who she was, and that got her taken off the street and beaten in the alley."

"Where was she going?"

"She didn't tell you? She was looking for you."

Joe scratched his head. "To take Whitfield off to jail?"

"We-l-l," Calico said, drawing out the word. "Eventually."

"Eventually?"

"She went for you before she was certain I had Whit in hand."

Quill raised his hand a fraction, drawing the sheriff's attention. "I believe Mrs. Fry wanted you to take me away," he said. "I admit I am still in the dark about that. I followed Miss Nash, er, *Calico,* to her room after she took Whitfield upstairs."

"You know him?" asked Joe. "His reputation?"

"No. Never heard of him."

"But you were concerned?"

Quill nodded, pleased that he was understood at last. "Exactly."

Joe cocked an eyebrow at Calico. "I guess he really didn't know who you were."

"Exactly," she said, echoing Quill. "He was interfering. That's why Mrs. Fry went to get you. When he followed me upstairs and carried on outside my room, I can assure you *that* is when the menfolk scattered. They did not want to be seen in the house if Whit got out."

"Understandable." He looked down at Whit. "He has been known to rampage. Kind of sorry looking now, what with Chick pinning him down like an unnatural lover." Joe knuckled his chin, thoughtful as he regarded Quill. "Good intentions don't precisely excuse your interference, although they do explain it. Maybe if Mrs. Fry had reached me before we arrived at this juncture, I might have been moved to take you in for a spell, just to keep the peace with her, you understand. I believe I mentioned she's a harridan."

Quill was sympathetic. "You did."

Joe's chest swelled as he filled his lungs with a deep breath. He released it slowly, heavily, as if it had weight and consequence. "Well, we are at this juncture, and I am inclined to let your interference pass. That all right with you, Calico?"

"It will have to be. You are the sheriff."

"So you do remember. I am never sure." He pointed to Chick. "What did you do to him?"

"Beat him about the head with my peashooter."

Joe laughed. "Well, he's twitching now. Quill, how about you pull him off Whit? Did I see a rope on the floor somewhere?"

"It's over here," said Quill. "Enough length to bind them both, separately or together."

"Oh, together. Yes, I like that. I surely do."

It took some prodding to bring them around, but eventually Nick Whitfield and Chick Tatters were on their feet, and after a humiliating shuffle down the main street of Falls Hollow, they were untethered so they could stumble into their individual cells.

Quill accepted a whiskey from the sheriff when it was offered. He was concerned that Joe Pepper's mood was too self-congratulatory, but when the man raised his glass and spoke, what he said was, "To Calico Nash. She does not disappoint." Quill tapped his glass to Joe's and they both drank.

"Another?" asked Joe.

Quill shook his head. "I've had enough."

"You staying in town tonight? It's getting late for you to be moving on."

"I hadn't planned on it, but now . . ." He nudged his hat back with a fingertip and regarded Joe thoughtfully. "Recommendation?"

"Hartford House. Nothing fancy, but the rooms are clean and they serve good food if you're inclined to eat breakfast there."

"All right."

Joe gave him directions. "You are leaving in the morning, right?"

"That is my intention."

"Yes, well, we've seen where intentions get you. Passing through, remember?" He leaned back in his chair and absently rubbed his knee. "What made you stop here in the first place?"

"I wanted a drink."

"That's what Sweeney's saloon is for."

"And the company of women."

"Ah, yes. The company of women. I reckon you did not expect to find the likes of Calico Nash."

"You reckon right." Quill folded his arms and stretched his legs. His dusty leather boots disappeared under the sheriff's desk. "How well do you know her?"

"About as well as anyone can, I suspect. We go back a ways. She was ten years old when I made her acquaintance. Funny little thing she was, all eyes and hair, hangin' on her pa's every word. I met her because of him. Bagger Nash and I served in the war together. The twenty-first out of Ohio. Came this way separately. I mustered out after Grant and Lee made peace, but Bagger stayed and took up with the cavalry. He was a scout during the war and liked it, so that's what he did."

"Army scout," Quill said softly, thoughtfully. It explained some things. "And you say she was hanging on his every word?"

"Every word. Every deed. She learned from him. Of course, Bagger was confronting a different situation out here. What he learned about tracking in the Western territories, he learned from the Indian scouts the Army employed. Calico absorbed it like a sponge."

"You know, she asked me if *I* was a bounty hunter."

Joe chuckled. "That sounds like her. If she was competing for a reward, she would want to know it."

"Makes sense, I suppose, but she was hired by Mrs. Fry. There is no bounty on Nick Whitfield."

Joe stopped rubbing his knee. He reached across the scarred oaken desk for a stack of papers, wet his thumb, and began sifting through them. "Huh," he said, studying one for a moment. He pulled it out and passed it to Quill. "Here's the leader of that rustling outfit I was telling you about."

Quill looked the reward poster over. The face staring back at him was quite ordinary, someone people would pass by without a second glance. The rustler's only distinguishing feature was his glasses. You did not see that often in a wanted poster, and Quill thought it was a reasonably good disguise. Once the man removed them, he would be all but invisible in a crowd. "Shelton area, right?"

"Good memory." He jerked his thumb at the wastebasket beside his desk. "You can throw it in there. We got him."

"With or without his glasses?"

"With. Turns out he can't see his hand in front of his face if he doesn't have them on."

"I thought they were a disguise. He looks like a mail clerk or an accountant." He crumpled the paper, tossed it in the basket, and accepted another notice from the sheriff. This time it was Nick Whitfield who stared back at him. The artist had drawn eyes that were dark, narrowed, and flat. The proportions of the man's broad features were correct, but they were set without expression. The effect was to make Whitfield seem dull, not threatening. It was not a particularly good likeness, but probably good enough for people who had met the man to identify him.

Quill whistled softly as he read the particulars. He looked up from the sketch and met Joe's eyes. "He robbed a bank? He's worth five hundred dollars because he robbed a bank?"

Joe nodded.

"And nothing at all because he beat a whore."

"I am not having that argument again," Joe said, sighing. "You heard me before. It's the way of the world. That notice came to my office a couple of days ago, while Calico was hiding out at Mrs. Fry's."

"Then she doesn't know about this."

"Nope."

"But you are going to tell her."

"Is that a question? Because I'm not sure I like it as a question. Of course I am going to tell her. It would be foolish, don't you think, to tell you and keep it from her?"

Quill thought so, too, but he had to be sure. He apologized to the sheriff for the slight on his integrity. Joe Pepper acknowledged the apology with a guttural utterance that might have meant anything. Quill chose to take it as acceptance. He returned Whitfield's likeness when the sheriff held out his hand for it.

"Shouldn't Miss Nash be here by now?" asked Quill. They had left her to settle up with Mrs. Fry and speak to the doctor. She promised to escort Amos to the jail once Doc Maine examined him. Surgery, if required, would be performed in one of the cells. The only person who objected to that was Amos, and Joe reminded him that he did not get a vote.

Joe looked past Quill to the window. Full-on darkness was closing in fast and the stores across the street were shuttered. Lamplight shone from windows above the stores, but it was insufficient for him to see movement on the street. Mostly what he saw was his office reflected back at him. He shrugged and rocked back in his chair. "She will be here directly. I imagine it is not easy getting the money she's owed out of Mrs. Fry. The old whore is not only a harridan. She is tightfisted to boot."

"I think she would object to being called old."

Joe snorted. "You've got that right."

"How old is Miss Nash?" Quill posed the question casually, but it was a clumsy segue and he felt the full force of Sheriff Pepper's shrewd gaze. There was a time he would have shifted uncomfortably under a look like that, but those days were long in the past, and the last six months spent in the employ of Ramsey Stonechurch had given him many opportunities to practice endurance. He suffered the look without any outward hint of embarrassment.

"Twenty-four, I believe. No, twenty-five. I seem to recall that she has an April birthday, not that it means anything to her. Bagger was one for making a fuss over it. That's how I remember she was ten when I met her for the first time. It was a few days after a party they had for her at the fort. She was still carrying around the present Bagger gave her. Wouldn't put it down. I think she slept with it."

"A doll," Quill guessed.

"You would think so, wouldn't you?" Joe shook his head. "No, it was a .44 caliber Henry repeating rifle. Had a twenty-four-inch barrel, but I swear, from stock to sight it was as tall as she was. Have you ever held a Henry?"

"I have. Not at ten years of age. My father would have judged it too heavy for me."

"That is because your father had some sense. Bagger didn't, not when it came to his little girl. Nine and a half pounds of lever action capable of firing thirty cartridges a minute if one took the time to get easy with it. You would be right to suspect Calico eventually got real easy with it."

"She has a reputation as an Annie Oakley."

Joe's dark eyebrows kicked up. "Better you keep that to yourself. She is itchin' to shoot you as it is. I would not give her cause. Follow?"

"I do. Thank you. You know, when she shot Amos, I thought she missed, but she didn't, did she? She meant to injure, not kill."

"That's right. Same as you, I suspect."

"What makes you say that?"

"Just a sense I get about you."

"Huh."

Joe's mouth twisted wryly at the noncommittal reply. "Am I wrong?"

"Not entirely, but I was aiming for his other leg."

The sheriff gave a bark of laughter. "Liar."

Quill merely lifted one lightly colored eyebrow and said nothing.

Smiling to himself, Joe opened one of his desk drawers and brought out a round green tin with a slightly dented lid and multiple scrapes along the circumference. "My wife dropped off cookies back when she was allowing me to have them. Gingersnaps. I like them because you can't tell if they're stale. She makes them hard enough to break a tooth if I'm not careful." He wrestled the lid off the tin, sniffed. "Smell fine. You want some?"

Quill had not eaten since breakfast, which consisted of coffee and a couple of day-old biscuits. The gingersnaps were probably not as hard. His mouth began to water as soon as Joe opened the tin. He reached for a cookie when the sheriff tipped the tin toward him.

"Take two," said Joe.

Quill was happy to oblige. He snapped one in half and plopped it in his mouth, turning it over with his tongue to soften it before he bit down. He noticed Joe Pepper did the same.

That was how Calico found them, slouched in their straight-backed chairs, legs extended, mouths full of cookie while they contemplated the one they had yet to eat as if it held the meaning of life. Perhaps it did, she reflected, giving Amos a little shove to propel him farther into the room. She remembered Mary Pepper's gingersnaps as being very good indeed.

They both rose to their feet, but not before they shoved the cookie of contemplation into their mouths. That amused her. "I hope you saved at least one for me."

"More than one. You got here in time. Who gave you trouble? Amos or Mrs. Fry?"

"Mrs. Fry. Tightfisted old whore." She saw Joe and Quill exchange amused glances, but she let it go. Holding up Amos's tether, she asked Joe, "Where do you want him?"

"We'll put him with Chick. Whit might kill him. He's in that kind of mood." He smiled at Amos, who recoiled at this news. "You heard me right. You keep away from him because I can't say how fast I'll get there if he puts his hands on you." He did not wait for Amos to confirm he understood. The truth was, Joe did not care. "I'll get the keys."

He walked to the door at the rear of his office, which led to the cells. He opened it with one hand and took down the ring of keys beside it with the other. "Give me the rope, Calico." He tossed the keys to Quill. "We will take Amos in."

"I can do it."

"I know, but let us do it anyway. Whit wants to kill you, and I swear he is mad enough to squeeze through the bars to do it."

"Thick neck. Skinny opening." She put a hand to her throat and pretended to choke herself. "He would be strangled."

"Probably, but you don't want to provoke him. Trust me. You want him alive." He waved Quill forward. "The rope?" Clearly pained, she gave it to him. "Have a cookie. Have several. You earned them."

"I am going to dunk them in your whiskey," she said sourly.

"Sounds awful, but you do as you like." He watched Calico walk behind his desk and take up his chair before he told Quill to proceed. He made Amos follow and then brought up the rear, prodding his prisoner forward while keeping him on a short leash.

By Quill's estimation, they were not gone more than two minutes, but it was much too long for Calico Nash to be left unattended at Joe Pepper's desk. She was holding up Nick Whitfield's wanted poster so the man's flat eyes and dull expression were turned toward them. In contrast, her green eyes were as brilliant as polished emeralds, and her expression was infinitely colder than those stones.

Quill returned the key ring to its peg and let his hand fall to his side. The sheriff was the target of her animus, but it was rolling off her in waves and he could not help but catch the incoming tide given his proximity to Joe Pepper.

Joe closed the door behind him. "About that," he said calmly. "I was going to tell you."

"Uh-huh."

He tipped his head sideways toward Quill. "Ask him."

"Why would I believe anything he has to tell me?"

Quill said, "Because lying doesn't come natural to me."

"Right. I remember. You have to work real hard at it."

Quill looked askance at Joe. He shrugged. "I tried."

"Not yet you haven't," said Joe. "Go on. Tell her."

Quill explained, "He showed me the

74

poster after we got here, and when I asked him if he intended to tell you about it, he was affronted."

Calico's eyes narrowed a fraction. "Affronted?"

"Insulted. Slighted. Offended."

She pressed the fingers of her free hand to her temple. "I swear I do not know who deserves a bullet more."

Joe raised one hand. "If I have a say, choose him. I'm telling you the truth, and he is just provoking."

"He has a point," Calico said, eyeing Quill. "I know what affronted means."

"I figured you did, but, well, the sheriff's right. I was being provoking."

Her eyebrows lifted sharply enough to create tiny furrows across her forehead. She shook her head sorrowfully. "Lying *doesn't* come natural to you."

"See?"

Sighing, Calico tossed Whitfield's reward notice aside. "All right, Joe. So you were going to tell me. Where do I have to take him to claim my money?"

"The reward was put up by the Jones and Prescott Bank in Bailey."

"Park County. That's not too far. I know the sheriff."

Joe nodded. "I will send him a wire in the

morning. Tell him to expect you in . . ." He paused, and Calico held up three fingers. "Three days, then. I will also send two deputies with you."

"Not necessary," she said.

Quill had the sense that it was more for form that she objected than out of any genuine resistance to the idea. To test his theory, he said, "I will go with you."

That pulled her straight up in her chair, although she had not been precisely slump-shouldered. "No." She said it firmly and in the manner of someone who would not brook discussion.

Quill was not sure if he was relieved or insulted. He decided what he felt was probably a little of both, a disquieting mix of emotion that made his belly clench, although he acknowledged it could have been hunger.

"Well, that's that," said Joe. "She doesn't want you. Besides, you're just passing through."

"On his way to Stonechurch," Calico told the sheriff.

"Lake County," Joe said. "That'd take you opposite of Bailey." He looked over at Calico, dismissing Quill. "I can give you Tom Hand, Buster Applegate, Christopher Byers, or Cooper Branch. Your pick."

She thought about it for a moment. "I remember Chris having good aim and a long fuse. Still true?"

"Sure is. Buster's about the same. Neither of them get riled much, and they will take their marching orders from you."

"All right. They can come. What's fair to give them?"

"The county's paying them, so you don't have to give them anything, but put forty in each man's pocket and they will be as devoted to you as two old coon dogs."

Calico wrinkled her freckled nose. "Maybe thirty would be better. I am fairly certain I do not want that much devotion. What about Amos and Chick? Is there a notice out for either of them?"

"No. Nothing like that's come across my desk. In fact, Whit seemed surprised when I showed him the reward poster. I think he believed he had made a clean job of it. A heartbeat was about as long as it took for him to try to go after Chick, but my sense was that Chick was also surprised. That makes me think Amos might have turned on Whit, but then, maybe not. It's hard to know what manner of thoughts go through the minds of miscreants like those three." He went over to the chair where Quill had been sitting and put himself in it. "What did Doc Maine say about Amos? Surgery?"

"Already done. There was a lot of carrying on, but the doctor persevered. I think he enjoyed himself a little too much. I do not fault him precisely, but I know it gave me pause about ever letting him take a slug out of me."

"Noted. Are you spending another night at the brothel?"

"No," she said flatly. "Marisa was moving back into her room before I had Amos out. I thought I would go to the Hartford."

"Why don't you stay with Mary and me tonight? You will be comfortable there, and no one will bother you." He was unaware that his eyes slid toward Quill until Calico followed the movement.

"He's staying there?" She jabbed her finger in Quill's direction. "You're staying there?"

"Joe recommended it. He did not extend an invitation to stay with him and his wife."

"You are still a stranger," Joe said affably. "My wife would not like it."

"Understandable," said Quill.

Calico's nostrils flared as she breathed in deeply. Her exhale was long and slow. "All right. Thank you, Joe. I am pleased that you asked, and I would like to see Mary again."

"Then it's settled. Do you mind holding

down the fort while I find Tom Hand? It was my turn to spend the night, but he will understand when I tell him who is here."

"Nick Whitfield is a prize," she said.

Joe gave her an odd look. "I was talking about you."

Quill would not have guessed that Calico Nash could be put to a blush, although she had the fair skin for it, but had he made a wager, he would have lost. Her fine, narrow face blossomed with rosy color.

And what he thought was, *Interesting.*

CHAPTER THREE

October 1888
Stonechurch, Colorado

"Have you tried talking to her?" asked Ramsey Stonechurch. "I told you yesterday to talk to her. You work for me. You recall that, don't you?"

Quill waited a beat before he responded. It was not always clear when Ramsey required an answer and when he was asking a question in order to provide his own answer. This time the silence stretched long enough that Quill was moved to say, "I do recall it, sir."

Ramsey threw up his hands, the picture of a man at his wit's end. His shoulders already filled the breadth of the large burgundy leather chair behind his desk, but now they lifted and bunched, stretching his black wool jacket at the seams. His turned-out palms were broad and square and his thick-knuckled fingers were splayed wide. A tide of red rose above his stiff shirt collar and disappeared under a meticulously trimmed salt-and-pepper beard. The color returned, rising to his cheeks, his forehead, and then slipped under his dark hair, visible only along the part line. He spoke slowly, stressing each word. "Then why the hell have you not done it?"

At the risk of stating the obvious and further inflaming his employer, Quill said, "She is your daughter, Mr. Stonechurch. I have no influence there. Ann would wonder why I'm interfering."

"Here is my point," Ramsey said, lowering his hands to the edge of his desk. He stood slowly, fingertips white against the dark walnut wood. When he was stiff-armed and leaning forward, he spoke again. "I am telling you to interfere. Do you understand? That is the nature of employer-employee relations. I pay you for services you provide for me."

"I understand," Quill said calmly. "Now will you please sit? If Ann walks in here and sees you this close to apoplexy, you will be supporting her primary reason for staying. Is that what you really want?" Ramsey remained still as stone for several long moments, putting Quill in mind of a gargoyle on the roof of a cathedral.

Ramsey's eyes narrowed, but he relaxed his arms, shoulders, and sighing heavily, eased himself back into his chair. After a moment, he said, "I do not think the state of my health is Ann's primary reason for staying."

"Can we agree to disagree on that count?"

"Probably not. You know I find it unsettling when people do not agree with me."

"Which is why you employ so many bootlickers." Quill arched an eyebrow and regarded Ramsey candidly. "You hired me to challenge you. That is what you said you wanted, and I took you at your word. Being surrounded by toadies does not mean you are respected; it means you are the head toad."

Quill noted that Ramsey's color had been receding until the "head toad" remark. He watched it flare again, but he did not back down. "Pardon me," he added. "It means you are the head toad, Mr. Stonechurch."

Ramsey picked up a letter opener and slapped it rhythmically against the open palm of his other hand while he stared hard at Quill. "Was I drunk when I hired you?"

"Not so it showed."

"Damn my tolerance." He tossed the letter opener aside. It skittered to the edge of the desk and stopped just short of falling over the side. Ramsey leaned over and drew it back. He set it parallel to his blotter. "If you won't speak to Ann, tell me what I can say to her that will persuade her to go east to school. She has her choice of colleges for women. Bryn Mawr. Vassar. Radcliffe. She wants nothing to do with any of them. Three years ago she talked of nothing else. She could not wait to leave Stonechurch. She has never been farther east than St. Louis. I was the one who had reservations then. Now that I want . . . no, *need* her to leave home, she will have none of it." He stopped, shaking his head. "Her life is in danger because of me."

"I understand." And he did. Three days ago Ann had tumbled from the depot's platform and onto the tracks as No. 486 was rolling in. She was immediately rescued by the miners crowding the platform, and her aunt had made a heroic leap to cover Ann's body with her own, necessitating the rescue of her as well, but the question of *how* Ann had fallen had not been satisfactorily answered. Ann blamed herself, for in her mind, she had gotten tangled in her skirts and must have made a clumsy attempt to disengage. She had no recollection of being jostled, and neither her father nor Quill had suggested that she might have been pushed. Her aunt's account of events was similarly unhelpful. It was an accident that was no accident at all. Quill knew it for what it was — a warning. And on this, he and Ramsey Stonechurch were of like minds.

As if he did not already know the answer, Quill asked, "What reason did she give you for wanting to stay?"

"Ach." Ramsey waved a hand dismissively. "She insists no one can take care of me as well as she can. There is no reasoning with her. I pointed out that her aunt does very well by me, but she claimed that Beatrice has not taken my best interests to heart because my sister-in-law says nothing about my whiskey and cigars. Thank God, is what I said. Ann did not find that amusing. She marched off and has not spoken to me since. We argued after dinner."

"When you asked for your whiskey and a cigar."

Ramsey thrust his chin forward, unrepentant.

"You have no shame," said Quill.

"Why should I? Dr. Pitman says there is no harm in it."

"I would call him a quack, but what he is, is a toady."

Ramsey's dark eyes narrowed as he stared suspiciously at Quill. "Did you speak to Ann after all? That is very close to what she said, except she called Pitman a sycophant."

"Your daughter has a better vocabulary than I do. I am not sure she will be improved by college."

"Mother of God. Did you say *that* to her?"

"I told you, I didn't talk to her, and she rarely approaches me for advice about you or anything else. I am fairly confident that she sees me as one of your sycophants. Probably the very worst of them since I am always nearby."

"She should be used to lawyers dogging my footsteps."

"Perhaps, but it does not mean she respects them for it, and you should keep in mind that I am not really your lawyer."

"You could be."

"No, I could not."

"You choose not."

"That's right, and this is an old argument. An old, settled argument."

Ramsey shrugged. "I don't see the harm in mentioning it now and again."

"The harm is that you will lower your guard as you become accustomed to me as a lawyer when you hired me as your bodyguard."

A deeply skeptical grunt came from the back of Ramsey's throat. "I think you are a better lawyer."

"Perhaps, but I have no interest there, and since I am charged with protecting you, it is better if you keep that in mind."

"Better for you, you mean."

"Only in the sense that it makes my job a little easier if you also remain alert. The consequence of you failing to do so could make you dead." Quill thought that Ramsey was going to raise a counterpoint after he mulled that over, so it was a pleasant surprise when he offered no objection and returned to the subject of his daughter and her rebellion.

"I think my daughter imagines herself in love," said Ramsey. "That's why she will have no part in leaving."

Quill had not expected that. He said nothing.

"Do not pretend that it had not occurred to you. You watch everything. Everyone. You must have observed her mooning about."

"Mooning? Ann? No, I have not observed that."

"Well, if that's true, you should not admit it. It does not inspire confidence in your ability to protect me."

"Your daughter is not trying to kill you."

"She might if we argue again as we did last night." Ramsey stroked his beard, thoughtful. "I want the name of the young man," he said finally. "I want you to find him and put him here." He pointed to the opposite side of his desk, directly in front of the chair where Quill sat. "Right here. In front of me. There will be a discussion."

Quill shook his head. "No."

"No?"

"I will not spy on your daughter."

"Investigate, not spy."

"Semantics. You will have to find someone else. I cannot protect you and follow her. Ann should go. Perhaps if you ask Mrs. Stonechurch what she knows."

"I already asked Beatrice. She says there is no one, but then she would. My sister-in-law's first order of business is to keep the peace."

"Yes. I would agree." It was what made Ramsey's sister-in-law an excellent syco-phant. He did not say so. The wiser course here was to keep that to himself. It was whispered about as fact that Beatrice Stone-church occupied one of the only two warm spots in what the miners acknowledged was Ramsey Stonechurch's stone cold heart. Ann Stonechurch resided in the other by virtue of being his daughter. Mrs. Stone-church came to be there by accident, the one that had killed her husband, Ramsey's

87

younger brother. Ramsey did not accept responsibility for the collapse of the Number 3 mine that buried Leonard Stonechurch for two days and left him unable to walk or draw a deep breath without coughing blood, but that did not mean he did not grieve for his brother or not think the collapse had claimed the wrong Stonechurch. Quill had it from Ann that her father grieved the loss of his brother's vitality, his humor, and most especially, his counsel, and it was during that time, when he saw Beatrice's unwavering, selfless devotion to her husband, that his sister-in-law came to take up permanent residence in his heart. But, Ann had hastened to add, when her Uncle Leo died just short of a year after the accident, it had been her father who had retreated to his office and did not emerge from his work or his whiskey for a week, and her Aunt Beatrice who seemed to regard the passing as a relief.

Quill had more experience with suffering and death than Ann Stonechurch, but he refrained from telling her that her Aunt Beatrice probably *was* relieved. Any comment he could have made about people mourning differently would have seemed patronizing, and her motive for telling him any of it was to express her concern for her father's health and not to cast aspersions on the aunt she loved dearly.

Ramsey snapped his fingers loudly enough to pull Quill's attention. "That's better," he said when Quill's blue-gray eyes refocused. "Now tell me what you were thinking." He held up his hand when it appeared that Quill meant to object. "Do not deny it. You did not hear a word I said until I brought you out of your trance. That you can think so deeply that you are unaware of your surroundings is another thing that does not inspire confidence."

"You were asking for a recommendation," Quill said. "I heard you. I was thinking about Ann and how she has, from time to time, expressed concerns about you. I had not realized until now how long it's been since she's done that."

"There is your proof that I am not the reason she won't leave. I am no longer first in her affection. I knew it. I was right."

"Maybe, and maybe she does not trust me to do right by you. No matter what you think, her concern is genuine."

"I do not doubt that it is genuine. I am saying it is no longer primary. There's a young man somewhere."

"All right. But I stand by my decision not to be the one to find him. As it happens, I do have a recommendation."

"Well? Out with it. I am supposed to be meeting with Raymond Garrison at the bank this morning. He does not like waiting, even for me."

"Katherine Nash," said Quill.

"Who is Katherine Nash?"

"I told you about her. The woman I met back in August when I was passing through Falls Hollow."

"Mother of God. You mean Calico Nash? Calico Nash, the bounty hunter?" Ramsey's brow creased. "Or is it huntress?"

"Hunter," Quill said. "Bounty *hunter*. I am almost certain she will threaten to shoot you if you call her the other. She does that a lot. Threaten, that is."

"She threatened you?"

"Several times."

Ramsey was philosophical about it. He shrugged. "I wanted to kill you at least once today, and we are not yet at the noon hour."

"There will be common ground, then."

"Not so fast. I am not certain I want a female of her particular ilk around my daughter."

"I am not sure she is of a particular ilk. She impressed me as one of no other kind. And we are in agreement that if Ann will not leave — for whatever reason — she

90

requires protection in her own right."

"Of course she does. But Calico Nash?"

Quill shrugged. "The decision is entirely up to you."

"I am glad to learn you know it. As you said, Ann is my daughter."

At that precise moment, the pocket doors to Ramsey's office parted and the daughter under scrutiny and discussion walked in. She was small in stature, taking her height and delicate bone structure from her deceased mother, but her stride, her ramrod spine, and the determined set of her jaw were all from her father. She marched up to his desk, laid a tri-folded piece of paper on the blotter in front of him, and waved an opened envelope under his nose. She withdrew the offending envelope and put it behind her back when Ramsey would have snatched it from her.

"What's this?" he asked, pointing to the paper.

"As if you did not know."

"Well, I don't. I would not have asked if I did. You know I can't abide wasting my breath."

The breadth of that untruth had Quill's eyebrows climbing halfway to his widow's peak. He knew he was fortunate neither Ramsey nor Ann spared him a glance because he could not have schooled his features quickly enough to avoid explaining himself. Anything he said would be seen as choosing sides, and in the end, blood being thicker, he would be the one they sided against. He could not do his job effectively if they pushed back at him. Ramsey alone was more than enough.

Ann Stonechurch had a pale, porcelain complexion that was made fairer by hair that was darker and thicker than her father's. She flushed brilliantly, coming close to the color Ramsey had displayed during his earlier apoplectic fit. Behind her back, the envelope fluttered as her hand shook.

"Read it, Father," she said. Her voice was tight, a little shrill. Absent was any hint of the melody that usually marked her tone. "And know I will have none of it."

Ramsey picked up the paper between a thumb and forefinger and shook it out gingerly, as if it might come suddenly alive and turn on him. When nothing like that happened, he held it with both hands and began to read. "This is from Smith College. You have been accepted. Ann, this is splendid."

The envelope dropped as she threw up her hands. "It is not splendid. I do not want to go. What I want is for you to promise me that you will stop making application on my behalf to *any* school."

"But, Ann. This is Smith."

"Father, I know. I can read. In fact, I read so well that I can study here on my own. I do not have to go anywhere."

Quill watched as Ann lowered her hands to her sides. Because her father was looking up at her, he did not see her fingers twisting in the folds of her skirt, but Quill did and gave Ann full marks for showing backbone in spite of her apprehension.

"I have been giving this considerable thought," she said. "What I am proposing is not the whim of a moment or a consequence of our argument last night. I believe it is entirely possible for me to acquire a most excellent education here. I have thus far, with the assistance of a governess, tutors, and of course, Aunt Beatrice, been the recipient of a fine education, and it was you who adamantly opposed me attending the school you built, staffed, and continue to fund in town."

Ramsey looked over at Quill. "Tell her. Tell her why it was not appropriate for her to attend the school I built, staffed, and continue to fund."

Quill was grateful for Ann speaking up before he had to.

"I do not want to hear Mr. McKenna's opinion on any matter since it merely echoes your own." Under her breath, she said, "Bootlicker."

Quill pressed a fist to his mouth and cleared his throat to cover his chuckle. Ramsey, he noted, was equally amused and trying hard not to show it.

"Mind yourself, Ann," said Ramsey.

Quill was aware he did not tell his daughter to apologize, probably because he was not sure she would. Quill harbored similar doubts.

Ramsey put down the letter. "Tell me about this proposal of yours."

Ann blinked. It was the only outward sign she gave that her father's turn of thought surprised her. "I have already begun to outline what I believe is a curriculum equal or superior to that which I might receive at any of the women's colleges. I can say that with confidence because I based my curriculum on the liberal arts studies offered by the various schools. I do not fool myself into thinking I can complete such an ambitious course of study on my own. Aunt Beatrice says there must be discussion, and I agree. I must be challenged to think in new ways about what I read. It will open my mind to experiencing the world in a different light."

"Experiencing what world?" Ramsey wanted to know. "I thought you were not going anywhere."

"Not now. Not at this moment, but someday. And when I do, I will have a deeper appreciation for the adventure of it."

"All right. Let us say that I approve your curriculum — and before we go any further, my approval of your curriculum is not negotiable. You must agree to it. I insist."

"I cannot do that. That would give you license to alter my studies in a way I might find abominable. We would arrive at this impasse again, both of us unhappier than we are now."

That gave Ramsey Stonechurch pause. He stared at his daughter, his world, as if he were seeing her in a new light. "Are you unhappy, Ann?"

Tears came unbidden. She was successful blinking them back, but her chin trembled. "I don't mean to be," she said. "I try hard not to be."

"Is there someone?" he asked. "Someone you don't want to leave behind?"

Ann's mouth opened a fraction. She gaped at her father and the flush was back in her cheeks.

Before she could speak, Ramsey said, "Mr.

McKenna thinks there might be a young man keeping you here."

Quill actually jerked in his chair. He glared at Ramsey in the brief moment he had before Ann rounded on him. His first thought was to defend himself. His second thought was to let it go. He went with his second thought.

"My father should be flattered that you think him young, Mr. McKenna, because I can assure you that he is the only man I do not want to leave behind."

"I beg your pardon, Miss Stonechurch, if I misspoke."

"If?" she asked haughtily. "*If* you misspoke? You most certainly did. I know that is precisely the sort of notion that would provoke my father to pitch a fit. How dare you compromise his health by entertaining that idea aloud and in his presence? As a lawyer, I thought you would know better than to make your case with no supporting evidence, and the reason I know you have no evidence is because what you suppose is not true. There is no young man."

"Ann," Ramsey said gently, "please calm yourself. Mr. McKenna knows he was in error. Don't you, Mr. McKenna?"

"I do," said Quill, but what he was thinking was the lady doth protest too much. He started to rise. "I have no place here. I believe your discussion would be better served if I left."

"Sit," said Ramsey.

"Stay," said Ann.

Quill regarded them sardonically, one brow arched, his mouth pulled to the side, and then he continued to the door.

"Come back here," Ramsey said. "I am relying on your counsel in this matter."

"Please," said Ann. "You figure largely in my ability to accomplish what I have set out to do."

Quill would have continued regardless of his employer's wishes, but Ann's appeal had his full attention. Still, he hesitated, and when he turned, it was done slowly, deliberately, and with the derisive smile still fixed to his face. Ramsey stared back at him, unmoved, but Ann had the grace to look sheepish. She was young, Quill reminded himself, and sheltered, and the grown-up airs she affected were to impress her father. He decided to return to his chair for Ann's sake and determined he would have it out with Ramsey at another time.

Ramsey waited until Quill was sitting before he asked his daughter, "What do you mean Mr. McKenna figures into your success?"

"I would like to know that as well," said Quill.

Ann folded her hands in front of her and spoke to her father in clear tones. "I cannot be left entirely to my own devices. I believe I mentioned that I must be challenged intellectually, and that is best done by people who bring knowledge and expertise to the subjects I intend to study. Mr. McKenna is one such person."

Quill cleared his throat because neither Stonechurch was looking in his direction. He was ignored, so he spoke up. "I am not one such person."

Ramsey kept looking at his daughter, but he tipped his head to indicate Quill. "He says he is not one such person."

"But he is." She glanced at Quill. "You are. You are easily the most educated man in and around Stonechurch." She said to her father, "That is no slight against you, Father, as you are knowledgeable in a great many things, but Mr. McKenna studied law at Princeton. He would be an excellent tutor."

"I would not be," said Quill.

"He says he would not be," said Ramsey. "And you could go to Smith."

"No, I cannot. I will not leave you."

"What if Mr. McKenna could do it but

does not want to? What then? He has other duties, you know."

"I am perfectly aware. But surely you can free him sufficiently to attend to my education."

Quill said, "I am sure he can't."

Ramsey was silent, thoughtful, but before his daughter became too hopeful, he shook his head. "Mr. McKenna is correct. I cannot make him available to you."

Quill heard the finality in Ramsey's tone, a tone that even Ann recognized as the end of the discussion. He considered what might be possible. "Katherine Nash," he said to himself. Then more loudly, "Katherine Nash might be persuaded to tutor you, Miss Stonechurch."

Ann pursed her lips. This had the effect of deepening the crescent dimples on either side of her mouth. "Who is Miss Nash?"

Almost simultaneously, Ramsey said, "I might not find her suitable."

Neither Quill nor Ann paid attention to him.

Ann rested her chin on her fist as she considered Quill's suggestion. "How do you know her?"

"We met once briefly, but I primarily know her by what I have heard from others. She is highly regarded."

99

"She has a liberal arts background?"

"I would definitely say that her education was liberal."

"All right. Do you think she will agree? Where is she now? How do we find her?"

"Leave all of that to me," said Quill.

Ramsey rapped his knuckles on the desk. "A point of order, if you please. I *still* have not agreed to this."

Ann bent and put her arms around her father's shoulders. She kissed him soundly on his cheek. "Of course you must agree, Father. We understand that. I will seek you out when you return from the bank. You can review my curriculum. When you see it, I think you will understand why Aunt Beatrice would be hopelessly out of her depth but fully in support of the endeavor. If you find that Miss Nash is suitably qualified and amenable, it is likely I will only need the occasional tutor to provide assistance in very specific areas."

She released her father and went to stand in front of Quill. She extended her arm to shake hands with him. "Thank you, Mr. McKenna. I am confident that you will persuade Miss Nash to come to Stonechurch. When you are not kowtowing to my father, it is your particular talent to be persuasive."

Quill released her hand. "Thank you. I think."

"Oh, it was a compliment." Turning, she fled the room, pausing only to slide the pocket doors closed behind her.

Ramsey Stonechurch was the first to fill the silence that followed. "What happened here?"

Quill avoided a direct reply. "What do you think happened?"

"I think I was outmaneuvered."

"She is your daughter," said Quill. "There is reason to be proud."

"She was good, wasn't she? I did not suspect that she could be so forward. I believe she must have practiced." He did not require a response and did not wait for one. "And then there is you. What do you have to say for yourself?"

"You should not have told her that I suspected it was a young man keeping her here, and you definitely should not have commanded me to sit as if I were your pet monkey. I will reluctantly tolerate the first, but speak to me again like that, and I will be gone."

"Seems to me you had your revenge. You forced my hand with this Calico Nash business."

"Believe that if you like, but we both know

you were considering the merits of it when Ann interrupted."

"I was in full agreement that protection for Ann is necessary but questioning the suitability of someone like Calico Nash."

Quill regarded Ramsey Stonechurch for several long moments, weighing his words, judging their consequence before he spoke. "This needs to be said because I cannot tell if you are denying yourself the truth or only denying it to me. Ann does not need someone *like* Calico Nash. She needs Calico Nash. Ann has provided us with the perfect cover for Miss Nash. You see that, don't you?"

Ramsey did not respond. Instead, he raised his pocket watch, examined it, and turned the face so Quill could see. "The bank, remember? My appointment with Raymond Garrison. I need to get to the bank."

"Did you hear me, Mr. Stonechurch?"

"I did indeed." Ramsey stood, put away the pocket watch, and nodded once at Quill. "You told my daughter you would take care of finding Miss Nash. God help you if you don't. God help you if she doesn't agree. I never asked you if you were a praying man, but if you're not, you should be."

Joe Pepper looked up as the door to his office was pushed open. A blast of cold air swept into the room along with an eddy of snowflakes and Calico Nash. He rose from behind his desk as she stomped clumps of wet snow from her boots. Her spurs jangled musically. She was wearing a heavy coat with the lambskin collar turned up around her ears and a green wool scarf wrapped around it to keep the collar in place. Her black Stetson with the telltale braided leather band was pulled low over her forehead. Her buckskin trousers were tucked into her boots. She crossed her arms and slapped at her shoulders, dislodging more snow from her coat.

"Put yourself by the stove," Joe said. "Coffee?"

"Yes. No need to trouble yourself. I'll get it. You get the whiskey." She tore off her gloves, shoved them in her pockets, and held her hands out to the stove. After turning them over a few times, she took down a cup from the shelf by the stove and poured coffee. She did not drink immediately, using the cup instead to continue to warm her hands. When Joe added whiskey, she thanked him. "I don't remember the last time I was this cold," she told him. "I suppose I have to count that as a good thing, else I would never go out in the snow again."

Joe nodded. "I know exactly what you mean." He stayed at her side until she sipped and pronounced the whiskey to coffee ratio a good one. He added a little whiskey to his own cup of coffee when he returned to his desk. "Have a seat when you have a mind to."

It was several minutes before Calico set her cup down to remove her scarf, hat, and coat. She did not hang them up, preferring to lay them out on a bench near the stove where they might absorb more heat. Afterward, she took back the cup and sat down across from Joe. She sipped, enjoying the warmth as it trickled over her tongue, down her throat, and settled in the pit of her stomach.

"When did you eat last?" asked Joe.

"I'm fine."

Joe reached for his stash of gingersnaps anyway. "Fresh," he said, holding up the tin. "Mary noticed my trousers were getting loose and she took sympathy on me." When he tipped the tin toward her, Calico reached in and came out with three.

"Where is Chris?" he asked. "I expected to see him on your heels. He found you, didn't he? I sent him out to do that."

"He did. I was in Kirkwood, staying with Edna and Walt Gravely. They're nice folks, comfortable to be around."

"Gravely. You brought in the man who murdered their son."

"I did, but we don't talk about that. They have other children, a few that are just youngsters. Sometimes I like to be around children."

"Really? I would not have guessed."

"I know. It surprises me. I was entertaining thoughts of moving on when Deputy Byers found me, so it worked to the advantage of both of us. He's taking care of the horses, by the way, and then he said he might stop in Sweeney's. He and I figured you wouldn't mind since we saw you in here through the window, and my business is with you." She stretched her legs and regarded Joe expectantly, her ginger eyebrows raised just a fraction. "What can I do for you, Joe? Chris said he didn't know what you wanted so there was no use speculating."

Joe opened the middle drawer of his desk and withdrew an envelope. He pushed it toward her. "You can see for yourself that I didn't open it. It arrived with a letter for me and I followed those instructions, the gist of which was to personally deliver that correspondence to you."

"Huh." She set her cup down and turned the envelope over in her hands. There was nothing to indicate where it came from. "Do you know who sent it?"

"I know who sent me my instructions, but I cannot be sure if he also penned your letter."

"Interesting. I do appreciate a mystery." She fanned herself lightly with the envelope and sniffed as if there might be a scent that would reveal a clue.

Frustrated, Joe pulled at his chin. "Open the damn thing, will you?"

"Patience. I could just take it with me and read it later."

"You are a cruel woman, Calico Nash."

She smiled. "I'm not. Not really." She slipped a short nail under the wax seal, broke it, and removed the letter. "Fine paper." She rubbed it with her fingertips. "Very fine." When she heard him sigh heavily, she said, "I do not receive many letters, Joe. I want to enjoy this." She waited until he sat back in his chair before she unfolded the paper and began reading.

Joe watched as Calico's eyebrows lifted, fell, came together, and lifted again. Her mouth never moved around the words so he had no idea what she was reading, but after her eyes darted over the first few lines, her lips parted and then never closed until she came to the end. When she was done, she lowered the letter slowly and stared at him. Had he ever known her to be dumbfounded? He didn't think so.

"What is it?" he asked. "What does it say?"

"It's from Ramsey Stonechurch," she said. "Is that who sent your instructions?"

Joe shook his head. "No. Quill McKenna wrote to me. Remember him?"

"Oh, yes. Apollo, the Sun God."

"What?"

She shrugged. "That's what I called him."

"To his face?"

"Lord, no. What would be the sense of giving a man already so full of himself another reason to beat his chest?"

"Are you sure you are remembering Quill McKenna?"

"Uh-huh. Brown hair, but mostly sun-licked, you know. Bit of a widow's peak. Had a light stubble on his jaw but no mustache to speak of. Blue-gray eyes. Tall, but not as tall as Nick Whitfield. Solid frame, lean not heavy." She put up her hands and held them about twenty inches apart. "Shoulders like so." The space between her hands narrowed. "Hips about like this. Good hands. Easy draw. Rolling walk and real light on his feet."

Joe's tone was a shade wry. "I guess you do remember him."

"Trust me, Joe. A man who looks like he does rides a chariot around the sun."

"Hmm. In that case, I found him to be surprisingly modest."

"He inserted himself into something he knew nothing about and never apologized to my satisfaction. There is nothing modest about that."

"Well," Joe said, "be that as it may, what does Quill McKenna have to do with Ramsey Stonechurch?"

"Stonechurch employs him. He does not say in what capacity, only that Mr. McKenna works for him and has recommended me for a position protecting his daughter. That is something out of the ordinary."

"You would consider it?"

"I would. He writes that I would have lodging in the house. My board is included. The salary is generous, which surprises me. I would not have expected generosity from Stonechurch. Then again, there will be Mr. McKenna to deal with, so I probably should ask for more."

Joe chuckled. "How old is the daughter? Does he say?"

"Seventeen. That is not so bad. I would not be like a nursemaid."

"How long does the engagement last?"

"There is no information about that, and no indication that he means to hire me. He wants me to present myself for an interview." She looked at the date on the letter. "He probably has hired someone else by now. This letter was written almost a month ago."

"It took some time to track you down. Chris and Buster didn't know where you were headed after you left them at the jail in Bailey."

"I was eager to see the last of Nick Whitfield."

"I thought that might be it." He pointed to the letter. "So what are you going to do about Stonechurch?"

Calico bit off a third of a gingersnap and absently brushed crumbs from the front of her vest. "Oh, I am going to go. If nothing else, meeting the pharaoh will be interesting."

"I have the sense that you don't think much of him."

"I should not have an opinion since I have never met the man, but I have never liked what I've heard about his mining practices. To be fair, it is not only him. It's all of them.

Eroding mountainsides with their water cannons, gouging the earth with explosives for their tunnels, and then abandoning it all when the silver, the copper, or the gold is gone. Maybe it's progress, for a time anyway. Some folks think so. Maybe I will come to see things his way after I hear him out."

Joe chuckled. "I am not holding my breath."

Calico smiled and winked at him. "I wouldn't either, Joe. I wouldn't either."

December 1888
Stonechurch, Colorado

Ann Stonechurch sat curled in a wing chair near the fireplace in the main parlor. She could feel the warmth of the flames on her face. She closed her eyes and welcomed the heat on her cheeks. If she summoned her imagination, she could pretend it was the sun she felt. In the summer, Stonechurch was surrounded by a verdant landscape. The mountains were there, of course, majestic snowcapped sentinels watching over the town, but there were months of pastoral perfection when the animals grazed on green slopes without effort, the hard foraging of the winter forgotten. Aspen leaves shimmered in the summer. Unburdened by snow, the boughs of every great pine were lifted to the sun.

It was not that she did not find beauty in a landscape blanketed by snow. She could. Today, though, it was especially difficult because the snow represented another obstacle on the path she had set for herself, and this obstacle was in every way outside of her influence.

Aunt Beatrice had offered encouragement when Ann first broached the idea of completing her higher-level studies in Stonechurch instead of attending one of the prestigious women's colleges in the East. Her aunt's main caution was for Ann to prepare thoroughly before facing her father.

With her aunt's approval of her plan, Ann worked on her father. She had been around mining long enough to know that a water cannon applied pressure to a hillside with blunt force. She also had observed canyons that had been scored deep into the earth's surface by relative trickles of water over the course of thousands of years. She determined then that she would be a trickle. Her father did not respond to blunt force, and she had time.

Quill McKenna's support was as unexpected as it was welcome. But for him, she would still be a tickle in her father's ear, something he would brush aside because it annoyed him. Thanks to Mr. McKenna, it had not come to that. He had plucked the name *"Katherine Nash"* out of the air and presented it as a gift. Time had seemed to slow to a crawl since then, and Ann knew herself to be impatient to set her eyes on this particular present.

Ann looked down at the book lying in her lap. It was not very interesting, but it was on the list of books that she had set for herself to read. She started at the top of the page for the third time.

"Oh, pardon me. I didn't realize you were in here." Quill began to back out of the parlor.

Ann closed the book and quickly put her feet down. She felt awkward of a sudden, uncertain what to do because she had not planned this encounter. When she spoke, her voice sounded slightly off its usual pitch. "No. Don't go. It is a boring treatise on population growth so you are not disturbing me in the least. Is there something you are looking for? Perhaps I can help you find it."

"Nothing like that. Your father and I have just come from the mine office. He went to his room. I heard the fire in here and thought I would warm myself at it."

"Then please do." She graciously waved him to the wing chair set at a conversational angle to hers. "Shall I pour you a drink? I can ring for tea if you like. I think there is still someone in the kitchen."

"No. The heat is enough."

"Very well." She set her book aside as Quill took up the chair. "I had it in my mind to speak to you as soon as my father let you out of his pocket."

Quill chuckled. "It must seem that I live there."

"Doesn't it to you?"

"I never thought about it."

"Perhaps you should, Mr. McKenna. My father will respect you more if you stand up to him."

"No, he won't."

Now Ann laughed. "No, you are right. He won't." She pointed to the pair of windows on the opposite side of the room. The velvet drapes were drawn back and the overcast sky seemed to push oppressively against the glass panes. "She is not coming, is she? Or do you think it is the weather that has impeded her journey?"

"I have no idea." His smile was sympathetic. "You have no use for that answer."

She sighed and shook her head. "None at all."

"You said you would take care of it. I assumed it would be done quickly."

"There is no hurrying Miss Nash. She chooses her, um, pupils, I suppose you would say, with care."

"You seem hesitant when you talk about her."

"Do I?" Not for the first time Quill silently cursed how hard it was for him to lie. He blamed his father, the Presbyterian minister, and his mother, the daughter of a Presbyterian minister. His brother had the reputation as the preacher's bad boy, and no matter how Quill tried to emulate his brother's sinning ways, it never quite took. Even when he did something downright awful, Israel was often punished for it, either because he stepped forward to take the blame, or he was held responsible for allowing Quill to do something everyone agreed was downright awful. Quill had finally concluded that the best course was to be, if not the good son, at least a better one, and spare Israel their father's rod on account of his behavior.

Quill held out his hands toward the fire and used the movement to cover shifting in the chair. "I believe I told you I do not know her well. I suppose that accounts for it."

"Mm-hmm. It certainly is one explanation."

Quill expected that she would elucidate and was very relieved when she did not.

114

Instead, Ann went in another direction.

"I am disappointed that she has not sent word one way or the other. Even if she cannot leave her current post, she could write to say that she was in receipt of Father's letter. She could let us know if she was considering the offer."

Quill was disappointed as well, but he did not say or show as much. Christmas had come and gone, and they were days away from the new year. He would have preferred to find her himself, but that was not possible. The last time he left Stonechurch, Ramsey had ventured out alone and come within inches of intercepting a bullet intended to stop his cold heart. It was the act of dropping to his knees to investigate what he considered was some peculiar vegetation that saved his life. Learning what happened upon his return, Quill made the decision that he could not leave again, no matter what family matter he was expected to resolve. God, but he wished he had taken up science instead of the law.

Quill said, "I could send another letter and try to find out if —"

He stopped when Beatrice Stonechurch appeared at the parlor's open doorway. She was a diminutive woman given to folding and unfolding her hands, a nervous tic that everyone kindly ignored. They were unfolded at the moment because she had them on either side of her head as she smoothed and patted her coffee-colored hair. Her fingertips fluttered, and then Quill realized all of her was a-flutter. He rose to his feet.

Ann also stood. "Aunt Beatrice? What is it? Father?"

"No. It is not your father at all. It is that woman. That woman has arrived, and she has come to the back door. What is to be done? Why would she come to the back door?"

Quill felt his lips twitch. What was it that Joe Pepper had said about her? Oh, yes. Calico Nash does not disappoint. And, Quill thought, she knew how to make an entrance.

CHAPTER FOUR

The cook was thrusting a cup of hot tea into Calico's hands when Quill and Ann arrived in the kitchen. Beatrice Stonechurch brought up the rear of their welcoming party.

"Oh, hello," said Calico. She directed the greeting to Quill, regarding him over the rim of her teacup as she hid her smile behind it. She looked over the young woman who stood beside him on the right, decided this must be Ann Stonechurch, and gave a cursory examination of the older woman standing behind them both. This was the older woman's second trip to the kitchen, and the cook had identified her as Mrs. Leonard Stonechurch, the widow of Ramsey Stonechurch's brother. Neither the cook, a stout and sturdy woman who introduced herself as Abigail Friend, nor any of her kitchen helpers, appeared to find it odd when Mrs. Stonechurch fled the room.

Calico found it odd, but said nothing, and now the woman, who at her full height stood several inches shy of Quill's shoulder, had returned with reinforcements, neither of whom had yet spoken a word. Ann Stonechurch, taller than her aunt but still on the petite side, was staring in a way that could most politely be called fascinated but was closer to stunned. Quill McKenna was grinning at her in that annoying way he had, as if he knew something she did not. That edge of secrecy in his smile would have been enough to contend with by itself, but the fact that sunshine seemed to spill from his parted lips was aggravating in the extreme.

Calico blew gently on her tea before she took a careful sip. Having made the first overture, she felt no need to speak up.

Quill stepped forward and around the kitchen table. He held out his hand with no expectation that Calico would take it. "Miss Nash," he said, tucking away his grin and putting her on the receiving end of a polite and proper smile. "On behalf of the Stonechurch family, welcome."

Calico set her cup down and thrust out her hand. When he engulfed it in his, she pointedly looked past Quill's shoulder at the only two Stonechurches in the room and raised her eyebrows. "They allow you to speak for them? It either indicates a remarkable lack of good sense or very poor manners. I feel certain it will not take me long to determine which it is." She removed her hand from his. "What do you do here?"

Before Quill could respond, Ann Stonechurch came around the table from the other side and put out her hand. "I am Ann Stonechurch," she said, lifting her chin. "It is a pleasure to meet you. Mr. McKenna has told me almost nothing about you, so I look forward to the time we will be spending together."

Calico appreciated the firm handshake and the tilt of the young woman's jaw. Now that Miss Stonechurch had recovered her poise, she seemed genuinely welcoming. Calico took it as a good omen.

Ann indicated her aunt, who was hovering closer to the door than the table. "You have met Aunt Beatrice?"

Because Calico judged the woman to be on the skittish side, she said, "We introduced ourselves earlier, and she observed my chill and wisely suggested tea." Calico picked up her cup again, sipped, and then thanked Mrs. Stonechurch.

Folding her hands, Beatrice looked quickly over at the cook before she responded. "Yes, the tea. Of course. You are welcome."

A small frown puckered Ann's brow, but she said, "Very good. My father does not yet know that you have arrived. I would be happy to show you to a room where you can change before you meet him."

Calico was tempted to ask what was wrong with what she was wearing, but she feared it might put Aunt Beatrice in a swoon and challenge Ann Stonechurch's composure. Quill might have flashed his grin again or — and this was more likely — simply shaken his head, but other than one of those brief signs to let her know he knew precisely what she was doing, he would have remained unmoved.

She had spoken with Mary Pepper about what she should wear for her interview with Ramsey Stonechurch, but in the end she had ignored Mary's advice and decided instead to let the pharaoh see exactly whom he was considering for his daughter's protector. Mary thought she had taken leave of her senses, but could not talk her out of wearing her buckskins, boots, and duster. Calico's only concession was that she packed her revolver in her trunk instead of wearing it. The trunk necessitated taking the train, which Calico supposed was also a concession, but as it was turning out be an exceptionally hard winter, she did not mind so much.

"I would like to see that room," she said. She would welcome cleaning up, shaking off the cinder dust of her journey, but she had no intention of changing clothes to make the acquaintance of Ramsey Stonechurch.

Quill said, "I'll carry your trunk. Ann, lead on."

Calico returned her cup to Mrs. Friend and then stooped to pick up her leather satchel. She did not argue about Quill taking the trunk. It was heavy, and she had paid a man playing checkers with the station agent to put it on his wagon and drive her, the trunk, and her bag to the Stonechurch mansion sitting squarely at the end of the long main street. Her driver was the one who assumed she was a back door sort of guest, and she had not cared, preferring instead to get out of the cold as quickly as possible.

The room she was shown was as fine as any that could be found in the costliest Denver hotel. After a second look around, she revised her opinion and considered it to be finer. The furniture was all dark mahogany, each piece polished so that it gleamed. The large wardrobe had brass handles, the bed's headboard was inlaid with extravagant scrollwork, and the narrow chest of drawers had porcelain knobs. A silk dressing screen was open in one corner of the room, and a long looking glass mounted in an elaborately carved frame stood next to it.

"Where do you want this?" asked Quill, referring to the trunk resting on his shoulder.

"Foot of the bed's fine." While he was setting it down, Calico pointed to the door beside the wardrobe. "Where does that lead?" she asked Ann.

"The bathing room." She walked over, opened the door, and allowed Calico to see inside. "Father stayed in a hotel in Georgetown, here in Colorado, I mean. Hot and cold running water and a bathtub that could be filled from the tap. He would not let it rest until he had the same. The house has grown like Topsy."

"I imagine it has," said Calico without any hint of sarcasm. She supposed if she were as rich as Midas, she might be tempted to have marble-topped sinks and a bathtub bigger than a horse trough. She dropped her satchel and went to have a closer look.

"All the linens you need are in the cupboard. Soap, too. If you prefer bath salts, I can have some sent up. One of the maids will be along directly to set a fire for you. Aunt Beatrice will already have seen to that. I will tell my father that you are here. How much time will you require?"

"Ten minutes. Maybe less."

Ann frowned. "Oh, but —"

Quill interrupted. "Miss Nash will need at least an hour." And before Calico could contradict him, he said, "Tell your father, Miss Stonechurch. He's been waiting almost as impatiently as you."

Ann nodded. She gave Calico a quick, encouraging smile, and hurried out.

As soon as Quill judged she was out of hearing range, he rounded on Calico. "I know you own at least one dress that would have been suitable for travel." When she simply stared at him, he reminded her. "Black and white. Stripes. You were wearing it the day I met you, or at least you were wearing it for part of the day."

"Well, I did not think it was suitable for travel, and neither would you if you had to wear it."

Quill walked over to the door, closed it, and leaned a shoulder against it to prevent a sudden intrusion by the maid coming to set the fire. "Do you really intend to wear trousers to sit for your interview?"

"Why shouldn't I? We will be talking about

protecting his daughter. He needs to know I can do it."

"He knows you can do it because I told him you can. He knows you're Calico Nash, and he knows your reputation. His daughter, however, knows none of that. To her, you are Katherine Nash, a teacher who is here to interview for a position as her private tutor. *That* is your role this time. No wig, no theatrical face paint to tart yourself up, but you do have to dress in a manner becoming a serious woman of studies."

Calico set her hands on her hips and glared at him. "Don't you think that should have been explained in someone's letter?"

"Until I saw you standing there in the kitchen, I thought it had."

"Obviously not."

Quill settled his blue-gray eyes on hers and held the stare, grim and sober. "I want Stonechurch to hire you. His daughter needs someone looking out for her as much as he does, perhaps more since hurting her would be the surest means of killing him. He and I believe there have already been warning shots across that bow."

"That's why you're here?" she asked. "You're his bodyguard?"

"Yes. Ann thinks I am his lawyer. Sometimes he likes to think the same thing."

"Mother of God," she said under her breath. She removed her hat, tossed it on the bed, and began to unbutton her long coat. "You will have to tell me all of it when we have more time. You need to go because I need to wash and change my clothes. And to be clear, the money is good, very good, but I don't have any qualifications as a teacher. Hell, I don't have a paper that says I graduated the eighth grade. What I know about the education of a young woman like Miss Stonechurch would not spill out of a thimble if I jammed my thumb in it."

"Let me worry about that."

Calico paused in unwinding her green woolen scarf. "Did I say I was worried? Because I'm not. I did not know anything about whoring either and I managed that well enough."

"That was for an evening. This will be weeks, even months."

"How long have you been here?"

"Ten months give or take a week."

"And is someone really trying to kill Stonechurch, or did he hire you as a precaution against that happening because he is so universally disliked?"

"There have been threats and two serious attempts."

She nodded thoughtfully, finished removing her scarf, and laid it on the bed. "All right. Go."

"Not just yet. Where is your pistol? I can see that it's not under your sleeve."

"In my bag."

Without asking permission, Quill opened the satchel. The derringer was lying on top. He took it. "A precaution. In the event someone else has hired you to shoot Ramsey in the interview."

"I do not think someone would have to hire me." In response to the wry look he gave her, she pointed to her trunk. "It is up to you if you want to seize my Colt. I won't be carrying it under my dress, but you might not take me at my word."

He opened the trunk, lifted the Colt Model 1877 double-action .38 caliber revolver by its pearl grip, and looked over his shoulder at Calico. "Lightning."

"That's what it's called. Shoots fast and true."

Quill replaced it in the trunk and closed the lid. "Do you have any other weapons?"

"There is a Winchester rifle in there under a false bottom." She shrugged when he cocked an eyebrow at her and slowly shook his head. "I think it is important to be prepared."

"Is there a cannon being delivered later?"

She gave him a flat smile and pointed to the door again. "Out."

He stood and pocketed the derringer. "Going." He opened the door and held it that way when Molly the maid appeared carrying kindling and a box of matches. He let her pass and paused another beat. "Thank you," he said.

"It's nothing, sir, but you are quite welcome," said Molly.

Quill did not correct the girl's impression that he was speaking to her. Over the top of the maid's head, he caught Calico's eye to make certain she knew that she was the one he was thanking. From the look of mild annoyance on her face, he guessed that it either did not matter to her or that she thought he was not moving fast enough. Congratulating himself for relieving her of her pistol, he ducked into the hallway.

Ramsey Stonechurch stood as the pocket doors to his study parted and Katherine Nash was shown in. He motioned her forward, waved his sister-in-law off, and invited her to sit.

"Miss Nash," he said, his dark brown eyes making a study of her from head to toe. She was wearing a simply tailored black wool gown, cinched at the waist by a black silk scarf that she wore as a belt. The gown had long sleeves, a white collar, and another silk scarf that was secured at her throat by a cameo brooch and fell down the center of the bodice like a man's ascot. "I think my sister-in-law was pulling my leg, which is astonishing since she has almost no sense of humor. I look forward to telling her that she made a very good job of it."

Calico had not yet taken the chair she was offered. One hand lay lightly across the curved back. "How do you mean, sir?" she asked as if she did not know.

He indicated the whole of her person with a sweep of his hand. "Your attire. Beatrice would have me believe you arrived in buckskin trousers and a Stetson and intended to sit for the interview in that mode of dress."

"Really? I can't imagine."

"It was difficult for me also. Please, sit."

Calico did and fixed a polite smile as he did the same. She waited for him to begin.

Ramsey picked up his letter opener and turned it over in his hand as he spoke. "I received the first threat on my life some twelve months back. It came at a time when there was no obvious reason for it. No accidents at the mines, no grumbling about wages or hours. I dismissed it."

Calico thought it was interesting that there

was no preamble to this information. Ramsey Stonechurch plunged in, expecting that she would know who he was and his role in the town. She did, but it rubbed her wrong that he was so confident of it.

"There was a second threat perhaps a month later, suggesting that I should leave town and turn over the operations to the miners. That was not going to happen, and when I gave no indication that it would, there was an accident with my rig that could have been fatal if I had not been able to leap free of it. It went over the hillside, injuring the horse so that she had to be put down. It was shortly after that that I hired Mr. McKenna. He says he knows you."

"We are acquainted," she said. "He should not presume to say he knows me."

Ramsey tapped the letter opener against the edge of the desk. His mien was thoughtful. "Yes. I take your point." The tapping stopped and he laid the opener aside. "Mr. McKenna and I were discussing the merits of my daughter having her own protection versus her leaving Stonechurch altogether when Ann came to me with a proposal. She suggested completing a curriculum of liberal arts studies right here at home. She does not want to leave me, she says. Concern for my health is the reason she gives. I think there is a young man somewhere pulling on her like a magnet, but whether or not that's true, she is adamant in her refusal to leave.

"Mr. McKenna had proposed your name before Ann arrived with her scheme, but I was not yet set on the matter. Once he heard Ann's intentions, he made a persuasive argument for you using the cover of educator to keep her safe. Naturally I prefer to have Ann out of harm's way, but I fail to see how that can be accomplished at present. What I think might turn the trick is if you could discover the identity of the young man. If he were, say, removed as an influence, Ann could then be persuaded to leave."

"Removed? Kill him, you mean?" Calico thought it was to his credit that Ramsey Stonechurch was startled by the question. At least he appeared to be, she amended as cynicism asserted itself.

"Hardly." He frowned deeply. "Would you do that?"

"Hardly."

"I confess that is a relief."

"Unless the young man proves to be a mortal threat to your daughter, of course, then I will shoot him, probably to wound, not kill, depending on the circumstances . . . and my mood at the time."

Ramsey blew out a long breath, watching her closely, trying to gauge how serious she was about the last thing she said. "I think I would like a drink. Sherry for you?"

"Whatever you are drinking will be fine."

"I am drinking whiskey."

"Then whiskey is fine."

He got up and went to the drinks cabinet, where he poured liquor into two cut-glass tumblers. He filled them evenly and still allowed her to choose. He did not return to his chair but hitched a hip on the edge of his desk instead. "I was thinking more in terms of a bribe. Money. A job away from here. Whatever would motivate him to leave."

"Have you and Mr. McKenna identified any candidates for your daughter's affection?"

"None. Mr. McKenna is not convinced that a young man such as I described exists. And to your next question, he has eliminated several men I proposed who might make threats against me but has not identified new ones. You would be charged with the same task. This person could be a danger to Ann."

"All right." She sipped her whiskey, smiled. "This is good. Very good."

"It is a pleasure to share a drink with a

woman who appreciates fine spirits."

She raised her glass slightly. "That appreciation comes from sampling too much liquor that could make you go blind."

Ramsey laughed with genuine enjoyment. "You really are Calico Nash. I haven't been entirely certain."

"It happens."

"Is it true that you tracked down Fairley Maxwell all the way to Brown's Hole and held him there until Dan Butler's posse caught up with you?"

"That is what the *Denver News* reported."

"And that is a modest reply."

She finished her drink and rolled the tumbler between her palms. "Do you have questions for me regarding my ability to take on this assignment, something that will help you determine whether or not hiring me is what you really want to do?"

"I appreciate you raising the subject. Actually, I do have questions. In order for this to work, Ann must be convinced that you are, in fact, a teacher. My daughter is quite a bright star, as was her dear mother, and if her suspicions are aroused, nothing will keep her from putting them to rest."

"A trait, I assume, that can be traced to you."

"And you would be right. My question,

then, is how will you manage this business of serving as Ann's tutor? Have you any experience in this regard?"

"All my experience is as a student, not as a teacher, unless you count the time I instructed Zeke Blackthorn on the proper way to clean and grease his rifle and how to shoot long range with it."

Ramsey cleared his throat. "No."

It was tempting to laugh outright, but Calico resisted the urge. "In that case, I stand by my first statement. I have only been a student. However, you need to know that I have had the good fortune to be the student of many different teachers, every one of them with considerable knowledge in their area of interest. Not *all* of my education has been in subjects that you and others would find, shall we say, unusual. I hasten to add that this view is largely on account of me being a woman and that the same tutelage in scouting, tracking, and shooting would not raise a single eyebrow if I were a man."

Ramsey withheld comment and merely said, "Go on."

"I do not want to misrepresent myself. What would pass for my formal education in no way approximates what your daughter has experienced, and as you said, she is a bright star. No one ever said that about me."

"Not even your father?"

"Not in my hearing, not that anyone has ever told me." She thought that he regarded her through eyes that were oddly sympathetic. It both surprised and discomfited her. "Do not mistake me, Mr. Stonechurch. No one has ever called me a dullard either. If there is a situation where I cannot hold my own, then I have not encountered it. That is not a boast. It is a fact."

Calico looked around the study and pointed out the leather-bound books that lined floor-to-ceiling shelves on two walls. "You have the tools I will require here to support the deception you have in mind. I will be a student all of my life. I enjoy reading, Mr. Stonechurch."

"Hmm." The sound vibrated at the back of Ramsey's throat. His expression remained considering. "Ann cannot know about the threats against me or that because of some recent events, Mr. McKenna and I suspect she is also a target."

"She was hurt?"

"Narrow escapes both times. A spill from the train platform and, more recently, the collapse of the book stacks in the town library that might have crushed her if her aunt had not pushed her out of the way."

"I understand. Warnings, then. To you."

"Ann already worries unnecessarily about my health, and any inkling that I am in danger will make her dig in her heels even deeper." Ramsey tapped his belly with his fingertips. "From time to time I experience severe discomfort of the stomach and . . . let us leave it at the stomach. My doctor has diagnosed an ulcer, for which he recommends the most vile-tasting concoction as was ever conceived. It is Dr. Pitman's contention that these spells of physical stress are also putting a strain on my heart." Beneath his mustache, his mouth twisted to one side, revealing his disgust. "He shared this with Ann and Beatrice, and now neither of them will let it be. The comfort I derive from the occasional glass of whiskey and a fine cigar has been seriously compromised. You smile, Miss Nash, but I assure you it is true.

"The first bout I experienced happened just days before the arrival of Mr. Mc-Kenna. Ann, who took charge of every aspect of my care during that time, argued that I should not be allowed out of bed to greet him. She was being overly cautious, of course, because under her care, I recovered quickly. No one else was allowed to do anything for me. Even her aunt, who provided exemplary care for my brother after his accident, was forbidden to help."

"Perhaps the doctor's snake oil also worked."

"Hah. I swallowed exactly two spoonfuls of the stuff. I dumped the contents when I was left alone and filled the bottle with chamomile tea, molasses, and a touch of whiskey. It still tastes vile, but at least I know what is in it and it will not kill me."

Calico smiled and there was no effort in it. No strain. That disturbed her. It was unexpected, as well as unwanted, that she felt something that might be akin to liking for the man.

Ramsey Stonechurch continued, "As I said, my druthers are to put Ann on a train and send her back East. I could probably get her there if shackles were not out of the question, but she would either make her way back or remain and hate me for the rest of my life."

"I do not know if you will welcome this observation, Mr. Stonechurch, but regardless of your daughter's reasons for staying here, what she has proposed is a rather elegant compromise."

"I would like to claim some influence," he said, "but I have no experience with elegance or compromise. What I do have is sense enough to know what is in my best interests. Right now, Miss Nash, that would be you."

Calico heard no dry humor there. He meant it as seriously as he said it. She stood when he did.

"The job is yours," he told her, holding out his hand.

Calico put out her hand in turn. "And I accept."

"Good." He held her hand a moment longer and then released it. "If it is to your liking, you may sit with us at dinner tonight, but we will all understand if you choose to take the evening meal in your room."

"It is kind of you to think of that. I do prefer to eat alone tonight."

"As you wish."

Calico stood. When she turned to leave, he fell in step beside her and escorted her to the doors. As she climbed the stairs to her room, she was struck by the sensation of his eyes following her all the way to the landing.

Quill was lounging comfortably on the padded window bench in Calico's room when she walked in, and he suppressed the urge to stand to greet her. At the very least, he suspected she would give him the gimlet eye. She might also threaten to shoot him. It was difficult to know the bent of her mind as she closed the door and leaned against it. She also closed her eyes and kept them closed while she sipped a breath of air and then expelled it slowly.

By his reckoning, a full thirty seconds passed before she looked in his direction. Her features were dominated by fatigue. If she was out of sorts with him, she was too tired to show it. Quill shifted from the corner of the bench and sat up a little straighter. One leg remained outstretched along the length of the seat, but he dropped the other over the side and extended it until his heel rested on the floor. His arms were crossed loosely in front of him, and he unfolded them and set his hands together in his lap.

"Do you want me to leave?" he asked. The shake of her head was so slight that he would have missed it if he had not been watching her closely. "Then will you sit down?"

"A moment," she said.

Quill realized she was looking more through him than at him. He waited for her eyes to focus and her thinking to catch up with the rest of her. She seemed very far away just then, and the distance did not close until she pressed three fingers to her temple and blinked several times.

"Ramsey Stonechurch is exhausting," she said, pushing away from the door. "You could have warned me." She crossed the room to the window seat, stared pointedly at his outstretched leg until he moved it, and then sat in the corner opposite him. Beneath her skirt, she drew her knees toward her chest and smoothed the material over them. She clasped her hands around her folded legs. "He is also not entirely unlikable. I did not expect that either."

Quill thought she looked as if she were still trying to make sense of it. "Would you have believed me if I told you that?"

"About him not being a complete despot? Certainly not."

"There you have it. Did he hire you? Ann is on tenterhooks."

She arched an eyebrow at him. "Interesting, then, that it is you who are here and not Miss Stonechurch."

"One of us respects closed doors."

Her smile was wry. "Of course. The answer to your question is yes, he did offer me the job. That saves me from going after Felix Marion. His brothers broke him out of jail. He was being held in Cheyenne, but there is thinking that the gang's moved south into Colorado. Joe Pepper offered me the chance. More trouble. Less money."

"So you would have joined a posse?"

"Maybe. I don't always. They make too much noise. But I might have offered to scout for them, depending on who was in charge." She looked at him oddly. "You seem relieved."

Quill did not realize he had given himself away. He did not shy away from the truth, not that he had any real choice. "I am. I suppose I wouldn't have been comfortable with the idea of you going after the Marion brothers on your own. If you scout for the posse, at least you would have them watching your back."

"Not that your comfort means anything to me, but have you ever ridden with a posse?"

"The largest. U.S. Army Cavalry." He was very much aware of her narrowing stare as she studied him for the lie. He held up his right hand as if he were prepared to swear to it.

"You just keep getting more interesting, Mr. McKenna," she said finally.

Quill did not think she sounded particularly pleased about it. The small vertical crease that had appeared between her eyebrows vanished, but she was still regarding him with more suspicion than curiosity. It was a look he knew from his first encounter with her.

"All right," she said. "I will allow that is a kind of posse because it speaks to my point. The boys do not always have your back. They get busy fast watching their own."

"Joe Pepper said your father was an Army scout."

"That's right."

He thought she might offer something more, but she did not and he let it go. "Did you have any other impressions of Ramsey Stonechurch besides deciding he is not entirely unlikable?"

"He left me with no doubt that he loves his daughter; however, he was not quite as ruthless as I expected he would be on the matter. At one point I thought he was telling me he would sanction the killing of the young man who supposedly has Ann's attention. He seemed genuinely taken aback that I would think that was what he meant. If I did not misread him, his reaction spoke well of him." Her eyes narrowed fractionally. "I am not a murderer."

"I did not represent you that way." He did not flinch from her hard stare, and she was the first to look away.

"He thinks he knows me because he's heard stories," she said.

"I imagine that's true for a lot of people who meet you."

"Well, they're mostly wrong. You thought I was —"

"Taller," he said dryly. "Yes, I remember."

Her mouth twisted to one side. "At least that was new. Usually it's some expression of surprise that I am a woman."

"The trousers, duster, and Stetson might have something to do with that."

"Hard riding calls for specific clothes."

"You took the train here."

"All right. I did. I was feeling contrary."

That admission made Quill grin.

"Don't do that," she said, staring at his mouth.

"Do what?"

"Smile like you swallowed the sun. It's not natural."

His grin actually deepened. He echoed her earlier observation, "I've never heard that before."

"Then there is something wrong with people. It's as if you have a mouthful of high noon. Somebody ought to have brought it to your attention by now."

A moment of stunned silence was followed by a staccato burst of laughter, and Quill did not get himself under control easily. The fact that Calico was staring stone-faced at him again struck him as more amusing than not. He could not quite flatten out his crooked smile.

Mildly nettled, Calico merely shook her head.

"Sorry," he said. When she responded with a derisive snort, it was all he could do not to start grinning all over again. To keep that from happening, he posed a question. "Was there any discussion of Ann's studies during the interview?"

"Yes. I had to set his mind at ease that I could be at least as good a teacher as Ann needs to avoid making her suspicious. I was convincing."

"I entertained no doubts that you would be."

"Well, there is still the matter of carrying it out. I don't fool myself. I told him I had an unconventional education, but only the broad strokes. Too many details, and he would have shown me the door."

Intrigued, Quill said, "One detail."

Calico's expression turned thoughtful. "All right. I learned my numbers counting cartridges."

That seemed reasonable enough to Quill. He had it from Joe Pepper that she had grown up at outposts. "I was thinking of a detail from your later education."

"Well, then, Mrs. Riggenbotham instructed me in matters of carnal knowledge by recounting whore stories."

Quill was not certain he had heard correctly. "*War* stories?"

"No. Whore stories. Mrs. Riggenbotham was not always the captain's wife."

"I see."

"You asked."

There was no getting around it. "I did. Please tell me you do not intend to instruct Ann in the way of . . ." His voice trailed off as he tried to collect his scattered thoughts and decide where he could safely turn his eyes.

Now it was Calico's turn to be amused. "You are blushing. There is something I don't see every day, especially from a man who introduced himself to me in a brothel. A cavalry officer to boot."

"Former," he said a bit stiffly even if he was grateful to have something else to talk about. "And I never said I was an officer."

"I know. But you were, weren't you? First impressions aside — because frankly, you looked vaguely disreputable on the occasion of our introduction — I am noticing more than a little spit and polish about you now.

Your suit, for instance, is fine. You are wearing good wool, and the fit tells me there is a tailor somewhere very pleased with himself. Your hair is somewhat overlong, but I think that is because you are particular about who cuts it, and your shoes have a shine I associate with officers turned out for a military ball. You hold yourself easy and you hold yourself straight, and you slip from one stance to the other without conscious thought because you have the knowledge of what is required at your fingertips. That always struck me as the mark of an officer. You can take orders and you can give them, but I've noticed that you prefer to give them."

Quill's mouth twisted to the side as he rubbed the back of his neck. His hair *was* overlong, and she was right about him being particular.

"Well?" she asked. "Were you?" When he did not answer, she snorted derisively. "You want to lie about it, don't you? I think you are trying to decide if you can get away with it."

She had read his mind exactly. His blue-gray eyes speared her knowing green ones. "You think you are clever."

"No, you think I am clever. I think I am observant . . . and perhaps a little clever."

He grunted softly. "Yes. I was an officer. Only a lieutenant, and not an ambitious one."

"Why did you leave?"

Quill shook his head. "Some other time." He checked his pocket watch. "Dinner is served promptly at seven."

"I was invited to the table, but I was given allowance to take my meal here. That is what I am going to do."

"That's probably wise. Ann will find it difficult to contain her excitement if you're there." He stood. "In the morning, then."

Calico woke up early. She lay still until she had her bearings and then listened for movement in the house. When she heard nothing in the hallway or below stairs, she slid more deeply under the bedcovers and smiled quite happily as she wallowed in the warmth. She wondered if she could accustom herself to the luxury of a thick mattress, blankets that did not itch, a pillow softer than a saddle, and clean cotton sheets. This was not a new imagining. She thought about it every time she was a guest in someone's home and less often when she was staying in one of the better hotels.

She turned it over in her mind, weighing what she would be surrendering for what she stood to gain. The argument she had with herself was more nuanced than deciding between two competing ideas. If it were only about sacrificing the outdoors and an itinerant life for comfort and confinement, she would take the life she knew, but there were other considerations, many of them complicated, at least in her mind.

Could she have a more permanent residence, for instance, and not be tethered to it? Would it limit her choices? She shied away from calling the residence a home as that word suggested a certain amount of domesticity, and that brought visions of aprons, feather dusters, and stove cooking. It also brought visions of a husband, children, and serving on a committee to raise money for new school primers or church hymnals. But if she settled into a hotel or boardinghouse, returning to it regularly when she was between assignments, she would have to advance money to keep the room available and there were no assurances that strangers would not use it while she was gone. She could not warm to that idea.

Calico pulled the pillow out from under her head and placed it squarely over her face. It muffled her rather loud groan of frustration. She remained like that for a few moments, considering whether or not she had stumbled upon an elegant compromise of her own by coming to Stonechurch, but before she was able to think it through, personal needs distracted her. Throwing off the pillow, then the bedcovers, Calico rolled out of bed and hurried barefooted to the bathing room.

She was still in there, completing her ablutions, wondering if Quill McKenna intended to return her derringer or if she would have to steal it back, when she heard someone enter her bedroom. She tensed, waited, and relaxed only when the maid announced that she had come to tend to the fire. She would have to get used to Ramsey's hired help coming and going without much in the way of forewarning. It was outside of the ordinary, and she was not sure she liked it. Her mouth twisted wryly and was reflected in the mirror above the washstand. The same could be said about Quill McKenna's coming and goings, she thought. The very same.

Calico dressed in the same clothes she had the evening before and added a black woolen shawl. The frost flowers on her windows were a sign the temperature had dipped several more degrees overnight, and she did not want to shiver uncontrollably in front of Ramsey Stonechurch or any of the rest of the family at the breakfast table.

Calico met Ann Stonechurch in the hall-way as Ann was coming out of her room. While it appeared to be coincidence that they left their rooms at the same time, Calico had the impression that Ann had been listening for her and timed her departure to make this meeting happen. The girl's fine features were flushed with what Calico imagined was suppressed excitement and her greeting came a bit too loudly. The surprise the girl affected was forced to the degree that it was no longer natural.

Calico pretended to notice none of it and greeted Ann warmly. "I am happy to know that I am not alone in being awake. Will you show me where I might find breakfast?"

"Of course, but you are very much mistaken if you think you and I are the only ones up." They started down the stairs. "Father rises earlier than anyone, and he will already have been in his study for hours. If he is not there, it is because he has gone to one of the mines — probably Number 1 — and in that case, Mr. McKenna will be with him."

"Why Number 1?"

"Oh, I imagine it is because there has been some trouble there. I don't know much about it. Father does not entertain those discussions when I am around. He says that is what Mr. McKenna's ears are for."

"But you know more than your father suspects." Calico said it as a matter of fact, and then she waited. Ann did not disappoint. First there was the sideways look that Calico caught out of the corner of her eye, and it was punctuated by a slender, secretive smile.

"The miners object to their wages. It had been thought for some time that the Number 1 mine would be played out, but a new vein was discovered. That is good news for the men as they continue to have work, but they also want a share of the profits. My father is adamantly opposed to what he calls a daft socialist experiment." She hesitated and then added in confidential tones, "He does not always say daft."

"I imagine not. So there is tension."

"Yes. Certainly."

"Violence?"

Ann shook her head vehemently. She stopped Calico at the entrance to the dining room by putting one hand on her forearm and spoke earnestly. "You must not repeat what I've told you. It will ruin everything, all of my plans. And you mustn't worry that if there is violence, it will touch us here. It won't."

"How can you be so certain?"

"Because my father will not allow it."

Calico's smile was gentle and her response meant to reassure. It did not matter what she believed; it only mattered what Ann believed. "Having met your father, I have every confidence that you are right."

"And you won't say anything?"

"No. Not a word to your father." It was a promise she could keep.

Ann and Calico were discussing Henry James's *Washington Square* when Quill entered the room. They nodded politely and then ignored him as he served himself from the sideboard. He sat beside Ann, spread his napkin in his lap, and tucked into his scrambled eggs. Although he did not show it, he was mildly amused by Ann's solemn recitation of what she considered the finer points of the novel. He wondered how they had come to be discussing this particular book. On the surface at least, the conflict between the heroine and her bullying father had a parallel in the skirmishes between Ann and Ramsey, but as Quill heard Ann go on, it seemed she had not made the connection.

A maid appeared bringing fresh coffee and Quill thanked her quietly. He used the cup to hide his smile as he watched Calico. He could not fault her for lack of interest in

Ann's monologue. She appeared to be listening deeply, as if there were meaning beneath the spoken words and the most important thing she could do right now was to hear what was not being said.

He started, splashing his fingers with coffee when Calico suddenly shifted her attention to him.

"What do you think, Mr. McKenna? Was Catherine Sloper's loyalty to her father misplaced as Ann suggests?"

"I would have had to read the book to have an opinion."

Ann said, "Oh, but I thought —"

"Never finished it." He set his cup down and spread honey on a second piece of toast. "*Treasure Island.* Now there is a book." He nudged Ann with his elbow. "Isn't that right? I know you liked it."

Ann blushed, but she spoke as though butter would not melt in her mouth. "It is a fine adventure, but I prefer the drama of relationships."

"The melodrama, you mean."

Calico said, "Do not respond to that, Miss Stonechurch. It is evident that Mr. McKenna is a philistine." Deep rolling laughter at her back startled her. She turned her head sharply even though she knew it was Ramsey Stonechurch who had come up behind her. He was smiling broadly as he rested his hands on the back of her chair.

"I think it is safe to say, Miss Nash, that Mr. McKenna has been called much worse than a philistine. Lawyer comes immediately to mind."

CHAPTER FIVE

Calico wondered if she looked as uncomfortable as she felt with Ramsey Stonechurch directly at her back. It disturbed her that she had not heard him enter or suspected that he was behind her until he spoke, and she had to ask herself if perhaps a single night spent in a comfortable bed was enough to dull her senses.

Ramsey addressed Ann. "Where is your aunt?"

Ann frowned and her eyes shifted guiltily to the end of the table, where Beatrice usually sat. It was abundantly clear to everyone that she had not noticed her aunt's absence until her father inquired. "I don't know." She pushed back from the table and began to rise. "But I will find out. Her nerves . . ." It was not necessary to finish the thought, as it seemed there was universal understanding. She smiled apologetically and excused herself. She paused only to kiss her father's

154

cheek on the way out.

Calico had hardly been aware of holding her breath until Ramsey stepped away from her chair to go to the sideboard. She exhaled softly but not as discreetly as she would have wished. She caught Quill's inquiring expression in the slight lift of his eyebrows. The table was too wide for her to kick him under it, although it was a temptation to try. It did not improve her mood that he seemed to have read her thoughts. He was practically beaming at her in that wholly unnatural way of his just before he bit down on his toast.

Ramsey was not privy to any of this as he helped himself to steak and eggs and a generous stack of silver dollar pancakes, and by the time he seated himself at the head of the table, Calico and Quill had stopped trading glances and were giving him their attention.

"We have a few minutes before Ann returns," he said. "I did not tell her yet that I have agreed to hire you, Miss Nash. She badgered me at dinner, and Mr. McKenna also, and she would have been at your door immediately if she had gotten her answer. I decided a lesson in patience was in order, and you deserved a peaceful evening after your journey."

Calico was grateful and she told him so, although she felt a twinge of sympathy for Ann, who was clearly anxious for an answer. Now she understood why. She looked at Ramsey, but her words were meant for Quill. "A peaceful evening was exactly what I needed."

"I do not understand why Father has not yet made his decision," Ann confided to Calico as they began a tour of the house. "He is being purposely disagreeable in the hope that I will change my mind."

"At the end of the day, he wants what he believes is best for you. It will help if you keep that in mind." Calico could see that Ann was hardly placated. Ramsey still had not told his daughter that he was in favor of the hiring. It seemed a tad cruel to Calico, but she allowed that Ramsey had his reasons. It did not set well that Quill McKenna appeared to be in lockstep with their employer — the toady. "I'm sorry. I should not have said that. You know it already. It must have sounded patronizing, and that was not my intention. I feel certain there will be a decision this afternoon." There had better be, she thought. This lesson in patience was becoming heavy-handed.

"You want the position, don't you?" Ann

asked suddenly.

"Yes, I do. I do not like to turn my back on an opportunity." Calico looked around the parlor as Ann ushered her inside. It was a warm, inviting room with dark walnut wainscoting, gold velvet drapes, and a large mantelpiece that displayed silver candlesticks and a collection of enameled boxes in a variety of sizes. There was enough seating for as many as a dozen guests, and the arrangement of furniture was such that it encouraged conversation in small groups. "This is quite a lovely room," she said. "Do you spend much time here?" Ann shook her head, and Calico thought she looked suspiciously close to tears.

"I will make it happen," she told Ann.

Ann's small chin stopped wobbling. "You will? You can?"

"Yes, Ann. I can and I will."

Calico had a thorough tour of the house through Ann's expressive, excited eyes and returned to her room well before luncheon. She was there only a short time before she was summoned — there was no other word for it — to Ramsey Stonechurch's study. It was Beatrice who had been sent to get her, and Calico did her best to set the woman at ease. Ramsey's sister-in-law was pleasant but not confident, and she chattered as opposed to engaging in conversation. Calico was grateful to leave her behind at the entrance to the study, and more grateful still that Quill McKenna was not waiting with the pharaoh.

"Close the doors," Ramsey said. He gestured to her to come forward but did not invite her to sit. "This need not take long, Miss Nash. It has come to my attention that perhaps I have been overzealous in my desire to teach my daughter a lesson in delayed gratification."

"Her aunt said something?"

"Beatrice? No. It was Mr. McKenna."

"Oh." Damn, and damn again. Couldn't he remain a toady? The job would have more to recommend it if he remained a toady.

"Yes, well. There you have it." His thick mustache lifted at the corners as he smiled broadly. "Do you want to tell Ann, or should I?"

Calico did not hesitate. "You tell her, sir. Every father deserves to be a hero to his daughter."

Ann practically bowled Quill over in the hallway as she was leaving her father's study. He made a show of staggering back, but except to give him an over-the-shoulder apology as she fled, he thought she barely noticed his performance. He was still smiling to himself when he walked into Ramsey's study. Ann had not taken the time to close the pocket doors. It did not matter who was responsible; that oversight always annoyed her father.

"I just saw Ann," said Quill. "Would I be correct that you finally told her you hired Miss Nash?"

"She brought a gun in here, Quill. Do you believe it? She brought a goddamn gun in here."

"Ann?"

Ramsey scowled. "No, of course not Ann. Calico Nash. She could have killed me."

"Huh. She carried in her revolver?"

"Not a revolver. A derringer. I spied the bulge under her sleeve."

"I'll be damned."

"Admiration is not what I am looking for."

"Well, it's hard not to be admiring. I took her pistol, so she either had a spare or she stole it back. Did she threaten you with it?"

"No."

Quill did not know what to say except, "I see." It was hard to keep amusement out of his tone.

"Oh, for God's sake, just sit down."

"She's not going to use it on you," said Quill. "It seems to me she is taking her responsibilities seriously. You should be satisfied with your decision."

"She is. I am."

"So you merely wanted to vent your spleen on me."

Ramsey Stonechurch knew nothing about being sheepish, so his expression remained unapologetic; however, his lips twitched and he gave up the scowl. "Your calm is infuriating, you know."

Quill sat. "I know it infuriates you, but I am not sure why that is. One would think you would want composure in a man charged with your protection."

"I do, but that doesn't mean I find it natural."

Quill thought he should probably begin a list. First it was his smile, and now his calm. He was surely a disappointment. "My father was a minister, Mr. Stonechurch. He knew how to vent his spleen from the pulpit and shower brimstone on the parishioners cowering in the last pew. You are not there yet."

"Not for lack of trying," said Ramsey. He opened the ledger on the desk and began to thumb through the pages. "Do you remember Frank Fordham giving this to me yesterday?" When Quill nodded that he did,

Ramsey went on. "I did not have an opportunity to examine it until early this morning, but I am discovering again that there is a good reason why I trust Frank with the business accounts. Since the new vein of ore was found in the Number 1 mine, Frank has been monitoring production. He made a comparison of the three mines we are currently operating and what he found is not encouraging."

Ramsey turned the ledger 180 degrees so that it faced Quill. "Look at it for yourself."

Quill pulled his chair closer to the desk. "Will I know what I'm seeing? I am not an accountant."

"This is not a balance sheet. These are production figures."

"All right." He examined the columns carefully, one for each mine. On the facing page there was also a month-to-month comparison of the previous year's production to the current mine yield. He could see the steady decrease in the Number 1 mine's production, a spike, and then a return to the earlier production numbers. There were fluctuations in the yields of the other mines, but Quill recognized that if he graphed the results over a year, even two, he would be able to draw a straight line between the points. The average yield remained the same.

"There is an upturn here in May when the new vein was found at Number 1, a slight increase the following month as expected, but then . . ." He looked over the figures again.

"But then?" Ramsey prompted.

"Production drops steadily. Slowly, to be sure, but steadily. It never reaches the previous lows, but it also does not reach the levels I would anticipate from a new vein."

"Look at that. You *do* know what you're seeing."

"What accounts for it?"

"You know what accounts for it. The men. They are not digging at the expected rate, not so slow that it would be noticed right way, but over time, and with Frank's attention to detail and how he set this up, the deceit of it all practically shouts out from the page."

Quill expected that explanation and was glad to get it out of the way so he could examine other possibilities. It was unlikely that Ramsey would entertain them for long, but Quill believed it was a necessary function of his own job.

"What else accounts for it?" he asked.

"Not a damn thing." Ramsey snatched the

book back and twisted it around again. "This is the miners doing this. My company. My men. It is an act of betrayal. They have no loyalty."

Quill waited for Ramsey to calm before he asked, "Can one man slow production on his own?"

"One? No. But one man can encourage others. That makes them all responsible."

"What if the vein is not as wide or as deep as you were led to believe?"

"It is." Ramsey closed the ledger and turned his head away as if he could no longer tolerate the sight of it. He closed his eyes briefly while he rubbed the bridge of his nose with a thumb and forefinger. "I saw the vein myself. I commissioned the survey. I know how to read a map, and before that I learned how to read a mountain. That's how Stonechurch Mining came to be."

Quill nodded. He knew the story of how Ramsey and Leonard Stonechurch came to make their first strike on Silver Knob following survey maps their grandfather made when he came through with Zebulon Pike in '06. They were young men when they came across silver, later gold, and still later, silver again. Mines played out because in the early days there was no machinery to uncover the ore or bring it up, and when the machines were invented that could do the job, there were few men with the resources to purchase and operate them. Eastern consortiums owned many of the mines, but Ramsey and his brother poured their profits into their holdings and stayed in Colorado. Ramsey thought people should appreciate that, but as time passed, and he became more distant from the daily operations while living like the lord of the manor at one end of the town, there were grumblings. There were resentments.

From what Quill could tell, the antipathies were isolated, not widespread. In spite of being known as a coldhearted bastard by some, there were plenty of people in Stonechurch who thought the sun rose and set according to their town's remaining founder. The help that Ramsey employed to run his house as efficiently as he ran his company were chief among them. It was Quill's opinion that Mrs. Pratt, the housekeeper, and Mrs. Friend, the cook, were more likely to surrender their firstborn than say a bad word about Ramsey Stonechurch.

"The machinery?" asked Quill. "Is it in working order? Have there been breakdowns?"

"Something is always breaking down," Ramsey replied. "I have no reports to

indicate that there has been more mainte-
nance at Number 1." He leaned back in his
chair and folded his arms. He thrust his
chin forward. "Go on. Try another one."

Quill thought if Ramsey had been wearing
gloves, he would have thrown one down.
"All right. What about a recording error?"
He raised both hands before Ramsey could
speak. "I am not talking about Frank. You
say he is meticulous, and I believe you, but
he does not count the cars as they come up
or weigh the ore or oversee the processing."

"Do you think an error like that would be
isolated to one mine?"

Quill admitted it did not seem likely, but
it did make him wonder about another possibility. "What if something is being deliberately recorded incorrectly? What if the
production is exactly what it should be, but
it is being recorded as less?"

"Embezzlement, you mean? Of the ore?"

Quill shrugged. "Is it possible?"

"That would be quite an operation, and it
doesn't really matter to me whether the men
are not bringing it up or whether they are
bringing it up and hauling it off in secret.
Either way, they are stealing from me. I
want you to find out who is behind it and
how it is being done."

"That means I would be away from the

house, away from you. You can't decide to go off on your own if I am at the mines. We know what happened the last time."

"You were gone for weeks then, not hours, and it doesn't matter. This is important, and I want you to take care of it. Besides, I have Calico Nash here. I am in hands every bit as capable as yours." He gave Quill a crooked smile. "And prettier ones, too."

"Hmm."

"Talk to her," said Ramsey. "Tell her what I want, and tell her not to ask for more money."

"I will tell her, but I am not responsible if she brings a bigger weapon to the table."

"Come in," called Calico, responding to the knock at her bedroom door. She was fairly certain that it was not Ann because she had left that young woman in the front parlor with a book. "You will have to decide if anything in all of literature has been as influential as this," she had explained, opening it to the first chapter and setting it in Ann's lap. " 'In the beginning God created the heaven and the earth.' I would be hard pressed to think of a better opening than that, although 'It was the best of times, it was the worst of times,' is very good, too."

Calico paused unpacking her trunk to see

who opened the door and was careful not to let her dismay show when she saw it was Beatrice Stonechurch. The woman stepped inside the room and then hovered there as if uncertain of her welcome. Calico decided to put that to rest.

"Please, won't you come in?" She pointed to the trunk and the clothes laid out neatly on the bed. "I am only unpacking. What can I do for you, Mrs. Stonechurch?"

Calico observed that upon taking another step forward, Beatrice clasped her hands together. The gesture made her small stature seem somehow even smaller. Her narrow shoulders appeared to collapse as she squeezed herself into a tinier space than she was meant to occupy. It was difficult to judge the woman's age, but Calico suspected she was younger than one might think at first blush, perhaps as much as a decade younger than her brother-in-law. The fine lines at her eyes and mouth were likely prematurely carved by her constant state of worry. It was the same with the creases in her forehead. They were always present but deepened when she raised her eyebrows. Her brown hair was thick and might have been called lustrous if it had been allowed to breathe, but Beatrice maintained it in tight topknot that contributed to her perpetually pinched expression. Calico would not have been surprised to learn that the ivory combs securing that knot were anchored just beneath her scalp instead of against it.

Beatrice had a trim, doll-like figure, curved precisely in the manner society — and Calico — admired, and in spite of her state of perpetual anxiety, or perhaps because of it, Beatrice Stonechurch looked out at the world through blue eyes that were unusually bright and attentive. Her smile, though genuine, was also tentative and faltered easily, but when it showed itself, it had the capacity to transform her features and leave the impression of a handsome, even lovely, woman in its wake.

Calico waited expectantly for Beatrice to speak. When the silence stretched for what seemed an inordinately long time, Calico prompted her with, "There was something you wanted to tell me, Mrs. Stonechurch?"

"Yes. Yes. You must call me Beatrice. Did I not say that when I came to take you to Ramsey's study earlier? I should have. I meant to. Leonard called me Bea. That is B-E-A, not B-E-E like the insect, although sometimes he would say it should be B-E-E because I moved so quickly from one thing to the next that he was sure he heard me

168

buzzing." She stopped abruptly to take a breath and then continued. "Please call me Beatrice."

Expecting there would be more after that pause for breath, Calico waited two full beats before she spoke. "Thank you, Beatrice. And I hope you will call me Katherine." It was less difficult to say than usual. Calico supposed it had something to do with the dress. Her experience had taught her that in some small way you became the person you were pretending to be.

"Yes. Yes, I will. That will be splendid." Another fine line appeared between her eyebrows as she pulled a frown. "You will not allow Ann to adopt that informality, will you? You are her teacher, not her friend. I helped my niece with her studies for many years, and while I love her as I would my own child, in the classroom our relationship was different, not that she did not always call me Aunt Beatrice — it would have been absurd to do otherwise — but she knew I was there for the specific purpose of instruction." A deep breath, and then, "I hope I have not offended."

"No," said Calico. "Not at all. I would be foolish not to value your opinion. I have been wondering if perhaps you see me as an interloper. My presence here cannot help but change your role in Ann's education. It would be natural if you felt some resentment."

Beatrice unclasped her hands and clasped them again. "No. No resentment. Perhaps someone without Ann's best interests at heart, someone who did not want her to be happy, might feel that way, but I am not that person. She reviewed her curriculum with me before she showed it to her father, and I approved it, knowing all the while that I could not be the teacher to help her move on. I encouraged my niece to pursue her plan. Encouraging Ann in any endeavor has always been my role. I do not see that changing." She took a quick breath, uncertain again. "Do you?"

"No. I certainly do not."

Beatrice exhaled softly, and her hands fell to her sides. "Good. That is very good. Excellent."

Calico waited a respectful beat, and when Beatrice merely continued to hover, she pointed to the clothing lying on the bed. "I wonder if you would recommend a dressmaker. I was not certain what I could expect when I left Falls Hollow."

"Oh, yes. Yes, I am happy to tell you that Stonechurch has two fine dressmakers: Mrs. Birden and Mrs. Neeley-Brown. I engage them alternately because their feelings are so easily hurt, and I do not want either one to think I have snubbed her. You might consider the same as it will go a long way to tempering tensions, and they will compete to offer you the best garment possible." Her smile appeared, and this time it was wily. "At least I have always found it to be so."

Appreciating Beatrice's craftiness in getting the better of the dressmakers, Calico chuckled. "I will certainly seek them out. Ann has offered to show me the town, or show me off to the town. I am not sure which it is."

"A little of both, I should think, although you must not imagine that my niece presents herself in a superior fashion about town because she is the daughter of Ramsey Stonechurch. Ann is modest and retiring in public. I do not know if she would engage in more activities in the community even if her father would permit it."

Calico intended to inquire about Beatrice's own activities in town, but there was no pause for breath this time, and Beatrice went on, returning to the subject of Calico's clothes.

"If you would rather," said Beatrice, "I could arrange for what remains of your wardrobe to be sent here. I would be happy to do it. Falls Hallow, did you say?"

"Hollow. Falls Hollow."

"And you were previously engaged there?"

"Yes." She did not elaborate. "As much as I appreciate your offer, I am set on having some new dresses. I do not think I will miss what I left behind." Which, in fact, was nothing.

Beatrice looked uncertain. "Very well, if you think that best." She brightened a bit. "I could accompany you and Ann tomorrow. I should like to visit Mrs. Birden myself about a new shirtwaist blouse. It is her turn to be engaged, you understand."

"I do. It will be a pleasure to have you come with us." Calico thought it was a wonder the lie did not stick in her throat. She was warming to Beatrice Stonechurch, but not to the idea of sharing Ann with her on the walk around town. Beatrice's presence would interfere with everything from conversation to introductions. Still, there was no polite way to refuse her. Calico heard herself say, "I would be grateful for any advice you could offer me."

When she witnessed Beatrice's sincere, uncomplicated smile, she was glad she had said it. It was only after Beatrice had departed that Calico wondered who she was becoming.

■ ■ ■ ■

Feeling put off her stride in the aftermath of Beatrice's visit, Calico struggled to find a polite tone when someone knocked at her door not more than thirty minutes later. Polite, she realized when she heard herself, did not equate to welcoming.

Quill stepped in the room.

"Oh, it's you." Calico turned back to the dresser and placed a pair of rolled stockings in the uppermost drawer. She removed another pair from on top of the dresser, gently rolled them around one hand, and placed them in the drawer as well.

"Settling in?" asked Quill.

"Trying to. I am besieged by interruptions."

"Really? I saw Ann in the parlor, and I know Ramsey is in his study because I came from there."

Calico chose another pair of stockings, but she did give him an over-the-shoulder glance while she wound them. "Beatrice . . . and now you."

Quill's approach was quiet, but not so quiet that Calico did not hear him coming. She spun around and threw the ball of stockings at him. He ducked and managed

173

to catch them anyway. "Do not try to sneak up on me. I don't appreciate it."

"What's wrong?"

She blinked. "I told you. I don't like people sneak —"

Quill shook his head, stopping her. "You snapped at me before that." He handed back her stockings. She squeezed them in a fist. "Was it Beatrice?"

Calico sighed. She relaxed her fingers and began to roll the stockings, smoothing them as she wound. "Since it seems it cannot possibly be you, then yes, it was Beatrice. But not precisely Beatrice. Her visit made me question what I am doing here."

"I thought that after speaking to Ramsey, that would be clear."

"The job is clear, but I'm not talking about that." Her eyes slipped away from his and she looked around the room. "I suppose I am saying I was more comfortable in Mrs. Fry's cathouse than I am here, and it was a burr under my saddle when I was only thinking it. Hearing it aloud, saying it to you, makes that burr a goddamn briar patch, and I am not thanking you for it."

"Do you want to back out?"

Insulted, her head snapped up. Her answer was swift. "No. I don't do that. I gave my word."

"All right."

"You should not have asked. If you knew me better, hell, if you knew me at all, you would not have asked."

"I apologize."

She shrugged, put the stockings away, and shut the drawer. Feeling cornered against the dresser, she slipped out sideways and moved to the bed. Quill did not follow. "Why are you here? Won't it raise someone's eyebrows if you are found in my room? I am painfully aware this is not Mrs. Fry's establishment, but are you?"

" 'Painfully aware' describes it pretty well."

"Then?"

"Mind if I sit?"

She gestured toward the window bench. "Suit yourself." She waited until he was seated before she perched on the edge of the bed and turned slightly in his direction.

"There has been some concern about the operation of one of the mines for a while."

"The Number 1. Ann told me that there is trouble there, something to do with sharing in the profits, she thinks. She pays attention, you know. It makes me wonder what she else she has heard."

"The threats, you mean."

"Yes, and how you and I figure into them.

She has one ear to the ground."

Quill leaned back against the window, stretched his legs, and crossed them at the ankles. He folded his arms against his chest and regarded Calico thoughtfully. "Ramsey wants to get to the bottom of why Number 1 is not producing ore at the level he expects. He will not listen for long to any explanation that is contrary to the one he believes is correct. He thinks there is one man who is rallying the others to slow their work, and if I can identify this man and move him out of the way, the mine will begin producing again."

"Move him out of the way? How will you do that?"

"I haven't gotten that far. I want to see if he exists first. There might be no single man leading the way. Ramsey never said the word 'union' in regard to this, but I have to believe it is at the back of his mind. He has educated himself about the growth of the organizations and the steps being taken to stop the formation of unions. He knows it's happening in other parts of the country. I have seen him pore over stories from Eastern newspapers, and he has strong opinions about it."

"Daft socialist experiment."

Quill nodded. "Something else you

learned from Ann?"

"Yes."

"Ramsey's voice carries to the rafters when he is ranting."

"It is no wonder she is concerned about his health."

"Exactly." He sighed. "Since I have been charged with discovering what's happening at the mine, I will be gone from the house more often. That will require you to keep an eye on Ramsey."

"Do you believe Ramsey is safe at home?"

"Yes. As long as he stays put. He gets it in his head that he has to leave and tears out of here like his hair's on fire." Quill regarded Calico's flaming tresses for a long moment. "Like yours."

Self-conscious, Calico tucked a loose strand behind her ear.

Quill cleared his throat and continued. "I've gotten used to listening for doors opening and closing, especially the front door because that's how he leaves and he usually slams it hard."

"I will keep that in mind." She rose and began to clear the bed of the remaining clothes.

"Do you need help?"

"No."

Quill did not offer again. She was firm

enough in her refusal that he thought if he touched anything, she might break his fingers or threaten to.

Calico opened the door to the wardrobe and began to place her things inside. "Does Ramsey have a candidate in mind? For the leader, I mean. Has he mentioned anyone?"

"No. And I didn't ask. I want to form my own opinion."

She nodded. "I was wondering about the house staff."

"My sense is that they are loyal and are happy to work in the big house, as they like to call it. They care that Ramsey Stone-church is respected in town. They believe it reflects poorly on them if he is not."

"They are probably right." She looked over the contents of the wardrobe now that everything was in place, and she was glad she would be visiting a dressmaker tomorrow. She told Quill about her plans. "So if you go to the mines tomorrow, Ramsey will have to go with you."

"He will probably want to. He can stay in his office there with Frank Fordham while I poke around. The men know me. It won't be unusual."

"Do they trust you? You do look like a lawyer. No one trusts a lawyer."

"Until they need one. You, on the other

178

hand, you look like a . . . ."

She waited, beginning to feel warm under his scrutiny. If he were smiling, she might have said something about the sun on her face, but he was not, just the opposite, in fact. His features were oddly solemn. She swallowed because that was what it took to move the lump from her throat and find her voice. "A teacher?" she asked.

He was still a long time answering, but finally he nodded. "Yes, exactly like a teacher."

"Yes, well, that is a good beginning. Appearance helps. I told you I had mostly cavalry wives to instruct me. I wasn't sure if I looked the part." Truly, she thought, it was easier to look the whore.

What she said made Quill curious about what she did not say. "What about your mother? Was she one of your teachers?"

"No."

Quill recognized when a door was being closed in his face. He did not try to push through. "Will you be joining us for dinner?"

"If that is what is expected, then yes."

"It is expected. The derringer is not."

Calico smiled crookedly. "He told you."

"Yes, he told me. You could have asked me for it." When she merely shrugged, he said, "You wanted him to see it, I think."

Calico did not respond to his observation. She asked, "Was he angry?"

"More annoyed than angry. He does not like surprises. He believes he should be able to anticipate every situation, every consequence."

Calico recognized something of herself in that description so she did not comment. "How old do you think he is? Do you know?"

"Fifty-two. Why?"

"Just wondering. Was he older or younger than his brother?"

"Older. Three years older. Leo would have been forty-nine this year. I remember that Beatrice remarked on it on the anniversary of his passing."

"But she is younger than that, isn't she?"

"Considerably. Ann told me her aunt was twelve years younger than her uncle."

"Thirty-seven, then," said Calico softly. "Has she shown any interest in marrying again?"

"Not that I am aware, and I believe I would be. She seems to be settled here, content with her situation. She is wealthy in her own right. Her husband's shares in Stonechurch Mining passed to her, and although she has nothing at all to do with the operation, she has never sold a single share to Ramsey. On paper, at least, he does not have controlling interest."

"So he might not want to encourage her to remarry."

"Probably not. It would have the potential to turn the business on its head. Why the curiosity about Beatrice?"

"I'm not sure. Just . . . something. Did I mention that Beatrice is accompanying Ann and me tomorrow?"

"No, but for God's sake, don't go looking for a husband for her." He grinned when Calico's jaw snapped shut. "Good. Concentrate on finding the object of Ann's affection." He paused. "If he even exists."

"Well, I certainly do not believe he haunts either of the dress shops we intend to visit. You know the town. Where should I be looking for young men?"

"The most suitable of them are employed by —" He stopped because Calico had raised her eyebrows.

"Who said anything about suitable? Ann is a seventeen-year-old female passing from girlhood to womanhood, and that, Mr. Mc-Kenna, is a transition where suitable is rarely a frame of reference. She will be entertaining notions of romantic love that would curl your hair. Swarthy rascals and outright villains will figure largely in her daydreams. I saw the dime novels she has tucked away in her room. Please, dismiss the idea of suitable from your mind and tell me where I should be looking for men who might have caught her eye."

Frowning, Quill scratched behind his ear as he considered his answer. "When you explain it like that, I guess you want to be around when the miners change shifts."

"She's been to the mines?"

"On occasion, but she doesn't have to be there to see the men coming and going. They all live in town. She only has to be present when they're on their way or coming back, and that's occurred many times."

"All right. I will be alert to that. It would be the afternoon change, wouldn't it?"

"Yes. The others are too early or too late. You will want to visit the mercantile and Smith's leather goods. The owners of both have sons that work regularly in the stores. One is about Ann's age. The other is twenty or so. There is also a boy at the feed store who always seems to be sweeping outside when I've been with Ann. I don't know that I ever thought about it before, but you will want to look for him."

She nodded.

There was silence then, comfortable as

first, but less so as it went on. Calico looked down at her hands. Quill looked at her. As so often is the way, when they finally spoke, it was at the same time.

"You first," Quill said.

Feeling somewhat foolish, she hesitated. When she looked up, she fixed her eyes on him. "I have been curious about why you recommended me to the pharaoh. What made you think on our short acquaintance that I would do this?"

"That you would do it? I was never sure about that. But that you could? That's different. I was confident."

"I understand about providing protection, but tutoring Ann?"

"I am prepared to cover for you there, if it comes to that. You held your own at breakfast with *Washington Square*."

"It is early days yet. She showed me her curriculum. Latin. Trigonometry. Renaissance art. Do you play poker, Mr. McKenna?"

"Quill. And yes, I do."

"Are you any good?" Before he could respond, she put up a hand. "Never mind. You cannot be. By your own admission you don't lie well, and what is a bluff except a lie of expression? Well, I lie very well, and I bluff like I lie. I like to win, but I can accept losing. I do not catch every miscreant I am chasing. I do not score a bull's-eye every time I shoot. I know there are faster draws than me, and I do not provoke a gunslinger to test his mettle. I will need to do a great deal of bluffing if I am going to pass muster with Ann, and you will have to hone your tutoring skills to help me succeed." She hammered him with a dead-on look. "And it would not hurt if you honed your prevaricating skills as well. You are pitiful. You lied at breakfast about never having read *Washington Square*. The only question I have is how many times you've read it."

Quill stared at her. "How in the — Never mind. The answer is twice."

"Pitiful."

"Uh-huh. On the other hand, I do know Latin, trigonometry, and have a better than passing acquaintance with the Renaissance. I swear I can help you there. You do not have to know everything, but begin with what you do."

In spite of her intention to guard her fences, she realized she was smiling. "You are not such a bad sort, Mr. McKenna."

"Glad to hear it," he said dryly. "It would be more welcome if you would call me Quill."

Although he was regarding her virtually

without expression, she felt sure there had been an overture of intimacy in his tone, an invitation. How else to explain the warmth she felt under her skin and the odd little skip in her heart? Her smile faded as she returned to guarding her fences.

CHAPTER SIX

Calico had visited more mining towns than she could properly recall. Some of them were no longer in existence, having been deserted by the inhabitants when there was nothing left to mine. In contrast to those ghost towns, or even those rough hamlets with some ore left to expose, Stonechurch had become a community. Everywhere Calico looked, she saw the influence of the Stonechurch brothers. It was most evident in the public buildings because they bore the Stonechurch name. These were not grand structures by any means. Unlike the mansion, which was stone, these buildings were all wood framed, but the exteriors were painted white, the windows were clean, and they all appeared to be in good repair. There was the Ezekiel Stonechurch Library, named after the grandfather who had explored the new territory with Pike. Not far away, but on the opposite side of the street, was the

Maud Wilson Stonechurch Schoolhouse, which Calico learned was named after Ann's mother. The building that served as a meeting hall, courtroom (when one was needed), and land office was also home to the town council — whose five members were duly elected after being endorsed by Ramsey Stonechurch. By necessity, it was the largest structure in town, and it had been renamed following the death of Ramsey's brother and was now the Leonard W. Stonechurch Town Hall. There was a jail, but the town's official lawman was saddled with the title of constable, and he was appointed by Ramsey Stonechurch, not elected by the populace.

Except for the Stonechurch Mining office, which was located rather unobtrusively at the end of Ann Street near the rail station, Calico noticed that none of the businesses had the Stonechurch name. There was Smith's Leather Goods, Hamilton's Mercantile, and Shriver's Apothecary. It seemed that every shop owner had taken his cue from Ramsey Stonechurch and attached his name to the business. Zimmer and Zimmer Laundry. Bartholow's Eatery. Dr. Pitman had a residence on the main street and a modest placard by his front door to indicate his profession. A similar placard marked the undertaker's home. Stonechurch had two barbers, two dressmakers, two churches, one livery, one blacksmith, and three saloons. Most surprising, the bank was not owned by Ramsey Stonechurch, and it bore the rather utilitarian name of Miner's Trust.

What Calico took away from her tour was that, although Stonechurch the community would live and die by the success of the mining operation, it was not quite the company town she had imagined it to be.

While her interest in the town was real, it did not turn Calico away from her purpose. She kept Ann at her side, although when she reflected on it later, it might have been more difficult to lose her. Ann proved to be shy in public, even a trifle backward, while Beatrice, in startling contrast to her demeanor at home, did not know a stranger and greeted everyone warmly, addressing them by name and making a personal inquiry that communicated genuine concern but also proved that she had been paying attention to whatever tidbit they had shared during a previous encounter.

Calico watched Ann Stonechurch respond to every overture politely. There was no faulting her manners; it was only that her discomfort lent her an air of reserve that could easily be misinterpreted as cool detachment. It probably did not help her cause that people were trying to engage her on the street bearing her name. Ann's youthful exuberance, her lively curiosity, was sadly absent here.

It occurred to Calico that if she were Ann's teacher in fact rather than fiction, it would fall to her to address these awkward social interactions. The mere thought stirred memories of sitting in a circle with the cavalry wives while they sharpened her conversational skills as they plied their needles. Under their tutelage she had grasped the niceties of social conventions and communication, and came to appreciate the necessity of them, but it was sitting around a campfire with her father, company privates, and the Indian scouts that prepared her for being able to comfortably carry on with just about anyone.

Ann Stonechurch, Calico decided, needed a campfire in the worst way.

That thought stayed with her on and off throughout the afternoon. It occupied her to the degree that she surrendered most of the decisions about her dresses to Beatrice, Ann, and Mrs. Birden. She did not put up much resistance when they encouraged her to order a third gown, although she did wonder what she would have to purchase from the other dressmaker to maintain the delicate balance. She allowed herself to be measured, poked, prodded, turned, twisted, and scrutinized. She survived it by imagining Quill McKenna's handsomely molded features with a bullet hole between his eyebrows. Sometimes she imagined him without the bullet hole, but in many ways that was more disturbing than being the subject of so much critical study.

He was an improbably attractive man. She had thought so from the first, and the first had not been when she opened the door to him at Mrs. Fry's. No, the first was when she had been standing at the top of the stairs looking over the guests crowding the parlor. She had not allowed her gaze to linger on him then, although it had been a sore temptation and resisting it had seemed somehow wrong.

She would not have been able to make out his features if he had not been looking up, but he was, and she clearly recalled the frisson of awareness in response to his open and frank stare. It was impossible to know the color of his eyes from where she stood, but their color had no bearing on how he looked out from them, and how he looked out from them made her keenly mindful just then of being a woman. Oddly enough, it was that moment of self-consciousness that nudged her forward and down the long staircase, and while she never looked in his direction again, his afterimage remained in her mind's eye, teasing her with its uncommon perfection.

Had she truly stared at him, she thought, she would have had to shade her eyes against the sunshine that glanced off his hair. It was also a mercy that he had not smiled because surely that would have struck her blind.

Even now, nothing about that seemed an exaggeration.

His hair and maddening grin aside, there was no other single feature deserving second notice on its own. Well, perhaps the widow's peak, although it was only evident when he raked back his hair. And one could make a case for the gemstone quality of his blue-gray eyes. Calico could even allow that some women, at least those drawn to villains, might find the cut of his jaw a point of interest, especially when it was defined by a day's stubble and lent him a vaguely disreputable look. His nose, though, she concluded with a certain amount of satisfaction, was just a nose, neither sharp nor soft, not hooked, never broken, neither long nor short, neither wide nor thin. It was ordinary.

Perfectly ordinary.

Calico came out of her reverie as the man with the perfectly ordinary nose walked into Mrs. Birden's shop and all the chatter around her stopped.

"Ladies," he said, tipping his hat as he greeted them. "And so we find you here."

The "we" he was referring to included Ramsey Stonechurch, who came in behind him a moment later.

Ann's mouth opened, Beatrice's hands clamped, and Calico's lips flattened. As a trio they covered a continuum of feeling: surprise, concern, and disapproval. Only Mrs. Birden was immediately welcoming and her effusiveness gave the other women cover as they gathered their wits.

Ann went to her father's side, stood on tiptoes, and bussed him on the cheek before she slipped her arm through his. She gave the arm a small squeeze. "I hope your presence means you intend to indulge Aunt Beatrice and me by approving new gowns. We have been through all the books looking for suitable garments for Miss Nash, and we are intrigued by the sporting clothes."

Calico caught the question in Quill's eye. She responded with a barely perceptible shake of her head.

"Sporting clothes?" asked Ramsey. "What

do you mean by sporting clothes?"

"You must know, Father. Tennis. Croquet. The costume one must have for riding a bicycle."

He raised a highly skeptical eyebrow. "Odd, but I have never heard you express the least interest in any of those things. I am unaware of you possessing the more critical sporting items, namely a racquet, a mallet, or a bicycle."

Ann heaved a mighty sigh. "Those were merely examples of sport. There are others."

Calico was certain that Ramsey could not raise his eyebrow any higher without a block and tackle, but he proved her wrong. She looked away quickly, pretending interest in a bolt of gray wool serge until she could temper her smile.

"Tell me about these others," he said.

"If you must know, archery and shooting."

Calico began to finger the fabric as though testing its strength, but she heard Quill clear his throat. Beside her, Beatrice drew in a soft but audible breath. Mrs. Birden tsked.

Ramsey Stonechurch said in stentorian tones, "Mother of God, spare me hell in a teacup. Absolutely not."

"Father!" Ann appealed to Calico. "Tell him, Miss Nash. Explain to him why these are perfectly reasonable feminine pursuits."

Calico grimaced, but her features were composed by the time she turned and lifted her head. As she expected, everyone was staring at her, but only Ann's expression was pleading. She faced her squarely and left no doubt that she would not be manipulated. "If I am going to explain anything, I will do so at the request of your father, and regardless, I will not be pressed into providing one in Mrs. Birden's establishment."

Ann flushed at the rebuke, but she took it on the chin, albeit a slightly wobbly one now. She released her father's arm. "You are right, and I am sorry."

Calico thought the apology was credibly sincere, and the way Ann's eyes darted from person to person, it was clear that she was begging everyone's pardon for the awkward moment.

"I believe I would like to step outside," said Ann. "Excuse me."

No one stopped her, but Calico immediately made to follow. It was Ramsey who put out an arm as she would have picked up her coat. "Let her go," he said. "I know my daughter. She needs a moment to cool those hot cheeks."

"But I should —"

He shook his head. "She won't move away

from the window. Give her a brief respite." When Calico made no further move to retrieve her coat, Ramsey lowered his arm and regarded his sister-in-law. "Ann said you were also interested in these sporting clothes. Was she telling me true or attempting to elicit your support?"

"Intrigued," said Beatrice, clapping her hands lightly together. "I do not think I am mistaken. The word she used was 'intrigued,' not 'interested,' and I can say without fear of being contradicted by either Miss Nash or Mrs. Birden that I was most definitely intrigued."

"But not interested, eh?"

"No. Goodness no. Not for myself. I imagine I would look quite foolish in sporting clothes. It seems to me that it is a fashion for younger women like Ann and Miss Nash. They would be very well suited to hemlines raised above the ankle and those darling little jackets that are cut just at the waist. Quite stylish and much more practical."

Ramsey remained suspicious. He said to Mrs. Birden, "Show me." And then he added to the room at large, "Not that my daughter will be carrying a quiver or raising a gun in my lifetime, but a bicycle is not out of the question."

Calico, who was watching Ann at the window, exchanged a glance with Quill as Mrs. Birden drew Ramsey closer to the table to examine her fashion catalogs. Beatrice Stonechurch unclasped her hands and made room for him.

Calico carefully sidled away. Not only was she not interested in the fashion plates, but in the main, she found them ridiculous. Women on the plains and prairies had been pulling the trigger on shotguns whenever they needed to, and she had never heard of one of them pausing to change into something more sporting.

She went to the dress shop's large window and looked out on Ann Street, observing the activity over Ann's right shoulder. The wide thoroughfare seemed to be home to every sort of industry, and as she stood there, the pedestrian traffic began to increase markedly. Here was the afternoon shift change, then, and even as she watched, Ann began to move with the tide, drifting away without purpose, like so much flotsam at the mercy of the current.

Quill was suddenly beside Calico, holding out her coat. "Your reticule?" When she nodded, he handed it to her. His approving quicksilver grin was how he communicated that he knew her derringer was inside.

Her response was to nod, and then she was out the door.

Calico dogged Ann's footsteps until the girl stepped sideways into the recessed alcove between the mercantile's pair of windows. She did not think she was mistaken that when Ann turned, there was both surprise and relief in her expression. That made her consider that Ann was not trying to hide, but rather that she had tucked herself into the alcove to get out of the way. It did not seem to be the behavior of someone anticipating a stolen moment with a passerby, but Calico also recognized it gave Ann a good vantage point from where she could observe everyone.

Calico joined her in the alcove and turned so that she also faced the street. "Your father asked Mrs. Birden to show him the sporting clothes."

Ann nodded but said nothing, and her fleeting smile was resigned, not hopeful.

"I did not encourage him. Your aunt had a hand in that."

Ann continued to stare straight ahead. "It doesn't matter. He will never permit me to learn to shoot or take up a bow."

"Do you really want to learn to use a bow?"

"No. I said that to distract him."

"So you are not interested in tennis, croquet, or riding a bicycle."

"I am not *un*interested, but what I want is to be accomplished with a gun."

"An Annie Oakley?"

Ann wrinkled her nose. "I do not want to join a Wild West show, if that's what you mean."

"God forbid. Why is it so important to you? I do not recall seeing anything of the sort in your extensive curriculum."

"It's there," she said. "Or at least the intent is there. Every one of the schools Father wants to send me to has courses to promote physical health and fitness."

"I suggest you reconsider the bicycle, then. I do not think it requires much in the way of fitness to shoot a gun."

"I suppose."

Calico did not think she sounded convinced. "I admit to being curious. Since you have given this some thought, who did you have in mind to teach you?"

"Mr. McKenna."

Calico was so rarely astonished that she had forgotten what a peculiar state of mind it was. She struggled to find words, and then to find words that were appropriate to say in the presence of this particular young lady.

She finally came up with, "Goodness," and recognized what a shamefully inadequate response it was when she heard it aloud.

Recovering her wits, Calico said, "Have you discussed this aspect of your education with Mr. McKenna?"

"I certainly intended to. To my regret, I put the cart before the horse. I did not expect to see him or my father walk into Mrs. Birden's. That has *never* happened. My enthusiasm for the sporting clothes outran my common sense."

Calico said nothing. It was a truth that everyone who had been in the dress shop could support.

"Do you have any advice for me?" asked Ann.

"Advice? About what?"

"About Mr. McKenna, of course. I need his cooperation."

"Aren't you putting the cart before the horse again? I think you need your father's approval."

"No. I cannot broach the subject with him, but if Mr. McKenna can be persuaded, he will encourage my father to see the sense of what I want. He has some influence there. I have witnessed it."

"Well, I have no influence with Mr. Mc-Kenna, and if you speak to him on this subject, I will be unhappy if my name comes into it."

"All right."

Calico stared at her young charge, suspicious of Ann's easy surrender. Her eyes narrowed thoughtfully. "You're going to chip away at him, aren't you?"

"Like a chisel on marble."

Calico laughed, encouraged. "Good girl. Shall we go back to the shop?" She put out a hand, indicating the street where the traffic had begun to dwindle and said casually, "Unless you are waiting for someone."

Ann frowned deeply. "What do you mean?"

Calico shrugged. "You were staring out so intently as the men were going by that I wondered if there wasn't perhaps someone you hoped to see."

"Did you? How peculiar. No, I was simply thinking."

Calico stepped out of the alcove and Ann fell in beside her. They turned in the direction of the dress shop. "Do you know them?" Calico asked. "The men who work for your father, I mean."

"The ones who work in the offices, yes, but not the miners. I recognize faces and know some by name. Father does not encourage familiarity. He thinks it is not proper." She smiled a trifle crookedly. "He is rather like a feudal lord in that regard. I have mostly become accustomed to it, but not without considerable frustration."

"I see," said Calico. And she did, all of it. As Ann pointed out, accustoming oneself to a different perspective was not without considerable frustration.

Calico waited until she heard Ramsey Stonechurch climb the stairs and go to his room before she left hers. Whether by design or habit, he was the last one to retire, and the wait for him to do so had seemed interminable. Calico read for a time, played solitaire, cleaned her Colt and then her rifle, turned down her bed, and poked at the logs in the fireplace at least a dozen more times than she needed to.

Ann had gone to her room immediately after dinner, and no one suggested she linger. Beatrice excused herself soon after, claiming she had a headache. As soon as the other women left, Calico sensed an impending interrogation, and she spoke up quickly to head Ramsey and Quill off, explaining she had to prepare for Ann's lessons and never giving them an opportunity to insert an objection.

She thought it was possible that Quill

might show up at her door, and she would have welcomed the opportunity to speak to him alone, but he never came. She learned from Molly, who had arrived with a tea tray at Beatrice's request, that Quill was gone from the house. Calico could only imagine that he had gone to one of the mines. It was late when he returned, but he still went to bed before Ramsey, and his footsteps never slowed as he walked past her room.

Calico hurried down the hallway when she heard Ramsey's door close. She had removed her shoes. Her woolen socks cushioned her footfalls, making her passage virtually silent. She wore a nightgown and a flannel robe and had confined her hair to a single plait that fell over her right shoulder. It was not her preference to have a confrontation in her nightclothes, but she had to be prepared if someone happened upon her in the hallway.

When she reached Quill's room, she did not hesitate. She turned the doorknob quickly and slipped inside. A single lamp burned on the nightstand beside the bed. The fire in the grate crackled but provided little in the way of light. Still, what was there was enough for her to see that the bed was unoccupied. The armchair facing the fire had its back to her. She expected that if

Quill were sitting there, he would have already said something. Nonetheless, she stepped forward carefully in the event he had fallen asleep in it. He had not.

Puzzled, Calico turned slowly as she remembered that his room was a mirror of hers, right down to the wardrobe on the opposite wall and the closed door beside it that led to a bathing room. She approached it, rapped lightly with her knuckles, and listened for a reply. She heard nothing.

After a brief debate in which she weighed the consequences of intruding against the consequences of inaction, she opened the door, poked her head inside, and withdrew it just as quickly. She quietly pulled the door shut and then knocked louder than before. Almost immediately there was splashing, some thrashing, and a few words that were largely unintelligible.

Good, she thought, removing herself to the bed. She had his attention.

It was not long before Quill appeared in the doorway. Water dripping from his tousled hair collected in the towel he had slung around his shoulders. He carried a shirt over one arm, his trousers over the other. He had hastily jammed his legs into a pair of gray flannel drawers and now they clung damply to his hips, thighs, and calves.

He was barefoot, he had yet to shave, and even in the meager light, his blue-gray eyes glowed like a wolf's.

His mouth flattened and a muscle worked in his jaw. Calico was heartily relieved by it, and she came within a cat's whisker of telling him so. Some bit of common sense asserted itself as she opened her mouth to speak, and she clamped her lips together. He would not have understood anyway, she thought, but a grin stamped on his face right now would have been gilding the lily.

"Start explaining."

"You know," she said conversationally, "I am considerably more civil when you intrude on me."

His expression did not change. He was giving her no quarter. "That is not an explanation."

"Prickly. Would you like to finish bathing? It seems a shame to let the water grow cold, and I don't mind waiting."

"Calico, I swear to God that I will —"

She put up a hand before he made a threat that he would feel compelled to carry out. "All right. I thought it would be obvious. I need to speak to you."

"Now? At this hour?"

"There was another hour that was better? You were holed up with our employer after dinner and then you left the house. It was already late when you returned, you did not stop at my room, and I decided it was wiser to wait to see you after Ramsey went to bed. He did that just a very little while ago."

"Then he is not asleep."

"Probably not, but if I had waited any longer, I would have been. I expected to have to wake you." When Quill did not admit that she had, she went on. "So here I am. Are you going to dress? You're dripping."

Quill looked down at himself at the same time a droplet of water from his elbow splashed on the floor by his foot. Regarding Calico sourly, he tossed his shirt and trousers onto the chair and finished drying his arms and chest. He rubbed his hair with the towel one more time before he slung it around his neck again. Ignoring his clothes, which answered her question about dressing, he remained in the doorway and leaned one shoulder against the jamb as he folded his arms against his chest.

"Wouldn't you be warmer closer to the fire?" When he merely continued to stare at her, she said, "I guess you're hot enough, leastways that's how I'm interpreting that look."

"Good for you. Now, what do you have to say?"

"Where did you go tonight?"

"To the Number 1 mine."

"I thought you might have. Ramsey stayed inside."

"He promised. When Ramsey and I were talking after dinner, he said something about a man named George Kittredge that made me think I should better acquaint myself with him." He paused, this time setting his jaw, and asked, "Again, what do you want?"

"You really do not like your bath interrupted." When she thought he might actually growl at her, she put out a hand. "I want to talk about Ann. I thought you should know what I learned this afternoon. It will be up to you to decide if you want to repeat it to Ramsey."

"Is this more about Ann having her ear to the ground? Because I've already told him about that."

"No." The space between her eyebrows puckered slightly. "Are you certain you don't want to put a shirt on? I think I see gooseflesh."

Sighing, Quill pushed away from the door frame and went to get his shirt. He threw off the towel, shrugged into the shirt, and buttoned it as he sat on the arm of the chair. "I don't know why I ever thought this was a good idea."

"Yes, you do." She smiled but did not elaborate. Instead, she said, "Tell me how it came to be that you and Ramsey ended up in Mrs. Birden's shop. Ann assured me that it has never happened before. And no, there is really nothing you can do except humor me. It will ease your mind if you recall that I have humored you on more than one occasion."

He was silent a moment, then, "No, I am not finding that as helpful as you seem to think."

Calico was not diverted. "Go on. Tell me."

"It is no great mystery. Ramsey and I were standing on the sidewalk outside the Stonechurch office. Frank Fordham was in the doorway and he wouldn't let us leave. There is always one more thing with Frank. I was listening to him, but I could see that Ramsey's attention was wandering. He kept glancing down the street, and then he suddenly decided he'd had enough and announced we were going. He did not say where, and I did not ask, but the dress shop wasn't our destination. We had just passed it when he stopped, backed up, and cupped his hands against the window so he could peer inside. The first I knew you were in the shop was when he told me."

"Huh."

Quill stretched his legs. "What?"

"How did he tell you?"

"I don't know. He said you were in the shop."

She fiddled with the end of her plait, brushing it lightly against her jaw as she thought. "I mean, did he say something like, 'There's Miss Nash.' Or did he mention his daughter first? 'Why, there is Ann. I should probably stop her before she spends all my money.' Maybe he saw Beatrice."

"Is this important?"

"I believe so."

"Let me think." Closing his eyes, he pinched the bridge of his nose with a thumb and forefinger. "He mentioned you first. Something like, 'Well, here's a piece of luck. Miss Nash is looking at fashion plates.' " He opened his eyes and stared at her. As understanding came to him, his eyebrows lifted a fraction. "He has an interest in you."

"See? I think that is important." Calico yanked at the quilt folded at the bottom of the bed and pulled it around her shoulders and across her lap. "It might not bother you, but it gives me gooseflesh." She regarded Quill thoughtfully. "Not that I could not accustom myself to the chill when the man is as wealthy as Ramsey Stonechurch."

"Mercenary."

That made her smile. "I *am* a gun for hire."

"He's twice your age."

She shrugged. "He wears it well."

"Hmm." He rubbed the back of his neck. "Did you suspect there was interest on his part before this afternoon?"

"I had an inkling at the interview."

"You didn't say anything."

"It was an inkling. Nothing will come of it, except that I will be careful not to encourage him. It is flattering, though, and my head is not easily turned."

"Gooseflesh already gone?"

"I believe it is. Do you suppose he would name something after me?"

"Probably. A park, maybe. Calico Commons."

She struck a thoughtful mien. "Perfect. Yes, I like that. Perhaps with a statue at its —"

"Well, don't start posing for it now. You are a proposal, ring, and ceremony away from marble immortality."

"I know. But I have always taken the long view."

One of Quill's eyebrows kicked up in a

perfectly skeptical arch before he stood and moved closer to the fireplace. He put his back to Calico while he poked at the embers and added a log, and when he was done, he continued to face the fire. No gooseflesh here, he thought. The chill he felt went all the way to his marrow.

He expected to find Calico staring at him when he finally turned around, but she was contemplating her left hand instead, fingers splayed, palm down, turning it ever so slightly, admiring the ring she imagined Ramsey Stonechurch would put there. "Diamond?" he asked dryly.

"With my eyes? Hardly. Emerald. A silver setting, I think. Mined right here in Stonechurch." When Quill said nothing, Calico looked up. His jaw was set in the way it had been earlier when he stood in the doorway. "Oh. It appears we are done with that."

He cocked an eyebrow at her.

"All right," she said. "We *are* done with that." She sighed. "I suppose you want me to tell you about my conversation with Ann now."

Quill neither confirmed nor denied it. His expression was not expectant. He simply waited.

"Ramsey Stonechurch was right," said

Calico. "There is someone keeping Ann here."

"She told you that? You saw him?"

"She did not tell me, not in plain words, but I certainly saw him. Her father will not be pleased, I think, because he is not the young man Ramsey imagines."

Quill groaned softly. "Ramsey won't be pleased about any of it, but at least tell me he is not twice her age."

"No. Not that. But there is no mistaking him for a young man."

"Not the boy who sweeps out the feed store, then."

"No. There is definitely interest on his part, but Ann did not appear to notice him. And you can cross off the Smith and Hamilton boys as well. She was equally awkward around each of them, but not in a girlish, shy sort of way." Calico was pensive. "Have you noticed that she is ill at ease around most people? I did not expect that. And I saw exactly the opposite with Beatrice. She greets everyone as a friend."

At the risk of being sidetracked, Quill still chose to answer. "What I noticed when I was with them was that Ann hung back with me and seemed to find pleasure that her aunt was so clearly enjoying herself."

Under her breath, Calico said, "Men."

"How's that again?"

She waved the question aside. "An observation. Nothing more."

Quill said, "If Ann did not give you a name, would you recognize this man if you saw him again?"

"Yes. He will be surprisingly easy to spot. That's always the way it is when the thing you're looking for is hiding in plain sight. You wonder how you could have possibly missed it because once you see it, you cannot *not* see it. You must have had that experience."

"Nothing's coming to mind."

"Perhaps it will. It's happened to me more than I like to admit, although admitting it keeps me open to the possibility that it will probably happen again. I set out on the trail once to find Boomer Groggins and take him back to the Denver jail. I was out thirty-three days, and the only nibbles came about when I was fishing — for fish. No one knew anything about where he was holed up, and I talked to his mama, his brothers, his cousins, half a dozen friends, and two women who claimed to be his fiancée. The smartest thing Boomer did when he made his escape was not telling anyone about his plans. There wasn't one of them who wouldn't have given him up for the reward money, and his fiancées would have given him up for nothing."

Quill felt a smile tug at his lips, and it was against his better judgment that he asked, "So where was he? I know you brought him in."

"When I got back to Denver, I found a hotel room, cleaned up, and went downstairs to get my first meal in thirty-three days that wasn't fish or hardtack. Guess who served it to me?"

Quill regarded her suspiciously. "No. You're making that up."

Calico held up her right hand. "Swear to God. I was irked some that there was a perfectly good plate of hot chicken and dumplings in front of me that would go cold if I left them, but since the jail was only two blocks up and one block over, I decided to enjoy my dinner. I was feeling a mite sluggish after that big meal, but my trigger finger didn't know that. I took him in and had dessert when I got back because I was feeling peckish again by then."

"What did you have?"

"As I recall, it was a generous slice of walnut cake."

A deep chuckle rumbled in his throat. "You really aren't making that up."

"I'm not, but what convinced you?"

"The walnut cake."

"Huh. Maybe the next time I tell that story, I'll start there."

Quill fell quiet. He stared at her. She sat on the edge of the bed still huddled in the quilt, her heels propped on the frame. Her toes wiggled in the thick woolen socks. Short strands of hair not tamed by her braid shone brightly in the lamplight. Her head was tilted a few degrees to the right as she looked at him inquiringly. The faintest hint of a smile pulled at the corners of her full lips. Her eyes were luminescent and keenly aware, and he saw the subtle change in her expression mirror his own. She took a short, shallow breath and softly bit her lower lip.

"Ah, hell," he said. He closed the distance between them before he had time to think better of it and pulled her to her feet. As he had anticipated, she was not tuckable. Staring at her lush mouth, only inches away now, he had just enough time to wonder why tuckability had ever been a consideration before his lips closed over hers.

He had no expectations about the kiss and had made no predictions about her reaction. He told himself he was prepared for anything. That turned out to be a lie.

Her lips were soft, pliant, and they parted on the smallest of sighs. She held herself very still as his mouth moved over hers the first time, but on the second pass, she gave back. There was pressure from her lips and intention also, and he understood it was the reflection of what she felt from him. That was good. He wanted her to feel his intention.

This kiss was not the impulse of a moment, no matter that it must have appeared exactly that way.

Quill's hands slipped under the quilt and nudged it off her shoulders. He slid his palms down her arms until they came level with the belt of her robe. He tugged, found the knot, and undid it. The robe fell open. The kiss deepened. His fingers walked inside and curved around her waist. He was reminded how slender she was. It was easy to forget that she was a slip of a woman, not fragile, never that, but delicate in the way a spider's web was delicate.

She lifted her arms to his shoulders. Her fingers twisted in the damp, curling ends of hair at his nape. Droplets of water slipped under his collar and slid down his back. He rolled his shoulders and shuddered. He swore he could taste a smile on her lips. It made him chuckle, and the vibration of his mouth on hers was all it took for her to take more of him. His tongue flicked across the ridge of her teeth and then met hers. Even if he had only imagined her smile, he was not mistaken about the hint of chamomile tea.

He sipped on her lips, her tongue, the very air she breathed. It was only when he felt her tug hard on his hair that he lifted his head. She sucked in a ragged breath, looked as if she might say something, but only stared at him instead.

"Uh-huh," he whispered, lowering his head again. "It's like that."

His hands tightened infinitesimally on her waist and slowly moved upward along her rib cage until his thumbs grazed the undersides of her small breasts. He rested them there when he felt her stiffen. He waited for her to relax, and she did by slow degrees, but even then he did not press. She moved against him. It was sweetly erotic, but he recognized experimentation, not experience, and he did not encourage her when she rubbed against his erection. She looked at him then, not startled, not in any way, but not certain either. It was her uncertainty that undid him. He leaned in, touched her forehead with his, and kept it there while his heartbeat slowed.

Later, he kissed her, and it was different this time. His mouth softened, his lips gentled, and he touched her on the corner of her lips, then her cheek, and then just below her ear. She turned her face into the crook of his neck and stayed there for a long time, her breath warm against his skin.

She separated from him, backed up to the bed, and simply folded. Quill stooped to pick up the quilt and remained there while he held it out to her.

Calico made a show of fanning her face with her hand. "I am warm enough, thank you."

He tossed the blanket at her anyway and stood. "Well, I certainly don't need it."

Calico was careful to keep her eyes on his face. "Uh, no. You don't."

"It seems Mrs. Riggenbotham's whore stories were lacking in certain details."

"There were no illustrations, if that's what you mean." Her eyes dropped to his groin. "Still, I grew up on military posts. I know what a cock looks like." She stared at the tent his made in his drawers until it twitched, and then her eyes flew to his face. "You did that on purpose."

"If you believe that, there are definitely holes in your education."

She huffed, but it was only for show and they both knew it. "I cannot believe you remembered Mrs. Riggenbotham's name."

Quill shrugged. "I remember lots of things that don't seem to matter until they do. Hard to figure out if it's a gift or a curse."

"Well, it's interesting."

He sat down on the wide arm of the chair again and folded his arms. "Is that good?"

"Good. Bad. I don't know. It's better than boring." Calico shoved the quilt off her lap and belted her robe. "And because there is always the risk of boring ourselves to the point of stupefication, there will be no more kissing." Before he could speak, she said, "Do you recall what we were talking about before you lunged at me?"

"Lunged? I didn't — Never mind. Yes, I recall. Walnut cake."

Calico's jaw snapped shut with an audible click. Her question had not been rhetorical. She really had lost her way. Stupified.

Unperturbed, Quill said, "You were making a point that things could be hidden in plain sight, and you were making that point in connection to Ann's young man, or rather the man who is not so young but has managed to engage her interest in spite of it. You said you would be able to recognize him when you see him again."

"Yes."

"Will I know him?"

"I am almost sure of it."

He nodded, thoughtful. "Can you arrange a meeting with him? Is that possible?"

"I can try, but I believe it will be awkward to confront him. He will not be expecting it."

"But you'll try?"

"I will." She got to her feet. "Come here with me. I want to show you something."

Quill followed her into the bathing room. She stopped in front of the washbasin and motioned to him to stand beside her. He did, and then he followed the path of her gaze as she looked directly into the mirror.

"There," she said, pointing beside her reflected image. "Don't look at me. Look there."

Quill did. He stared at his reflection for a long moment, his eyes never wavering from the blue-gray pair in front of him, and was eventually rewarded by the odd experience of watching comprehension dawn in his own eyes.

"Damn me," he said under his breath. "God damn me."

"That seems rather harsh," said Calico.

His eyes shifted sideways, and he held her gaze in the mirror. "Are you sure it's me? You said she didn't say so in plain language."

"I'm sure." She took him by the wrist.

"Let's go back to the bedroom, where it's warmer."

Quill shook her off and snapped, "I don't need to be led like a dog on a leash."

Calico paused, nodded, and then she left the room. It was several minutes before he returned. Calico was standing at the fireplace, and she did not give ground when he came up beside her.

"I'm sorry," he said.

"I embarrassed you."

"You gave me every opportunity to figure it out for myself, right down to that story about capturing Boomer Groggins."

"Maybe it wasn't the right example. Maybe I should have told you one about how hard it is to see what's under your own nose. Like the time I —"

Quill's short laugh was rich with self-mockery. "Perhaps later. I have it now."

"Yes, of course."

"Tell me how you ferreted this out in three days."

"All right. I picked up on some things that made me realize Ann changed her mind about college in the East a while back. A long while back, actually. Probably about ten minutes after she clapped eyes on you, and the only reason it took her ten minutes to make the decision is because she lost her

220

mind there for a bit. It's not your fault. I figure you likely smiled at her, being all polite the way you are when you're not barging into someone's room or trying to sneak up behind them, and she was a goner right then and there."

"You know you are being ridiculous."

"What's ridiculous is that, smart as you are, you don't know it."

He sighed. "Go on."

"Well, Ann's smart, too, and she knew better than to make it obvious by telling her father right then that she was going to stay in Stonechurch. She's shy in some ways, so I would guess she skittered out of your way in the beginning. I think you noticed and wanted her to feel comfortable. You probably made sure you spoke to her in passing, had a kind word for her now and again, showed an interest in whatever she was talking about at meals. Does that sound about right?"

It sounded exactly right. Quill swallowed a groan.

"While that's going on, Ann is making her plan. You don't think she came up with the curriculum on the spur of the moment, do you? She's a deep one. That took some serious study. She never thought it would be easy."

"There's something you don't know. Ann never was one to seek me out much. On the occasions she did, it was because she was worried about her father or she was out of sorts with Beatrice. I can count on my fingers the number of times we were alone for more than five or ten minutes."

"I'm sure. No wonder she is trying to find a way to spend time with you. She could not keep speaking on the same two subjects forever, and she was confined by her youth, her sense of propriety, and concern about raising her father's suspicions — and yours."

Quill grimaced, pushed his fingers through his hair. "She's a child."

"That is the first I've ever heard you say so, and I don't think you really treated her that way."

"I didn't treat her like —"

Calico turned her head toward him and cocked a fiery brow. "Like me?" she asked. "Like a whore?"

Quill stared at the flames. "You have a knack for getting under my skin, Calico, and not always in a good way. I was going to say I didn't treat her like a woman full grown."

"Oh."

"Yes," he said. "Oh."

"First love is complicated," said Calico.

He nodded. "We need to find her a beau."

"I thought of that. From what I observed today, it is very slim pickings. This herd's been culled."

That raised a small smile. "What did she say to you this afternoon that tipped the scales? There must have been something."

"Mm. Shooting lessons."

"I hope you didn't encourage that. It took me better than half an hour after dinner to direct Ramsey to another subject. If Ann cares about his welfare, she will not light his fuse again."

"I did not encourage her, but I did ask her who she thought was going to teach her to shoot. Do we need to return to the mirror?"

He practically recoiled. "She said she wanted me to teach her?"

"She did. She was set on it, as a matter of fact. And that's when I knew I had drawn to an inside straight." When Quill could only stare at her, not moving, not blinking, she offered up a slim, sympathetic smile. "You, Mr. McKenna, have yourself a sweetheart."

CHAPTER SEVEN

Calico began to feel restless at the end of her first week. By day fifteen, she was contemplating escape. At the end of her first month, with too much of nothing physical to do, her skin began to crawl. And if it was not a fact, then she was hallucinating. Although she entertained notions of leaving this job behind and taking another, it was never a serious consideration. It did, however, make for a diverting daydream.

Probably because she recently told the story about Boomer Groggins to Quill, sometimes she thought about the thirty-three days she spent pursuing him. Never once in all that time did she feel as twitchy as she did after a week in Stonechurch. And it was only getting worse.

She could point to several factors impacting her current state of agitation. Ramsey's attention had not abated, and while his overtures tended to be subtle, she was aware of how his eyes tracked her movements, even at the dinner table when she was engaged in as ordinary an activity as raising a glass to her lips. Her assignment required her to meet with Ramsey and report on matters related to Ann's education and on her own progress in identifying Ann's attachment. She tried to keep the meetings short, as there was little enough to tell him about Ann's studies day to day, and everything she had to say about identifying the young man was a barefaced lie.

Ann Stonechurch was inexhaustable. Her delicate features and fine manners tended to disguise the fact that she had inherited her father's tenacity. Whether Ann was in her studies or outside of them, Calico had encountered men bound for prison, some facing the hangman's rope, who were less relentless in their quest for freedom than Ramsey's daughter was in the pursuit of getting her way. Ann had not changed her mind about learning to shoot, nor had she changed her mind about wanting Quill McKenna to teach her. As far as Calico could tell, she showed no signs of surrendering. Mentoring a kindred spirit was demanding work, and most nights Calico crawled into bed drained of all thought. Strangely enough, she was content with it.

Beatrice was relentless in a manner peculiar to her. She was relentlessly pleasant, and there were encounters with her that left Calico's teeth aching and others that left her unaccountably sad. When she realized that she was avoiding Beatrice, she made it a point to seek her out instead. Beatrice seemed to welcome the attention, and Calico had a source of information for all things Stonechurch.

Quill McKenna did not come to her room again, and she did not visit his. They had agreed on the occasion of their last meeting not to tell Ramsey what she had learned about the object of Ann's affection. Quill told her he wasn't certain he liked being referred to as an object, and she had threatened to use him for target practice. Thus, their business was satisfactorily concluded.

It had not occurred to Calico that it marked the last moments they would spend any length of time together in private. They caught each other in passing, exchanged information as it came to them, but by and large their conversations occurred in the presence of others. Calico was uncertain why Quill did not show up at her door, but she suspected it was for the same reason she did not announce herself at his.

The kiss had changed things, and she was

a little sorry she had lost a sparring partner, but she did not regret the fact of the kiss. She wondered if he did. That would be a damn shame because all in all it was a very nice kiss. Pleasant. Well, splendid really. Curl-your-toes perfect, if she was being honest. Even now, she could touch her fingertips to her lips and recapture the feel of his mouth on hers. At odd moments she would catch herself doing exactly that and feel so foolish that she coughed or cleared her throat to hide the truth from herself.

It was not that kissing was exactly a novel experience, just one she had not practiced. Like shooting, it required a target. Unlike shooting, the target had to be taller than a bottle and more interesting than a clay pigeon. Quill McKenna met both qualifications, but Calico had reservations about using him for practice. In light of what he had said about not liking the reference to himself as an object, it was doubtful that he would agree to it anyway. He would be more likely to trust her with a gun in her hand and an apple on his head.

Picturing that raised Calico's smile. It was the first time in days that it did not feel forced. She closed the book in her lap and stared at the fire while she thought about that. As much as the Stonechurches, individually and collectively, contributed to her restive state, and as often as she fidgeted when she thought of Quill or Quill's kiss, nothing influenced her mood to the degree that being confined did.

She was certainly not a prisoner. She merely felt like one. It was not enough for her to walk down one side of Ann Street and up the other. Ann, Calico was surprised to learn, did not ride and demonstrated no interest in the activity when Calico offered riding lessons. The future purchase of riding clothes was not a big enough carrot to entice her. Calico was disappointed. Even with Ann in tow, riding would have given her respite. It felt as if she had been cut off from a sure, but temporary, avenue of escape.

Calico's need to be out of the house led her to accept Ramsey's invitation to visit the mines on day ten. She knew it was a mistake before she said yes but heard herself agree to it anyway. Sometimes common sense did not serve one's desires and that was just the way it was. Quill had tried to make it a foursome by inquiring if he and Ann might go along. Ramsey was having none of that. Neither was Ann for that matter. Calico shared a padded leather seat with Ramsey in his comfortably sprung rig, and

Quill was left to keep an eye on Ann while avoiding her at the same time. Calico was sure that of the two them, she had had the better afternoon. Still, at the end of the day she felt selfish for it and came to the difficult conclusion that she could not do it again. Ramsey asked her to join him on two more occasions, but she had plausible excuses each time. Ramsey had no choice but to take Quill with him; otherwise the true intent of his invitation to her would have been revealed. For reasons that were entirely his own, he was not prepared to express his interest overtly.

Calico rested the back of her head against the chair. The front parlor was a comfortable room. When one was alone there, it invited restfulness. She closed her eyes. She was hardly aware of the faint smile still stamped on her lips as she thought about slipping out at night and walking deep into the trees until the pine boughs were thick enough to hide her from even the moonlight. If she called on her imagination, she could hear the crunch of crusty snow beneath her feet and catch the scent of pine. The birds were sleeping, but there was movement around her, stealthy foxes and wily raccoons in search of prey. A sudden gust of wind dropped pinecones out of the trees, and they landed with enough force to *pop! pop!* all around her.

Calico sat up straight and suddenly. Her book had fallen off her lap but she knew that was not the sound she had imagined. It was when embers exploded in the fireplace, creating a shower of sparks, that she understood the real source of what she had heard. Again, she wondered if she was growing soft. In the not so distant past, she would have invented gunfire to explain the noise, not falling pinecones.

"Why, here you are."

Calico came close to launching herself out of the chair. "Beatrice!" She swiveled in her seat. "I didn't hear you come in." But she had, she realized, and wondered if the woman was the stealthy fox or the wily raccoon.

"Oh, I frightened you, didn't I? Goodness, I did not mean to do that." She pressed her hands together, this time in the manner of someone praying for forgiveness. "I came to see if you wanted tea before you retire. A nice chamomile is a sleep tonic; at least I find it so."

"You are kind to think of it, but I will pass this evening. I don't think it settles well in my stomach."

"Really? That is odd. Most people find it

soothing, but perhaps tea with ginger root will suit you better."

"Perhaps, but another night. You caught me catnapping, which proves I am ready enough for sleep without any help." She leaned forward, scooped up her book, and stood. "Has everyone else retired?"

"Goodness, no. My brother-in-law is always the last to go to bed. He works entirely too hard. Ann is in her room, studying, I'm sure, not sleeping, and I just left Mr. McKenna in the kitchen, where he is writing down Mrs. Friend's recipe for orange layer cake. He intends to send it to his mother."

"He has a mother?" As soon as it was out, she wished she had not said it. More than her words, it was her tone that caused Beatrice to stare at her oddly.

"Yes, dear, of course he has a mother, one I should very much like to meet, given the fact that she has raised such an agreeable son as our Mr. McKenna."

"Hmm."

"In the event it had not occurred to you, he has a father also. A minister. He writes to his parents regularly. I know because I carry the post back and forth. There is a brother, but Mr. McKenna does not speak of him often, and usually it is about the past." Her voice fell to a whisper. "I think the brother has been on the wrong side of the law for quite some time. It was back in August, I believe, that Mr. McKenna had to leave Stonechurch on a family matter. He was gone longer than expected, and Ramsey was unhappy about it. He said something under his breath that he probably wishes he had kept to himself."

"What did he say?"

Beatrice hesitated. She fussed with a loose brown tendril that had escaped her topknot. "I suppose since I've told you this much . . ." She made a steeple of her fingers. "Ramsey said he should have been left to rot in jail."

"I see," said Calico.

"What a trial it must be for his parents. And poor Mr. McKenna. A lawyer."

"A trial for him as well," Calico said wryly.

"Oh, my." Beatrice's blue eyes brightened momentarily as she caught the humor of it, but then she looked away as if embarrassed by a lapse in her judgment.

Lord, Calico thought, Beatrice Stonechurch needed to allow herself a human moment. She tucked her book under her arm and stifled a yawn. "I think I will go to my room now. I look forward to seeing you at breakfast."

■ ■ ■ ■

By Calico's reckoning, there were at least four hours remaining before sunlight would steal across the horizon when she left the house. It was plenty of time; she would be satisfied with half that.

She left by the back door, but before she stepped off the porch, she stretched her arms wide and filled her lungs with crisp mountain air. Snow covered the ground, but there were enough tracks going to and from the house that she was able to mask her own. It was nothing more than the kind of precaution that she was used to taking. It seemed unlikely that anyone had heard her leave. She was cautious by nature.

Calico followed the route that she had walked earlier in her mind's eye, up the gradual incline of the hillside, past the junipers, and deep into the cover of the ponderosas. She walked with deliberate care until her eyes accustomed themselves to the dark, and then she picked up her pace, quickening her stride even as the grade steepened. She only paused occasionally and only when she wanted to look over her shoulder. When she spied lamplight winking at her from town, she moved on. When she finally confronted darkness, she stopped and spread the blanket she carried in a roll on her back on the ground. Then she sat. Then she lay down. And then she stared through a narrow space in the pines and imagined the sky opening up to her.

She stayed in just that position, her breath misting, her nostrils flaring slightly as she took in the scent of the earth and open space.

It was cold, of course, uncomfortably so, and her blanket provided almost no barrier, but that hardly mattered at the outset. In any other circumstance, she would have built a small fire and huddled close to it. She also would have had another blanket, her saddle for a pillow, and hot stones to place near her feet.

It would have been heaven. And although she allowed that her bed back at the house was very nearly so, it simply was not the same. It was only when her teeth began to chatter that she admitted to the advantages of comfort over cold.

"You are certifiable as a danger to yourself," Quill said.

Calico blamed her chattering teeth for not having heard his approach. She threw a forearm over her eyes. "You know, it was not so long ago that people couldn't sneak up on me. Go away."

Quill ignored her. "Just what in the hell do you think you're doing out here?"

"I'm recollecting that it's been fifteen years give or take since I've spent more than five days indoors, and I was sick then. Cholera outbreak. I am not used to being indoors, Quill, not for days on end. I needed to have the sky over my head."

Quill was not unsympathetic. He skirted the bottom edge of the blanket and hunkered down beside her. "Did it have to be now? In the middle of the night?"

"It can't be in the middle of the day, now can it? There's Ann."

He laid a gloved hand on her shoulder. "You're shaking, Calico. You can't stay here. You have to get up."

She knew he was right, but except for the movements she couldn't help, she stayed exactly as she was.

"Please."

She would never be able to say what it was about the way he voiced that single word that made her uncover her eyes and stare at him, yet that is what she was moved to do. His hand slid from the curve of her shoulder to under it. She was already so stiff that she accepted his assistance without comment.

"Let me have your hands."

She dutifully gave them over.

Quill removed her gloves, rubbed her hands hard between his, and then held the gloves open so she could slip her hands inside.

"Will you come back with me?"

Calico looked up and found a patch of sky. What she wanted was for him to go away. What she said was, "I want a little longer." Out of the corner of her eye, she saw Quill nod. "How did you find me?"

"I saw you leave."

"I didn't realize anyone was still awake."

"Couldn't sleep tonight. I was sitting at the window bench."

She nodded. "Nothing feels quite right anymore. I haven't fired a weapon since I arrived, and I can't see that there will be an opportunity to do so. That's not good. I need to stay sharp. I need to know I'm sharp."

"I understand."

"I don't think you do. How did you follow me? I was careful. I stepped in tracks made by other people. You shouldn't have been able to find me, and yet you did. Here I am, and somehow I've lost my way."

Quill let a moment pass and then said quietly, "Whose tracks did you imagine you

236

were stepping in, Calico?"

Her eyes widened. *"Yours?"*

He shrugged, nodded. "I do understand." He stood and extended his hand. "Let me help you up."

Calico hesitated, but in the end she placed her hand in his and allowed him to pull her to her feet. "Thank you." When he released her hand, she shook loose the kinks and frozen joints. She crossed her arms, slapped her shoulders, and jumped in place.

Quill picked up her blanket, rolled it, and when she turned around, he strapped it to her back. "You travel light. I usually bring a couple more blankets than this. Do you have a flask?"

She shook her head. "I don't own one."

"Luckily I do. Better yet, I brought it." He reached in his wool coat and pulled out a silver flask. "This is Ramsey's best whiskey, so enjoy it." He opened it and handed it to her.

Calico put the flask to her lips, tilted it, and took a deep pull. The whiskey was warm in her mouth and still warmer as it slid smoothly to the pit of her stomach. "That *is* good." She pressed her lips together to contain the heat. "Mmm."

"Have another," he said when she would have returned the flask.

She did. "Thank you." This time he took it from her and slipped it back in his coat. "You're not having any?" she asked.

"One of us should be sober on the trek back, and I noticed you didn't eat much at dinner. You're going to feel it."

"Unlikely. I was raised on it. Mother's milk."

Quill was skeptical and it showed. "Bravado? Exaggeration? A good bit of both, I'd say."

"Actually, not much of either. Apparently I was a colicky baby."

"Oddly enough, I have no trouble believing that."

Calico jabbed him with her elbow, not hard, just enough to let him know she was alert and listening.

"Come on. Let's go." He turned and started off, and she fell into step beside him.

"Why were you awake?" she asked.

Quill glanced sideways at her. "I was puzzling out the problem of Ramsey's Number 1 mine. I think the men are loosely organized, but if there is a leader, I haven't been able to identify him, and I believe if there were a leader, the men would be better organized."

"You mentioned a name. George . . . George . . ." She shook her head. "No. I

238

can't bring it up."

"George Kittredge."

She held up her right hand and snapped her fingers, or rather she tried. "It's the gloves."

"Uh-huh. About Mr. Kittredge . . . he has been working for Stonechurch Mining for eighteen years. He remembers when Ann was born, how proud and excited Ramsey was at the time, and what a celebration there was that night. Drinks all around, that sort of thing. It's the kind of story a man might share if he wants to prove his loyalty or point out a personal connection."

Quill stopped, lifted a low bough out of the way, and let Calico pass under it before he followed. "Mr. Kittredge is in charge of the crew that lays down explosives. He got his experience during the war, blowing up bridges, rails, and munitions strongholds. He wiggled all ten of his fingers at me as proof that he is good at his job. Came west with the railroad and ended up here. He seems settled, has a wife, children. I don't take him for someone who likes to stir the pot."

"So he is not a candidate for organizing the men."

"No, but I think he suspects something is going on. He hedged, wouldn't say anything straight out, and I mostly listened. He mentioned that he's been having problems with the explosives. Orders not filled properly. Damaged fuses. Wet dynamite. He says he complains, things get better for a time, and then the problem comes around again."

"That would go a ways to explaining why the vein isn't delivering the ore Ramsey expects, but wouldn't there be problems at the other mines? I would think they would order all the explosives from the same place."

"I asked him why he doesn't borrow what he needs from another crew at another mine. That's when I learned he and his men are the only ones working with explosives. It's been that way for a long time. They go from mine to mine as needed, and right now the Number 1 mine is the only one requiring a fire in the hole."

"Do the explosives arrive damaged or are they damaged in storage?"

"I don't know. Kittredge stopped talking. He got skittish as he went on. Started to think better of what he was saying."

"But you said he's complained. Someone must know."

"I said that *he* says he complained. He sounded credible, but I don't know who he reported it to, and if I ask too many times, or ask the wrong people, it will get around. No one will speak to me, or if they do, it will be hard to trust what they say."

"Have you told Ramsey?"

"No. That's what I was trying to puzzle out."

"It's his company. Seems as if it's something he should know."

"Yes, well, it's not entirely his company. Beatrice owns half, remember?"

"I'm not sure why that's important."

"It's important because she has an interest even if she doesn't put her hand in day to day. She leaves the decision making to him, but she pays attention to the operation. She asks questions. I know because I've been in the room when she's come to Ramsey on one matter or another. She has a distinctive perspective on Stonechurch Mining. The operation is personal for both of them, but Beatrice has a different view of the men working for them. She knows the miners by name, knows their families, knows whose wife is going to have a baby and whose father is ill. She visits men who have been injured. She makes sure their families are cared for. Ramsey supports the school, but she knows the children. He gives money to the library, but she heads the committee that chooses the books."

Calico said, "I'm realizing I don't know her at all. I was aware that the shopkeepers were happy to see her, but I assumed that was at least in part because she spent money with them. I observed she spoke to everyone who came in and out of the stores, but I didn't realize she was as familiar with the miners."

"Did you know that she visits the mines more often than Ramsey?"

"She's never mentioned it."

"Probably because she's been doing it for so long that it's a matter of routine to her. Maybe a couple of times a month. She takes things when she goes. Breads and cakes. Little sandwiches that you would expect to have at tea. Jellies and jams. Bandages. Liniments. Salves. Woolen socks. Gloves. The men flock to her."

Calico tugged on Quill's coat at the elbow, stopping him in his tracks. She stared at him, looking for the lie. "Little sandwiches?" she asked, raising her eyebrows. "Truly?"

"Truly. I swear. The miners love them."

Shaking her head, Calico released his coat. They began walking again. "She is not precisely as she seems, is she? I am appreciating that about her."

"It is not making too much of it to say that the men adore her."

"And you think she is sympathetic to them."

"I'm not certain she would be in favor of me digging into this matter too deeply. Ramsey hasn't shared his suspicions with her."

"I think I understand why, but the company's losses are her losses, too."

"There is no denying that. What is less clear is how much she would care about it. I'm not suggesting that she would be complacent if the company was facing bankruptcy, but that's not the case here. The losses are small compared to the gains. She might find it acceptable if she thought the men had something to gain."

Calico was quiet for a long time, then, "No wonder you were awake."

"Hmm."

Calico stopped as they broke through the trees, reluctant to return in spite of the cold. She stamped her feet.

"Do you want another drink?"

She shook her head. "How often do you go out at night?"

"Since you've been here, only once. Before then, every three or four days if I could. Never less than once a week. I'm surprised you tolerated the indoors for as long as you have, unless this is not your first time?"

"No, this is the first I've wandered off."
When he started to go, she said, "Not just
yet. I have a question."

"It can't wait?" When her expression
clearly communicated it could not, he said,
"Go ahead."

"What about Ann? Does she never accompany Beatrice to the mines?"

"No, never. Not that I'm aware."

"Hmm."

"What are you thinking?"

She shrugged. "I'm not sure. I can't
decide if it's odd or understandable."

"Why odd?"

"Beatrice dotes on Ann. It seems it would
be in her nature to invite Ann to join her.
Then again, perhaps Beatrice has asked her
and Ann has not wanted to go."

"Or, and this seems equally likely, Ramsey
forbids it."

"Why would he do that?"

Her genuine confusion made him chuckle.
"You do realize that it is your upbringing
that is out of the ordinary, don't you?"

Calico bristled. "I don't know why you
would say that."

Quill stared at her, trying to make out her
features in the darkness. Finally, he said, "I
can't tell if you're serious."

"What is extraordinary about being raised

to care for myself, tolerate those who are different from me, and expect folks to behave like they have some sense?"

This time Quill's chuckle was absent of humor. "Everything about that seems extraordinary. My brother believes the Lord will provide, my mother's tolerance is limited to people who agree with her, and my minister father expects folks to behave as if Satan's whispering in their ear."

"I can't tell if you're serious," she said, echoing him.

"Oh, I assure you I am. And if Ramsey doesn't want his daughter associating with the miners, who can be rough and unruly as the mood strikes them, it's not the most unreasonable thing he's ever done. He would stand with society on this one, and you would stand alone. Well, mostly alone."

Calico was unconvinced. "If you say so."

"Do you really want to argue about it now?" He swore the shudder that went through her shook the ground under his feet. It was answer enough. "Stubborn woman. Come on."

It was when they reached the relative warmth of the kitchen that Calico felt the full effects of the whiskey. She swayed on her feet as Quill nudged her into the room. "Ooh." She put a hand out to steady herself and found the table.

Quill stopped her from pulling out a chair by putting his hands on her waist and moving her toward the back stairs. "Mother's milk," he said under his breath. "I don't think so. You're drunk."

"Am not."

"*Sh.* Whisper."

"Am not," she repeated, this time quietly.

Quill decided the better course was not to call her a liar. He unstrapped the blanket roll from her back and stayed close behind her as they climbed the stairs. With a little physical guidance and some prompts in her ear, he managed to get Calico inside her room without anyone else coming out of theirs.

Calico removed her hat and tossed it behind her. Quill caught it, leaving her to cross the room unassisted. Spinning around with more grace in her mind than in reality, Calico collapsed backward on the bed. "Ooh." She blinked rapidly and pressed her fingertips to her temple. "I should not have done that."

Rolling his eyes, Quill dropped her Stetson on the trunk lid and then went around the bed to where she was sprawled on top of it. Her splayed legs were hanging over the side. "Boots first," he said, and hunkered down.

"I can do that."

"Uh-huh." He pulled them off and set them gently on the floor. "Socks on or off?"

"Off."

Quill removed them and dropped them inside her boots. He pulled off his gloves, stuffed them in his pockets, and then rubbed each of her feet between his hands. When he judged they were warm enough, he tugged on her little toes to see if she was still awake.

"Hey," she said. "Why'd you do that?"

"Because I could." He took her by the ankles and lifted her legs as he stood, then he shifted her ninety degrees so she was lengthwise on the bed instead of crosswise. This had the effect of twisting her duster so he leaned over and began unbuttoning it. She slapped at his hands, not hard, but just to let him know she was protesting. He ignored her. Once he had wrestled the jacket off, he removed her gloves and warmed her hands as he had warmed her feet. He thought she might have sighed, but because she was Calico Nash, he thought it was just as likely that she had sworn at him. Shaking his head, he yanked the blankets from under her, pulled them over her, and tucked her in.

He thought her eyes were closed, but

when he finished, she was looking at him. "Warm enough?"

"Mm." She tugged on the covers until they were at her chin. "Toasty."

Quill could not tell if her smile was sleepy or drunken. Probably a little of both, he decided. "I'm going to see to the fire." He turned to go, but she caught him by the hand. "What is it?"

"I don't know." And she didn't. She felt oddly disconnected from her thoughts. They tumbled, flitted, but she could neither follow one nor catch it when it landed. "Will you sit with me?"

Quill's eyes shifted from her to the chair. "Let me take care of the fire first."

Calico was slow to release his hand, and when she did, she felt bereft. To see him better, she rose up on her elbows and stayed that way while he stirred the fire and added wood. It seemed to her that he remained there overlong, staring at his handiwork, but eventually he turned and came to the bed. It was only when he was standing beside her that she realized she had been holding her breath.

"If you like, I can move that chair closer to the bed," he said.

She lay back again and smoothed the blankets. "No. Leave it there."

He nodded and started to retreat.

"No," she said when she understood he meant to sit in it no matter where it was. "I want you to sit here. With me."

Quill turned and stepped sideways out of the line of the firelight. His eyes narrowed fractionally as he studied her features. She did not look as if she was up to mischief, but neither did she look particularly innocent. "You have a good poker face."

"I do," she said agreeably.

"I still think you're drunk."

"I'll let you know when I'm drunk."

Quill took off his hat and coat and put them on the window bench. He ran a hand through his hair. "Wouldn't it be better if you behaved like you have some sense?"

Calico patted the space beside her. "Wouldn't it be better if you behaved like Old Scratch was whisperin' in your ear?"

"Damn," he said under his breath. And then he sat. "Move over, I need more room."

Calico scooted sideways while Quill made a quarter turn toward her and drew up a knee so he could rest it on the bed. "Better?" she asked.

He ignored the question and asked his own. "Do you ever not get your way?"

"Of course."

"Name one time."

She didn't have to think about it. "I offered to give Ann riding lessons, and she turned me down."

"Did she tell you she's afraid of horses?"

"No. Is she?"

"Uh-huh."

Calico sighed. "Well, there you have it. My motive was completely selfish, but you already know that. I wanted a reason to get out of the house."

"Maybe there is something I can do about that."

"Really?"

"Maybe. No promises." Quill glimpsed her hopeful expression before she schooled her features. "No promises," he said firmly.

Calico slipped one arm free of the blankets and found his hand. She wrapped her fingers around his and squeezed.

He merely grunted softly, noncommittally.

She opened her fingers but did not withdraw her hand. There was a short silence. She could not guess what he was thinking, but she decided to say what was on her mind. "Men have kissed me before."

Quill blinked. "I know," he said slowly. "I was one of them. Did you think I forgot?"

"No. At least I hoped not. It's all right to say that, isn't it? That I hoped you didn't forget?" She sighed heavily. "This is like set-

250

ting out in the dark with no notion of the lay of the land. Seems I'm already running headlong into my first obstacle what with you sitting there like the great stony face of a mountain."

"I was only waiting for you to draw a breath. The answer to your question is yes. It's all right to say that you hoped I didn't forget."

She nodded. "I guess that's good. That you didn't forget and that I can speak my mind about it."

"Yes," he said, careful not to smile. "Both those things are good."

Catching something vaguely patronizing in his tone, she regarded him suspiciously. "You just spoke to me as if I were a child. There is no convincing you I am not drunk."

"Tipsy, then."

"If you like." She waved her hand airily. "Now about the other. I thought you should know that those men who kissed me, well, I kissed them back. Most of them."

Quill knew he shouldn't ask, but the devil was whispering in his ear. "The ones you didn't kiss back . . . what did you do?"

"I walloped one with my first reader. I was six and he was eight."

"That happens," Quill said philosophically.

"The other fellow I marched off to jail at the end of my Colt."

"For kissing you? That seems excessive. Please tell me you were not six."

"Funny. He was a felon who thought he had a way with women, whether they wanted him to have his way or not. It was a real pleasure taking him in."

"Good for you."

She smiled a trifle lopsidedly, proud of what she'd done and a little embarrassed that she had shared it. "So there you have it. I am not inexperienced."

"And you thought that was important to tell me."

"Yes. It occurred to me that you might have thought differently." She shrugged. "Did you?"

"I did."

"Ah-hah."

Laughter rumbled deep in his throat. "Ah-hah? Do you think we would still be kissing if I had gauged your experience better?"

Calico sobered, after a fashion. "I didn't think that . . . exactly."

"Hmm."

"But I've noticed that when you're not barging in where you don't belong, or sneaking up on a body, you're real mannerly."

"You think I need some encouragement?"

"Don't you?"

"Not as much as you're offering."

Her eyebrows lifted. "Then why haven't you kissed me?"

"Aren't you worried that we'll get bored with it? Bored to the point of stupefication, I think you said."

"I said that because I shouldn't want you. I don't even want to like you."

In vino veritas," Quill said, shaking his head. "I know. Don't you think I know? Here it is, Calico, the truth: If I kiss you now, it won't end there. Not this time. I don't mind if you take me for a gentleman, but you should not mistake me for a saint." The look he gave her was significant for its knowing. "And it's already too late for you to bluff. Your poker face doesn't work when you're flushed to the roots of your hair."

Still, she tried. "Of course I'm flushed. These blankets are tucked around me so I can't move, and that fire is blazing. I'm still wearing all my clothes, and you poured whiskey down my —"

Quill said, not unkindly, "Shut up, Calico." He bent and put his lips to hers.

She made a small sound, not protesting, just startled. She welcomed the pressure of his mouth. It held her still in a way the tight cocoon of blankets could not. It comforted and excited, and it seemed perfectly reasonable just then that his kiss should do both.

When he released her, drawing back just a hairsbreadth to change position, she lifted her head, reluctant to let him go. Her mouth brushed his jaw. His stubble was rough against her sensitive, slightly swollen lips, but the sensation tickled more than stung. She followed the line of his jaw to the hollow behind his ear, and then she whispered, "One of us is on the wrong side of the blankets." His soft chuckle made her smile; his breath was warm against her neck.

Neither of them attempted to deal with the wrong side/right side of the blanket problem. A tangle was inevitable. What they avoided was the argument about it.

Quill caught her chin with his fingertips and lifted it a fraction. Her lips parted. The narrow, dark space between them was an invitation. Their sweetly puckered outline was a promise.

"You are all temptation," he said, and then he plundered her mouth.

Calico welcomed him, welcomed the deep, driving force of that kiss, the way it covered her, took her over, took her under, and made her so very grateful she was a woman to this man. She lifted her arm that was still outside the blankets and rubbed his back with her palm. His shoulders bunched under her touch. A shudder tripped along the length of his spine. He moved closer. It was as if she had pulled a trigger.

She liked that.

Calico stretched, arched her back. She wanted to be against him; she wanted to be flush to his taut frame. The blankets were an annoyance. Their clothes were genuine obstacles.

She freed her other arm from out of the cocoon and slid her hand between their bodies. Three buttons fastened his jacket and she undid them easily. Further exploration revealed four buttons on his vest, and she worked on those from top to bottom. When she found six buttons on his shirt, she actually groaned and pushed at his shoulders in frustration.

"You are more buttoned up than an undertaker."

Quill levered himself on one elbow and regarded her handiwork. "You seem to be doing all right. Do you want help?"

Calico put up a hand, pretending to shield her eyes from his grin. "My God, Quill, even in this light your teeth gleam." When he abruptly laughed, she clapped that hand over his mouth. "Shh. You will wake some-one."

He circled her wrist and removed her hand, but not before he kissed the heart of her palm. That quieted her. He moved her hand to his shirtfront and waited for her fingers to begin to fiddle with a button. "One at a time," he said, releasing her.

A small crease appeared between Calico's eyebrows as she worked. "This is like picking a lock, only harder." She nudged his breastbone with the heel of her hand when she felt a chuckle rumbling in his chest. He never gave sound to it, so she didn't hit him again. When she was done, she felt a measure of satisfaction out of all proportion to what she had accomplished . . . until she discovered the buttons on his union suit. "This is what explosives are for," she muttered.

"You are frightening, do you know that?" He pushed her hand out of the way and finished the job himself. As soon as he was done, her hand slipped inside the opening and lay against his skin. He sucked in a breath. "Your fingers are still cold."

"Why do you think they were so clumsy with the buttons? I'm warming them." Before he could stop her, she turned so she could get her other hand inside. "This is nice. You're like a furnace. Should have known, you swallowing the sun and all."

"Uh-huh. That must be it." He might have said more, had been considering it anyway, but her palms began to slip upward across his chest. If he was warming her up, then she was doing the same to him.

Calico parted the material wider. She leaned in and kissed him in the space she made between her hands. She did it again and again, each kiss a little higher on his chest than the last, until she reached the hollow below his throat. Lifting her head, she kissed him on the mouth.

Quill let her topple him onto his back. She rolled so she was partially covering him with the blankets and her body. This time he was the one cocooned. As confinements went, this one had a lot to recommend it. He waited to see what she would do.

For a time, she merely held his gaze. Direct. Steady. He did not feint. Neither did she. The narrowest of smiles signaled her intent. Satisfaction for her. Anticipation for him. She lowered her head and touched the corner of his mouth where his faint dimple lived. Her lips slid over his. The tip of her tongue traced the crease on the first pass and filled it on the second. She pressed; he drew her in. The kiss was deep and wet and soft. Pleasure blossomed and then lingered.

Calico held his head in her hands, her fingers threaded deeply in his hair. She ran her tongue along the sensitive underside of his lip and traced the ridge of his teeth. She feasted on his mouth. He tasted faintly of peppermint. She realized she probably tasted of whiskey. Kisses should always taste so fine.

Quill did not try to take command, and she was grateful for that. He seemed to understand that she needed to set the pace, and the pace she set was unhurried. She wanted to explore, and for a long time he was content to let her have her way . . . until he wasn't.

His move was sudden, the effect, arresting. He wrestled his arms free, took Calico by the shoulders, and pushed her onto her back. While she was struggling up to her elbows, he sat up and shrugged out of his jacket. He tossed it to the foot of the bed, where it slid over the side. His vest was next, and it went the way of his jacket.

"Now you," he said, turning on her.

Calico's eyes widened at the predatory gleam in his. She pointed to his chest. "Um. Shouldn't you take off your shirt?"

He arched one eyebrow. "Do you want

help?" When she shook her head, he tugged at the blankets so she could get her arms under them. She wriggled like a worm on a hook until she produced her leather vest. He flipped it over his shoulder. It landed on the trunk at the foot of the bed. "Now unbutton your shirt."

She hesitated.

"Or I can do it."

Calico's hands slipped under the blanket again. Her fingers were clumsy, but the cold did not account for it. What followed consisted of contortions and squirming, but she removed her shirt and showed it to him.

He looked at it, grinned. "You're a step ahead. Lucky me."

Realizing he had only told her to unbutton the shirt, Calico threw it at his head.

"Now, see, that's where you're different," he said after he dragged it down over his face. "I figure a lot of women would have fought to get this back." He pitched it over his shoulder.

"And I figure them for ninnies. You were going to get it anyway."

He bent his head and dropped a swift kiss on her parted lips. "Yes, indeed. I surely was." Quill removed his shirt and held it up. "In the interest of fairness." He gave it the same careless toss he had given hers, but before he lay beside her again, he took off his boots.

Calico regarded his feet with a raised eyebrow. "What about your socks?"

"My feet will get cold." When she continued to stare at them unsympathetically, he shrugged, and yanked them off. There was no way Calico was going to hold on to the covers after that, which, he supposed, had been her plan all along. The inevitable tangle happened then, but compromise eventually begat comfort.

Quill's hand curved around Calico's waist. With minimal pressure at his fingertips, he urged her closer. He plucked at the fabric he encountered. "Are you wearing a union suit?"

"It was cold outside."

Shaking his head, Quill found the uppermost button. He paused and whispered, "I'm better with corset strings."

"I'm sure," she said dryly.

"But I know how these work."

Calico didn't say a word. There was a hitch in her breath as he unfastened the first button. His fingertips scraped her skin. She expected to see sparks. By the time he'd finished unfastening all the buttons, she expected her flesh to ignite.

His hand slipped inside the flannel and

lay against her rib cage. His thumb made a pass just short of the underside of her breast. It didn't matter that he hadn't touched her breast; it only mattered that it felt as if he had. Her nipple swelled. She wanted him to make another pass with his thumb, this one directly over her aureole. She wanted his thumbnail to flick the little soldier until it stood at attention. Every pass he made brought him closer, and then he was cupping her breast. It would be now, she thought, closing her eyes. It would be now.

But it wasn't his thumb that she felt dart across her nipple.

It was his tongue.

CHAPTER EIGHT

Calico felt herself pulled as taut as a bow. The length of her body arched. Her heels dug into the mattress. The back of her head dug into the pillow. He rolled her nipple between his lips. He sipped, sucked, and she felt a contraction deep inside her. Her skin prickled, and sensations she had no name for flooded her. Waves of heat were chased by cooler ones. Whiskey and peppermint. What he was doing to her was deliciously carnal and wonderfully wicked.

She was glad for the devil whispering in his ear.

Her fingers pushed into his hair. They fluttered once and then they were still. She tried to hold him when he wanted to lift his head. She heard him chuckle, felt the vibration of it against her skin, and then he slid his mouth sideways into the valley between her breasts, and climbed out the other side. He caught her untried nipple in his lips and tugged. She thought he might have said something about fairness, but she couldn't be sure, and she didn't care anyway. Not just then.

He laved her aureole with his tongue. Calico concentrated on the slightly abrasive nature of his touch. Sand over velvet. Like his voice. His touch was like his voice, mesmerizing. In a different frame of mind, a twenty-mule team could not have dragged that admission from her, but if he had asked now, she would have told him. He could have asked her anything and she would have told him true.

When she felt him push against her hands this time, she let him go. He had changed her perspective. She understood now that she was the beneficiary of giving him his way, and everything was easy after that. It was not often she was content to follow someone else's directions.

"Look at me," he said.

She did. He was not smiling. It was impossible to make out the color of his eyes, but the way he looked out of them was intense.

"You don't want to miss anything."

He was right. She didn't. Calico nodded.

"Good." He kissed her. "Very good." He kissed her again.

When he was done, Calico realized she

had missed a good deal. The top of her union suit was bunched around her waist, and she had no idea how he had made that happen. She did not dwell on it long. Couldn't. He was tugging on it now and that captured all of her attention.

"Lift your hips."

She did. Quill rolled the suit over her hips, past her thighs, and then he disappeared under the blankets to finish the job. The union suit appeared. Quill didn't.

She felt his lips at the side of her right knee, his fingers under it. He dragged his mouth a few inches higher. His hand curled around her thigh. She knew it was as black as pitch under the blanket, but he was having no difficulty finding his way. He was climbing her like ivy.

"Raise your knees."

She did. He moved between them, separating them farther. With knees lifted, the blankets tented him and she could no longer see movement or watch his progress. Her hips jerked involuntarily when he kissed her mons. The rosy flush that eventually colored all of her started there.

Quill did not linger, not with his mouth. He made a pass across her belly, took some care with her navel, and then attended again to each breast in turn. When his head finally reappeared, Calico's eyes were open but infinitely darker than they had been. They were also vaguely unfocused.

That did not last. They came sharply to attention when his hand slid between her thighs and he eased two fingers inside her.

"That's right," he said, his lips hovering just about her mouth. "Make them wet for me."

She did. Slick with dew, Calico contracted around him. Groaning softly, he thrust his hand more firmly against her. She pushed back. He kissed her then, echoing the movement with his tongue in her mouth. Once again, she pushed back.

Her fingers scrabbled at the sheet, clutching it in her fists, but when he told her to put her arms around him, she clutched him instead. Sounds she did not recognize as her own rose from the back of her throat. Her mouth hummed against his lips. Her body hummed against the length of his. She felt his erection pressing. She wanted it pressing inside her.

He eased his hand away and lifted his head. "I know you know," he whispered. "But are you ready?"

"I'm ready," she whispered back.

Quill showed the first signs of impatience as he tried and failed to unbutton the front

265

flap of his union suit. When he swore softly, Calico helped him push it over his hips instead. She cradled him between her thighs. He lifted his hips. Without thinking, she angled hers to meet him. Her fingers grazed his cock, then circled it, and finally guided him to her.

Oh, yes. She was ready.

He levered himself on his elbows and thrust, not deeply at first. That came later. He tried to be careful, but she was impatient and, as was her custom, was bent on having her way. When she winced and dug her fingers into his shoulders like talons, he paused to give her another chance to accommodate his entry. He also did not pass on the opportunity to give her a sardonic look.

Calico came within a moment of answering his mockery by sticking her tongue out, but he began to move, and she nearly sank her teeth into it. She reared up and nipped him on the neck instead.

He grit his teeth and growled in her ear. It sent a shiver all the way to her toes.

She uncurled her fingers and smoothed over the crescent indentations in his flesh. Her hands slid down his back on either side of his spine and came to rest at the small of it. When he moved, she felt it first in him and then in herself. It made his thrust seem fuller somehow, made the experience richer, made her feel as if she were not merely taking part of him, but all of him. She was not sure she *should* feel that way. It was premature, possibly unwise, but denying it would have been wrong. She did not want these moments to be less than they were.

She was glad he had told her to open her eyes. He was beautiful. Strained, his features were masterfully cut. They showed in sharper relief than usual and the symmetry held. His eyes were dark, impenetrable at their centers, and firelight cast one side of his face in a pale orange glow. His thatch of hair absorbed the light. His face reflected it. She raised her hand and cupped his cheek cautiously. There was heat, and he was the source of all of it.

Sparks rose in a spiral from the point of their joining. They were familiar to her. She had felt them earlier, but they had faded, become a memory. They did not fade this time. They were white hot, delicately sharp, and they pricked her as they skittered across her skin. Her muscles jumped, twitched, but it never occurred to her to try to avoid it. What she wanted was to feel it more deeply.

Calico dug in her heels as the exquisite

stirrings of pure pleasure flooded, and then overwhelmed her. She would have cried out if he had not covered his mouth with hers. He swallowed whatever unintelligible thing she might have said and took the spasm that rocked her body and made it his.

His thrusts quickened, his breathing sharpened, and he buried his face in the curve of her neck as his body jerked. He did not try to avoid coming inside her, and he was deep when it happened. He nipped her flesh as she had done to him, but then he kissed her there and turned the feral attack into a moment of tenderness.

Quill felt her stiffen. Apparently tenderness was what she wasn't ready for.

He did not want to move, but he did. In consideration of his weight and her silence, Quill rolled onto his back and tugged his union suit over his hips and up to the level of his waist. His heart was still thumping in his chest but slower now, and what had been a thundering in his head had quieted to a dull and distant roar. He was aware that Calico lay unmoving. The blankets did not stir once he was settled. Nowhere did their bodies touch, but heat radiated between them.

He had no idea what she might be thinking, and he did not spend a moment guessing. Instead, he asked, "Are you all right?" When she did not answer, he turned on his side, raised himself on an elbow, and regarded her profile. The shadow that he cast made it difficult to clearly see her features, but he could tell she was not sleeping. The opposite seemed to be true. Her stillness was a consequence of how alert she was. He thought she might come out of her skin if he touched her. She certainly would leap out of the bed. He kept his hands to himself and prompted her. "Calico?"

Her response was barely a whisper. "I think I might be bleeding."

"Ah."

"Ah? Is that all?"

"This is a new conversation for me."

"For me, too. And I am the one bleeding."

"It might not be blood. It might be me."

"You?"

"My seed."

"Oh."

"Mm. What would you like me to do?"

"Leave."

"Besides that."

"Then I don't know."

"What if I light the lamp? At least then you will be able to see."

She hesitated. "Where will you be while

I'm looking?"

"On the other side of the room, if you like. With my back turned."

"All right."

Quill raised the covers enough to swing his legs over the side of the bed as he sat up. He found matches in the bedside table's single drawer, lit the lamp, and adjusted the wick. He checked with her to make sure the light was adequate before he walked to the fireplace. He warmed his hands while he waited to hear the results of her examination. It did not occur to him that she would not say anything, so he was surprised when he caught her out of the corner of his eye making a beeline for the bathing room.

He got to the door in time for her to shut it firmly in his face. The tail of the sheet she had wrapped herself in got trapped between the frame and door. He stared at it, considering what he wanted to do, but then she took matters into her own hands. He heard her swearing softly as she cracked open the door and yanked on the sheet. He might have gotten a toehold before she closed it again, but he did not even try. He waited on his side of the door and listened for a while before he returned to the bedside.

He shrugged into the rest of his union suit, buttoned it up. He found his shirt and put it on and then gathered her clothes, folded them, and placed them at the foot of the bed. He opened her wardrobe and removed a cotton shift and her robe. He hung them on the bathing room's doorknob so they were within her easy reach. Inside that room, he heard the water stop running. It did not seem to him that enough time had elapsed for her to fill the tub.

Quill knocked. "Are you all right?" She murmured something he could not make out. "May I come in?"

"No!"

He heard that. "Then I won't. I have your nightgown and robe hanging right here when you want them." It was shortly afterward that the door opened a fraction.

"Step back," she said.

He did. "They're on the knob."

Calico slipped her hand through the opening and felt for her belongings. She clutched both articles in her fist and pulled them inside. This time she made certain everything cleared the door before she closed it.

Quill waited for her on the window bench. When she finally reappeared, he stood. She did not try to mask her annoyance. "I told you I would do anything besides leave."

"I remember."

"You didn't take me at my word?"

"I didn't take you for being so patient."

"And I never figured you for a coward."

Calico bristled. "I am not a coward."

"Are you saying you weren't in there longer than you had to be? You were hoping I would give up and be gone."

Her chin came up. "Well, if I was — and I'm not saying I was — it didn't work. You're still here." Barefooted, she stalked to the bed and unfastened her robe. She dropped it where she stood. Throwing back the covers, she crawled in, set her back against the headboard, and drew the blankets up to her waist. "If you must know, the sheet was stained. I had to wash it out."

He doubted that the activity accounted for all of her time in the bathing room, but he decided the wiser course was not to challenge her. He'd called her a coward and lived. No sense tempting fate.

"It won't dry in there," he said. "Not by the time the maid who sees to your room arrives. What if I bring it in here, lay it over the chair close to the fire?"

"Or I could just make the bed before Molly gets here. I usually do, you know. I'm not used to people tidying up after me."

Quill gave her a long, contemplative look before he got to his feet. "I don't know if you could be more stubborn."

"I could try," she said under her breath.

"I heard that," he said, but he was already headed for the adjoining room and he didn't pause to look back at her. She would not have been pleased that he was grinning.

Calico did not look in his direction when he returned with the sheet over his arm, nor when he snapped it out and draped it over the chair.

Quill pushed the chair closer to the fire. "You don't have to be embarrassed. In medieval times the lord of the manor would have waved a bloody sheet from his window to show everyone his bride had been a virgin. Or so I've read." He turned in time to get a pillow in the face. He caught it before it dropped to the floor. "I suppose I deserved that."

"There's no supposing about it."

He nodded and carried the pillow back to the bed. He stood at the side, waiting, hoping he had already proved his well of patience was deeper than hers. She did not extend her invitation in words. Rather, she moved over and returned the space he had previously occupied. He lifted the covers himself and stuffed the pillow she'd thrown at him behind his back as he sat. Quite deliberately, he sat close enough to brush shoulders, and took it as a good sign when she did not scoot away.

Of course she could have only been trying to prove she was not a coward.

"There were several things wrong with your story," she said.

"Oh." His eyebrows lifted. "We're going to talk about that?"

She went on as if he had not spoken, ticking off her points on her fingers. "First, we are not living in medieval times. Second, you are not lord of this or any other manor. Third, I am not your bride. And fourth, I was not embarrassed."

"I will stipulate to the accuracy of the first three items, if you will agree that the fourth is a bald-faced lie."

"Stipulate?" Her cheeks puffed as she blew out a breath. "You don't have to pretend to be a lawyer here. In fact, I'd prefer that you didn't."

"All right," he said easily. "But do you agree?"

"That I was embarrassed? Yes, I will agree, but you shouldn't mistake it for being ashamed. I wasn't ashamed."

"I should hope not."

"Mrs. Riggenbotham told me it could happen."

"I thought she might have."

"She also said it doesn't always. I was hoping that I'd be an exception."

That made him curious. He looked sideways at her. "Why?" He saw her hesitate then shrug.

"I suppose because you wouldn't have known for sure that you were the first. It seems like something you would take real serious, probably feel some sort of obligation. I didn't want to be responsible for that."

"Hmm. We see it a little differently. I don't think you are responsible for how I feel about anything."

"So you don't feel an obligation."

"I didn't say that. I said you're not responsible if I do."

"But I don't want you to be beholden."

"That's not up to you."

"You are worse than stubborn," she said. "You are deliberately provoking."

"Look at me, Calico."

"Not if you're grinning."

"I'm not."

She turned her head. His face was very close to hers.

"You are not responsible," he said. "And I am serious about this." He lifted the underside of her chin with his fingertips, tilting her head and lowering his own. He kissed her then. At first it was hardly more than the suggestion of a kiss. His lips brushed hers, gentle and careful. Her mouth softened, parted, but the tenor of the kiss remained unchanged.

He was deliberately provoking.

Quill let his fingers fall away. Calico's head did not drop a fraction. Her lips were pliant and the kiss was no longer something being done to her. She was returning it with the same care and gentleness that he had shown her. He wanted it to linger, to last long beyond this moment, but there was something else he wanted as well. It was then that he drew back and searched her face. He could tell that she had never closed her eyes. He couldn't help himself; it made him smile.

Her lips twitched, quirked, and in spite of her efforts to make it otherwise, they unfolded into a wide smile. "It's like a yawn," she said, staring at his mouth. "It's contagious."

Quill passed a hand over the lower half of his face. When his mouth was revealed again, the smile was gone.

Calico sobered as well.

He said, "I want you to promise that under no circumstances will you cut me out."

"Cut you out? I don't understand."

"I think you do. You tried to get rid of me earlier. Given the chance, you'll try it again. That's why I want your word."

"I told you, I was embarrassed."

"I know what you said, and I know you will always have a reason. I want to have a say. I want your word."

Her eyebrows puckered as she frowned. "Why would you even believe me?"

"Are you saying I shouldn't?"

"No. I'm saying that —" She stopped, shook her head. "Never mind. You've got my thinking all twisted. That's a lawyer trick."

"Sorry."

"Hmm." She continued to regard him with suspicion.

"Your word," he said again.

"You are like a hound with the blood scent."

"Uh-huh."

Calico said nothing. Her eyes never wavered from his, but she did blink first. Swearing softly under her breath, she threw up her hands. "All right. I give you my word."

"Say all of it. You have to say all of it."

"I will not cut you out."

"Under any circumstances."

"I will not cut you out under any circum-

277

stances." She pointed a finger at him. "And just see if you don't regret it."

Quill was philosophical. "Well, that's something for me to think about, isn't it?"

"You should have thought of it before you extracted my promise."

"I did not have a gun to your head."

"Would you have left this bed if I hadn't given it?"

"No."

"And there is my point exactly."

"Do you want me to leave?"

Calico's lips parted as her jaw sagged. She required a moment to regain the power of speech. "It didn't work the last time I asked you. Why would it work now?"

"Because I am the one asking. You can pretty much depend on me to be open to your answer if I'm putting the question to you."

Abruptly, she slid down the headboard, yanked the pillow from under her neck, and placed it squarely over her face. She then proceeded to groan loudly into it.

Quill waited until she was quiet for almost a minute before he lifted one corner of the pillow. "So do you want me to leave?"

She tore the pillow out of his hand and crossed her arms over it. This time she used it to smother her laughter. She had to give it up when it became almost impossible to breathe. He was a gauzy figure when she looked up, and she had to dash tears from her eyes to see him more clearly.

"I could cheerfully kill you," she told him, hugging the pillow to her chest. She hiccupped softly. "I swear I could."

"I believe you." He stretched out beside her, turning on his side to look at her closely. "You were laughing, weren't you? I wasn't sure at first."

"You don't sound as if you're sure now." She took pity on him, although she had no explanation for it. "Yes, I was laughing. I'm tired and cranky and I don't think I am going to be able to sleep, and you were buzzing in my ear like a bee I could not swat for fear of knocking myself out, and it was all just . . ." She hiccupped again. "Just . . ."

"Too much?"

She nodded. When she closed her eyes, tears leaked from under her lashes. Her face crumpled. She started to bring the pillow up over her face again, but he stopped her. She did not resist when he took it away, nor did she stop him when he drew her into his arms. She curled into him. His chin rested against her head. He stroked her hair. He never once told her to hush. He never once said everything would be all right. How could he have known that anyway? He did not know why she was crying.

Neither did she.

Quill did not know how long he held her, but he knew he held long after she quieted. She must have been comforted in his arms, or at least comfortable, because he released her as soon as he felt her try to draw back. He did not want to make that hard for her.

He supposed this circumstance would be a good test of the promise she had made. He could not imagine that she cried often, and probably never openly, and she would likely be embarrassed. He waited to see if she told him to leave.

Calico lifted her head while Quill put the pillow under it. She used a corner of one of the quilts to dab at her eyes and blinked rapidly to fan the ones that threatened. Her smile was watery and apologetic, and she did not quite meet Quill's eyes when she looked up at him.

"That has never happened to me before," she said. "Is that what is meant by hysterics?"

"The very definition, I believe."

She sniffed, nodded thoughtfully. "If it happens again, I want your promise that you will put me down. I do not want to end my days in an asylum."

"I doubt either of those two endings will be necessary."

"Your promise."

"You have it."

"Use your gun and don't let me see it."

"You have my promise to put you down. You don't get to tell me how to do it." Before she could argue, Quill lifted the covers and rolled out of bed.

"Where are you going? You're not leaving, are you? If you go, I want it recorded wherever you are keeping score on these things, that I did not ask you to leave."

Quill looked sideways at her as he bent to retrieve the coat he had dropped on the window seat. He tapped the side of his head with a forefinger. "Noting it right now."

"You trust that? You should probably write it down."

Ignoring her, he held up his coat, patted down the pockets, and retrieved his flask. "Hair of the dog," he said, holding it out as he approached the bed. He uncapped it and handed it to her. When she took it from him, he crawled back in. "Go on. Drink up."

She took a good swallow and handed the flask back. "At least you didn't say it would calm my nerves."

He raised the flask to his lips and drank deeply before he capped it again and set it beside the lamp.

"Why did you take a drink?"

"Well, if I have to have a reason, I figure it'll calm my nerves."

Calico's soft groan did not require a pillow stopper. She flopped on her back and was still shaking her head when he finally made himself comfortable beside her. "Are you going to sleep here?"

"No, but I am going to wait until I know you're sleeping."

"I knew it. I bet you feel obliged. See? It has begun. You shouldn't have followed me. And you definitely shouldn't have brought a flask."

"Is it the worst thing you can imagine that someone wants to look out for you?"

"No," she said. "But then when I was twelve, I imagined a two-headed dragon that breathed blue and green sulfur fire, had a scorpion tail full of poison, and was herding me toward the edge of a canyon."

Quill could picture it. "That sounds bad. Something at dinner not set right with you? Was it chicken?"

She shook her head. "Peyote."

Now it was Quill who groaned softly. "I don't want to know." He heard her quiet laugh and then just quiet. He slipped an arm under her, drew her close, and she fit

herself against him as if she had been doing
it for years.

Lying down the way they were, Quill
discovered she was tuckable after all.

Calico awoke as soon as the maid opened
the door. She sat straight up. The room
swam briefly, but she recognized it as more
a consequence of bolting upright than of
drink. Quill was gone. She had known that
immediately upon waking. What she did not
know was if he had taken all the evidence of
his recent occupancy with him. Her eyes
darted to the window seat, the foot of her
bed, the floor, and finally the chair. Everything was gone, even the sheet. She found it
after exploring under the covers. He had
not precisely made the bed around her, but
he certainly had made the attempt.

And all the while, she had slept like the
dead.

"Just the fire, please, Molly," she told the
maid. "Am I the last to be awake this morning?"

"No, Miss Nash," said Molly. She rolled
the wood she carried in her plump arms
onto the marble apron and set new kindling
to bring the fire up. "Mr. Stonechurch is
up, of course, and Mr. McKenna, but the
ladies are still in their rooms. Miss Ann is

reading, and Mrs. Stonechurch is not feeling well, so I believe she will not be down for breakfast."

"What is Mrs. Stonechurch's complaint?"

"Dyspepsia, she calls it. She's delicate that way."

Calico could not tell if Molly thought Beatrice was delicate because of her word choice, using "dyspepsia" when she might have said "upset stomach," or if she meant Beatrice herself was delicate. Calico decided it did not matter. They were both true. "What is she taking for it?" she asked.

"Mrs. Friend is brewing one of Mrs. Stonechurch's special teas right now. It will be something with ginger and peppermint. It always is for stomach ailments. She gives it to Mr. Stonechurch when he is having a time of it. Now when her husband was bedfast, she gave him meadowsweet with a dash of cayenne. Poured it down him by the gallon for the terrible ache in his joints after that awful accident." Molly sighed so heavily that ashes scattered in the grate. "That was a time, I can tell you. A terrible time."

Molly stood, brushed her hands on her apron, and then turned to Calico. "Will there be anything else? I could run water for your bath. It's a pleasure to say that. Run water. I have to pump and haul it by the bucket at home. This house is a miracle of mechanics. Did you know there's talk of using the boiler to heat every room? I don't know how it would work, but it'd be just fine with me if I don't have to lay fires every morning."

"But would you still have a job?"

Molly's eyes matched the saucer roundness of her face. "Oh. Now there's something to keep me up all night, same as Mrs. Stonechurch." She pressed her hands against her belly and frowned. "Do you know, I think I'm feeling a touch dyspeptic?"

Calico swiveled to the edge of the bed. "Perhaps some of the tea will help." As casually as she could, she asked, "Did I hear you correctly? Mrs. Stonechurch was up all night?"

Molly nodded. She picked up Calico's robe and brought it to her. "That's what she told me. I imagine she slept for a time and doesn't remember, but she said she tried reading, writing letters, even paced a bit, and nothing helped settle her stomach."

"I wonder why she didn't make a cup of tea?"

"I asked her the very same thing. I think she was a little embarrassed to tell me, but she did, and I said I understood, because I do."

"And?" asked Calico.

"And it's the noises, you see. You must have heard them. Pipes bang. Floorboards creak often enough that you can imagine someone's stepping on them. When it's very cold, the wood makes a sound like a gunshot. It's windy on this knoll. Even in summer, you can hear whispering in the pines, and it slips right in under the windows so as you'd swear there's a presence at your bedside." She shrugged. "Leastways, that's what Mrs. Stonechurch says. Arriving in the wee hours as I do, I've heard it, too. And the voices, same as she did, but early on I came to realize that Mr. Stonechurch talks to himself when he's working, and what with him rising before sunup, it was him I was hearing."

"Mrs. Stonechurch must know that as well."

"She does. That's why I think she felt a little foolish telling me. I tried to put her at ease. I told her I wouldn't have gone to the kitchen either."

"That was good of you."

Molly nodded slowly, thoughtful. "Maybe you'll remember that if she forgets. I'm saying that just in case Mr. Stonechurch figures out how to put heat in the rooms and there's no longer a job for me. I might need a recommendation."

Calico promised that she would and shooed Molly out. The tub proved to be a temptation she could not resist, and she turned on the taps while she made the bed. Quill had put away the clothes she'd worn to go outside. She had not given them a thought last night, but they would have raised Molly's eyebrows this morning. Calico's eyes strayed to the bedside table. The flask of whiskey was also gone. She was a little sorry about that.

Slipping into the tub, she lay back and sluiced water over her shoulders. She looked down at her breasts. Her pale skin bore the rosy evidence of Quill's stubble until the heat of the water created a flush that covered it. She touched fingertips to her lips. Had Molly noticed they were swollen? She could still feel the press of Quill's mouth there, a stamp that would not fade for some time. It was a slightly different sensation between her legs, because there she was aware of a tender emptiness. Her hand slid from her mouth, to her breast, to her belly, and came to rest on her mons. Much as he had done, she made a gentle exploration. Her skin was sensitive. The bud between the folds of skin was especially so. She avoided a second pass across it; the sharpness of the pleasure was too much like pain.

Calico let her hand drift across the curve of her thigh and fall deeper into the water. She laid her head against the lip of the claw-footed tub and closed her eyes. It would have been easy to slide back into sleep if it hadn't been for Molly's interruption, or rather Molly's rambling during her interruption. Calico had never thought she would welcome ignorance over knowledge, but she found herself dangerously close to entertaining that notion now.

Beatrice Stonechurch had been awake last night, all night if she was to be believed. The woman, who was frequently late to the breakfast table because she happily reported she slept very well, was awake all night with a stomach ailment. The thought of it was enough to make Calico's stomach roil. She decided right then that she would have peppermint tea at breakfast.

She would have to tell Quill. There was really no question of keeping it to herself. If Beatrice had seen anything, heard anything, and was thinking about repeating it, he was entitled to share her anxiety. Fair was fair.

With that, Calico gulped air and slid deeply under the water.

Ramsey and Quill stood as Calico entered

the dining room. Ann looked up, beamed, and said, "I finished *Far from the Madding Crowd* last night. I could hardly sleep for wanting to discuss it with you."

Calico responded with what she hoped was better than a wan smile. *Was everyone awake last night?* "Good. I look forward to it also." She took the chair Quill held out for her and accepted Ramsey's offer to make a plate for her at the sideboard. She managed to thank them both warmly while avoiding eye contact. She remembered that Quill had called her a coward, and for the first time, she felt like one.

The plate that Ramsey set in front of her was filled with more than she ate at three breakfasts. She stared at it, unsure how she would manage, but gamely picked up her fork.

Across the table, Ann chuckled. "Father pays no attention to what anyone eats. He thinks we all consume food as he does."

Ramsey sat and tucked into his second helping of eggs. "I do not think about it at all," he said. "It's fuel. What is there to think about?"

Ann shrugged helplessly. Her mouth dimpled as she winked at Calico. "See?"

"I do."

Ramsey waved his empty fork with a flourish. "Enough about that. Miss Nash. Ann. Mr. McKenna came to me with the most startling proposition this morning. Even more startling, at least to me, is that I have agreed to it. Whether you will do the same remains to be seen, but I will warn you that it includes you both or neither of you."

Ann and Calico stared at him and then at each other. They shrugged simultaneously, mutually agreeable in their silence.

"What is it, Father?" asked Ann.

While Ann's attention was on her father, Calico stole a sideways glance at Quill. He was enjoying gooseberry jam on toast and giving nothing else away. She looked back at Ramsey, who like a good showman was delaying the big reveal by pouring a measure of cream into his coffee.

"Father!"

Ramsey pulled his cup and saucer closer in the event his daughter was tempted to stir it for him. "All right. It's this: Mr. Mc-Kenna has proposed to instruct you on the proper use of firearms." His eyes, absent of all amusement, darted in Calico's direction. "Both of you. At the same time."

Calico saw Ann's enthusiasm deflate when she heard this last condition, but the young woman quickly recovered herself, leaping from her chair to throw her arms around her father's neck. Calico realized Quill must have seen Ann's initial reaction also, because he nudged her foot under the table. Calico kicked him back.

"Well," said Ramsey, making no attempt to free himself from his daughter's clutches. "I know how Ann feels about the offer, Miss Nash, but I have no idea what your thoughts are."

Ann's presence forced Calico to accept the proposal with caution. It was with a decided lack of eagerness that she said, "It is certainly a generous offer, and one that you must have given considerable thought to before you agreed, I don't know if I am —"

Ann broke in. "Oh, but you must, Miss Nash. You heard Father. We must both agree to take lessons. I thought we already had. And you did say it could be a woman's pursuit as well as man's."

"I did, but I think I must have meant some other woman's pursuit, not mine."

Ann disengaged from Ramsey and straightened, her disappointment keen. She rested one hand on her father's shoulder. "I hope you do not mean that."

"I do mean it," she said firmly. "But you should not take it as a refusal. I intended to say that I do not know if I am truly prepared to hold a gun, let alone shoot one. I suppose we shall find out, won't we?" She gave Ann a slightly reproving smile that became warm as she turned to Ramsey. "Thank you, Mr. Stonechurch. Of course I accept."

Ramsey jerked his chin at Quill. "He made a compelling case. The man's a damn fine lawyer —"

"Father!"

"A fine lawyer," he amended, patting Ann's hand. "Which is precisely why I hired him."

Calico watched Ann. She had not yet thanked Quill, and Calico was unsure if she would seize the opening her father had given her. The young woman was nodding. Her eyes were brighter than they had been, but her smile was diffident.

"Yes," said Ann softly. "Thank you, Mr. McKenna. I would be pleased to learn to be so persuasive in my arguments."

Ramsey's brow beetled as he regarded Ann. "If I hear even one of his lawyer tricks coming from you, our arrangement is finished."

Alarmed, Ann said, "You would fire him?"

"No. Of course not. I would disown you."

Ann's lips pursed in disapproval, but she bent and kissed him on the cheek anyway. "You are a beast, Father, but I love you in spite of it."

Ramsey ruffled her hair before she straightened. "And you're a good daughter."

Calico thanked Quill as Ann returned to her seat. It was a modest thank-you, something she might say in response to having been passed the jam. It was impossible just then to express anything approximating the joy she truly felt. She would be outdoors. She would have a gun in her hand. She would stay sharp.

Quill McKenna had solved her problem, and Ann Stonechurch had the satisfaction of believing she'd won the day, which in fact, she had. All in all, a splendid outcome. Calico's plate no longer looked as full as when Ramsey had set it in front of her. Appetite returning ever so slightly, she dug in.

Ann was hardly able to stay present during her studies. Her eagerness to begin shooting practice was a palpable thing.

"I don't think we will be firing guns today," Calico told her. She redirected Ann's attention to a passage in the Thomas Hardy novel that Ann had looked forward to discussing earlier. Now the girl could not seem to recall a single salient point. The names of the characters sometimes eluded her.

"Why wouldn't we?" asked Ann. "Mr. McKenna said we would have the lesson today."

"I cannot be sure, but I think there are things he will want to teach us before we take aim at anything. Have you held a gun before?"

Ann shook her head. "No, Father has never allowed it, but you must have seen the guns in the case in the rear parlor. I studied those."

"I have seen them, and I think they are older weapons. Antiques."

"Some are certainly from the war. The oldest piece belonged to my great-grandfather. He carried it when he came exploring with Pike."

"Then it must be at least eighty years old. I do not intend to shoot with that. It might explode upon discharge."

Ann laughed. "That doesn't seem likely. You are worrying too much, Miss Nash. You could be excited about this. Didn't you tell me you are open to new experiences? Well, here you are on the cusp of one."

"I suppose."

"Besides, neither of us will be firing Great-Grandfather's pistol. That would give my father apoplexy. I heard Mr. McKenna say that we will be using his guns. I did not know he had more than one, and I only know about that because he was wearing it when he came back this past August."

"Your aunt told me he was gone for a while."

Ann nodded. "Family matters, I think. No one spoke to me. Frequently they don't. You probably know more about it than I do."

Sensing Ann was fishing, Calico said nothing.

Ann sighed and directed her eyes to the passage Calico wanted her to read. She did not read it, though. She said, "What do you think of Mr. McKenna?"

If Calico had not been anticipating a conversational turn like this, she might have given a start. Instead she injected a note of shrewdness in her tone, as if she were only now coming to see which way this wind was blowing. "Ann? Have you an affection for Mr. McKenna?"

Ann's head snapped up. She was wide-eyed and blushing. In spite of those signs, she said, "No! No, why would you think so? I was asking *you* what you thought of him."

"I know," Calico said gently. "It struck me that you might have reasons for asking that are not so obvious. Am I wrong?"

"Most definitely. I asked because . . . well, I just asked. Everything is not for interpreting. Take this book, for instance. I believe dissection of every character's motives does not illuminate the story but rather detracts from it. In my estimation, they are all very silly anyway."

And with that, they were back on task. Calico did not think Ann would stray from it again, at least not with a line of questioning that had anything to do with Quill McKenna.

After lessons with Ann were over, Calico went to find Ramsey Stonechurch. He was not in his study as she expected, but Quill was. She hesitated when he waved her inside, but the sardonic look he gave her was not one she could refuse.

"Where is Mr. Stonechurch?" she asked, sliding the pocket doors closed behind her. "I came to see him."

"I figured."

"You're sitting at his desk. Does he know?"

"Not only does he know, but he invited me to." He set down the newspaper he was reading and leaned back in his chair. "He's with Beatrice. He intercepted her luncheon tray and decided to take his meal with her." Quill checked his pocket watch. "Hmm. I did not realize it was so late. I thought he would be down by now."

Calico stepped closer to the desk. "She might be giving him an earful. This morning I learned from Molly that Beatrice was up most, if not all, of the night."

"Dyspepsia. So I heard."

"Yes, but what do you think *she* heard?"

"Probably nothing. You were a very quiet lover." He mocked her by holding up his hands to ward off anything she found to throw at him.

Calico put herself into one of the chairs on the opposite side of the desk instead. "It's dangerous to be too predictable."

"I will keep that in mind. You look lovely, by the way. I wanted to tell you that at breakfast. Is that one of the gowns from Mrs. Birden's shop?"

It was of so little importance what she wore, that Calico had to look down at herself to recall what she had chosen that morning. It was the dove gray dress she had asked Mrs. Birden to make for her. It had a delicate edge of lace at the throat and wrists and no other adornment. She liked it for its plain and simple lines, but she wore it with a green shawl Beatrice had insisted that she purchase. The shawl was closed with her cameo brooch.

"Yes," she said. "Mrs. Birden made it for me."

"Well, you look lovely in it."

"Oh, stop. It drains the color from my face, which is why Beatrice made me buy the shawl. She said it was on account of the house being cold, but I had already heard her whisper to Mrs. Birden that the gray washed my complexion so completely the freckles hardly showed. I thought that would be something in the color's favor, but apparently not."

Amused, Quill said, "You know, when you run on like that, you sound just like her."

Ignoring that, Calico regarded him frankly. "I did not think I was all that quiet."

"I'd know a little more about that than you would, wouldn't I?"

"I spent eight days in a whorehouse," she said dryly. "Do you think I wasn't paying attention?"

He laughed. "All right. You have me there. But you shouldn't necessarily use what you heard there as a gauge. I am certain you were quieter than the majority of Mrs. Fry's girls."

Calico's stare drifted away as she turned thoughtful. "Why were you there that evening?"

"Joe Pepper asked me the same thing. I wanted a drink, and I wanted company."

"I know that," she said. "I didn't ask it

298

very well, but I meant why were you passing through Falls Hollow in the first place? What took you away from Stonechurch? You had a job here. You don't strike me as someone who would have abandoned it on a whim."

Quill looked at his watch again. "I need to find Ann. I told her we would be starting around three."

"She'll find you. It can't be much later than two thirty."

"Two thirty-three."

"As I said . . ."

Quill set his hands in his lap, folded them, and tapped his thumbs together as he thought. Finally, he said, "In your travels, have you ever come across one Buck McKay?"

"No. I know the name, though. Robberies, if memory serves. Not trains. Not banks. Something . . . no, I can't quite bring it to mind. I remember his territory, though. Illinois. Indiana. Missouri. That's probably why our paths never crossed."

"He's been known to make forays into Kansas."

Calico snapped her fingers. "Buck McKay. He was running crooked games on Mississippi riverboats. I heard they threw him overboard."

"You *do* remember him."

"He didn't drown."

"No. And no one shot him either, which they would have been well within their rights to do."

"There was something else, I think. More recently. It might be what happened in Kansas."

"Probably. It was in the papers. He set up a traveling tent church, passed himself off as a man of God, although of no particular denomination, and bilked a succession of congregations out of their offerings. He promised the money would be used to build a more permanent structure. He moved on every time."

"You went after him? You told me you weren't a bounty hunter."

"I'm not. He was arrested, tried, and found guilty. I went to see if I could get him moved from Kansas to an Illinois prison as a favor to his parents."

"How could you do it? Wouldn't you really have to be a lawyer?"

"I am a lawyer, Calico, just one who doesn't much care for practicing it." Quill did not waste a second. While she was recovering from that blow, he gave the other. "As for why I would do a favor for his parents, it's both simple and complicated. They are my parents, too."

She stared at him. "Then . . ."

"That's right. Buck McKay is my older brother."

CHAPTER NINE

Ann Stonechurch accepted the weapon Quill placed like an offering in her open palms. She hefted it, accustoming herself to the weight. "What kind of gun is this?"

"A Colt .44 caliber centerfire. It's a popular model. If Constable Hobbes carried a gun, that would be a good choice. That's a four-inch barrel, and I would appreciate if you didn't point it at me."

"I am not even holding it correctly," protested Ann.

"It's not loaded either. And none of that matters. That's a pearl grip so have a care." Quill turned to Calico. The three of them were sitting at a table in the back parlor. The round walnut table, used for cards when Ramsey invited assemblymen, railroad officials, and sometimes the constable and the town council, bore evidence of cigars that had burned too long or the white rings of glasses left to sweat. No amount of polishing could erase the suggestion that deals had been made here and money had exchanged hands, sometimes with cards in play, sometimes without. "Try this," he said, passing Calico her own gun. "See how it fits."

Calico held it gingerly as if it might discharge in spite of Quill's promise that it was not loaded. She had wondered if he would take the revolver from her room or had another of his own. Here was proof that he had been going through her things again. She studied her weapon and then looked at Ann's. "It seems as if the barrel on this might be longer."

"Good eye, Miss Nash. That's a four-and-three-quarters-inch barrel. Also a Colt, but a .38-40 caliber. The grip is ivory." He held out his hand. "Here. Let me show you how to hold it." He palmed it, adjusted his grip, thumb on the hammer, finger on the trigger, and aimed at the ripening apple in a still life painting above the gun case. "It would be unusual for you to be aiming at a target that high, but you get the idea."

Ann mimicked Quill's grip and aim. "Maybe I am standing at the bottom of the staircase and the scoundrel is coming down the steps toward me. He is a dark-haired villain with a scar at one corner of his

303

mouth. It makes him seem as if he is smiling when he is not. He uses it to draw me in, make himself seem less threatening, but I know the truth. I pull the trigger and —"

Calico said, "Ann, what are you reading that is not on the list we discussed? And please put that down."

Ann slowly lowered the Colt. Her cheeks were flushed. "It is heavier than I thought it would be."

"Ann?"

"Oh, very well. The latest Nat Church adventure arrived in the mail a few days ago."

Quill said, "*Nat Church and the Chinese Box*? I would like to read that."

Calico said primly, "Do not encourage her, Mr. McKenna."

Quill gave every indication that he was abashed. "You should not be reading that tripe," he said to Ann.

She nodded solemnly. "I'm sure you're right." She mouthed the words, "I will give it to you later."

"I heard that," said Calico. She set her gun on the table and gave Quill her full attention. "What else should we know?"

Quill instructed them on how to clean the gun properly. He pointed out the safety features and demonstrated how to load the guns, explaining that they used different cartridges. Ann wanted to know why he owned guns that did not use the same bullets. It was a reasonable question, and he saw Calico smirk as he was searching for an explanation that would not give him away as a liar. Before his hesitation became obvious, he said, "The one Miss Nash is holding was given to me by someone who had no use for it any longer."

Ann, still very much under the influence of Nat Church dime novels, sat up straighter and asked with unbecoming eagerness, "Because he is dead? Because you killed him?"

"No," said Quill. "Because he . . . well, he . . ."

"Retired," said Calico. "I believe you told me you had a Colt that once belonged to the Teller County sheriff. This must be it."

Although Quill was on firmer footing thanks to Calico, he still only trusted himself to nod.

"Oh," said Ann, her narrow shoulders sagging.

"I cannot imagine why you are disappointed," said Calico. "I'm sure the sheriff killed some miscreants with it."

Seeing that his young student was mollified for the time being, Quill continued the lesson.

Ann was animated at dinner as she answered her father's questions about the first lesson. It was clear to Calico that she had hung on Quill's every word, but she was not as certain that it was as evident to Quill or, more important, to Ramsey. Calico reminded herself that Ann's attention made her a good student, even if it was for the wrong reasons. She felt more confident after seeing Ann handle the Colt than she could have imagined she would be.

Quill, it turned out, was a good instructor. More than once during his demonstrations, Calico was put in mind of her father. She had been much younger than Ann when she learned to use a gun, but the manner in which she had been taught was virtually the same. Bagger Nash's first concern for his daughter was her safety. When the weapon she was using made her arms sag with fatigue, Bagger used to make her promise not to shoot herself in the foot. For some reason that always made her laugh, and Bagger would relieve her of the gun when she was too weak to resist.

As Calico had predicted, Quill did not take them outside. The first lesson never included target practice. The first lesson was about respect. Although Ann was disappointed, Calico thought she had taken the lesson Quill meant to teach to heart.

Ann finally wound down as dessert was being served. That was Ramsey's opportunity to ask about her other lessons, and those questions he directed at Calico.

"I wish Beatrice felt well enough to join us," he said, "because I had this bit of intelligence from her. She tells me that you have instructed my daughter to read the Bible."

Calico blinked. Of all the things he might have mentioned about Ann's studies, this was easily the most unexpected, and she could infer from his tone that he was not pleased. "Yes, I have."

"I do not recall seeing it on her list of recommended reading."

Neither was a Nat Church dime novel, Calico wanted to say, but apparently that was of lesser concern, if it was even known. She realized she must have telegraphed her thoughts because Ann was trying to catch her eye. It was clear she was pleading not to be given up.

Calico said, "I thought I was given leave as her teacher to modify the list as I deemed appropriate. You have objections to the Bible in its entirety, or is it a particular book?"

"I do not have objections, not precisely, but I would certainly like to hear the purpose of it."

"The purpose? It has been a source of inspiration for art, music, poetry, and literature. My hope in having Ann read the Bible is that she will come to recognize its influence in the arts, from works by Da Vinci to Handel to Chaucer."

Ramsey stroked his beard, thoughtful as he regarded Calico. "You surprise me, Miss Nash. Clearly you have given this careful consideration."

"That I surprise you in any way, Mr. Stonechurch, is not a compliment. It means you have underestimated me and that makes me wonder why you hired me as your daughter's teacher."

His hand fell away from his beard, and he pointed a finger at Calico, not aggressively, only to underscore his argument. "And *that* is why I hired you." He looked at his daughter. "Did you observe how she makes her case? You can learn that from her, not from Mr. McKenna." He picked up his fork and stabbed his sponge cake. "Now, what book of the Bible are you currently reading, and have you reached the passage where I part the Red Sea?"

"I wanted to tell him he was the serpent in the garden," said Calico, cinching her robe around her waist. "I suppose that's why you set your heel down on my toes."

Quill was sitting comfortably on Calico's window bench, his back in one corner of the niche and his long legs stretched across the padded seat. It was after midnight, but Ramsey had retired to his room early, citing stomach discomfort, so Quill felt safe bearding the lioness without fear of interruption. "Actually, I thought you might call him Ramses."

Calico groaned softly. "Why did I not think of it? I doubt I will ever be given a more perfect opportunity than the one I missed."

"It's true. You are losing your edge."

She eyed him narrowly. "Not amusing."

"A little amusing."

Her narrow-eyed stare remained unchanged.

"All right," he said agreeably. "Not amusing."

Calico grinned. She carefully turned the upholstered chair away from the fire so that it faced Quill and sat, drawing her legs up to one side and covering her bare feet with the hem of her robe. "Do you think he has a real objection to Ann reading the Bible, or was there some other reason that he brought it up?"

"Truth? I think he likes to bait you. It's part of his courting ritual."

"Hmm. Yours, too." Quill looked as if he might object but then seemed to think better of it. "That's right," she said. "You do it, too. Ramsey, though, asked me to go riding again. He wants to show me more of the land surrounding Stonechurch tomorrow."

"Whatever he shows you, you can be sure he owns it."

"I figured as much."

"Did you give him an answer?"

"I told him yes. I offered reasons why it would be difficult. Ann's lessons. Your shooting instruction. I even fabricated a need to visit Mrs. Neeley-Brown's dress shop to make up for the dresses I bought from Mrs. Birden. He has better aim than I do; he shot them all down."

"He won't be taking you in a rig this time. You'll be on horseback."

"I know. That is the part I'll be looking forward to. I really do need to order riding clothes. I don't ride sidesaddle and I dislike wearing trousers under my skirt, but that is what I will have to do."

"You're all right with this?"

"Right enough. I won't be distracted, if that is a concern. I know it will be up to me to watch out for him. I'll take my gun. He can carry my rifle in his scabbard." She gave him a considering look. "You'll be here with Ann. How do you feel about that?"

"I think I can count on Beatrice to provide plenty of distractions. She is feeling better, by the way. I visited her after dinner."

Calico tried to read his expression. It was inscrutable. "Did she mention anything?"

"She mentioned lots of things, but no, nothing that you're wondering about. Besides, if she had heard something, she would be more likely to mention it to Ramsey than to me."

"Maybe she did. Maybe that's why he asked me to go riding."

"You think he's going to interrogate you?"

"He might."

"I could understand your concern if he began questioning me. I'm the one who can't lie. You will be fine."

She huffed softly. "I find that a little insulting."

"It's not his business," said Quill. "We work for him. He does not own us."

"I think he would disagree. Don't forget

where we are. This is Stonechurch. What he doesn't own outright, he finds ways to control. Yes, I know the shops are privately owned, but surely you realize Ramsey has only to stop buying their products to ruin them. They depend on his patronage as if he is some English lord and they are tenant farmers and villagers." She set her chin on one fist. Her brow wrinkled. "I believe I will point Ann toward studying the Revolution. I am certain there is a lesson that we can debate at dinner."

"I am not sure Ramsey is as petty-minded as you seem to believe. The man wants a legacy, and he is wise enough to know you do not ruin the very people you are expecting to erect your statue."

Calico's chin came up. "You *are* persuasive."

He shrugged modestly.

"Why don't you want to practice law?"

"Too confining. The courtroom, the offices, the procedures."

"The rules of law."

"Yes. In short, the rules of law. The irony is that I mustered out of the Army for similar reasons, although I didn't understand it at the time. I thought studying the law would allow me to right wrongs, so I was slow to comprehend that the law can also protect wrongs, even nurture them."

"You are talking about the Indian campaigns."

"Yes, and more. There was so much more. Sometimes I think they could have survived the campaigns. What they could not survive was the law. Our law. All of it created to serve us." He chuckled softly, without a shred of humor. "My views did not make me a popular counselor."

The curve of Calico's mouth was faint, sympathetic, and a trifle sad. Her eyes held his and she willed him to see her sincerity. "Perhaps not, but they make you a good man."

"I don't know about that."

"Shut up and accept the fact that I do."

That made him laugh, and this time amusement touched every note of it. "Would you consider coming over here and telling me I'm a good man?"

"Not even for a second."

Another chuckle rumbled deep in his throat. "You are a hard woman, Calico Nash."

"I have been told that before, but usually he is in shackles." She pretended not to be moved by the sunlight in his grin, but there was a stirring between her thighs that made her want to squirm. She held herself very still instead. "When Ann interrupted this afternoon, you were telling me about Buck McKay."

"I wondered when you would retrace your steps on that trail."

"Well, here I am."

"His name is Israel. Israel McKenna. I can't tell you how he came to be called Buck, but it was not a family nickname. The first I heard it was in connection with a gambling debt he acquired when he was sixteen, so it might have had something to do with bucking the tiger. You're familiar with faro?"

"I am."

He nodded. "A couple of men showed up at our house looking for Buck McKenna because he owed them money. They could have just as easily shot him, but they were sympathetic to his age. They merely wanted their money. My father paid and delivered a strong lecture on the evils of gambling."

"The lecture? Was it delivered to the men or your brother?"

"To the men. My brother, when he returned home six days later, got a slightly different lecture in the woodshed. He came out striped but unbowed, and I remember thinking that there was no punishment so harsh that he would be changed by it. Israel

314

would have fared better if our father had
given up hope that he could be saved. He
suffered a lot of beatings because Father
expected sin but believed in redemption."

Quill rubbed his jaw as he cast his mind
back. "There were other incidents, more
than my parents ever knew. Petty thefts.
Extortion. Israel got better at what he did.
It was usually some minor thing that tripped
him up. There was talk of moving, but we
never did. My parents received sympathy
from the community, not censure. It was
remarkable. No fault was ever attached to
them. In fact, very little blame ever attached
itself to Israel. I should also mention that
he is engaging, charming, and extraordinarily likable."

Calico put up a hand. "Just tell me this. Is
he prettier than you?"

"I don't know how to answer that."

"Let me put it another way. Are you prettier than he is?"

"No."

She sighed. "It's hard to imagine, but it
explains a good deal." She tapped an ear-
lobe. "The lamplight is dim, so it is difficult
to judge, but I think your ears are turning
red."

Quill resisted touching them. If the light
were any better, she would see that his face

315

was flaming. He went on. "Israel left home at eighteen. He set out without telling anyone where he was going. We heard about a Buck McKay now and again but never thought we were listening to stories about Israel. McKenna. McKay. We should have known, or at least suspected, but that came much later. I already told you the kinds of things he was doing. He scraped by. He escaped by."

"Didn't you tell me your brother thought the Lord would provide?"

"That's Israel. If it's there, the Lord provided it for his taking."

"I see. A somewhat twisted interpretation. Did you get him moved to a cell closer to your parents?"

"I did, but only because my parents agreed to pay for his board. Kansas was not about to pay to house him in a Cook County jail, and without payment, Cook County was happy to leave him where he was."

"So you all work together to rescue him."

"Oh, he does all right rescuing himself."

"What do you mean?"

"He got off the train in Missouri."

"Got off the —" She stopped because Quill was already nodding.

"That's right. He escaped. Somewhere near Jefferson City is what I heard. And that's the last I heard. He'll surface again. He always does."

Calico said nothing for a time. She did not hear bitterness, merely resignation. "Do you want me to find him?"

Quill's answer was swift. "No!" A moment later, he said it again, more softly this time. "No. There are federal marshals looking for him. Let them find him."

"Most of those lawmen don't know the territory they're appointed to. They probably won't be successful. Is there a reward?"

"Not for the marshals. I believe they're motivated by the fact that Israel escaped the custody of one of their own."

"Oh. That's embarrassing for them."

"Yes."

"Um, just because I have a curious nature, Quill, I was, um, wondering —"

"Three hundred dollars."

"Oh."

"Hardly worth your time."

"I was not going to make time for it. I was curious, just like I said."

"Uh-huh."

She shrugged off his disbelief. "Why is the reward so small?"

"First, he's never killed anyone. Second, to keep bounty hunters away. The marshals really do want to bring him in."

"What about you? What do you want?"

"I want him to stop. Just stop."

"And what do your parents want?"

"That's easy. They want to save his soul. That's the thing about faith. If you believe, if you really believe, you don't surrender it for the likes of Buck McKay. If my father admitted that Israel could not be saved, it would make his life a bigger fraud than any ever perpetrated by his firstborn. He has never said that. He can't. But I believe that's what he thinks. It is no different for my mother."

"Are they proud of you, Quill?"

"Sometimes I think they are, not that it's ever been said, but Israel is the prodigal son." He shook his head a little helplessly. "Or he could be if he ever went home."

"Beatrice says you write to your parents."

"Does she? I guess she would know. She carries posts to and from town." Quill shifted his position on the bench, dropping one leg to the floor and stretching it out at an angle. "What about you, Calico? Was your father proud of you?"

"He was. He told me, too."

"You never mention your mother."

"I didn't know her. Childbirth fever. I was only days old when she died. My father said she passed holding me in her arms. I was

318

swaddled in Kelly green calico that she intended to use for a dress. She was the one who named me Katherine after her mother, but the way my father always told it, she died calling me Calico. That's why I'm partial to it."

"I like it, too."

The curve of her lips was bittersweet. "I have a cameo brooch that belonged to her. I've never needed any other jewelry."

"No, you don't."

She stared at him. "What you said earlier, about me going to where you are and telling you that you're a good man?"

"Yes? You're reconsidering?"

"Not reconsidering. I didn't consider it before. I told you that."

"So you are only considering now."

"Actually, I just finished. I've made my decision." She did not tease him by sitting there another moment. She got up and went to him. He made a place for her between his splayed legs. She sat and took his hands in hers. "You are a good man." She leaned in, found his mouth with hers, and kissed him lightly on the lips. "And while it pains me some to say it, I don't exactly regret that you chased after me back at Mrs. Fry's cathouse."

"Careful, Calico. Compliments like that

will turn my head."

She leaned in again and whispered against his mouth, "We don't want that." She slipped her hands out of his and raised her arms. She draped her arms over his shoulders, fit herself to him when he pulled her close, and then kissed him until they were both breathless.

Smiling, she took one of his hands and urged him to his feet when she got to hers. She would have led him to the bed, but he never gave her the chance. Calico emitted a soft, girlish squeal when he suddenly picked her up.

"What was that?" he asked, straight-faced as he looked down at her. Her eyes were wide, the centers darkening. "Did you hear it?"

"I didn't hear anything."

"Hmm." He carried her the short distance to the bed and unceremoniously dropped her, satisfied when she squealed again. Quill stepped out of her reach when she sat up and tried to catch his sleeve. "Warm a place for me while I undress. And take off that robe."

It was a reasonable plan and Calico went along with it. By the time he had stripped down to his flannel drawers, she was ready for him. She held up the covers just enough to let him slip under them. He immediately tried warming his icy toes between her toasty feet. "Stop that!" she whispered. A residual chuckle made the command less forceful than she would have liked. She quickly drew up her knees and gave his chest a little push.

Quill caught her by the wrist and gave her arm a gentle tug, setting it around his waist. He edged closer and her knees unfolded and made room for him beside her. His fingers walked down her collarbone from her shoulder to her neck and then made a half circle to her nape. He found her thick braid and brought it forward. When he pulled at the black grosgrain ribbon securing it, she clapped a hand over his.

"You do not want to do that," she said.

"I don't?"

"My hair has a life separate from my own. It will be everywhere."

"I accept the challenge." He could see that she remained doubtful, but her hand fell away from his, and he removed the ribbon. He tucked it under her pillow and then began to weave his fingers through her plait, loosening it as he went. "I wanted to do this last night."

Her voice was no more than a whisper, husky at the edges. "Why didn't you?"

"I don't know."

She nodded, accepting it. "There were things I wanted to do and didn't."

His fingers stopped. Arrested by her confession, Quill's eyes shifted from Calico's flaming hair to her flaming face. "For instance?"

She tapped the hollow between his collarbones. "I wanted to kiss you here." Her fingertips drifted lower, following his breastbone. "And here." Her hand spread wide across his chest. "Here and here." She curled her fingers into a loose fist and dragged her knuckles down his flat belly. His skin retracted as he sucked in a breath. She stopped at his navel. "Here, too."

Emboldened by his silence and the steadiness of his stare, Calico's fist opened as slowly as a blossoming flower and then her hand slipped below the waistband of his drawers. She followed the arrow of hair to his groin and stayed it there. She leaned into him just enough to set her lips against his, and said, "I wanted to put my mouth here." And to make certain there was no mistaking her intent, her fingers closed in a fist again, this time around his cock. It twitched and swelled in her hand. Her eyebrows lifted and she gave him an arch look.

Quill said, "It has a life separate from my own. It will be everywhere."

Calico's fist applied pressure. "It better not be."

It turned out that laughter was a considerably powerful aphrodisiac. They traded kisses and quips in equal measure. Either was capable of raising a chuckle or a groan. All of it was wickedly amusing.

She had her way with him. Quill did not even pretend to object when she straddled his hips. Her fiery hair, finally freed from the braid, hung in waves on either side of her face each time she bent to kiss him. She worked her way down his body, pressing her lips against his skin in all the places she promised and in some that she hadn't. When he pointed that out, she told him frankly that his body was a canvas, her mouth was a brush, and she was overwhelmed by inspiration. His chest heaved with laughter, nearly dislodging her, and she was forced to clamp a hand over his mouth and ride it out. When he quieted and she removed her hand, he apologized for the distraction and said he hoped she would continue to be inspired.

Apparently she was, because she found a particularly ticklish spot on his chest and tortured him with the damp edge of her tongue. She also found another spot not far below the first that was raised and smooth and shaped like a starburst. She kissed it gently, tenderly, without comment, and then she moved on.

She lowered herself so she could she lay flush to his body and peppered his chest and belly with kisses until she disappeared under the covers. Her hands found him first and that was very good. Then she found him with her mouth and that was even better.

Her mouth felt almost cool against his hot skin. Blood engorged his cock. His pulse beat thrummed in his ears, in his chest, and where she held him with her lips. Curiosity motivated her exploration, but his pleasure kept her there. She sucked, licked, laved him with her tongue. She heard the sounds he could not swallow and the ones that lodged in his throat. His hips jerked. She took him deeper. She cupped his balls and squeezed.

That was when Quill dragged her out from under the blankets. In a move she was helpless to counter, he had her on her back and secured under his weight. Her shift was twisted around her thighs, and she scrabbled with the fabric to yank it higher. He pressed his advantage only long enough to bury himself inside her. He levered himself on his elbows, hips lifting just a fraction, and then thrust hard and deep. She grabbed his shoulders for purchase, her short nails scoring thin crescents in his flesh.

Quill held himself still. He felt the effort of denial across his shoulder blades where the muscles in his back were pulled taut. He clenched his jaw. His nostrils flared when he sucked in a breath. He held that breath, heart hammering. The whole of his body was a single, jangling nerve.

Calico understood then that he was waiting for her. She did not know how she knew that, just that she did. She cupped the side of his face, drew her thumb across his cheek, and she smiled at him.

"Let go," she said softly. "Let go."

It was her smile as much as her words that did him in. She tripped the nerve and pleasure swamped him. His hips pumped shallowly. He threw back his head, neck and spine arching, and then he gave a shout that had Calico groping for a pillow as his body shuddered. She never used it. The tension that had held him together slowly seeped away and he lowered himself onto her.

"God," he said softly. It was as much an expulsion of air as an expression of astonishment. "Was that all Mrs. Riggenbotham's doing?"

Calico sifted through his hair with her

fingertips. "Her accounts were descriptive, but the whores at Mrs. Fry's were also instructive."

"So it would seem." He chuckled when she rapped him on the shoulder with her knuckles. He started to ease away from her, but she stopped him.

"Not just now," she said.

"I'm too heavy for you."

"Not just now you're not."

He nodded, but he was still careful not to crush her. "Do you ever think about Nick Whitfield?"

"No more than any other man I helped put behind bars. Why?"

"I wondered if he might not be a little more special than most."

"Special? Why would he be?"

Quill sighed. "Because he's the reason we met."

"Oh, that."

"Yes, that."

She tipped her head, trying to see his face better. "Are you disappointed?"

"Just wondering how you thought about it."

Calico smoothed his hair with her palm and then wound her finger around a thick strand at his nape and tugged. When he lifted his head, she said, "I guess I don't think about it. I'm sorry." And she was. The thing that was on her mind, the thing she did think about but would not allow herself to say, was that she and Quill were meant to cross paths. It would have happened with or with Nick Whitfield. She believed that some things were destined; she did not believe that meant they were forever.

Calico slipped out of bed first and went to the bathing room to wash. Quill was standing outside the door when she came out. By the warmth of the room, she could tell that he had stoked the fire. She moved aside to let him in and went to the fireplace. It was not long before he joined her there. He stood behind her and slid his arms around her waist. He rubbed his chin against her hair. His stubble created static. Single strands of her colorful hair separated themselves and were lifted into the air. They both felt a shock. He jerked his chin up. She ducked her head.

"I'll be more careful," he said, smoothing her hair with his palm. He braided it loosely before his arms circled her waist again. He folded his hands. She leaned back against him. "I wish you weren't riding out with Stonechurch tomorrow."

"It's done. I need to be out. Really out. Confinement to this house is nearly intolerable. I don't know how Beatrice could stay in her room all day."

"She had company. Ramsey. Me. Anne spent a little time there, mostly to tell her about the guns, I think. Did you go?"

"I poked my head in. She was sleeping on the chaise. There was a book on the floor at her side, and a basket of knitting beside that. I imagine that's how she wiled the hours away."

"She had a delivery from the druggist this evening. You were in the front parlor with Ann when it arrived. Powders, although Mrs. Stonechurch prefers her teas. Molly must have let it out that she wasn't feeling well."

"Hmm. Will you take Ann out to practice shooting tomorrow?"

"Not until you get back. I can't imagine that Beatrice will want to go with us, and I am not going out by myself. You know you will have to pretend to be clumsy with your gun for a while."

"I know. I thought I did well today."

"You did."

"If you set up targets, I can miss all of them simply by shooting at another target of my choosing. Ann will never know."

He gave her a squeeze. "A very good plan."

In spite of the heat from the fire, she

shivered slightly. His embrace could do that to her.

"Back to bed," he said.

She didn't protest, didn't explain that it wasn't the cold that had touched her. Everything she felt when she was with him was outside her experience. Destiny aside, she was not prepared to make herself more vulnerable than she already had. She did not know if she would ever be ready for that. There was no going back, but it did not necessarily follow that she was prepared to go forward. She was not even certain what forward would look like, only that her stomach clenched when her mind started to make that journey.

Calico let him lead her to the bed. She got in and moved to the shallow depression that was hers. When she rolled onto her back and looked up at him, she saw that he had no intention of following. "You're leaving?"

He nodded. "Sleep. We both should get some."

She did not argue. She judged it was better if she did not accustom herself to sleeping beside him. And as she watched him leave, it occurred to her that his thinking was probably not so different. When he closed the door and went forward without her, this time it was her heart that clenched.

Calico rode a bay that Ramsey secured for her from the livery. The mare was gentle, almost lethargic, and Calico wished he had chosen a more spirited animal. Her name suited her, though. She was called Daisy. In Calico's estimation, the only name more appropriate would have been Lazy Daisy.

Ramsey had a well-groomed black gelding with a wide white stripe down his nose and around his eyes. It made the animal look as if he were wearing a mask. Fittingly, he was called Bandit.

Ramsey held up his mount to wait for Calico. He used the moment to breathe deeply, taking in the fresh, crisp air until his chest expanded. He looked around him. Everything was brighter against the heavenly blue of a cloudless sky. The snowcaps gleamed white. The icy needles of the ponderosas glinted like emeralds. In the distance, outside of his view, he could hear the echo of men and machinery. His mines. His land. His life.

He smiled a trifle apologetically when Calico came abreast of him. "She is not frisky, is she?"

"Frisky? No. She is certainly not that."

"I told Mr. Calhoun, who owns the livery,

that I wanted a horse suitable for my daughter's teacher. You're probably wishing I had told him it was for Calico Nash."

Calico patted her mare's neck. Daisy actually preened. "She's not used to being ridden hard. It's all right. We aren't in a hurry, are we?"

"No. Not in any hurry at all." He turned up the lamb's wool collar on his coat and then pointed out a break in the trees up ahead. "We're going that way. I want to show you the mountain spring. On a day like today you will think it's spilling diamonds over the rocks."

The route he took her on was wide enough for them to go side by side. Ramsey held the gelding back so Daisy would stay with him. Calico's eyes darted left and right, not so much observing the scenery as looking through it.

"What do you think is going to happen out here?" he asked her.

"I hope nothing."

"When someone took a shot at me, I was on the eastern side of my property, every bit of seven miles from town, twelve from where we are now."

"Doesn't mean we won't be followed."

Ramsey shrugged. "You're doing what I'm paying you for, I suppose."

"That's right."

He nodded. "How did you come to be a bounty hunter?"

"I couldn't find work as a teacher."

"All right," he chuckled. "So you don't want to talk about yourself. I suppose I understand that, but it makes it difficult for me to say something about me."

Calico figured he would blast right through that obstacle. When he cleared his throat, she knew she was right. That sound was the equivalent of lighting the fuse.

"I don't know if my daughter told you, but her mother died when she was two. Cholera."

Calico did not say so, but she wondered if it was the same outbreak that had nearly killed her. The timing was right, and she had been at a Colorado outpost then. "I'm sorry. No, Ann has never said anything about it."

"I thought I would lose her, but the illness passed her by. Beatrice became sick and survived. I did also. My brother was like Ann. He nursed all of us." He cleared his throat again. "When Maud died, it crossed my mind to leave the mountain. Leo talked me out of it. Beatrice helped raise my daughter. I had my work . . . have my work. I married late; I was thirty when I took Maud for my wife, and thirty-five when we had Ann. Maud had trouble keeping a baby; she lost three. Ann was a miracle to us."

Calico was not sure what to say, but she thought some sort of response was in order. "She is a lovely and accomplished young woman. I have to believe your wife would be pleased with how you've done."

"I believe so, too, although no small amount of the credit belongs to my sister-in-law." Ramsey urged Bandit over a fallen log, while Calico let Daisy go around it. When they were abreast again, he said, "Lately I've been thinking that I might want to marry again. Ann is older and will be leaving home, no matter what she thinks to the contrary. My brother's gone. I want to share —"

"Beatrice!" said Calico.

"Where?" Ramsey turned right and left in his saddle, looking hard through the trees and toward the clearing for his sister-in-law.

Calico shook her head. "No. I didn't mean that she was here. I meant that it must be Beatrice you want to marry. I think it's wonderful. She is such a good woman. Devoted to you, to your daughter. And you already share ownership of Stonechurch Mining. Quill told me. That's what you were going to say, weren't you? That you want to share it with her as a husband?"

Calico could see that Ramsey Stonechurch was struck silent by her assumption. She pressed on before he gathered his wits and corrected her mistake. "I asked Quill if he knew whether Beatrice had ever expressed an interest in remarrying. He said he did not think she had, but now I believe I understand why. She strikes me as too timid to be obvious about her affections, but it seems clear where they lie. I hope you will ask her soon. I can keep a secret about almost everything, but probably not about this."

Calico pressed her heels into Daisy's sides and gave the mare a reason to pick up her pace. She moved ahead of Ramsey and crossed from the trees into the open. "I will try, though," she told Ramsey. "I wonder if Ann suspects your intentions. You know, it might be the very reason she did not want to go away. She would not like to be at college when you make the announcement. She would hate it even more to miss the wedding."

The sunlight on the snow was blinding. Calico had to squint and raise one gloved hand to shield her eyes from the glare. Farther ahead she could see the mountain stream that Ramsey had mentioned. He was not exaggerating about the spring spilling diamonds over the rocks. Every water droplet glistened.

She glanced behind her and saw Ramsey was closing the gap between them. She grasped for something else to say that would make these moments so awkward for him that he could not possibly unburden himself of a marriage proposal.

"The view is breathtaking," she said, nudging Daisy forward again. Ramsey drew alongside her anyway, and she silently cursed the indolent Lazy Daisy. She kept her hand up to her brow and wished the silly little velvet hat she was forced to wear had the brim of her Stetson. "It is too bad that Ann doesn't ride. I think she would like to see —"

It was almost too late by the time Calico saw the long, dark shadow against a milk white crest of snow to register what it was and act on it. She made a grab for the rifle in Ramsey's scabbard and missed because her sudden movement made Bandit crow hop. The gelding threw his unprepared rider off. Calico leaned as far sideways as she could and still stay in her saddle. She caught Bandit's reins, yanked hard, and kept him from trampling Ramsey.

She did not immediately feel the bullet that creased her arm just below the shoulder. It was still extended for balance when she heard the long-barreled rifle's report. That's when she understood what the burning sensation was. She threw herself from the saddle, not the least worried that Daisy would do anything but step over her.

"We've got to get back to the trees," she shouted at Ramsey. "Are you all right? Can you walk?"

Except to nod, he didn't move.

"You've got to get to your feet, take Daisy by the reins — she won't bolt — and use her for cover to get to the trees." Another bullet dug into the ground between them. They were sprayed by snow and bits of frozen dirt. "Now, Mr. Stonechurch! Now!"

"You're bleeding! You're hurt!"

"Go!" Calico scrambled to her knees, cursing her skirt when it impeded her progress, and grabbed Daisy's reins. She tugged sideways and brought the mare around and then shoved the reins at Ramsey. "I will kill you myself if you don't go now," she said, gritting her teeth.

He took the reins in his fist, stumbled to his feet as another bullet slammed the ground near Calico's left shoulder. He hesitated. She had not flinched, and for a moment he thought the bullet had struck her, but then he saw her unbuttoning her coat to make her gun accessible. He did not know if she meant to make good on her threat, but he did not stay to find out.

Calico clicked her tongue against her teeth loud enough to get Bandit's attention. He was skittish, afraid, but for reasons she would never understand, he responded to her call. "Here, boy. That's a good fellow." He put his nose down near her head, snuffling, and for a few precious moments blocked her from direct fire. "Sweet, smart Bandit. He didn't know how to take charge of you, did he?" She patted his nose. He shook his head and the reins dropped within her reach. "That's it. Stay still, sweet lad. Yes, you are so very bright." She jumped to her feet, grabbed Bandit's bridle to steady him and herself, and when they were both ready, she seized the pommel in her fist and pulled herself into the saddle. She never sat up. Lying low, she whipped the reins, and held on as Bandit charged the trees.

By the time they reached the house, they had rehearsed what they would say. They had arrived at the explanation stage only after considerable wrangling. There was no talking Ramsey out of taking responsibility for shooting her. He remained adamant that neither Ann nor Beatrice should be party to the truth. Ann would never leave, and Beatrice would be a tangled skein of nerves. Calico gave in because she did not have a better idea. It was hardly plausible that she had shot herself in the same arm she used to handle a gun. Still, it rankled that Ramsey would make himself look foolish on her behalf. She had no expectation that the story would not become fodder for the town, and for a while at least, he would be the object of snickering, perhaps even sneering, and that did not set well with her because it was undeserved.

At Calico's insistence, they dismounted some fifty yards from the house and tethered their mounts in the trees. Quill could come out later, she told Ramsey, and retrieve her scabbard and rifle before the animals were returned to the livery, but she did not want to risk either Ann or Beatrice seeing a weapon that they knew he did not own. The presence of the Colt could be explained away, but her Winchester rifle was something else again.

"Are you able to walk?" asked Ramsey, looking her over.

"It's my arm, not my legs. And it's only a flesh wound." She handed him her revolver. "Take this. You should be holding it when we get there."

He accepted the gun, but he continued to regard her injury doubtfully. "You say it's a flesh wound, but you won't let me see it. Your coat sleeve is soaked with blood. I don't think you know how bad it is."

"Maybe not, but it's not getting better while we stand here jawing about it. If it will help you move on, you can take my arm. My *good* arm."

Ramsey stepped up to her left side and slipped his arm through hers. "There's one more thing," he said as they began walking. "About what I was saying before I was shot at, or more accurately, what you were saying . . . I think it would be better if . . ." His voice trailed off. He shook his head and did not resume speaking.

"I won't say a word, Mr. Stonechurch. Forget anything I said to the contrary. I can keep a secret, even about this."

His cheeks puffed as he exhaled. "It's just that what I started to say . . . well, I don't think you . . ."

"I won't say a word," she told him again. "Let's leave it at that."

CHAPTER TEN

Beatrice Stonechurch backed into Calico's room carrying a tray of tea and sand tarts. She turned, revealing her treasure, and immediately realized she had arrived with too little refreshment.

"Oh, well, this won't do," she said, her eyes darting from Calico to Quill and back again. "I did not know that Mr. McKenna was here. I would have brought another cup."

Calico beckoned her to come closer to the bed. "Mr. McKenna just arrived, but he has already informed me that he does not intend to stay long. Isn't that right, Mr. Mc-Kenna?"

Quill did not answer. Instead, he stood and relieved Beatrice of the tea tray. He set it on the bedside table. In addition to the delicately painted china pot and creamer, there was only one cup and saucer and three dainty cookies. "You weren't going to have tea, Mrs. Stonechurch?" he asked.

"No. Conversation perhaps, but not tea. That's a special blend of white willow bark and meadowsweet. I added a touch of licorice to give it more fragrance and flavor. I find that helps. It's for her fever, you understand, and the discomfort she still has with her arm." Expecting a protest from Calico, Beatrice gave her a stern look and waggled a finger at her for good measure.

"Do not deny it. I see for myself how you favor your arm." She moved like a sprite, smoothly inserting herself between Calico in the bed and Quill standing right beside it. He had to give way to her or have his toes trampled. She put the back of one hand to Calico's forehead. "As I thought, dear. You are fevered."

"Your fingers are cold, Beatrice."

"That's because you are so warm," Beatrice went on, shaking her head. "I don't like it. That Ramsey could be so careless, it still rankles, and I have not kept how I feel about it from him. This idea of learning to shoot makes no sense to me. This is a peaceful mining town, not Deadwood or Tombstone. Ramsey and Leonard did not stand for the kind of wild nonsense that went on in Leadville in its heyday. Even Constable Hobbes does not wear a gun. He has always maintained that his stick is enough to keep the peace."

Beatrice turned suddenly. She was too short to look Quill squarely in the eye, but by sharply lifting her chin, she gave him an eyeful anyway. "I blame you, too, Mr. Mc-Kenna. Ramsey told me you persuaded him that there was no harm in allowing my niece and Miss Nash to learn to shoot, and we all see what's come of that, don't we?"

"I blame myself," Quill said, contrite.

Beatrice humphed lightly. His penitent mien took some of the wind from her sails. She turned back to Calico. "I cannot apologize for feeling so strongly about this. Ann knows how I feel, too."

Calico said, "You have not mentioned me. I share in the blame. I could have refused Mr. Stonechurch's invitation to ride his property. Certainly I should have not seized on the opportunity to take Mr. McKenna's gun and asked for a lesson."

"I am not convinced the lesson was your idea, although I understand that you might want to protect Ramsey. It would be like him to try to impress you. Ann told me that you were not comfortable with the gun at the first lesson, so it seems unlikely that you would have been eager for another."

Calico pressed three fingers to her temple

and gently massaged it. "I understand how you arrived at that conclusion, but you would be incorrect. I *did* ask for the lesson."

Beatrice gave in gracefully. "If you say so. I am going to pour you some tea and stay long enough to see you drink it, and then I promise I will be gone and you and Mr. McKenna may talk." She gave Quill an over-the-shoulder glance. "As long as you do not overstay your welcome."

Quill crossed his heart.

Calico accepted the cup of tea and held it in both hands as she lifted it to her lips. At the first taste, she wrinkled her nose.

"Too much sugar?" asked Beatrice.

"No. I think it must be the licorice. I'm sorry, but I don't care for it."

"I will leave it out next time. Go on, drink up. I promise it is better for you than anything Dr. Pitman will want to give you. The man trusts his laudanum, but it has no healing powers."

"Mm," Calico murmured. With Beatrice watching, she tipped her head and drained the cup.

"I'll leave the cookies," Beatrice said. She set them aside and presented the tray to Calico for her to return the cup. "I will come back later to check on you. Mr. Mc-

Kenna, I will see you at dinner."

Quill nodded and escorted her to the door and opened it for her. He watched her go, closing the door when she reached the stairs. Even then he did not move away until he was certain she was not returning.

When he stood at Calico's bedside again, he leaned forward and put his hand against her forehead as Beatrice had done. "I think Beatrice is right. You have a fever."

Calico knocked his hand aside and set her own hand against her brow. She shook her head. "Stop hovering. I think you both are making too much of it. I would not call this a fever."

Quill shrugged and sat in the rocker that had been moved into her room to accommodate company. He scooted closer to the bed and set his heels on the bed frame. "Maybe I'll send for Dr. Pitman regardless of what Beatrice decides."

"Don't. I mean it. Too much fuss has already been made. I can barely tolerate my own company let alone the parade that comes in and out of here."

That arrested his attention. He cocked an eyebrow at her. "Do you want me to leave?"

"Yes. No. I don't know. I am just in a mood. This is not a wound that should be keeping me bedridden. I do not understand it. I had less discomfort after Dr. Pitman stitched it up than I have now."

"That might have been the laudanum. He gave you a good first dose. You slept for the better part of what was left of the day."

She ignored him. "It cannot be infected. He took care to clean out the wound. I watched him pick out threads from my blouse and coat sleeves."

"I know. I watched you watching him. Most people would not have had the stomach for that."

"Well, I know you don't, or you would have been watching him."

Not offended in the least, Quill grinned at her.

"Truthfully," she said, "I had a harder time stomaching Beatrice's tea. I am glad she took it away. I would have had to pour it down the sink." She chose a cookie, wincing as she reached for it with her injured arm. "It cannot be infected," she said.

"That's the second time you've said that. Are you trying to convince me or yourself?"

Calico bit down hard on the cookie. "I change the dressing regularly. I am so well rested that I am tired from it. I drink the teas and use the poultices. If all of that has been in vain, I will shoot myself, and do a better job of it than that sniper in the rocks did."

"In fairness, he was aiming at Ramsey."

"Which goes to my point of doing a better job." She put the remainder of the sand tart in her mouth and chewed.

"Crumb," said Quill, touching one corner of his mouth. "Other side. That's it. May I look at your arm?"

"Don't you want a cookie?"

"I know obfuscation when I hear it."

"Who said, 'First thing we do, let's kill all the lawyers'?"

"Shakespeare put the words in the mouth of a villain named Dick the Butcher."

"Are you certain he was a villain? It seems as if the idea might have merit."

"He suggested it so he and his friends could get away with anything they liked."

"Oh. I thought it meant something else."

"Hmm. Most people do. Now let me see your arm. Notice that I am not asking."

Calico folded the blankets to her lap and untied the belt of her robe. She did not refuse Quill's assistance when it came to getting her arm out of it. She wore a sleeveless shift to make changing the dressings easier.

Quill stared at the bandage that wrapped several times around her upper arm. The portion that covered the sutures was stained brown while the rest of the cotton gauze was white. The stain did not look as if it was dried blood, but he could not imagine what else it might be. He asked about it as he began to unwind the gauze.

"It's a tincture that I swab over the sutures when I change the dressing. Echinacea, I think, and I'm sure some other herbs. The Indian scouts used things like this for healing. My father trusted them more than the Army doctors, so I stand with Beatrice on this."

"Beatrice gave you this? Not Dr. Pitman?"

Calico nodded. "She is right about him. He would give me laudanum and maybe some snake oil with enough alcohol in it to arouse the interest of a temperance league, but he has nothing as helpful in his black bag as Beatrice has in her jars."

Quill remained doubtful, and the feeling only increased when he got a look at her wound. He shook his head. The bullet had done more than merely crease her flesh, although that was how she liked to describe it. Before the sutures, the gash was just better than a half-inch wide. It was four inches long. To call it a flesh wound hardly seemed accurate. Calico simply did not have that much flesh. The bullet could just have as easily shattered her bone.

The sutures were taut because the flesh they were trying to hold together was swollen under them. The tincture that discolored the bandage was a transparent brown wash across the wound. Beneath it, her skin was purpling.

"Calico? Did it look like this the last time you changed the dressing?"

She had not yet looked at it, had been watching him instead, and had seen the truth she had not been able to admit. She cast her eyes down. The initial injury had been easier to look at than what she was seeing now.

"No," she said on a thread of sound. She closed her eyes and set her head back against the headboard. "God, no."

"But you had an idea something was wrong."

"I might have."

"Uh-huh." The rocker scraped the floor as he pushed it out of the way. "I'm going to wash that up, dress it myself, and then I am sending someone for Dr. Pitman. Do you have more bandages?"

"In the washstand."

He stalked off to the bathing room, but not before throwing the discolored, tainted bandage in the fire. "I am looking after you from now on. Beatrice knows what she knows, and that does not include anything about treating gunshot wounds."

Calico did not argue. In truth, she was weary of Beatrice's flitting and fluttering. Beatrice was not anything if not a woman of good intention.

She opened her eyes when she felt Quill beside her. He had a basin of water that he set on the small, square table, crushing the sand tarts. She did not think he even noticed.

"Can you turn a little this way?"

She did. She also sucked in a breath between her teeth when he applied a warm, wet compress to the wound. He held it there for one long minute before he began to gently bathe the injury.

"Listen to me, Calico. I need to remove the stitches. I'm softening the threads so I can clean in the seam. There's going to be blood . . . and worse. If you don't want me to do it, I will send for Dr. Pitman now, but this needs to be tended soon. Tell me what you want. It's your choice."

"After you clean it, can you stitch it again?"

"Yes. There are no needles here like the ones the doctor used, but I can do it. I know where Beatrice keeps her sewing box. I only have to get it."

"Then do it. I want you to do it." He nodded, warmed the compress in the basin
again, and placed it over the sutures. "Hold
that there. I won't be long." He turned to
go, but she stopped him.

"Bring your flask."

"I can do better than that."

To keep herself distracted from thinking
about what Quill was going to do, she
counted off the seconds until he returned.
She stopped at 578. She couldn't be sure
that she had not repeated herself a time or
two, so she decided that ten minutes was
about right.

Quill kicked the door behind him. He had
Beatrice's enameled sewing box under one
arm and a bottle of whiskey under the other.
He juggled the bottle, dropping it into his
hand, and held it up for her to see. "Kentucky bourbon."

"Did Ramsey give that to you?"

"Nobody gave me anything. No one
knows. Anyway, they both owe you." He set
the box on the floor by the bed and the
bourbon on a corner of the table. "Ramsey
because he was foolish for taking you out
there in the first place, and —"

"I told you," she whispered, "I think he
really invited me out there so he could

propose."

"That doesn't make anything right in my book." He removed the compress and dropped it in the basin, and then he searched the box for the smallest pair of scissors he could find. When he found them, he held them up to show her. His thumb and index finger barely fit through the grips. He tested them experimentally and judged they would work. Apparently, so did she. Her uncertain frown disappeared.

Calico moved over to give him room to sit. She held her elbow to keep her injured arm steady.

"You don't have to look," he said as he began snipping. "I wouldn't look if I didn't have to."

"I am not looking, and you are a fool."

"You know, I am persuaded that a fool can serve an important purpose."

"Oh? And what's that?"

"Well, distraction is the one that it's serving now." He snipped and pulled out the last of the thread. "Done. Don't look yet. I have to open the scab." He set the scissors down and used the compress to separate the skin.

Calico recoiled at the putrid smell of pus, but she looked down at the open wound anyway. She wrinkled her nose. "Why aren't you making a face?"

"You're looking. You shouldn't be."

"I'm looking at you. Why aren't you making a face?"

"I am. This is it." He applied the warm cloth just below the wound and pressed it carefully upward. He kept pressing it, evacuating the pus.

Calico looked away again. "How did you get the cicatrix on your chest?" she asked. "I know it's from a bullet, but what happened?"

Quill concentrated on what he was doing, but he answered her question so that she would not. "What happened was Hammer Smith. Michael is what his parents called him, but everyone else knew him as Hammer. I don't know why criminals are partial to taking nicknames, but I've made a little study of it, and it seems they are. Boomer Groggins. Chick Tatters. Buck McKay. Billy the Kid. Should I go on?"

"Definitely . . ." She gritted her teeth and curled the fingers of her injured hand into a fist. ". . . not."

"Take a breath," he instructed. "A deep one. Let it out slowly."

She did. It helped.

"So Hammer's playing cards with four friends in a saloon in Barboursville. Sam

Petry's place. I am having a drink, waiting for the game to end so I can ask Hammer what he knows about some cattle missing from the Clinton ranch. I thought we would have a discussion, make sure I had my facts right, before I took him in."

"You said you weren't a bounty hunter."

"And I'm saying it again. I'm not. Now pay attention." He tossed the soiled compress on the floor and exchanged it for a clean one, soaking it first, and then squeezing out the excess water. He continued working. "The game ended, it looked as if Hammer had done well, and he ordered a whiskey. I picked it up from the bar and took it over to him. Told him it was on me if we could have a chat. He seemed to figure that was a fair trade, so he invited me to sit. I was dragging a chair over when he shot me. I never saw him take a drink, but I was told later that he had and that he wasn't partial to Sam's watered-down whiskey. I wasn't partial to being shot, so I shot him back. I don't remember anything after that. His friends ran off, Sam brought the doc, and the town put me up in a nice boarding-house until I recovered. Turned out, Hammer wasn't real popular."

Calico realized suddenly that Quill was done cleaning her wound. She hadn't felt a thing as he had finished up. He had the bottle of bourbon in his hand, not the compress.

He folded over a corner of the quilt and gave it to her. "Bite down on that, unless you want a pillow."

"What about the bourbon?"

"In a moment. Go ahead. Bite down."

She did, and was glad she did, because there was no warning as he poured fine Kentucky whiskey into her wound. Tears came to her eyes and every muscle in her face hurt as she squeezed them all as tightly as she could. The pain never really passed, but it did become endurable. She tore the quilt out of her mouth and opened her eyes. Quill was dangling the bottle in front of her.

"You can clobber me with it or drink it. Lady's choice."

"Give me that." Without thinking, she tried to take it with her dominant hand and the movement set all of her nerves humming. Beads of blood reappeared along the gash in her arm. Grimacing, she took the bottle in her left hand while Quill attended to the bleeding. "I am going to drink myself stupid."

"Good," he said, unperturbed. "That will put us on equal footing, me being a fool and all."

She paused in lifting the bottle to her lips. "I didn't mean that. Or rather, I meant it kindly."

He glanced up at her, smiled. "So you say now." He finished dabbing blood from the wound. "Go on. Drink. You won't feel any less pain, but you won't mind it as much."

She nodded, set the bottle against her mouth, and drank deeply. Her eyes watered as heat burst in her throat and belly. She had to blink to clear her vision, and when she had a good look at what Quill was doing, she could see he was expertly threading a needle.

"This is the best thread Beatrice has for this." He held it up, examined it. "It might be better than what the doctor used. I do wish I had his needle, though. The curve. It helps." He looked over at her. "Ready?"

"You've done this before, haven't you?"

"Mm-hmm. Those Army doctors your father didn't trust? I helped them set bones, stitch wounds, remove arrowheads. I got good enough at it that they requested me." He shrugged. "You do whatever you have to do on a campaign, but it's all right if you want to change your mind about me doing this. I can send for Pitman."

"No." She drank from the bottle again before she gave it over. She needed to free her good arm to hold the other steady. "Go on. Take a drink if you like."

He did and then set the bottle on the floor. "My hands will be even steadier if you're not watching me."

She chuckled quietly. He made it so easy for her to look the other way that she did.

Quill never looked up from his work, even when he heard Calico wince or the sound of air hissing through her clenched teeth. There were moments that he paused to let her catch her breath or still her twitching arm, but those moments were few and brief. He wanted to be done, and he could not imagine that Calico felt any differently.

When he had cut the last thread, he dropped the needle in the basin, and reached for the bourbon. He passed it to Calico without taking any for himself and supported her elbow while she drank. "I am going to make a sling for you. The stitches will hold better if you keep the arm immobile."

"Do what you like," she said airily, waving him off with the bottle. "Whatever you like."

He leaned over and kissed her on the forehead before he stood. Satisfied that she was well on her way to stupid, he picked up the basin and carried it into the bathing room. He came back with a thin towel, which he folded into a triangle and then fashioned into a decent sling. She was unusually cooperative as he put it on and only protested halfheartedly when he relieved her of the bottle.

"I'll find something better for the sling later. I have an idea."

Nodding agreeably, Calico asked, "Aren't you going to wrap a bandage around your work?"

"Later. I want to watch it for a while, and fresh air is probably better than covering it up."

"Somethin' we agree on."

"Mm." He looked over at her. Her green eyes shone a little too brightly, although he was uncertain whether the source was drink or pain. He decided it was probably both. "You should rest."

It was surprisingly easy to give in. "All right." She looked at her wounded arm again. "What should I say to Beatrice when she wants to give me a plaster or a poultice or some other such thing?"

"I will talk to Beatrice. And Ramsey. I need to explain about the bourbon." He stood, swiped cookie crumbs from the nightstand into his palm, and dusted them off in the fire. He came back for the bottle, the sewing box, and a second look at Calico's arm. His stitches were holding and the predominant color along the length of the wound was no longer purple. "I will come back after dinner. What should I tell Mrs. Friend to make for you?"

"Soup. Whatever she is serving the family."

He nodded. "I will be with Ramsey for a while, and then I am going into town." When she started to protest, he stopped her. "Ramsey and Ann will be fine here; they are not your responsibility for the time being." Quill did not give her an opportunity to argue. He exited quickly.

Ramsey was sitting with Frank Fordham when Quill entered the study. He had not bothered to knock and both men looked up at the intrusion, Frank in surprise, Ramsey in annoyance.

Quill did not apologize for interrupting. "I need a moment of your time." He spoke to Ramsey, but his eyes darted to Frank and then to the doors. The company accountant was halfway to his feet before Ramsey stopped him.

"Just a minute, Frank," Ramsey said, holding up his large, square palm. He pointed to the chair and Frank sat down again. Ramsey jerked his chin at Quill. "As it happens, Mr. McKenna, I also need a moment of your time. Mr. Fordham and I are looking over a list of men that were recently hired and —"

"I promise I will review it when I get back from town. I'm leaving, but I need to speak to you first."

Ramsey nodded to Frank. "It's all right. Wait in the front parlor. It seems this won't take long."

When Frank was gone, Quill closed the doors and approached Ramsey's desk. He did not sit. What he did was set the bottle of bourbon down. Hard.

Ramsey did not flinch. "This is about Miss Nash," he said.

Quill nodded shortly. "From now on, I am the *only* person who is going to take care of her. I will ask for Dr. Pitman's help if I think I need it. Under no circumstance is Mrs. Stonechurch to tend that wound with her herbs and barks."

Ramsey frowned so deeply that his eyebrows came together in a single line. "Beatrice? Has she done something?"

"Meaning well is not the same as doing good. She has no experience with gunshot wounds, and she has more faith in her remedies than in Pitman. She either did not recognize the infection that was developing or she thought she could manage it. Neither is acceptable. I am going to speak to her about it, but I wanted you to know."

Ramsey put up a hand and shook his head. "Don't. It will be better if I talk to her. She gave my brother excellent care. I don't want her to mistake your concern for an insult."

Quill drank in a slow, calming breath. "I don't want that either, but you have to speak to her today."

"I will."

Quill watched Ramsey's eyes drift to the bourbon. "That was to make Calico not care so much about the pain. I had to open the wound, drain it, clean it, and suture it again."

Ramsey paled a little. "I didn't know. I saw her this morning. She never complained."

"She doesn't. She won't. There's been no one for her to complain to for a long time. I don't think it occurs to her."

"She saved my life," he said quietly, distantly, as if the fact of it still stunned him.

"She did. And she bears you no ill will because she was the one who got shot. I am the one holding that against you. Do you understand?" He slapped the table when

Ramsey did not respond. "Do you understand?"

Ramsey nodded. He looked up, held Quill's hard stare. "Perhaps better than you think I do. You suggested her to me because you wanted to see her again. You seized an opportunity." Ramsey's gaze turned shrewd. "You don't only blame me for what happened. You blame yourself."

"Not because she got shot. I did not stop you from taking that ride. That's what I blame myself for. I told you she wouldn't be able to arm herself properly. Hell, you were carrying her rifle. You put the both of you at risk because there were appearances you wanted to maintain."

Shaking his head, Quill stepped away from the desk. "You need to think about how much longer you want to keep your daughter in the dark. Beatrice, too." He started for the door, paused, and turned back. "And there is something else you need to know. You were right that there is someone who has caught your daughter's interest. Calico figured it out almost right away. She left it up to me to tell you when I thought the time was right. I am thinking that it is now."

Ramsey Stonechurch moved to the edge of his chair, his back ramrod straight. "And? Who is it?"

"Me, sir. Your daughter's infatuation appears to be with me." Quill walked out then, ignoring Ramsey's bellow, demanding that he return.

Quill came back in time to change for dinner. He checked on Calico before he went downstairs. She was sleeping, so he left the flat parcel from Mrs. Birden's dress shop on the rocker and did not disturb her.

Conversation at dinner was largely limited to what passed between Ann and Beatrice. Ramsey and Quill responded to questions put to them by either of the woman but said nothing to each other. Quill thought Ann looked eager to be gone from the table. Beatrice was harder to read, but she excused herself when Ann did, so Quill figured she was equally glad to have somewhere to go.

Ramsey and Quill did not speak while the table was being cleared and neither of them tried to leave. It was only when the door had been closed and they were alone that Ramsey stood.

"Drink?" he asked, walking over to the cabinet. "I know there is an open bottle of bourbon here somewhere."

"Thank you. Yes." A minute later Quill had a drink in his hand. Ramsey tapped it lightly with his own before he returned to his chair.

"I will begin," said Ramsey. "I spoke to Beatrice. She was horrified at the prospect that her remedies may have done more harm than good."

"They did no good."

Ramsey lifted his hand a fraction. "Please, let me have my say. You already made your opinion clear." When Quill nodded, Ramsey went on. "As I said, she was horrified. You should consider allowing her to provide teas. Everyone in the house knows they are efficacious." He patted the general area of his stomach. "She will want to talk to you later to apologize. I ask that you hear her out, be patient with her. Forgive her. I hope you will encourage Miss Nash to do the same."

"I won't have to. Miss Nash will do all those things on her own."

Ramsey pressed his lips together, nodded. "You were also right about something, Mr. McKenna. I was wrong not to heed your advice about not inviting Miss Nash to go riding. I did not use good judgment there, and she paid for it. You know why I did it, don't you?"

Quill hesitated, wondering if he should admit that he did. After a moment, he said, "Yes, sir. You are fond of her."

"Fond?" Ramsey's short laugh mocked

363

himself. "That makes me sound rather avuncular, doesn't it? It is damn lowering to be thought of in that light. Older. Harmless. Foolish. My interests were romantic, but I don't suppose I cut a dashing figure." He laughed at himself again. "Cut a dashing figure. I *am* old, or else I am susceptible to the same nonsense delivered by the writers of dime novels as my daughter." Shrugging, he sipped his drink. "Does she know?"

"Ann?"

"No," he said somewhat impatiently. "Not Ann. We will get to her later. I meant Miss Nash. Calico."

Quill did not pretend not to know what Ramsey was talking about. "She suspects."

"So if you know that, it means that the two of you have talked about it." He sighed. "That is even more lowering." One of his wiry eyebrows arched. "Did she tell you what we were discussing when the first shot was fired?"

"Yes." Seeing Ramsey's dismay and genuine discomfort, Quill took a breath and reached deep for the lie. "She said she was explaining the merits of a Winchester over a Remington repeater and you were arguing the opposite view. Ironic, then, that someone would take a shot at you while you were debating which rifle was better."

Ramsey was slow to respond. He studied Quill over the rim of his tumbler. "Yes. Ironic."

Quill said, "You should sort this out with Calico."

"I don't think there is anything to sort out. I know which way the wind is blowing, and it is not in my direction."

Quill said nothing. He finished his drink.

"More?" asked Ramsey.

"No. I think we need to discuss your daughter. You understand that whatever she imagines she feels for me, it is not reciprocated."

Ramsey knocked back what remained of his drink. He got up and poured another finger. "I would go so far as to wager that when you were in uniform, you cut a damn dashing figure."

"That was quite a few years ago."

"Jesus, Quill. What are you now? Thirty?"

"About that."

Ramsey added another splash to his glass. "Jesus," he muttered again.

Quill said, "You should know that I intend to spend more time with Calico while she is healing, and sooner or later Ann and Beatrice, Mrs. Friend, Mrs. Pratt, Molly, and everyone else in and out of this house will take notice and have something to say about it. If Calico's right about Ann, then she —"

"Oh, she's right. I'm calling myself three kinds of an idiot for not seeing it, but the scales have been lifted from my eyes. My little girl is going to have her heart broken just like her father."

Quill cleared his throat. "I don't think —"

"Don't assume you know what's going on in here." Ramsey tapped his chest with his forefinger. "I was — am — a damn sight more than fond of Miss Nash."

Quill was not certain what he could or should say to that.

Ramsey rested an elbow on the sideboard. He tapped his tumbler lightly against the polished top. "Maybe Miss Nash could speak to her. Soften the blow. She would be sensible about it."

"Ann?"

"Calico. Oh, hell, they would both be sensible. If I understand anything about how this works, they will skewer you and congratulate themselves on being too smart to be taken in by your goddamn dashing figure."

Quill put his hand up, extended his fore-finger. "A point of clarification. How much did you have to drink *before* dinner?"

■ ■ ■ ■

"I have newspapers for you," said Quill, pulling a week's worth of folded dailies out from under his arm. "Where do you want them?"

Calico patted the space to her left. "*Rocky Mountain News?*"

"Uh-huh." He set them down, felt her forehead with the back of his hand, and looked over the tray across her lap. She had finished most of her soup. A few noodles and bits of chicken were left, but the broth was gone. Half of a roll remained beside her bowl. He pointed to it. "Is that half of the only roll you had, or did you already eat one?"

"Ate one. With elderberry jam."

"Good." He saw the teapot on the table. "Did Beatrice bring that?"

"No, Ann. That and more sand tarts." She looked up at him. "Ann said you were unusually quiet this evening at dinner. She thinks Beatrice is afraid of you."

"I was angry with Ramsey. It got away from me. I tried to be civil, but I don't know . . . I will speak to Beatrice. Apologize. Tell her she can bring you those teas she swears by."

367

Calico grimaced. "You do not have to mention the teas." Her eyes darted to the seat of the rocker. "I am curious about the parcel. You left it, didn't you?"

"I did. It's what I went to town for. You were sleeping when I brought it in."

"I wish you had woken me. I was so sure you were going to return with Dr. Pitman that I made myself fall asleep out of sheer cussedness."

Quill took her tray and set it aside. "And I was so sure it was the bourbon." He picked up the brown paper parcel by its string and dropped it in her lap. "Don't expect too much. It's something practical."

"It doesn't matter what it is. The fact that it's anything at all is . . ." She shook her head and quickly looked down at the package. She tugged at the string, careful not to make a knot of it. When she was done, she drew the string out slowly and wound it around her wrist, tucking in the end so it would not unravel. When he asked her about it, she shrugged and told him she might have use for it, and then she turned the parcel over and folded back the paper.

"Oh," she said. "Oh." There was no other sound she could move past the lump in her throat. She looked up at him then, her glistening eyes an exact match for the bright green calico fabric in her lap.

When she said nothing, he explained somewhat diffidently, "It's to make a sling."

She nodded jerkily and offered a watery smile.

"I . . . I, um, I remembered what you said about the swaddling cloth."

Calico nodded again, tried to speak, and . . . nothing. She knuckled her eyes before tears dripped on the fabric.

"I never figured you for a watering can."

She chuckled unevenly, sniffed, and accepted the handkerchief he thrust at her.

"Just so you're not tempted to use the material," he told her.

Calico dabbed at her eyes, blew her nose, and gave him a sideways look. "As if I would." She folded the handkerchief and tucked it under the tray on the table. "Put it on for me."

"Of course." Quill thought his voice sounded slightly off, husky, even a bit rough as though he had not spoken in a long time. He did not dwell on it, helping her out of the sling she was wearing instead. He was already folding the calico when she stopped him.

"No," she said, putting a hand over his. "I want you to wrap my wound. You said you would later, and it is later now. If it bleeds, it will ruin this cloth. I don't want that. Please."

"I can buy another length of —" Quill stopped because he could see that was not going to satisfy her. "All right." He used his teeth to cut a tear in the towel, and then he rent it into four wide strips. He covered her wound with one, secured it, and resumed fashioning the sling. When he was done, he helped her into it, setting the angle so her hand lay just above her heart. "Is it too tight?" He had knotted it at the side of her neck.

"No."

Quill chose another strip of towel, folded it several times, and inserted the pad under the knot. Satisfied, he moved to the rocker.

Calico ran her palm over the cotton fabric from her wrist to her elbow and back again. "Thank you," she said. "I don't think I thanked you before."

"You did. You just didn't know it."

She pressed her lips together and nodded.

He pushed the rocker back and set his heels against the bed frame. "You should know what Ramsey and I discussed after dinner, most of it anyway." He reviewed his conversation, treading carefully when it came to Ramsey's feelings for her. There was nothing to be gained by repeating what was essentially the man's declaration of love for Calico, and moreover, it would have been wrong. What was in a man's heart should not be grist for the mill.

When Quill finished, he looked at Calico expectantly. "Well, what do you think?"

She did not hesitate to tell him. "What I think is that you and Ramsey are lily-livered."

"Lily-livered?"

"Gutless. Craven. Cowardly."

He put up a hand. "I know what it means. I do not know why you think it's true."

"What else would you call someone who cannot face a young woman and talk frankly about her tenderhearted, but ill-advised, attachment to a man who is better than ten years her senior?"

"Sensible?"

Calico rolled her eyes. "Spineless. There's a word. Shame on you for turning over that responsibility to me."

"I believe I felt shame. Ramsey was not feeling anything but his liquor. You hold it better than he does."

"Flattery will not work here."

"I was not trying to —" He frowned, thoughtful. "Hmm. Maybe I was."

Calico groped for one of the folded newspapers at her side with every intention of throwing it at him, but when she picked it up, she realized it was too flimsy to have any impact. She dropped it and pointed to her sling. "You know, I could slip my derringer in here and you would be none the wiser until I was pointing it at your heart."

He grinned broadly. "You *are* feeling better."

She groaned softly. "You really are impervious to threats. Ramsey was right about one thing. When I speak to Ann, I am going to skewer you, and I am going to invite her to do the same."

CHAPTER ELEVEN

Over the course of the following week, and under Quill's watchful eye, Calico's wound closed and began to heal remarkably well. Beatrice Stonechurch credited her teas, and Calico did not have the heart to tell her that except for those occasions when Beatrice hovered while she drained her cup, she generally emptied the teapot into the sink.

Beginning the day after Quill sutured her wound, Calico regularly left her room. She took her meals in the dining room again, sat with Ann in the front parlor for studies and her own reading pleasure, resumed being instructed on how to handle a weapon in the rear parlor, and perched on a stool in the kitchen so she could observe Mrs. Friend making bread, pastries, stew, and soups. Mrs. Friend found her interest a curiosity, but she was happy for the company, and Calico never had to explain that what she knew about cooking was limited to chuck wagon fare and those things that could be prepared outdoors over an open fire.

She bided her time approaching Ann, waiting for an opportunity to present itself. It finally came about because Ann walked in on her reading the romantic dime novel adventures of Felicity Ravenwood. There was no hiding it from her, so Calico owned up to her guilty pleasure.

After that, it was surprisingly easy to talk about first loves, romantic love, love at first sight, and love everlasting. Calico listened more than she contributed, and asked many more questions than she answered, all of which had the consequence of Ann taking notice of what she said when she did speak, even taking some of it to heart. They never spoke about Quill, not directly. Ann talked about the *idea* of him, and sometimes about the *ideal* of him, and Calico heard as much curiosity as she did longing. It was when their conversation turned to reality that the skewering began.

When Calico shared some of that conversation with Quill, she found considerable satisfaction in pointing out that it was Ann who inserted the first skewer.

Quill shuffled the papers in his lap as he regarded Calico with a skeptical eye. "She thinks I'm a scoundrel now?"

"Not just you. All men. And not 'scoundrel' in any romantic sense."

"Scoundrels are romantic?"

"Only in Felicity Ravenwood's world. Have you been listening at all? Ann has come to her senses. Her perspective is practical, thoughtful, and you no longer figure into her notions of what would make a suitable match. You should be overjoyed."

A small crease appeared between his eyebrows. "I am not sure I like being a scoundrel."

"Oh, that is the least of it." She put up a hand. "You do not want to know."

Quill agreed that he probably did not. "It sounds as if you both were sensible about it. Ramsey said you would be."

Except to humph quietly, Calico made no comment. "What do have over there?" she said, gesturing to the papers in his lap. It was late, minutes shy of eleven, and to Calico's eyes Quill did not look as if he had been sleeping long or restfully in quite some time. Although there was no good reason for it as far as she was concerned, he spent most of the last seven nights napping in the rocker, the armchair, or stretched out on the floor beside her. The one time he had joined her in bed, they had collided in their sleep, and her injury had gotten the worst of it. The searing pain made her bolt upright, and she barely managed to stop from crying out. There was no reasoning with Quill that it was not his fault, and he remained convinced that if she had shouted, it would have awakened everyone up and down the hall as well as the dead.

Quill lifted his papers and squared them off. "I can do this in my room or downstairs if I am keeping you up."

"I didn't say that you were. I asked what they are."

His lips parted around a long exhalation of air. "Something that I promised Ramsey I would review last week and never got around to it. I forgot. He forgot. Frank Fordham remembered. He came by asking for them."

"And yet, I still don't know what they are. Is it a secret?"

"No. The most important paper here is a list of the men that Frank wants to hire. Ramsey asked me to compare it to a list of known agitators."

Calico's eyebrows lifted. "Agitators? You mean men who want trade unions. And where does that list come from?"

"I had a premonition you weren't going to like that." When her eyebrows did not lower even a fraction, he continued. "The names come from all over, actually. Ramsey has more connections than the Union Pacific. It is not only the mine owners who share information. Ramsey hears from the likes of Carnegie, Morgan, and Rockefeller. He knows who is stirring trouble — his view, not necessarily always mine — in Chicago stockyards, in the Appalachian mines, and in the shipyards on both coasts. There's a movement and it scares him, I think. It scares all of them, so they make lists."

"I *don't* like it. Next they will be rounding them up. Moving them to reservations." She snorted and reached for the cup of tea on the bedside table. It was cold, but she didn't care. She gulped it down. Almost immediately she was pressing her palm against her midriff.

"Are you all right?"

"I drank it too fast. I do that sometimes when I'm agitated. I should know better. It's the chamomile, one of Beatrice's least offensive brews, but it doesn't always settle well in my stomach." That said, her stomach rumbled and roiled. Her eyes widened. "Oh, dear. Here it comes." She rapidly tapped her chest with her palm but made no effort to cover her mouth.

The air she expelled came out in a loud, long, and most unladylike burp. It was only in the aftermath that she remembered to press her fingertips to her lips.

Quill regarded her with interest. "Well," he said matter-of-factly. "Everything seems to be working."

"Mm." She caught her breath and swallowed. "My father would have cuffed me for that if we were out scouting. Too much noise, he'd have said. Now if that had happened while we were trading stories with the other scouts, he'd have clapped me hard on the back and congratulated me for what he would have called 'an excellent peptic outburst.' It tended to hurt a little either way, so I'm grateful you weren't moved to hit me."

Quill said, "Did the Army command know you were out scouting with your father?"

"No. And when I got better at it, sometimes my father didn't know. I did not like being left behind."

"You've never told me how you found your way to bounty hunting."

"When I was fifteen, my father was diagnosed with consumption. He didn't hear that from an Army doctor. A shaman told him. He was fairly adept at hiding it, although I came to believe the commander eventually figured it out. Whether he pretended not to know because it served my father's purpose or his own, I can't speak to that. I tried to talk some sense into him about leaving for better climes, but he was set as hard and fast in his ways as a tick on your belly. Refused to move to Arizona, where the air might have improved him. He liked the mountains. Liked the plains. He did not want anything to do with the desert. He died in my seventeenth year while he was hunting down a renegade Army deserter. I buried him, mourned him, and took up his job. In my mind it was the best way to honor him. I tracked down the deserter and escorted him to Fort Bent, where no one knew me. I had some idea about passing as a man — don't laugh, it's been done — but I never was too keen on it and didn't try very hard."

She held up her hands in an attitude of helplessness. "The fact is I like being a woman. I just want to do mostly what interests a man."

"Maybe what you really want is the choice."

Calico thought about that. "Could be. Men have a lot of choices."

"So what happened at Fort Bent?"

"Nothing. Everything happened afterward. I returned to Fort Collins. By the time I arrived, they had had word from Fort Bent. They knew about my father and that I had captured and taken in the deserter. There was some talk about me staying on with one of the families, but I didn't want that. My father had some savings, which were turned over to me. I took his guns, some of his clothes, all of our books. They gave me his horse, which I had brought back. I bought a new saddle, a good pack animal, and I headed out for the nearest town where I could find a marshal or a sheriff and the wanted notices. It was four months before I had my first bounty, but I never wanted for anything during that time." She paused and shook her head slightly, remembering. "That's not true. I wanted for company. I wanted for my father."

Quill nodded.

"He taught me most everything I needed to survive, but he did not teach me how to be alone. I had to learn that. I could hunt, so I ate well. It was never a problem to find water. I knew what plants I could eat. I had books, all of which I had read, but I read them again as time allowed. That helped. Bagger believed reading elevated the soul. Sometimes it seemed to me that it did.

Leaves of Grass. Do you know it?"

"I do."

"It was my companion. My edition was small. It fit in my pocket, and I carried it with me, not on the packhorse. Whitman should be read outdoors, Bagger said, and I think he was right. It helped."

Quill imagined Calico sitting hunched in front of a small fire, Whitman's book in her hand. Her face would be illuminated by the fire, and the pages would be illuminated by her grace. Her lips would move as she read because she would want to hear the words aloud. She probably knew whole passages by rote, but she would hold the book out anyway and take care with every word, every nuance.

He wondered if she would share that experience with him. If he invited her to lie with him in the deep grass, would she come? Would she read to him if he asked? *There is something in staying close to men and women and looking on them, and in the contact and odor of them, that pleases the soul well, All things please the soul, but these please the soul well.* He wanted to be out of doors with her, blanketed by sunshine and nothing else, alone and together, naked in the celebration of what was right and fine between a man and a woman.

They would sing the body electric.

He blinked. Calico was looking at him oddly. He managed a lopsided, somewhat self-conscious, smile.

"Where did you go?" she asked. "For a while, you were not in this room."

"You remember the place where I found you that night you left the house? I went there."

"Really?"

"You were with me. Actually there were three of us. You. Me. Walt Whitman."

"You are a dangerous man, Mr. McKenna."

"I thought I was a scoundrel."

"That, too. Now where are those newspapers you brought me?"

"On the chest on top of the ones I brought you a week ago."

She looked past the foot of the bed. "So they are." She refused his offer to retrieve them. The sling was a nuisance as she attempted to crawl to the end of the bed, and feeling as graceless as a three-legged cat, she pulled her arm out of it.

"I saw that."

Calico ignored him, grabbed the entire stack of dailies, and scooted back to the head of the bed. She made herself comfortable and arranged the sling so it lay like a scarf around her neck and shoulders. She stretched her arm experimentally, which she did off and on throughout the day, although never in front of Quill. When she glanced over at him, he was staring at his work, but there was the narrowest of smiles on his lips.

Because she had nothing substantial to toss at his head, she proceeded to sift through the newspapers, looking for a story that she had started to read some time ago and never finished. Her eyes skimmed the pages for some mention of the Palace Variety Theatre and Gambling Parlor. Bat Masterson's new establishment was engaging vaudeville acts from the East, and Calico thought she might like to read what the fuss was about.

It was on her way to finding that article that her eyes fell on another. She had purposely avoided reading the crime report column, which dutifully logged the names of those arrested for drunkenness, depravity, and dealing from the bottom of a deck. She especially did not want to see the name of someone she had taken in appear again as the perpetrator of a new crime. That did not happen often, but when it did, she blamed the lawyers. It seemed to her that on those occasions they had sense for the law and little for justice. The juries were hopelessly confused.

But none of that was what pulled her attention this time.

"Mercy," she whispered, rattling the *Rocky* in her hands. "Lord have mercy." She held the newspaper closer as she reread the offending column. "If this does not move me off this mountain, I must truly be in love." Behind the paper, Calico shook her head slowly. "Huh. I did *not* expect to come to that realization in this manner."

"Imagine my surprise," came the wry reply.

Calico lowered the newspaper until she could see Quill over the top. His head was bent as he continued to study his lists. "Maybe I didn't mean I was in love with you."

"Mm-hmm."

Shaking her head, she said, "I do not understand it, but I find your confidence to be one of your most attractive qualities." He looked up then and dazzled her with a cocky grin. "But I will never get used to that."

Still grinning, Quill dropped his work on the floor. The papers scattered. He stepped over them to get to the bed. She was already moving over to make room for him when he reached her. He sat down, removed his shoes and his jacket, and then positioned himself so he was against the headboard beside her.

He leaned over, careful not to jostle her arm, and kissed her proffered cheek. "Now show me what prompted you to make that rather extraordinary declaration."

"Was it extraordinary? I couldn't tell."

"Calico." He flicked at one corner of the paper she was still holding. "The *Rocky*?"

"What? Oh. Yes, of course." She passed the broadsheet-style paper to him and pointed out the story. "I imagine you are waiting for a similar bolt of lightning to strike you, although I think it would be good of you to tell me if you hear any thunder in the distance. Having said it aloud, it feels a little like I am wearing my undergarments on the outside. It's not precisely uncomfortable, but it's the kind of thing that's bound to attract notice."

"Hmm. Let me read this, and then I will be happy to report on the weather."

She poked him in the arm with her elbow, which made her wince and him regard her with a raised eyebrow and no sympathy. After that, she rested her head on his shoulder and let him be.

"Damn," he said under his breath. "Damn and damn. How does this happen? How

385

does our friend Nick Whitfield break out of jail? I would have thought he'd find it difficult to break an egg."

"Read on."

Quill did. A moment later, he said, "Of course. Chick Tatters." His eyes darted down the page. "I don't see Amos Bennett's name here. I thought the three of them worked together."

"So did I, but I don't think Amos and Whit were longtime associates. Do you remember Joe Pepper telling us that Amos might have been the one who gave Whit's name to the law after he — Whitfield — robbed that bank in Bailey?"

"I'm recalling that now."

"Whit was the only one I escorted to the Bailey jail. I never saw a notice for the other two. I figure Whit never turned on Chick Tatters because he was counting on him to get him out. Whether Amos helped or not probably doesn't matter any longer. It's hard to believe that Whit wouldn't have killed him by now." She pointed out the paper's publication date. "This paper was days old when you gave it to me. Now it's been almost a month. Amos Bennett is dead."

Quill did not disagree. He read through the article again and then folded the paper.

He used it to indicate all the other newspapers fanned out across the blankets and Calico's lap. "I think we need to look through all of these. Whit might have already been caught."

She sighed. "I am not hopeful, especially since there is no mention of a reward, but you are right, we have to look." She quickly ordered the papers chronologically, putting the oldest on the top. She handed it to him and took the next one for herself. They both began to read.

They were four papers down when Quill came across the notice of Amos Bennett's demise. The authorities suspected the hapless Amos had drowned trying to cross the rapidly rising waters of Bessemer Creek. There was no reason given as to why they suspected that, but since two of Joe Pepper's deputies were involved with the retrieval and identification of the body, Quill and Calico reasoned they believed Amos had been trying to flee Whit and Tatters.

Calico discarded another issue with no new information. "I confess I am more hopeful that Whit's been captured knowing that Joe Pepper and his men were out looking for him." She plucked the next paper in the stack and opened it to the arrest log and crime stories.

Quill also chose another and skimmed the front page. "Calico? Who knows you are here?"

"Joe Pepper knows because we talked about it when he passed your letter on. His wife knows because she helped me choose some clothes. I don't know who they might have told. Truthfully, I don't know why they would have told anyone, but I never asked them not to."

"Hmm."

"Is it important?" She turned her head and was confronted by Quill's patently disbelieving expression. "Oh. You think because Whit chased down Amos Bennett, he will come after me? I doubt it. First, we are only suspecting that Whit was responsible, and second, as long as there are banks to rob and whores to beat, he will always have something better to do."

"Are you saying that to ease my mind or your own?"

Calico did not reply.

Quill caught her by the chin when she would have looked away. He held her widening eyes. "Uh-huh. I thought so. Listen to me, Calico. I don't want you pretending that the possibility doesn't exist because you're harboring some notion that you are protecting me. I know it's been a long time since anyone's looked out for you, so maybe that is why the idea of it makes you skittish, but that's one aspect of love that you are going to have to accustom yourself to. Do you understand?"

She blinked. Her lips parted, but she breathed in, not out. She had no words, not even one.

"Here it is, Calico. That thunderstorm you were talking about earlier? Well, it passed over my head a long time ago. Lightning hit close enough to make me jump when you appeared on the balcony of Mrs. Fry's cathouse. I had another jolt when you gave me hell for interfering in your business — and that was when I still thought you were a brunette."

She frowned deeply.

He shrugged, said matter-of-factly, "Until you, I always thought I was partial to blondes."

Now she had words, but he kept going before she could speak.

"Obviously I didn't know my own mind because there were other things I was wrong about."

Calico's eyes narrowed.

"That's right. Your eyes. Green, not blue. And you're tall, so the curves are kind of long and gentle, not deep. Then it turned out that you have hair like a flame and dart about as if it's really on fire. You threatened me — several times as I recall — and you clobbered Chick Tatters without blinking an eye. You carried a derringer, you were pretending to be a whore, and you tied Nick Whitfield up like you had been roping and wrangling all of your life."

Quill tilted his head and studied her face. "Do you truly believe there was a moment after I left you in Falls Hollow that I was not thinking about how I was going to find you again? I was here when lightning struck, and you were nowhere around."

Calico cupped the hand that still held her chin and lowered it, squeezing gently. "Oh my."

"So now you know."

She nodded. She had known, of course, but she had not *known.* Not like this. "I suppose you will want to read the rest of the papers now."

Quill slid down the headboard and brought Calico with him. The *Rocky Mountain News* crumpled and crinkled noisily all around them as they nested. "What papers?" he asked in the moment before he bore down on her.

They began without urgency. Their confessions made, neither had a reason to

390

hurry. Pleasure was in the exploration of their promise to each other. It was in the touch of her fingertips across his brow and in the way his lips moved at the hollow below her ear. She unbuttoned his vest and peeled back his shirt. He removed the sling she had fashioned into a scarf and wrapped it loosely around her wrists. She stared at him, but she did not resist then or when he lifted her hands and placed them above her head. One by one, he unfastened the small buttons that closed the neckline of her nightgown. He kissed her everywhere her skin was revealed. Her flesh was warm, and it warmed him.

She looked down, watched the crown of his head move lower. He parted her gown and took the tip of one breast in his mouth. His tongue darted across her nipple. When he sucked, her breath hitched, and she held it until he released her. At that moment she did not care if she ever breathed again. She would have gladly drowned in pleasure.

She raised her bound arms and circled his neck. She thought about swaddling cloths, thought about swaddling him. He took her other breast, teased it with his lips and tongue and then with his hot breath. She scrabbled his hair and twisted the curling ends around her forefingers. It was like swimming in sunshine.

He unfastened his trousers. She tugged on her gown. He moved between her legs and she prepared a cradle for him, raising her knees, hugging him with her thighs. He knew her body, the long and gentle curves. She thought about that as he came into her, about that and other things, and they all made her smile. She was a redhead every-where, and she welcomed him into the fire.

The tempo changed. It had to. Where there had been no urgency, now there was need and it pressed them to want more, to search for it and claim it. He rocked her with each thrust, and she met him measure for full measure. The bed groaned. The headboard banged against the wall. Neither of them heard any of it. There was their breathing first, and then there were words.

She said, "Ah. Like that. Just like that."

And he said, "Hold me."

"Mm." She contracted everywhere she could, but especially *there.*

He moaned softly, far back in his throat where he could feel the vibration. "That's it. You know. You always know."

A sound she was unfamiliar with bubbled to her lips. He bent his head and it tickled his ear. She said, "I love you." The whisper made his heart stutter and tripped his pulse.

There was a rush like an avalanche in his head and he cried out as he came deeply into her.

He lay still, moved slowly, and slipped a hand between their bodies. The touch was precisely what he thought it would be. Electric. Her body jerked, froze, and then jerked again. He could almost feel her falling away from him. He let her go, waiting until the last possible moment to seize her in his arms and hold her close.

They were comforted by their silence, by the crackle of the fire and the rustling of papers. The covers were in disarray, tangled and bunched. One of the pillows was now at the foot of the bed. There were copies of the *Rocky Mountain News* on the floor and under their feet. The bedside table was several more inches from the bed than it had been. The oil lamp on top of the table was precariously close to the edge. Quill was wearing the green calico like a neckerchief, and one of Calico's sutures had broken.

They noticed these things gradually. He pointed out one, she another. They laughed with very little sound. It was in his smile, in her eyes. He stretched large and wide; she stretched with feline grace that captivated him.

"What is that around your ankle?" he asked, squinting to get a better look at it before she tucked it under the quilt.

She shrugged. "It's just . . . something."

"Let me see it."

"I am not moving. You'll have to."

He was too curious to let it go, so he sat up and swept back the quilt. She raised her leg and made a circle with her nicely turned ankle to show off what she was wearing around it. It was a narrow braid, and at first, because of the pale color, he thought it might be made from a lock of his hair. "That's not mine, is —" He broke off, patting the back of his head in a search for cropped locks.

"No, it's not yours. It's not hair." She regarded his halo of golden highlights with interest. "But now that you —"

"Not amusing," he said. He caught her under the knee and drew it back until he could grasp her ankle. He ran his thumb along the braid. "This is string. You made a braid of string. Why would you do that?"

She reached up and tugged on the calico neckerchief that she had been inspired to tie around his throat. It came away easily and she smoothed and folded the fabric. When she was done, she looked at him and waited patiently for him to understand.

When it came to him, he looked from her to the calico she was holding and simply shook his head. He lowered her leg and drew the quilt over it. "I even asked you why you were saving the package string."

"And I told you I might need it."

"Did you know what you were going to do with it then?"

She nodded faintly. "I saved the brown paper wrapper, too."

"Calico."

"What you did, Quill. It's precious to me. Every bit of it."

Quill lay back and offered his shoulder. She put her head down and then lifted it long enough to slip the folded fabric under her cheek. He said dryly, "It has so many uses."

"Be quiet," she said. "It's perfect."

When Calico awoke, it was not yet dawn. The oil lamp was still lit and resting on the bedside table, but the table was no longer at her bedside. Quill had moved it beside the armchair, where he was now sitting. She could see him clearly in three-quarter profile as he bent over his reading. His concentration was all for his task. Twin vertical creases had appeared between his eyebrows; his lips were rolled inward and pressed together in a flat line. He knuckled the stubble on his jaw as he read. Occasionally his mouth would pull to one side.

She lay as she was, not moving, content to watch him from beneath lowered lashes and sleep-swollen eyelids. Looking on him now, Calico realized that she had become accustomed to his smile, his laughter, and the tilt of his head, which was somehow wry and curious at the same time. She tried to recall if she had ever seen him long in this particular pose, serious, intent, sober. His face was also transformed by this manner, but differently, and she saw the man who was deeply attentive, intelligent, not only clever, and naturally thoughtful in his outlook.

Lord, how she loved him. It occurred to her that she would be changed by it, that it could hardly be helped, but she did not dwell on it. If she allowed herself to wander down that path for very long, she would confront an entire thorn patch of problems that she would rather avoid for the present. She was happy to let her mind drift.

She realized she must have done something to give herself away, a contented sigh perhaps or a change in her breathing, because Quill looked up from his reading and caught her watching him. She stretched and smiled sleepily. It was no good pretending that she was not replete in the aftermath of their lovemaking when she most certainly was.

"How long have you been working?" she asked, raising herself on an elbow.

"I don't know. Awhile."

"You didn't sleep?"

"I did."

"What's wrong?" She glimpsed one corner of the bright calico under her arm. If she were not already alert to Quill's mood, it would have made her smile. She tucked it beneath her pillow, out of sight. "Quill?"

"I've read through all the papers," he said. "I went downstairs to Ramsey's study and found a couple of issues we didn't have. He also had a few recent issues of the *Denver Post* so I read through those as well."

"And?"

"Those deputies who accompanied you and Whitfield to the Bailey jail?"

Calico felt a stirring of alarm. It kept her still. "Yes. Christopher Byers and Buster Applegate. What about them?"

"The *Post* reported that Applegate was grievously wounded during a shootout in Royal Canyon. Byers — they refer to him as Kit in the account — was killed. Joe Pepper was heading the posse. He was also wounded, but the reporter indicates he is expected to survive. No one else was hurt, and the posse turned back to Falls Hollow without making a capture."

"What about Buster?"

Quill shook his head. "I can't find any mention of him after that first account, but then we don't have every issue. He could have survived."

Calico twisted the sheet in her fingers. "It's clear from the account that the posse was chasing Whit?"

"Yes. Tatters, too. They were still together then. No one in the posse could say with certainty that either was wounded. There was no blood trail to follow even if the posse had been inclined to go on, so that seems to indicate that Whit and Tatters escaped unharmed."

"I know Royal Canyon," said Calico. "It wasn't Whit and Tatters who escaped. It was Joe Pepper and his men. They were ambushed. I am as certain of it as I am that Thursday will follow Wednesday. Maybe the posse was closing in, narrowing the gap so much that they spooked Whit. He decided to make a stand but on his terms. The canyon's narrow with just a finger of water running through the floor, and there are plenty of niches in the rock to hide out. It's hard to climb, though. The best way to get to the hidey-holes is to take a route down from the top. It'd be like shooting fish in a barrel."

Quill picked up where Calico left off. "So you think Whit and Tatters put down some signs at the mouth of the canyon — a few so the posse could be fooled into believing they'd gotten lucky — and then covered their tracks on an easier path to the top."

"I think exactly that. Look who they picked off. Byers. Applegate." Her voice hitched suddenly. A long moment passed before she could get out the last name. "Joe."

"They targeted them."

"Yes."

"Were you aware that either of them was that good a shot?"

"No. But you know that bragging rights and notoriety tend to go to a man with a fast draw, and that doesn't apply here. A rifle changes things. With a good site and a steady hand, a man who can barely get his gun out of his holster in close quarters has a dead-on aim at a hundred yards. It could be we are just finding out how good they are."

Quill said nothing. He dropped his head back and stared at the ceiling.

"What are you thinking?" she asked.

"Nothing profound or insightful, I assure you. I'm thinking I don't like it. I don't like any part of it."

"I understand."

One of his eyebrows lifted. "Do you? You have a role in this. If I were Nick Whitfield, I would regard you as having the largest role."

"There's Mrs. Fry."

He turned to face her fully, his expression grave. "She's gone, Calico. Dead. I read it in one of the papers I found in Ramsey's study; it was only a couple of lines, easy to miss if I had not been reading everything closely. A madam's death is not worth much ink."

"Dead?" Calico sat up, crossed her legs tailor-fashion, and drew one of the quilts around her. She rubbed her temples, trying to take it in.

Quill continued. "We didn't ask ourselves why Joe Pepper was heading the hunt. Whitfield broke out of a jail in Bailey. That's not Pepper's territory. He got a posse together when Mrs. Fry's brothel burned to the ground with her inside it. There was so little information that I am not certain who might have died with her and who might have escaped. No cause is given for the fire; no one is named as having set it." There was no need to say more. She was nodding, the truth borne home.

"The order of events," she said slowly. "I am confused. Amos's body was found before or after the fire?"

"After. I made a chronology." He moved all the papers on his lap to the table except for the one on top. He stood and carried it to Calico. "Here. It's the best I could do given that we do not have every newspaper and the reporting is erratic. There were events happening in Denver proper that were judged to be more important. Rightly so."

"A bounty on Whitfield and Tatters would have gotten everyone's attention."

"You're right, but the bank in Bailey already put up one reward. You know. You collected it. It's easier to get reward money when a robbery's been committed than when a life's been taken."

"So as long as they stay out of banks, they can —" She stopped herself. The truth was too depressing to be said aloud. She looked over Quill's chronology as he returned to his chair. "The escape. The fire. Joe Pepper puts his posse together. Amos's body is found. What's this? I can't read this." She squinted as she tried to make out his scribbling. "Something about a brand. A brood."

"A brawl," said Quill. "There was a fight in a little mining town called Reidsville that began in a saloon and spilled out into the street. There were injuries. Arrests. One name caught my attention. Charles Tattersall. I thought it might be Chick. As you said, neither man is good with a gun in close quarters. That's when they use their fists. Brawlers, both of them. The town isn't far from where Amos was found. Maybe ten miles as the crow flies. I know it's all supposition, but I figured I should write it down."

She nodded. "Charles Tattersall. Maybe it is Chick. He wouldn't have been in jail very long. The timeline still holds." She pointed to the item following the last downward arrow. "Royal Canyon."

"Nothing that I can find since then makes me think they are anywhere except laying low."

Calico laid the paper on the bed beside her. "I find it odd that Joe did not send word to me. He would not do that as a rule, but about this, I think it would have occurred to him that I should know."

"Maybe it did, and he did not have time to see it through."

"You're probably right. I wonder who is

out looking for Whit and Tatters now."

"With no reward, I suspect marshals will be appointed to take up the chase. Also, there were deputies who survived the ambush. Tom Hand. Cooper Branch."

"They will be needed for general law enforcement. Joe Pepper will not be able to spare them. You're probably right. It will be marshals."

"Do you wish you were one of them?"

"A marshal?" She laughed, wryly amused. "Wouldn't that be something? No, I don't think I would care to be one of them, even supposing they would have me." She regarded Quill candidly. "What do you think we should do? I believe you've been giving it some thought. You've been awake longer than I have."

"I am going to speak to Ramsey about you leaving Stonechurch."

"I see. You are not even going to ask me what I want to do?"

"I would be surprised if you wanted anything other than another confrontation with Nick Whitfield. The problem, as I see it, is that you will not get as close to him as you did the last time. He is not likely to accept a drink from you when he can end your life from a hundred yards away."

Calico laid her palm across her wounded

arm. "Perhaps he's already tried . . . and failed."

Quill closed his eyes briefly and nodded. "I had the same thought. All the more reason for you to leave."

"We don't know that he did this to me, and I am not going to act on supposition. How would they even know I am here?"

"That's why I asked you who might know. You said you told Joe and Mary Pepper and anyone they might have told. How hard do you think it would be for Whit to learn your location if, say, Mary was threatened?"

"That is pure speculation, and I don't like it. I was hired because it is Ramsey Stonechurch's life that is in danger, and Nick Whitfield and Chick Tatters have nothing at all to do with that. How could they have possibly known that Ramsey and I would be riding that morning? And in that particular direction? I did not know it myself until we set out. I'm not sure that Ramsey knew the night before where we would go."

"He knew. He told Beatrice."

"He told her?"

"He did. Ramsey does not keep much from her. For him it is about atonement. His brother's accident, his death, Ramsey holds himself responsible. He confided as much to me once. It was a whiskey confession, which made it more believable in my estimation."

Calico threw off the quilt and pushed out of bed. Barefoot, she crossed the room quickly and threw herself into Quill's lap. He barely had time to get his arms out to ease her down. She wriggled, which, oddly, was not as pleasant as he could have wished. It felt, for a moment at least, like a punishment.

Calico looped her arms around his neck. "I am not leaving, Quill McKenna. I cannot stop you from speaking to Ramsey, and I probably cannot persuade him to keep me on if you advise against it, but I can decide what I will do if it comes to that, and it will not be getting on the next train out of town. The Jordans operate a boardinghouse on Ann Street that looks to be comfortable and well maintained. And if there is no room to let, I can always sleep outdoors. I might even prefer it."

"Why do I feel as if I am being threatened?"

"I don't know."

He regarded her skeptically from under raised eyebrows.

"I want us to do this together, Quill. Whatever it is that's to be done, we should be doing it together. You said I had to accustom myself to the idea of you looking out for me, and now I am saying that you need to do the same."

"Calico, I am not the one Whit will be coming for."

"You were there."

"He was out cold most of the time I was in the room. I helped Joe Pepper get him on his feet, walk him down the street, and put him into a cell. He doesn't know who I am."

"Chick Tatters does. He will remember you."

Quill had no argument for that. His arms tightened around her.

Calico touched her forehead to his. "I did not come to Stonechurch because the great Ramses asked me to. I came because this is where you were, and maybe I didn't know it at the time, or wouldn't allow myself to be open to the notion, but I know it now. I know this, too: I am staying because this is where you are. If you are afraid of losing me, Quill, then you need to stop trying to push me out the door."

CHAPTER TWELVE

Quill set the lists he had reviewed on Ramsey's desk. "I did not find any names common to the men Mr. Fordham wants to hire and the men you believe are agitators. I apologize it took so long to get to it."

Ramsey waved the apology aside. "I told Frank to go ahead and hire them. If there's trouble, so be it. Besides, Beatrice — you know how she is — says she's met most of them and approves of the lot. It would not surprise me to learn that every one of them is a family man with babies to feed. That is the sort of interview my sister-in-law likes to conduct." He had a fond smile for the memory of that discussion before he laid his pen on top of the papers and sat back. His brow beetled when his gaze settled on Quill. He pointed to a chair. "You look awful. Sit." When Quill went down without an argument, he said, "You are as rumpled as an unmade bed. Did you sleep? Is it Miss

Nash? Has something happened?"

Quill rubbed the bridge of his nose as he slid lower in the chair. His legs were extended so far forward that the toes of his shoes nudged Ramsey's desk. "Miss Nash's health is excellent. She is ready to pick up her gun again. Her rifle, also. She made a convincing argument that she needs to test her strength and her skills. She is not comfortable saying she can protect Ann if she does not know her limits."

"Understandable. What was your objection?"

"I had several, but in the end it came down to her not going out alone. Her arm is not as strong as she thinks it is. She will tire quickly."

"I will accompany her, of course."

"And draw fire?" Quill shook his head. "That is not the answer, not when we don't know how it happened that someone came to be lying in wait for you. I am going to go with her. I believe you and Ann are perfectly safe if you stay here. You are the only person I am telling in advance that we will be leaving. No one else is to know. No one. Say nothing until our absence is noticed."

"What do I say then?"

"Anything you like. I don't care."

"Where will you be going?"

"She agreed I could choose the place, and I have not decided. In fact, I don't intend to make that decision until we are on our way."

"That seems overly cautious, but very well. How do I send help if it's needed? I have no reason to believe that anything untoward will happen, but I should be prepared, shouldn't I?"

Quill nodded slowly as he considered this. "All right," he said at last. "I can tell you that we will return within three hours of leaving, and I will alert you when we are ready to go."

"All right." He waved Quill off. "Go. You have time to change before breakfast. No one presents himself at my table looking like you do. It's unappetizing."

George Kittredge bent over the crate from California Powder Works and pried open the lid with a crowbar. He was not a man given to profanity as a rule, but when he saw the condition of the dynamite, he swore loudly enough to make himself the object of notice. He laid the lid on the ground and held on to the crowbar. He hunkered beside the crate marked on all four sides with the bold letters of the company's most popular product: HERCULES.

George was a compact man, short, narrow, and firmly muscled. He liked to tell the men who worked under him that he was ideally suited to be an explosives man. Not only was he shaped like a cylinder, but he was born one part of the good earth, three parts nitroglycerin, and had a blasting cap for a head. In short, he was a stick of dynamite, stable when properly handled, unpredictable when treated without respect, and powerfully volatile when someone lit his fuse and let it burn.

"Cavanaugh! Shepard! Over here. Now!" He jabbed his forefinger at the ground on either side of the crate. He thought he heard one of them say something that sounded like fire in the hole, but he ignored it. Damn right, there was fire in the hole. When they were standing in their respective places, he said, "Look at this. What do you see?"

They hunkered beside the crate as he had and looked at, but did not touch, the dynamite. It was packed twelve sticks across, twelve sticks deep. One hundred forty-four sticks, each one powerful enough to take a man's life. Working in concert, they would take out the side of a mountain.

Cavanaugh, squat and sturdy with a coarse black beard and mustache, was the first to whistle softly. Shepard, slim and wiry, scratched the back of his balding head.

"Crystals," said Shepard.

"That's right," said Kittredge. Small white crystals dusted all twelve sticks of dynamite on the top row. "You know what this means, don't you?"

"Sure," Cavanaugh said. "It means the crate was turned at least once in storage and then left upside down. Can't think how else the crystals could have ended up on top unless the top was the bottom for a while."

"For a long while," said Shepard. "Crystals generally settle to the bottom."

Kittredge used the tip of the crowbar to gingerly turn over the lid. Hundreds of crystals glinted in the sunlight. "And all over the lid — and now some are on the ground."

Shepard, who was hunkered closest to the lid, shuffled backward. "Careful with that crowbar."

Kittredge swore again, this time softly. "There's a reason these crates need to be turned," he said, his jaw clenching and un-clenching.

Cavanaugh and Shepard knew that reason. They were looking at it. But they did not interrupt Kittredge's rant. It was better to let him have his say.

"Nitroglycerin weeps. It weeps like the

newly widowed, and we will have more than our share of those if there are more cases in storage like this. Dammit, fellas, what the hell is happening here?"

The fellas exchanged glances and simply shook their heads. They had been working with dynamite long enough to respect the highly explosive nature of its primary component, nitroglycerin. In its pure form, nitro was extraordinarily sensitive to freezing temperatures and shock. Transporting it, even in small amounts, was a job given to men with a death wish. The one part sawdust, wood pulp, or crushed shells in every stick of dynamite provided a degree of stabilization for the nitro.

Over time, though, nitro could seep through the packing material, causing crystals to form on the sticks. The crystals, then, were nitro returned to its pure form, and they settled at the bottom of the crates, thus requiring that the crates be turned regularly. Turning kept the nitro more evenly distributed within each stick and eliminated or reduced the weeping effect and the formation of explosive crystals.

"We were supposed to set charges in Number 1 this afternoon," said Kittredge. "I don't like the looks of this." Using the crowbar, he very carefully pushed one of the crystals on the ground off to the side, and then pushed the lid out farther of the way. Without warning, he pounded the nitro crystal with the tip of the crowbar.

It blew a divot out of the dirt.

He looked at his men. "We are going to have to go through all the crates in storage, save what we can, and do a controlled explosion of the rest." He chuckled shortly, without humor. "Controlled. Like trying to control an earthquake, that's what I'm thinking."

Shepard nodded, clearly unhappy. "I think we are going to need help."

"Don't want a lot of men in storage at once," said Kittredge. "I'll go. It's my responsibility. The rest should be volunteers. We'll work in shifts."

"What about the new fellas? You think we can trust them to know what they're doing? I get a little jumpy about working with new fellas." Shepard put out his hands and showed twitchy fingers. "See? I hardly trust myself when I'm like this."

Kittredge gave him a sour look and made no comment about his hands. "What new fellas? No one told me that I had new men on the crew. I knew Mr. Fordham made some hires, but I didn't ask for anyone."

Cavanaugh poked a stubby finger off to

his left where half a dozen men were crowded in a semicircle with their backs turned. The object of their interest was hidden from view, but it was evident that they were jostling for position and stretching one arm, sometimes two, toward a point at the center.

"What the hell are they doing?" asked Kittredge, getting to his feet. He jerked his sharp chin at the group and waved them over even though none of them was looking in his direction. "Hey! You! All of you! Look here!" When a couple of them shifted and turned, a gap was created so that Kittredge could see past them to the center.

"Oh, crikey," Shepard said. "It's Mrs. Stonechurch, and she's got a basket with her. I think that's a . . . by God it is! She's got crullers, boss. Crullers!"

George Kittredge shouldered Shepard out of the way and went straight for his crew, Beatrice Stonechurch, and the crullers. He whipped off his hat as the men parted to make room for him. He ignored the muttering that accompanied his intrusion. His men knew he was a fool for crullers.

"Mrs. Stonechurch," he said, smiling so broadly a gap in his lower molars was on display. "It is always a pleasure to see you, but I am going to have to ask you to step back a piece. May I escort you over there to the footbridge? I would be right pleased to carry your basket for you."

"You are without conscience, Mr. Kittredge," said Beatrice, dimpling. Her blue eyes brightened merrily as she made to protect her treasure. "Trying to steal my basket from right under my nose. Look at your men. They think you are taking advantage of your position."

"I am. They already have crullers."

She started to open the lid of her wicker basket but stopped when Kittredge shook his head. The light in her eyes dimmed as she frowned. "Why, you are serious. You truly need me to move."

He nodded. "Just to the footbridge, ma'am. That should be sufficient for now." He darted a look at the group, four of whom he knew, and two whom he did not. He forked two fingers and pointed to the unknown pair. "Come with me. The rest of you go see Shepard and Cavanaugh and come up with a plan. Oh, and for goodness' sakes, take them some crullers." He nodded to Beatrice to open the basket, and once she had handed over two, he indicated they needed to move on.

"We are having a bit of a problem with Hercules," he told Beatrice, taking her elbow as they walked over rough, rocky ground. Mud, most of it frozen, some of it not, connected patches of snow and ice, adding a challenge to their nearly 100-yard trek. On their way, they skirted a rusting water cannon, rocky outcroppings, mounds of snow and ice, and ditches like troughs. George stopped when they reached the footbridge. It was a narrow, crudely constructed wooden affair that was not built to cross a body of water. It was erected to span a crevice in the mountainside that was conservatively estimated to be some 120 feet deep. George leaned an elbow against an end rail and waited to be offered a cruller.

Beatrice stood well back from the edge of the crevice beside a mound of shoveled snow that was almost as tall as she was. She asked, "What sort of problem? Do you truly think you can say something like that and it will be the end of it?" A fur-trimmed hood framed her face. It also tickled her cheeks. She handed her basket to George Kittredge and pushed the hood back. Her cheeks immediately blossomed with color, compliments of the cold. When there was no response to her question, she said, "I like to know these things, Mr. Kittredge. I have an interest beyond seeing you men are well fed and taken care of." She smiled, removing any possible sting that might have been attached to her words. "Please. Have a cruller."

He explained the problem to her and the men standing behind her while he ate. "So I am looking for volunteers to examine the crates we still have in the underground storage."

"Do we need to find a new supplier?"

He shook his head. "This is not something that happened before Hercules was shipped. And I am confident it did not occur in transit. We created the problem by storing it without regularly rotating the crates."

"How does that happen?"

Kittredge chomped down hard on his cruller. "I will be investigating that. There is a schedule. Obviously it was not followed." He looked past her shoulders to the pair of men who were hanging back. "I understand you were assigned to my crew. Who are you?"

The shorter of the pair was still half a head taller than George Kittredge. He stepped forward and put out a hand. "Name's Rocky Castro."

Kittredge looked him over. The man had broad, square cut features, a mud-colored beard in need of grooming, and dark eyes

417

that were bright and eager in their regard. His smile was a bit too engaging to suit Kittredge, who never had a good first impression when a man was trying so hard to make a good first impression. "Mr. Castro."

"Rocky."

"Rocky," said Kittredge, ending the handshake. "What is your experience with explosives? Why did Mr. Fordham put you on my crew?"

Beatrice said, "I believe I will leave you now, Mr. Kittredge. Your business certainly takes precedence over mine. Mr. Castro. Mr. White. Do not let yourself be intimidated by Mr. Kittredge. He is naturally concerned about everyone's safety." She took back her basket and invited all three men to help themselves one more time before she confidently crossed the bridge and headed into town.

When she was gone, Kittredge turned his attention to the man he had not yet met. "You're White?"

The big man nodded. He thrust a hand at Kittredge. "Marcus White."

Kittredge watched as his hand disappeared in White's large grasp. The man could have easily crushed his fingers, but he made no attempt to show strength. George Kittredge liked that. He needed men with finesse, not ham-fisted laborers. "Good to meet you. You are already acquainted with Mrs. Stonechurch?"

"Met her when I was looking for a job. Introduced myself again when she came with the basket. Real nice lady. Good crullers, too." His eyes darted to the bridge, his expression considering. "Might be I'd even cross that bridge for one if I had to."

Kittredge gave the end rail a hard shake, and the entire bridge rattled. "Fine piece of engineering." He waved a forefinger back and forth between the pair. "You two come as a set? Know each other from somewhere?" He watched them look at each other with some surprise. It was White who spoke up.

"Never met until we were standing in line waiting to hear about a job."

"Experience?"

"Worked in and around the Leadville mines for a couple of years. Had my own crew for a time, but frankly, I am better at taking orders than giving them. Did not like having my orders questioned." He turned his thumb in on himself and tapped his barrel chest. "People expect a fight from me on account of my size, but I'd rather use my head."

Kittredge merely nodded. He turned to Castro. "You?"

"Worked mostly for the railroad. There are still a lot of spurs to be built in these mountains. That's what I was doing." He shrugged. "Heard about Stonechurch Mining when I was working up around Reidsville. Thought I would look into it."

Kittredge looked them over again. "You heard what I was telling Mrs. Stonechurch?" When they both nodded, he continued. "Then you understand the situation. I am looking for volunteers to open the crates in storage and see what we can use and what we have to destroy before it destroys us. Either of you interested in doing that?"

Marcus White carelessly shrugged his broad shoulders. "Why not?" He lifted his hands and wiggled all ten of his digits. "I probably have more of these than I need."

Calico lowered her Colt and regarded her target with disgust. The empty bourbon bottle that Quill had set out for her remained precisely where he'd placed it. The stump it was standing on had not fared so well. The bark was splintered and ragged. The tree behind it and another slightly to the left also bore witness to the fact that her aim was not what it had been.

She looked askance at Quill. He was leaning against the thick, furrowed bark of a Douglas fir, arms folded, hipshot, and one ankle crossing the other. "Well?" she asked. "You're thinking it. You might as well say it."

"If you know what I am thinking, I am going to save my breath. Are you done?"

The Colt was an anchor pulling on every one of the joints in her arm. Her wrist, elbow, and shoulder all ached. She felt the strain in the muscles of her upper arm and neck. Her fingers were stiff, partly with cold, partly because she had pushed herself far past her endurance. Quill had suggested after twenty minutes that she stop, and her response had been to roundly ignore him. He did not make the suggestion a second time. In fact, he spoke very little after that. She did not blame him.

She had not fared any better with the Winchester. The recoil of the rifle's butt made her arm judder. After firing it only a few times, she knew she had to return it to the scabbard.

Frustration made her muscles tense. "I want to have a tantrum. I want to scream and cry and stamp my feet."

"Do you think it would help? I'm asking because, frankly, you look bone deep mean and you still have that gun in your hand."

She turned toward him and shook her head slowly, regretfully. "I don't think I can lift it one more time."

"I see that it would put a strain on you, but I am in a provoking frame of mind right now, and even though you haven't come close but two or three times to hitting that bottle, you did real well with the stump. Since I am a fair size bigger —"

"And with a whole lot less sense."

"That, too. I guess you'd be able to hit something on me if you felt you had to."

"I guess that'd be true."

"Uh-huh. So why don't you let me take your gun for you? That would be in the interest of self-preservation. Mine. Not yours."

Calico breathed in and nodded slowly as she exhaled. "I suppose that would be all right." She did not try to raise her arm. "You will have to —"

Quill pushed away from the tree. "I've got it. This first." He removed her gun belt before he took the Colt out of her hand. He walked over to his horse, laid the belt over the saddle, and slipped the Colt into the holster. When he returned to her side, he slipped his arm under hers and gestured to the stump. "Come on. You can sit a spell.

There's no shame in that. You need to rest your arm before we ride back. I want to make sure you can handle the reins."

She opened her mouth to argue, thought better of it, and fell into step beside him. "I did not expect to be as fast or as accurate as I was, but I did not expect to embarrass myself."

"I suppose how you think about it depends on your vantage point. I thought you did yourself proud right up until the moment your stubborn self got in the way of your sensible self."

"Oh, so that's what happened."

"Looked like it from where I was standing." Quill released Calico when they reached the stump. He swept the bottle aside and offered her the seat. "Do you want a drink?"

She leaned over and looked at the bottle lying on its side. It was indeed empty.

Quill laughed and showed her the flask he had been carrying inside his coat. "Here. Did you think I would risk a good bottle of bourbon on the chance you *wouldn't* hit it? That would have been insulting to you and a crime against the bourbon."

She arched an eyebrow and held out a hand for the flask. He uncapped it for her before he gave it over. Raising it to her lips, she asked, "When do you think we can come out again?"

"That's a different question than asking me when I think you will be ready."

Calico tipped the flask and took a good swallow. Her eyes watered. She handed back the flask and swiped at her eyes as she caught her breath. "All right. When do you think I will be ready?"

"What are you willing to do to prepare yourself?"

"What do you mean?"

"I mean that Beatrice has some ideas about exercises that will strengthen your arm, and she would like the opportunity to help you."

"When did she say that?"

"She didn't. Ann did." He held up a hand when Calico would have interrupted. "Hear me out. Ann was informative, and she reminded me that I bear some responsibility for Beatrice not coming forward. Understandably, my insistence that I be the only one to look after you made her reluctant to broach the subject with either one of us. It has also been true that when she asks you about your arm, you have a tendency to dismiss it as nothing. It is not nothing, and you are your own worst enemy there."

Calico recognized the truth of that. "What

does she want me to do?"

"Ann wasn't specific. I don't know if she knows precisely what Beatrice would recommend, but Ann also reminded me that her aunt did much more than ply Leonard Stonechurch with healing teas. His legs were crushed in the accident, and he never drew an easy breath after he was rescued. Ann says that once his bones knit, Beatrice exercised his legs for him. She did something to help him improve the strength of his lungs. Beatrice Stonechurch might look fragile, but she is tenacious. She refused to let him waste away in bed."

Calico glanced at her injured arm and raised it experimentally. Deep fatigue had set in the muscles. She set her hand in her lap to support it. "Should I speak to her?"

"I think so. At least listen to what she has to say. Calico, I was watching you shoot. Your problem with accuracy this afternoon was never your eye. It was your strength. Your stance, your concentration, your awareness of your surroundings, all of that came as naturally to you as breathing. You struggled with your grip first, then holding your weapon steady, and finally with your own irritation."

She sighed heavily. "I don't think I could have hit the proverbial broad side of a barn."

He grinned. "You were considerably better than that." He took a drink and slipped the flask inside his coat. "We should be getting back. I told Ramsey to give us a few hours before he raised the alarm."

"Wait. Aren't you going to shoot?"

"I hadn't thought about it."

"Don't you practice?"

He shrugged. "Not much." He did think about that. "Not ever."

"Are you that good?"

"It's that boring."

She could only shake her head. "Show me what you can do." She leaned over and picked up the bottle. Standing, she placed it on the stump.

Quill protested as she started walking away. "I shot Amos Bennett in the leg. Remember that?"

She turned and said cheekily, "I remember that you told Joe Pepper you were aiming for Amos's *other* leg. I want to see if that's true." Then she kept on walking.

Quill took his position in the tramped circle of snow that Calico had occupied and unbuttoned his long coat. He swept it back on the right side to reveal his Colt. He unstrapped it before he looked over at her. She had stepped several feet to the side but had not retreated to the tree. "Do you want me to draw and shoot, or shoot with my gun already out?"

"You do whatever makes you —"

Quill drew his gun, fired. The bottle jumped and shattered.

"— think you can hit the target," she said slowly.

"I pulled that a little to the left," he said, holstering his weapon. "Maybe I should do some target practice."

Calico was still staring at the shards of broken glass glinting on the surface of the snow while Quill was already heading for their horses. "Stop right there, Mr. Quill McKenna."

He stopped, turned, his features impassive. "Yes?"

Calico's green eyes narrowed. "Where did you learn to shoot like that?"

"I was in the Army, remember?"

"I knew soldiers who did not know the butt of a gun from the barrel, so that is an inadequate explanation."

"My father taught me," he said. "When he wasn't preparing sermons or ministering to the wicked and the ill, he liked to be outdoors. He hunted to put meat on the table, and he took Israel and me with him when we were old enough to carry a rifle." He shrugged. "That's it. No different than how you learned."

Calico did not try to hide the fact that she was still suspicious. "Maybe. Maybe not. If you don't practice, how did you come to be that good?"

"I don't know that I am that good."

"I know what I saw, and I know how to judge it. You are exactly that good."

Quill was silent, thinking. After a few moments, he said, "Well, my father called it a preternatural bent. It was not a compliment. He didn't trust that my talent wasn't the devil's doing, and he was certain I would come to grief for having it."

"And your brother? Does Israel have the same bent?"

"No, but he's done his best to prove that you can come to grief without it." He smiled wryly. "If my father ever saw the irony there, he's never said as much."

Calico walked up to him, raised herself slightly on her toes, and kissed him on the mouth. "I appreciate the irony, and I am in awe of your gift. If I thought for a moment that I could be the shot you are, I might be envious, but what you can do is something extraordinary."

"It's probably a little important that I'm good at it, Calico, but it's still only shooting."

"What was it you said to me not so very long ago? Oh, yes. 'I suppose how you think about things depends on your vantage point.' Well, from where I'm standing, it's a mighty fine thing that you can do. It's just a guess, you understand, but I'm thinking with that kind of aim, you've probably spared more lives than you've taken."

Quill did not respond to that. What he said was, "Let's go home."

It was not home, of course, but in a way that Calico could neither quite define nor wanted to dwell on, it was beginning to feel something like that.

CHAPTER THIRTEEN

Nick Whitfield and Chick Tatters had a week's pay in their pockets and gave in to the urge to take a decent meal in a restaurant instead of stealing scraps from what was thrown out of one. Their choices were limited, but they settled on Bartholow's Eatery because it had a large front window with a good view of the street. They took a table close to it but not directly beside it. There was no point in making themselves the object of passing glances.

They both ordered chicken and dumplings, a side of carrots, and asked for extra bread and beer. When the waitress was gone, Whit eyed Chick's half-empty glass and reminded him to go easy.

"I know you like it," said Whit. "But I can't say that I've ever seen it like you back. A commotion like the one you caused in Reidsville could have powerful ramifications if it happens here."

"You mean like we won't get paid real money."

"That's one. There are others." Whit's eyes darted toward a corner at the rear of the restaurant and waited for Chick to follow his gaze. When he did, he said, "That's the town lawman sitting there. Hobbes, I believe is his name. He was pointed out to me this afternoon when we were shufflin' those cases around."

Chick nodded. "Good to know, but I don't have any plans to start a ruckus." He chuckled. "Especially not one with a man carrying a stick. Lordy, whatever would I do?"

"You never have plans. It just sorta happens — that's what I've been noticing." He lowered his voice until it reached its most menacing pitch. "And you better not have your gun tucked in the back of your trousers. We talked about that. No weapons. Not yet."

Chick picked up his glass and sipped his beer as dainty-like as a debutante. He put out a pinkie just to piss with his friend.

Whit's menace faded, replaced by a genial smile. "Tonight while you're sleeping, I'm going to break that finger."

Uncertain, but alarmed now, Chick pulled his pinkie back. "C'mon, Nick, there ain't no cause to do that. I was only having some fun with you. And I ain't carrying."

Whitfield placed his large hands flat on the table as he leaned forward. He spoke softly. "Call me that again, and I will do more than break your finger. You understand?"

Chick Tatters's narrow face drained of color. He did not nod. He did not move.

"Well?"

Whispering, Chick said, "I forget your name."

"Jesus Christ." When he saw Chick frown, he said, "That's not my name, you idiot. I'm Marcus White."

"Right. Yeah, I remember now."

"I just told it to you."

"Uh-huh."

Whit itched to grab Chick by the throat, but he leaned back and snagged a thick slice of warm bread instead. Still speaking quietly so his deep, rumbling voice did not carry beyond their table, he said, "How the hell did you come up with Rocky?"

"How'd you think? We're in the middle of the mountains."

"That's what I was afraid of. Your parents name you Rocky, or is that a sobriquet?"

"I don't know about that sober part, but I figure my parents named me Simon Peter

Castro, and called me Rocky on account of Simon Peter being the rock and all. That's from the Bible."

"Amazing," Whit said under his breath. "No other word for it."

"Astonishing," Chick said helpfully. "That'd be what you call a cinnamon."

"Uh-huh. Let's leave it at amazing."

"Sure, Marcus." He grinned. "See?" And feeling confident with his memory, he raised his glass and asked for another beer.

Nick Whitfield turned his chair a few degrees so he was no longer squarely facing his partner. It was not widely known that he and Chick Tatters were distantly related through their mothers' side of the family. Their familial connection rarely came up in conversation, and when it did, it was because Chick raised it, usually harking back to some incident in their childhood. Back then, long before Whit had grown into his oversized hands and feet and filled out the promise of his large-boned frame, it was Chick who had been the leader of their kinship boys gang, and Chick who had used his fists to great effect defending Whit from his tormentors. The head blows Chick had received in those early years of acting as the defender had gradually taken their toll, leaving him a couple of bullets shy of a full load.

Whit reminded himself of that now. There was no denying that he had an obligation to Chick Tatters, but there was also no denying that some days were harder than others to live up to it.

Chick followed Whit's example and turned his chair an equal number of degrees toward the window. He was more comfortable with the lawman at his back anyway. There was no way of knowing if there was a wanted notice with his face on it posted in the constable's office.

"Well, look there, Marcus," said Chick. He started to raise his hand to point, thought better of it, and lowered again. He wrapped his fingers around his glass of beer, figuring they were safer with something to occupy them. "That's her, ain't it?"

Whitfield murmured agreement. He had noticed the pair of women walking along the opposite side of the street before Chick had. He would have been happier if Chick had not seen them. It was bound to lead to a conversation that he would rather have take place elsewhere. It was hard to turn Chick once he had the bit between his teeth.

"Seems kind of provincial."

"Providential," said Whit. "That'd be another cinnamon."

"How about that." He nodded, impressed.

"So what do you want to do? It's like she's teasing us."

Whitfield shook his shaggy head. "Teasing us? Think. She doesn't know we're here. The two of them are probably going into that shop over there. The one with the gown in the window. See how their steps are slowing?" Even as he was speaking, the women were making a turn toward the shop's door. A moment later, they were inside.

"Gone," said Chick. "Feels like a missed opportunity."

"To do what?"

Chick shrugged. "Shoot one, take the other."

"On Main Street. In the daylight. In front of more witnesses than I can count on my fingers. That does not sound workable to me. This is why you are not supposed to have a gun."

"I don't. I swear. I was considering what might have been. Anyway, it's not Main Street. They call it Ann Street. You know, after her. I saw a signpost."

Whit sighed. He was glad for the interruption of their waitress bringing plates of hot food and another beer for Chick. He thanked her and slid his chair closer to the table. "She puts me a little in mind of my Rosalie." He tapped his jacket pocket where

435

he kept his sister's photograph.

"There's a resemblance," said Chick and immediately changed the subject. "Have you thought about how hard this is going to be?"

"It's timing."

"Hmm. Hey, you should call me Rocky more often. Get used to it." He picked up his fork and speared a dumpling. "Probably would help me get used to it, too."

"All right, Rocky. I can do that."

Chick grinned and tried not to stare at the hand Whit still had over the photograph. He plopped the dumpling in his mouth and then spoke around it. "I have to tell you, Marcus, I am not real fond of this job."

"It's a little late, don't you think, to be saying that? You could have spoken up weeks ago."

"Huh? We only got moved to Kittredge's crew yesterday."

Whit's features cleared as he realized which job Chick was talking about.

"That's right. Dynamite, Marcus. We are working with dynamite. Crates and crates of it. Must be thousands of sticks. When's the last time you touched dynamite before yesterday?"

"I'd have to say it was when we opened that safe on the express mail car between

Omaha and Fort Kearney."

"That's what I'm remembering, and that was a ways back. And come to think of it, how come I wasn't invited to join you at the bank in Bailey?"

"No one was. It was a spur-of-the-moment decision when I was passing through." He forked some chicken. "Do I have to remind you that there were consequences? That's why my likeness was on the posters. You can bet it wasn't because of that Falls Hollow whore. Anyway, it turned out to be a good thing. I needed you to break me out of jail."

"Amos helped," Chick said.

"I told you, Amos had a piece in me getting caught, but I blame myself, too. I was feeling pretty good about what I'd done on my own, and hubris was my downfall. I said something about it, and then so did he. That was wrong. I should never have trusted him the way I do you."

"That's 'cause we're kin."

"Probably is."

The truth of that settled over them and they ate in silence for a time. It was Chick who finally broke it.

"Still, don't like working with Hercules," he said, sopping up gravy with a chunk of bread. "Especially what that Kittredge fella has us doing now. You know how dangerous

437

it is, don't you? Those nitro crystals." He lifted his hands, palms out, fingers spread, and parted them slowly. "Boom. We could be dead before we get to what we came for."

"Then we will have to be careful, won't we?"

Chick lowered his hands. "Real careful." He jerked his chin toward the shop across the way. "What do you think they're doing in there that takes so long?"

Whit made a beak with his hand and opened and closed it several times. "They're women," he said. "Only two ways I know to shut them up." He closed his hand into a fist and gave it a shake. "One's like this."

"What's the other?"

"Eight hard inches of what I've got between my legs."

"So you *are* carrying your gun."

Too astonished to speak, Whitfield stared at Chick for a long moment before his laughter boomed as hard and loud as a nitro crystal explosion.

Calico and Beatrice shared a sofa in the front parlor while Ann sat across from them in one of the chairs. Ann was reading, or mostly pretending to. She had no particular interest in the exercises that her aunt was showing Miss Nash. She was reflecting back on an interesting encounter at the livery when she had been introduced to a gentle mare named Daisy and a gentler young man named Boone Abbot, who worked in the livery grooming and feeding the animals and mucking the stalls.

Ann knew she must have seen Boone Abbot around Stonechurch before, but she could not remember a particular time or place or a single pleasantry they might have exchanged. Until he was standing beside her while she was tentatively stroking Daisy's nose, he had not existed in her world, not even in her imagination. She blamed the dime novels for that. It was precisely as Miss Nash had warned her: too many scoundrels and too few good men.

Was Boone Abbot a good man? she wondered. He seemed as if he might be. He was not shy, but he spoke quietly, and when he saw she was as skittish around him as she was around Daisy, he kept a respectful distance. At first he even talked to her through Daisy, and his voice drew her in so that she was the one who stepped closer. She did not mind when Daisy began to nuzzle her, and she did not notice when Miss Nash walked away, and she could not clearly recall when she joined the conversation Boone was having with Daisy, yet all of that had happened.

He was tall and straight and had an easy smile that reminded her of Quill McKenna. Similarity ended there. Boone Abbot had hair the color of a polished chestnut and eyes that closely matched it. He had a narrow face and a nose that was a shade too big for it. The bump on the bridge gave it distinction. She must have stared at it, she thought, because he rubbed it now and then with his knuckle, and she wondered if he was self-conscious. He should not have been. She thought he was very fine. Very fine indeed.

It was only when he was escorting her back to Miss Nash that she realized Boone Abbot walked with a slightly uneven gait. She wondered about it, but she did not ask. It did not change how she thought of him. It was as unimportant to her as the bump on his nose.

Beatrice was demonstrating how Calico should rotate her arm in small and large circles when Ann said, "Why have I never met Boone Abbot before?"

Both women turned to look at her. Beatrice's features evidenced some surprise, while Calico's evidenced mild interest.

"Well, I don't know," said Beatrice. "Boone's always been around. He is Abigail and James Abbot's third son, but their fourth child. He has an older sister and a younger one, and then there are more boys. I believe there are seven children in all. Hardy family. No deaths to the usual diseases that afflict so many during childhood." She took Calico's wrist and raised it, encouraging her to start the clockwise circles. "Are you saying you met Boone Abbot?" she asked. "Or was it a rhetorical question, dear?"

"I met him. Miss Nash introduced us."

Beatrice looked askance at Calico and received verification that this was true. She raised her eyebrows a fraction. "Tell me about it. I should like to hear how that came about."

Ann said, "Miss Nash recently pointed out to me that while I am able to employ all the requisite social graces in my home, I am neither comfortable nor confident outside of it."

"That is simply not true," Beatrice said stoutly. "You have beautiful manners. Everyone says so."

"Aunt Beatrice," said Ann. "I know you say that as a kindness, but Miss Nash is right. I say very little when we are out."

"Perhaps that is because I say too much. Is that it? Have I done you wrong?"

"No. Not at all. And Miss Nash never suggested that you did. The point is that she realized that I should have lessons outside of the classroom."

"Shooting? Have we returned to that?"

When Ann did not respond, Calico realized she was looking to her for help. She stopped rotating her arm. "This has nothing at all to do with those lessons, but if you hope we are done with them because of my unfortunate accident, I am afraid you are mistaken. This is something else entirely. Ann has been practicing conversing with me as if I were Mrs. Neeley-Brown or Mrs. Birden or Mr. Zimmer from the laundry. She would like to step forward instead of hanging back, and she would like to know more about the people she passes and never sees. She wants to be more like you in that regard, Beatrice. Ann admires the way you can speak to anyone and that you know something about everyone."

Beatrice's hands came together; her fingers twisted. She moved to the edge of the sofa cushion, perching there like a fluttering bird. "Oh, but I had not realized. Ann, you are such a good hostess to your father's guests. You always know what to say to make them welcome. I am certain you impress them. And these are important people to

Stonechurch Mining. My chatter embarrasses me when they are around. I can say quite truthfully that I am happy to excuse myself when Ramsey wants to discuss business matters."

Ann said, "It is not hard to be gracious to them when they expect nothing from me except that I be gracious. They would be alarmed if I expressed an interest in the company, and I am not certain their alarm would be any greater than my father's."

"Are you interested, Ann?" asked Beatrice.

"Of course I am, but that is for another discussion. Right now I want to talk about Boone Abbot. What do you know about him? Besides the fact that he is the third son?"

Beatrice waved at Calico again to resume her exercises. "Well, he is certainly a nice young man. And conscientious. He has that in his favor. When I rent a rig, he always goes over the leather seat with a cloth and helps me manage that first step. I would even go so far as to call him gallant."

Ann closed her book and put it aside. She leaned in, her expression earnest as only a youthful countenance can be. "I thought the very same thing, Aunt Beatrice. The very same."

Calico continued to rotate her arm in

smaller circles as she quietly excused herself. She was careful to walk around the back of the sofa and not between Ann and Beatrice. She smiled to herself when neither aunt nor niece made a conversational pause to bid her good night, and that smile was still lingering when she reached her bedroom.

Quill turned up the collar of his coat. Tonight the wind seemed strong enough to tunnel through the mountain. It would not, of course, but as it came roaring through the crevice under his feet, he thought it was capable of lifting the ramshackle footbridge off its moorings. It was an unsettling thought, and he picked up his pace to reach solid ground.

George Kittredge was not at home. Quill had already stopped there with a basket of warm crullers for the entire Kittredge clan. Beatrice had given him the idea when she mentioned her activities the day before. Ramsey had been unusually quiet at dinner that night and merely pushed his food around his plate while Beatrice held court with her news about the men and their families. Quill could not tell if Ramsey was uninterested or if he was on the cusp of not feeling well. Ann broached the subject of his health at one point, but Ramsey dismissed her concerns. After that, no more was said.

Quill approached the entrance to the tunnel where the dynamite was stored. This was George Kittredge's domain. He could often be found within a few yards of the entrance, speaking to one or more of his crew. It was typical for him to be leaning over a survey map of the mountain and the mines, pointing out where the charges would be placed for the next blast. He was meticulous, and Quill had seen firsthand that he was respected not only for the breadth of his knowledge but also for his willingness to share in the difficult and dangerous tasks.

That meant, Quill supposed, that Kittredge was deep inside the tunnel where storage for the dynamite had been carved out of the rock. Because of the nitroglycerin's sensitivity to freezing temperatures, underground storage was a necessity in the mountains. There was no one at the entrance, which was not the general practice. Several lanterns were hanging on pegs driven into the mountainside for the purpose of lighting the way. Quill took one down and held it out as he stepped inside the timbered adit.

Lanterns lighted the passage at regular

intervals, but Quill estimated he had been making a gradual descent over fifty yards before he encountered a light moving toward him. He stopped, waited. There was one lantern, but two men. He recognized both of them when they came upon him, but he only knew the name of the shorter of the pair.

"Mr. Cavanaugh," he said, nodding once. His eyes swiveled to the other man. "I'm sorry. Mr. —"

"Shepard. Jim Shepard." He regarded Quill doubtfully. "I have to say, Mr. McKenna, that our boss isn't going to like that you're here. It wouldn't be right for me not to warn you to turn around."

"I stand warned." He pointed to the crate in Cavanaugh's hands. "It's a little late for blasting, isn't it?"

"Trying to prevent one," Dave Cavanaugh said. He set the crate carefully on his shoulder. "If you need to know more than that, you'll have to talk to Mr. Kittredge."

Quill eyed the crate. "I plan to."

Shepard said, "If you don't mind me asking, if you don't know what's going on, then what brings you here? It's a little late for lawyering, isn't it?"

"Mr. Stonechurch works day and night, same as you. There is no such time as a little late when he takes to an idea." Quill observed that this seemed to satisfy both men. He hoped they would be well outside of the tunnel when they realized he had provided no real information. He, on the other hand, had been given a tidbit that whet his appetite.

Quill found George Kittredge in one of the deeper storage chambers. There was only one other man working with him. Quill had seen him around, but like Jim Shepard, he could not put a name to the face. He nodded a greeting when the young man looked up from his task. He was kneeling beside an open crate of dynamite but had been examining the upside-down lid.

Quill took a step closer to see what he was studying, and it was then that Kittredge noticed him and ordered him back.

"Can't say that I am surprised to see you, but I thought it would be earlier," said Kittredge. "I wondered if she would say something. God knows, I haven't had the time. I suppose she did."

Quill figured he was referring to Beatrice. He had no idea what she was supposed to have said. She had shared odds and ends about the men and their families, but nothing specifically about the mining operation. Ramsey had not mentioned anything, so if he knew what was going on, which seemed unlikely, he was keeping it to himself for now, which seemed even more unlikely.

Quill said, "She did say she was here yesterday afternoon. I take it you did not get your fair share of crullers. I dropped a basket off at your home."

"Well, you can be sure I won't get my fair share of those." He lifted his hat, ran a hand through his hair, and darted a glance sideways at the man kneeling on the ground. "Joshua. Seems like you could use a break to stretch your legs about now. Go on. Leave that. I'll tend to it. See if you can do anything to help the other two."

Neither man spoke until Joshua's footfalls had faded in the corridor. Quill said, "He's one of the Abbots, isn't he?"

"Uh-huh. Good lad. All the Abbots are; most of them work for Stonechurch. One of the boys works in the livery."

Quill realized that's why Joshua seemed especially familiar. "Boone. Why doesn't he work here?"

George Kittredge pointed to the open crate. The lantern light was sufficient to make the dynamite sticks sparkle. "Nitro," George said succinctly. "Boone Abbot should be dead."

CHAPTER FOURTEEN

Calico slipped lower into the tub when she heard the door to the bedroom open and close. "In here," she called out. She almost added Quill's name, but held back on the sudden suspicion that he was not the person who had just entered. She stared at the open bathing room doorway waiting to see who would appear.

"Beatrice." Calico blinked, sat up straight, and drew her knees toward her chest. She hugged them. "Has something happened? Is it Ann? Mr. Stonechurch?"

Beatrice politely stepped back from the doorway. "I asked Mrs. Pratt to steam some towels. I have them here. You should wrap them around your arm. They will relax and soothe your muscles. Where shall I put them?"

"There is a stool in here. You can bring them in and put them on it." She smiled faintly as Beatrice hurried and set the towels down. Her eyes remained averted for the whole of her intrusion. "Thank you," said Calico. "It was thoughtful of you to bring them yourself. I hope you are on your way to bed and did not make a special trip."

Beatrice cast her eyes at the floor. Her hands were knotted. "I am on my way to bed, but I had a reason other than the towels for coming here. I truly need to speak to you about what you did on Ann's behalf today."

"There's really no need to thank me. I was happy to —" She stopped because Beatrice was shaking her head. "Oh, you are not here to thank me, are you?"

"No. No, I am not, and I am sorry for it because I know your intentions were the very best."

"Well, I thought they were. Would you mind waiting for me in the other room? I will only be a few minutes."

Beatrice's answer was to scurry out. Calico finished washing and wrung out her hair. She dried off, finger combed her hair, and slipped into a sleeveless shift. She tested one of the steamed towels for heat before she wrapped it around her arm. She left the others on the stool when she went out to greet Beatrice.

Calico expected to find that Beatrice had

at least tried to make herself comfortable, but the woman was standing beside the armchair instead of sitting in it. Calico did not comment and went straight to the wardrobe, where she chose a pair of gray woolen socks. She sat on the window bench and put them on.

Sighing almost inaudibly, she asked, "What have I done?"

"Perhaps I am making something out of nothing," said Beatrice. "Before I go on, I suppose I should ask you if you spoke to Ramsey about Boone Abbot."

"No. I didn't. It never occurred to me."

"I was afraid of that, although certainly I hoped I was wrong. My brother-in-law will never approve any connection between Ann and the young Mr. Abbot. He is likely to be apoplectic when he hears they spoke."

"I don't understand. I know I left the conversation early, but you were speaking favorably of Boone while I was still present."

"Oh. Oh, I see. You are confusing what I think about Boone with what Ramsey will think. Oddly enough, we are not of similar minds. In my estimation, Boone Abbot is a perfectly fine young man, wholly acceptable as a friend to Ann. I regard him as one of my husband's saviors. Ramsey regards him as an unwelcome reminder of the tragedy that eventually claimed Leo."

"I have noticed that Boone limps, but I never inquired about the cause. I might have guessed that it had something to do with the horses, but I think you are telling me it was the mines."

Short brown ringlets framed Beatrice's face. They bounced as she nodded. "Boone worked in the Number 3 mine where Leonard was visiting the day of the accident. He was learning about how to handle dynamite and set charges under George Kittredge's guidance, but on that particular day he was a laborer in Number 3. I have this account of what happened from my husband so I have no reason to doubt it. Young Boone Abbot, and he was just seventeen then, spied a bundle of dynamite wedged between timber and rock in the side tunnel where he was digging. Most of the bundle was buried, so the fact that he saw it at all I've always believed is akin to a miracle."

"It was sabotage?"

"No. No, nothing of the sort. An oversight. It had been set there months earlier by George and his men. For whatever reason, it did not detonate with the other charges. The tunnel was excavated, timbers erected, and no one found the bundle until Boone.

He did what he was supposed to do. He alerted men deeper in the tunnel to get out, and he went to find Mr. Kittredge."

Beatrice paused. "You should have a robe on, dear. You're shivering."

Rather than argue, Calico began to rise.

"I will get it. Stay where you are."

It was then that Calico understood that Beatrice needed something to do. She needed a distraction from her own story before she could continue. Calico took the robe, thanked her, and waited patiently for her to begin again.

Beatrice sat in the armchair, perched much as she had been on the parlor sofa except that she was still now, not fluttering. "Mr. Kittredge was at one of the other mines, too far away to fetch quickly. Boone found Ramsey and asked him to come and look at what he had found. Ramsey was occupied on another matter and asked Leonard to go instead."

Beatrice's head tilted as she regarded Calico. "Do you know anything about dynamite, dear?" When Calico shook her head, Beatrice said, "Of course you don't. Why would you? It's only when mining has been in your blood as long as it's been in mine that you begin to learn things you mostly wished you did not know." She shrugged and her smile was rueful. "Over time, dynamite sweats. I've heard the men say it weeps like the newly widowed, but I have never cared for that expression. Dynamite is a man's invention, and so it sweats."

"Nitroglycerin," said Calico.

"Yes. So you do know something. It sweats nitro and forms explosive crystals. That's what Boone saw on the bundle in the rock. He understood it had to be extracted with expert care. My husband understood that as well, but he was under the misapprehension that he could do it himself. It is hard to say if Ramsey would have chosen a more cautious course and waited for Mr. Kittredge to return, but since Ramsey did not accompany Boone, it is only a matter of speculation. Leo never asked that question. I do. I keep it in my heart, but I have asked myself it many, many times."

Moved by Beatrice's confession, Calico nodded slowly. In her place, she would ask the same question, and she would ask it aloud.

"Leonard had the good sense to send Boone away while he worked, but Boone either did not get far or did not go far, and the collapse of the tunnel trapped him as well. My husband was not standing close to the dynamite when it exploded. He had started back to get a tool. He and Boone were separated by three yards of rock and timber. They could hear but not see each other. They thought they would die there and each man prayed independently that he would be the first to go. Neither wanted to die alone, you see. Sometimes I think it was the fear of that that kept them alive. Boone's leg was trapped in a gap between the rocks. It was horribly twisted, they said when they found him, but it wasn't crushed. He did not want to leave Leo, but they had to take him out of the tunnel. His poor mother. She waited with me and we both wept when he was carried out. She did not want to leave my side just as her boy did not want to leave Leo. I insisted that she go, of course, but her oldest boys stayed with me. It was another thirty-six hours before they lifted Leo out of the rubble."

Imagining the horror of it, Calico closed her eyes briefly. "How awful for all of you."

"It's past," Beatrice said after a moment. "It's behind us. Most of us."

Calico said, "Mr. Stonechurch."

"Yes, my brother-in-law is changed. He must live with the fact that Boone came for him and he sent his brother in his stead. Leo never blamed Ramsey. My husband told Ramsey many times that there was nothing to forgive except that Ramsey forgive himself and forget about what might have been."

"But he cannot."

"Cannot. Will not. Thinks he should not. I have no answer for how he chooses to grieve."

Calico scooted into a corner of the bench and drew her legs up and to the side. "Why doesn't Ann know about Boone Abbot?"

Beatrice's blue eyes clouded briefly as she frowned. "Oh, I see. Yes. I did not explain that as well as I might have. I see that now. Ann doesn't know because Ramsey forbade talking about the accident around her. He believed that she did not need to know details because she would be frightened that the same might happen to him. He did not want to spend hours, days, weeks, reassuring her."

"Isn't it possible the opposite could be true? That by knowing details, she would understand how unlikely it was that this particular accident would happen again."

"There was no reasoning with him, and frankly, I did not try very hard. I did not like talking about it either, so keeping Ann away from it suited me as well."

There was a sharp edge to Beatrice's tone that Calico had not heard before. "I apologize. I did not mean to sound critical." Calico watched as Beatrice seemed to draw in on herself, somehow becoming smaller than she had been a moment earlier. Her shoulders hunched, her chin dropped, and her fingers folded in a gentle handclasp. She looked uncertain, not anxious.

Beatrice sighed quietly. "It is still difficult to discuss, but I came here to do that. I should not shy away from the unpleasantness. I do not want you to think Ramsey is unfeeling or inattentive, and I think I may have given you that impression."

"I have some idea of how much he cares for his daughter."

"Yes. He certainly does, which is why I believe he will be unhappy to learn she has been introduced to Boone Abbot. You should not mention it to him."

"But you said —"

"It doesn't matter. To Ramsey he is a reminder. I cannot say it more plainly than that. Boone would be working with George Kittredge if Ramsey would stand for it. He won't. Boone seems to have made peace with it. I have noticed he has a way with the animals, and his mother is certainly glad he is no longer working in the mines."

"Did you try to discourage Ann at all after I left you downstairs?"

"No. Heavens no. Coward that I am, I left that for you to do."

Calico smiled wanly. Why were there no problems here that she could settle with a gun?

The house was quiet when Quill entered. From outside, he had seen lamps burning in Ramsey's study and Calico's bedroom, but when he knocked lightly on the pocket doors of the study, there was no answer. He parted them, looked inside, and did not see Ramsey at his desk. The lamp, he thought, would extinguish itself soon enough so he let it be and headed upstairs. He paused outside Calico's room but elected to go to his own to change first.

The first thing he did when he was inside his room was to cross to the bed and light the lamp beside it. He shook out the match and tossed it into the fireplace. No one had laid a fire for him, so he did it now to stay warm while he stripped out of his clothes and cleaned up. He was dusty from his trek into the tunnel but at least he was not carrying nitro crystals on his clothing. George Kittredge could not say the same. The man could not return home until he had been picked clean of every one of them.

Quill took the lamp into the bathroom,

where he stripped down and washed up. He left everything in a pile on the floor, pulled on clean drawers and warm woolen socks, and padded back into the bedroom. He was glad he was holding the oil lamp in both hands; otherwise he might have dropped it when he was brought up short by the sight of Calico curled under the covers on his bed.

He could not imagine how he had not seen her earlier, but he also hadn't heard her enter. Her hair was fanned out across the pillow in all its brilliant color. Her eyes were closed, and her cheek rested against the back of one hand. Quill turned back the lamp until only a thread of light was visible. He set it down and went around to the other side of the bed. Raising the blankets, he slipped under them and carefully stretched out. He had just finished making a comfortable depression for himself when Calico turned over and faced him. Her eyes did not open just then. That happened when she drew up her knees and bumped his.

"Hello," he said. He was unreasonably glad he had left that slender flame burning in the lamp. She was beautiful in the cast of golden light and Quill's eyes drank her in.

"Hello," she said, smiling sleepily. "I did not think you would be gone so long."

"Neither did I."

"Is everything all right?"

"That's a conversation that can wait until morning."

She nodded faintly. "I suppose that's an answer of a kind."

"Hmm. Sleep. That's what can't wait."

Her eyes roamed his face and finally settled on his mouth. "Or . . ."

"Yes, well, there is always 'or' . . ."

She laughed without making a sound, and the vibration of it was still on her lips when he leaned forward and kissed her. They edged closer, looking for accommodation of knees and thighs. He raised her shift. She loosened the string on his drawers. His fingertips sought the velvet smooth skin of her hip; she searched out the flat of his belly.

They kissed slowly, deeply, drawing out the pleasure, finding the nuances of taste and smell and touch. Their play was sweetly erotic. He bit gently down on her lower lip. She made a sweep across his upper lip with her tongue. He hummed against her mouth; she whimpered against his.

She tugged at the ribbon that held the neckline of her shift in place, and then she took his hand and laid it over her breast. She guided his thumb across her nipple. He teased it until it was a bud before he replaced his hand with hers. He waited, and the color of his eyes turned smoky in the waiting. Her fingers were still for a long time, but then her hand slowly began to move and she grazed her skin with her nails.

"Oh," she said on a thread of sound, and he answered in kind.

She raised her knee when he nudged her with his. He made room for his thigh between hers. She was conscious of the opening he created, conscious of the way she had parted her legs for him. He did not press his advantage, if indeed he had one. He simply stayed as he was, perfectly composed, watching her touch herself in all the ways he liked to touch her.

He moved the strap of her shift over her shoulder. "What's this?"

She realized he was touching the damp towel still wrapped around her upper arm. "Later," she whispered. "Take it off."

He did and pushed it over the edge of the bed. He leaned over and laid his mouth against the puckered flesh of her healing wound.

"If only that were all it took to make it better," she said. She moved her hand from her belly to his chest and found the raised starburst of flesh that was his scar. "I wish I had known you then. I would have tended to you."

"Tend to me now," he said, and so she did.

She took him in hand and angled her hips and invited him to come into her. She was wet, made that way first by his hand and then by hers, but he did not rush his fences. He advanced slowly, taking her by fractions, daring her not to push back.

They remained on their sides facing each other. The novelty of the position lent their lovemaking new intimacy. He slipped his fingers deeply into her fiery hair. Heavy strands of it licked at his skin. He could imagine heat where none existed. She removed her hand from where they were joined and let it slide over his abdomen and chest, grazing his skin with her nails so lightly that he shivered. She felt the movement inside and it tripped a like response. The last thing they were was cold, but the shiver moved them blindly toward more heat.

For her it was feeling his smile against her mouth as he turned her on her back. For him it was the contraction of her body as she clung to him in every way possible.

Even afterward she would not let him leave her. "A little longer," she said when he would have withdrawn. She liked the small

462

movements he made because he could not help them as she could not help hers. Here, in his arms, was a place she felt safe surrendering the illusion of control. And it was an illusion, she reminded herself, and one she welcomed for the order and sense of predictability it brought her. Sometimes she needed that, and sometimes, like now, she could let it go.

Their breathing calmed, and when he lifted himself a second time, she made no protest. He fell on his back beside her and she moved her head to the cradle he made for her against his shoulder. She wriggled some as she adjusted her shift so it was no longer bunched around her hips. She also raised the fallen straps and tugged on the ribbon at the neckline to make it a more modest opening.

"Are you quite finished?" he asked when she had settled in for the second time.

"Mm."

He chose to believe that meant that she was. He idly stroked her upper arm with his fingertips. Her palm lay without moving on his chest. They lay in that fashion for a long time before he asked, "Do you ever think about a life different from the one you know now?"

The question made her heart jump. "How

do you mean?"

"I'm not sure. Just . . . different."

"Sometimes," she said. "Sometimes I think about it."

He waited to see if she would elaborate, but she did not. What she did was turn the question on him.

"Do you?" she asked.

"I do. Not often, but sometimes. Like you."

She waited as he had and sensed his caution in the silence. Suddenly she said, "I think about a place I can go back to."

"There's no place like that for you now?"

"No. Not really. I've got some money saved. Stashed, on account of not trusting banks." She thought he might laugh at that, but he didn't. That eased her enough to say, "I might buy a parcel. Enough space to open my bedroll and stretch my toes. Maybe . . . someday."

He was quiet for a long time before he said, "I have a place."

She realized she had never once considered that he might be from somewhere. "I've always thought about you as just passing through on your way to somewhere else."

"I have a spread south of Denver, just outside a little town called Temptation. A house, stable, some outbuildings, and about eight hundred head of cattle. I move around, same as you, but that is where I return."

"Does your place have a name?"

"Eden."

"Eden," she repeated softly. "Of course. What else would you call a spread outside of Temptation?"

"I never claimed to be much for originality."

She smiled sleepily. "Is it hard for you to leave behind?"

"It's still a place, not home. Not yet, not for me. I have a wrangler and some hired hands taking care of it."

He inhaled deeply and then slowly released the breath. "You haven't asked me what would make Eden home."

"No, I haven't."

"All right," he said, pressing his lips against her hair. "Maybe neither of us is ready to say it out loud."

Calico closed her eyes and felt the press of tears behind her lids. She did not try to understand them. They simply *were.* When she finally fell asleep, it was because she could not make the journey between Temptation and Eden one more time.

Quill heard his name. He sat up straight,

blinked, and patted the space beside him. Calico was no longer in his bed. Had she called him?

"Mr. McKenna!" Not his first name. Not Calico, then. Ann? He shook off the dregs of sleep as he moved off the bed. "Coming!" he called out, looking around for his clothes. He remembered leaving them on the bathroom floor and went to get them. He did not even question why Calico was standing where his clothes had been. She had them in her arms and offered them up. They did not speak as she helped him into his shirt and then gave him his trousers. He put on his shoes, kissed her on the cheek, and left her standing precisely where he found her. It was yet another explanation that would have to wait.

Quill opened the bedroom door. It was indeed Ann Stonechurch in the hallway. The dim light made her face seem even paler than it was. Her eyes were wide, almost wild with fear, and her hands flapped like a startled bird's wings as she spoke.

"Please. You have to come with me. It's Father. Something's happened. Something awful."

He joined her in the hallway and took a step toward Ramsey's room. She grabbed his arm and shook her head frantically.

"Where is he?" asked Quill.

Ann pulled him toward the stairs. "In his study. He never went to bed."

Quill removed her hand from his arm so he could take the lead. He leaped down the steps two and three at a time and reached the study well before Ann. She had left the doors parted and he hurried inside. The room was exactly as it had been earlier when he had only poked his head inside. Ramsey was not at his desk. Quill turned to look at Ann. He could not catch her eye because she flew past him on her way to the far side of her father's desk, the side that was not in Quill's line of sight.

He went after her. She was already beginning to kneel when he caught up to her. He dropped to his knees beside her and her father.

"Is he breathing?" asked Ann. "He was breathing when I found him."

"Sh." Quill bent his head so his ear was near Ramsey's open mouth. He laid his palm on Ramsey's chest to feel for the rise and fall. "Yes," he told Ann. "He's breathing. He was like this when you found him?"

She nodded. "I shook him, tried to rouse him, but I never moved him. I went to get you."

"Where is your aunt?"

"Sleeping."

"Get her. Miss Nash, too. They should be here with you while I go for Dr. Pitman."

Ann stood, but she did not leave. "What is wrong with him?"

Quill only knew what *wasn't* wrong with him. There were no obvious wounds, no blood pooling under his body. His features were still symmetrical, nothing sagged or drooped. When Quill raised Ramsey's eyelids, the pupils responded to the introduction of light. "I don't know, Ann. Bring your aunt."

Ann backed away and then fled.

As soon as she was gone, Quill bent over Ramsey again. He did not listen to the older man's breathing this time. Instead, he smelled his breath. It was vaguely sour with the scent of vomitus, but Quill saw no evidence for it on the carpet. There was another odor as well, but not one Quill could identify. He looked around for an overturned glass or one that was nearly empty. There was none, and no plate either. The scent continued to elude him.

Quill turned Ramsey on his side. The lack of any response was discouraging. He wondered how long Ramsey had been lying there. It was certainly possible that he had been there when Quill had looked in earlier.

Quill knew he had no reason to suspect that anything was wrong at that time, but that did not stop him from being frustrated with himself. He could have done more. The lamp had been burning. He could have stepped inside and looked around. If he had, he would know whether Ramsey had been lying unconscious in the room then or if his collapse had only recently happened.

Above him, he heard doors open and close, footsteps treading more heavily than was their custom. The distinctly feminine voices drew nearer. Quill stood just as all three women appeared on the threshold. They let Ann reach her father first.

"You moved him," she said, kneeling. "Should you have done that?"

Quill did not answer her. He was looking at Beatrice, and when she nodded, he knew that she understood. "Do what you need to do to make him comfortable. I am going for Dr. Pitman." He caught Calico's hand surreptitiously and squeezed it as he brushed past her. "I won't be gone a moment longer than I have to be."

Ann tugged on her aunt's hand. "What is wrong with him? Is it his heart?"

From Calico's perspective, Ann may as well have tugged on her aunt's heart. Beatrice's porcelain complexion turned ashen, and the gray cast made her look impossibly fragile.

Beatrice responded to the tug by joining her niece on the carpet. Unaware of what Quill had done, Beatrice went through the same motions but in the end had nothing to add that enlightened.

Calico pointed to the sofa at the rear of the study. "Should we put him there? Mr. McKenna said we should make him comfortable."

"I don't think we should move him," said Ann. "What if we hurt him?"

"All right," Calico said. "We won't move him. I will get a pillow for his head, though."

"Oh, yes. Do that. He looks so uncomfortable. His neck . . ." Ann's voice trailed off as she considered the awkward angle of her father's neck. "Do you think he might have broken something? Perhaps when he fell?"

Calico had already retrieved a pillow from the sofa and now she hugged it to her midriff as she waited for Beatrice's pronouncement.

"Ann, there is nothing wrong with his neck that a pillow will not improve." Beatrice waved Calico over and took the pillow from her. She gently lifted Ramsey's head and slipped the pillow under it. "There. Do you see? I believe his color is already getting better."

Calico thought this last was wishful thinking. Ramsey's cheeks had a cherry glow to
them. Calico had seen the like before and
could not recall that it was ever a sign that
a change for the better was coming. Ann,
though, nodded and was calmed by her
aunt's words. There was some good in that,
Calico decided. Ann Stonechurch was a
rapidly unraveling bundle of nerves.

Beatrice rose to her feet and pushed
Ramsey's chair closer to where he lay. She
sat. Ann stayed on the floor beside her
father. Calico moved to the chair she usually occupied when she was Ramsey's guest.

None of them spoke. Ramsey did not stir.
The waiting was interminable.

Because Calico's attention was for what
was happening outside the walls of the
home, she was the first to hear Quill's approach. His voice had become unmistakable
to her. Without announcing her intent, she
got up and went to the front door to let him
in.

Dr. Pitman stamped his feet as he entered.
Snow fell off his shoes in clumps and dusted
the floor when he removed his coat and hat.
Calico took the items from him and held
out her hand for Quill's things as well.

"Mr. Stonechurch's study," she told the

471

doctor, and he hefted his leather bag and hurried on. To Quill she said, "If there's been any change, it hasn't been for the better."

He nodded. "Ann?"

"Sick with fear." She put the coats and hats in the front parlor while Quill waited for her. "Do you know something you're not saying?"

He touched her arm and held her up. He spoke quietly. "No. Nothing firm. Suspicions only."

"Did you share them with Pitman?"

"No. They are probably nothing, and I want to hear him out first."

"All right. Then I will do the same."

Quill did not have an opportunity to ask what she meant by that. By the time the question occurred to him, she had stepped away and was preceding him into the study.

Abraham Pitman was in his late forties, but he suffered from stiff joints that made him navigate like a much older man. The prospect of getting down on his knees to examine Ramsey Stonechurch was daunting. He placed one hand on the edge of Ramsey's desk and the other on the chair that Beatrice had vacated and lowered himself carefully beside his patient. He winced as his knees touched the floor, but

472

he did not complain.

He wore gold-rimmed spectacles that had a tendency to slip down his nose because he had no bridge to speak of. It had long been his habit to push at them whether they were in place or not. He did this before he opened his case and removed a stethoscope.

His examination was efficient and conducted without comment. He listened to Ramsey's breathing, checked his heart and lungs, his pupils, his reflexes, made a sweep of his mouth with a hooked forefinger, and clapped him hard on the back. He tapped Ramsey's liver, his midsection, and listened to his bowels. He checked for broken bones and bruising, and when he was finished, he was no closer to making a diagnosis than when he entered the room.

"Mr. Stonechurch can be moved. There is no reason not to put him in his bed. Is there anyone in the house who can help?"

Ann shook her head. "None of the help live here. You know that. They've all gone home."

Calico spoke up. "We only need to make a litter. There will be little problem managing after that. Mr. McKenna? Will you come with me?"

Quill followed her out of the study. "You have an idea?"

"Bed slats and a couple of blankets."

"That will work."

They returned to the study with the makeshift litter in under ten minutes. Quill rolled Ramsey onto it. Dr. Pitman insisted on keeping Ramsey on his side, so they placed pillows at his back to use as a stopper. Quill took one end and Beatrice and Calico each held a slat at the other.

Once they put Ramsey in bed, the women stepped outside the room while Quill and Dr. Pitman stripped him out of his clothes and into a nightshirt. When they were permitted to return, Ann and Beatrice rearranged the blankets, tucking and smoothing and fussing unnecessarily because they needed something to do.

"Miss Nash, will you fetch a basin for me?"

"Certainly." Calico disappeared into the bathing room to get one.

Dr. Pitman pushed his spectacles over his sloped nose. "I was able to force a mild purgative down his throat. If it works, his stomach will involuntarily spasm and he will purge the toxins. It is the only thing I can think to try. If it is his ulcer, there will be blood." He took the basin from Calico's hands and placed it on the bed close to Ramsey's turned head. "He must not be left alone. He will need help with the purge. Under no circumstances can he be allowed to breathe in what his stomach is trying to reject."

He took a moment to look at each member of his audience in turn. "Do you understand?" When there were nods all around, he continued. "I propose taking the first shift as it will likely happen soon. I don't suppose that any of you will sleep well for what remains of the night, but I would gladly take a cup of coffee if it were offered."

"Of course," said Beatrice. "Yes, of course. I should have already made the offer. I will bring it directly. Anyone else? No? Very well." With a last look at Ramsey, she left.

"What sort of toxins?" asked Ann. "What did you mean by that?"

"Oh, it could be anything. Let's begin with Ramsey's last meal, which I assume was dinner."

Quill said, "I did not see anything to suggest he ate something later."

"Well, then, let us go forward with dinner. What did he eat?"

Ann put her hands together in the same way her aunt so often did. "What we all ate. Potato soup. Baked fish with hollandaise sauce. Cole slaw." Her delicate features started to crumple. "This is ridiculous.

None of us is ill. What is happening to him?"

Calico moved to stand beside Ann. She gently laid a hand on the girl's back at the shoulder and addressed the doctor. "I do not think that Mr. Stonechurch has done justice to a meal in quite some time. Ann is correct that we all eat the same things, but he eats less these days. Remember, Ann? You even remarked on it at dinner the other evening. You asked him if he was feeling well."

Dr. Pitman patted his own well-rounded belly. "Perhaps he is looking out for this. I have advised that he do so."

"Perhaps," Calico said, unconvinced.

"Well?" He directed his question at everyone. "Has he complained? He certainly did not seek me out."

Quill said, "I spend the most time with him. He's made no more than his usual number of comments about his . . ." He paused, searching for a word that would not offend Ann's sensibilities. "His rumblings."

"He might have said more to my aunt," said Ann.

"That is certainly possible. Likely, in fact. Mrs. Stonechurch has more remedies for dyspepsia than the apothecary. I will ask her when she returns." Dr. Pitman's spectacles had slipped again. This time he regarded the others over the rims. "Go. Rest as best you can. Ann, that is especially necessary for you. Ask your aunt to make you some chamomile."

She nodded slowly, the hint of a rueful smile shaping her lips. "I was on my way to the kitchen to make that for myself," she said to no one in particular. "I was restless, couldn't sleep. That's why I was downstairs and why I noticed the lamp burning in my father's study. I went in to extinguish it and found him lying on the floor." She turned sharply in the doctor's direction. "Will he recover? If this is because of something he ate tonight, will he recover?"

Pitman's shoulders rose and fell. "I will do my best by your father," he said. "And the rest will be in God's hands."

Ann nodded sharply and fled the room, blinking back tears.

Calico and Quill exchanged glances. Without a word passing between them, they were comfortable believing they had reached agreement. It was Quill who addressed Pitman. "Do you believe his condition can be attributed to something he ingested at a single meal?"

The doctor gave Quill a considering look and then darted a glance at Calico. "Miss Nash. Perhaps if you would go to Miss

Stonechurch, you could be a comfort to her."

Quill said, "You will not get rid of her that easily. She stays and hears whatever you have to say. I can assure you, it is what Mr. Stonechurch would want."

"I don't understand."

"You don't have to. What I require is that you trust me and, by extension, that you trust her. Your patient does. He hired us to protect him and his family, and you can see that we are failing. Now, before Beatrice returns, tell me what you are really thinking."

Abraham Pitman did not surrender his skepticism easily. "Trust you? Trust you over Beatrice Stonechurch? Over Ann? Why would I do that on your say-so?"

Calico took a step forward, loosened the belt of her robe, and tugged on the right sleeve to reveal the long scar across her upper arm. "This was not the result of Ramsey Stonechurch misfiring his weapon, Dr. Pitman, and I believe that there has always been some part of you that suspected as much." Calico had no idea if that was true or not, but she erred on the side of the man having a measure of common sense. "I was shot because I was with Mr. Stonechurch. The bullet I took was meant for him. Ann and Beatrice do not know that because Mr. Stonechurch kept it from them." She yanked up the sleeve of her robe. "Now, tell Mr. McKenna what he wants to know before I strangle you with your stethoscope."

Appalled more than alarmed, Pitman's eyes widened over the top of his spectacles.

Quill said, "Usually Calico threatens to shoot someone, so I would say this is progress."

Pitman's mouth snapped shut and then slowly parted. "Calico? Miss Nash is Calico Nash?" His mistake was in putting the question to Quill. He had to take a step back as Calico took a menacing step forward. He put out his hands defensively. "I apologize," he said, although he had no clear idea what he was apologizing for. "I just thought you would be —"

"Taller?"

"No. Not that. I thought you would be mud fence ugly."

Calico threw up her hands as she walked away. "Talk to him, Quill. I will look out for Beatrice." She went as far as the doorway and stood there, acting as sentinel for Beatrice's approach.

Dr. Pitman gave Quill his attention, though from time to time he cast a wary eye in Calico's direction.

Quill said, "You understand you do not repeat what you've just learned."

The doctor's head bobbed several times and very quickly. "Who are you?"

"Still Quill McKenna. Nobody special." Behind him, he heard Calico snort. It warmed him some. "Now that we are done with the unpleasantness of threats, I need to know what you do."

"It's not food poisoning," he said. "Not the way we tend to think of it. But do I believe he's been poisoned? Yes. Small quantities over time would be my guess. He did not eat a poisonous mushroom, for instance. That would have killed him quickly. It's possible he ingested more tonight and that is what caused his coma. But what led up to it? That took time. Patience."

"Specific knowledge?"

"I would say so, yes." It was when Quill raised an eyebrow that the doctor seemed to hear what he had just said. He shook his head and even lifted a hand as though he could push the words out of the way. "I am making no accusation. Absolutely none."

"But she could do it."

"No. She could not, and you will not get me to say so." He pointed to Calico's back

and whispered, "Even under threat of violence."

"All right," Quill said agreeably. "What
kind of poison? I caught a scent that I could
not identify."

From the doorway, Calico said, "Ask him
why Ramsey's cheeks are cherry red."

Quill did not repeat the question. He
simply gave the doctor another inquiring
look.

"Drink, most likely. Too much of it. He
likes his whiskey."

Calico slapped the doorjamb hard with
the flat of her hand. She turned then because she knew she could expect that she
had the attention of both men. "It is *not*
from drink. I've seen this before, or something very like it. He's had trouble breathing. He's still having trouble."

"I examined his lungs."

"I know you did. I saw you. I can see his
chest moving. He's breathing, but not
breathing." Frustrated because she did not
have the knowledge to explain any better,
she turned her back on the doctor again.

Pitman stepped closer to his patient and
set his stethoscope against Ramsey's heart
and then moved it to his back to listen to
his lungs again. His proximity made him
the first to be aware that the purgative was

about to work. He pushed the basin close to Ramsey's mouth and held the man's head. His patient's body began to spasm. Ramsey's legs jerked and bent at the knees. They were drawn involuntarily toward his chest. His arms flailed, contracted, and he would have dislodged the basin if Quill had not stepped in to help restrain him.

The retching was difficult to listen to. Sounds that did not seem at all human came from deep inside him. He soiled himself, and he continued to heave after it was clear he had emptied the contents of his stomach.

Calico crossed the threshold into the hallway and closed the door behind her as the men went about the business of cleaning Ramsey and changing the sheets. Quill came to get her when he and the doctor finished. He carried the soiled linens in his arms.

"Beatrice?" he asked.

Calico shook her head. "Give me those. I'll take them to the laundry tub and see what's keeping her."

Quill did not argue. He quickly made a bundle of the linens and passed it to Calico. "I think the purge helped," he said.

"Good."

Her terse reply caused him to give her a

second look. "Calico? What is it?"

"It could be an accident, you know. Not intentional. She might have —"

Quill put a hand on her shoulder. "You heard Dr. Pitman. Ramsey was poisoned over time. I am not sure how that indicates an accident."

"I don't want it to be true."

"I know. I like her, too."

Calico did not comment. She hefted the bundle. "I better go. I suppose it will be a test of Dr. Pitman's confidence if he drinks the coffee she's preparing."

Quill watched her go. She took the back stairs to the kitchen. He waited until he was certain Beatrice was not coming up by the main staircase before he returned to the room. He trusted that Calico would find Lucrezia Borgia still in the kitchen fussing over Dr. Pitman's coffee while she calculated her next move.

"Any change?" asked Quill, approaching the bed.

The doctor did not answer the question directly. "I believe there is reason to hope." Now that Ramsey's stomach had been purged, he could lie on his back. Pitman changed the warm compress he had placed across his patient's forehead. He also wiped Ramsey's face and wet his lips.

"I told Calico that the purge seemed to help. Was I lying?"

"No. But then I am also questioning myself. It can be hard to gauge improvement against hopefulness."

"I understand."

Pitman laid the used compress on the lip of a basin of fresh water. He closed his medical bag. "So you are not Mr. Stonechurch's attorney."

"No, but not for lack of an offer on his part."

The doctor turned and faced Quill. "And Mr. Stonechurch really hired you to . . . what? Keep him safe?"

Quill glanced at Ramsey. Failure weighed heavily. "All evidence to the contrary, yes."

"You have been living here for quite a while. What happened that prompted Mr. Stonechurch to seek you out?"

"Anonymous threats, but you're mistaken about him seeking me out. I found him."

Pitman frowned. "How does that happen?"

"He told someone about the threats, someone who took them more seriously than he did. That person came to me and I went to Mr. Stonechurch."

"Then you've done this before."

"I have."

"Calico Nash?"

"To look after Ann. You know there were . . . let's call them mishaps."

The doctor nodded as he sank slowly into the armchair. He absently rubbed his left knee. "I had no idea she was in real danger."

"No one does. That was the way Mr. Stonechurch wanted it."

"I wondered about you living here at the house, but then I know how Ramsey Stonechurch works. I decided that he wanted you at his beck and call at all hours."

"You were not wrong. As it happens, I am a lawyer."

"Oh. And Calico Nash is a teacher?"

"No. She's a bounty hunter."

Pitman removed his spectacles and cleaned them on the sleeve of his jacket. "It is a little overwhelming."

"I can see that."

He nodded slowly and returned his spectacles to his face. "Elderberry," he said quietly.

"How is that again?"

"Elderberry. The leaves, stems, roots are all poisonous. The boiled berries are harmless, but the other parts of the plant must be removed. Anyone who makes jams, pies, and wine with elderberries knows that. I recommend and use an elderberry tonic for rheumatism. The apothecary keeps a supply."

"You think that's what Ramsey ate?"

"I cannot be certain, but the symptoms fit. Miss Nash mentioned loss of appetite, which he would naturally experience because of mild nausea and other unpleasant symptoms. He would be uncomfortable, but he would not be alarmed."

"Dyspepsia," said Quill.

"Yes, that would be the logical conclusion. If he had come to me, it would have been mine. I had already diagnosed an ulcer."

"I do not mean this as an insult, but in this house, you would be the second opinion. He would have gone to his sister-in-law first."

"Without a doubt. Beatrice Stonechurch has educated herself on the healing herbs. She knows tonics and tinctures and teas. I would trust her to nurse me if I were unwell. You know she cared for her husband from the moment he was carried out of the mine until his death. I never said as much — I would not have dared — but I did not believe Leo would live a full week. She had almost twelve months with him, and had it not been for his lungs, she could have had longer. She made remarkable strides with improving his leg strength —"

"I am aware," Quill interrupted. "I want to hear about these other symptoms."

"The flush in his cheeks. That's telling." He put out a hand when Quill would have interrupted again. "I know what I said to Miss Nash, but please appreciate how difficult this is for me. I will do right by my patient, but to be put in the position of accusing Beatrice, that I cannot do. What Miss Nash observed is the result of Mr. Stonechurch not being able to use the air he is breathing. The toxins in the elderberry affect the body's capacity to carry oxygen. He would have experienced shortness of breath on previous occasions, but since the symptoms can pass if he ingested only small amounts, he would think it was his heart. About tonight, all I can say is that if he has even half the determination of his brother, he will recover. I will never think that he cannot."

"I want to believe that." Quill glanced at the open doorway, frowned. "I need to go downstairs. Someone should be bringing your coffee by now."

"I was thinking the same thing. Go on. I will call for you if I need help. And Ann is close by."

Quill nodded. He left the doctor changing

Ramsey's compress yet again and followed Calico's back stairs route to the kitchen. The quiet that met him as he neared the bottom of the steps put him on alert. By the time he reached the door, every hair on the back of his neck was standing up.

He pushed through cautiously. A lighted oil lamp on the table was casting its dim light in a small circle around it. The stove had not been fired. There was no evidence of a coffee canister or the pot anywhere in the room. The cups and saucers were all accounted for in the dish cupboard.

He stood still, listened, and when he heard nothing, he decided there was only one direction worth pursuing. He headed for the back door off the mudroom and found it was blocked.

Calico's body lay sprawled across the threshold.

CHAPTER FIFTEEN

Quill went back for the lamp and set it on the floor beside Calico. There was no obvious injury. He ran his fingers through her hair and over her scalp. He found a small lump near the crown of her head but no blood. She had been cracked hard enough to knock her unconscious but her assailant had stopped at one blow.

Quill laid one hand on Calico's shoulder and shook her while he said her name. She moaned softly the second time he gave her a shake and opened her eyes on the third. He gave her a moment to collect herself, which for Calico involved cursing and self-recrimination, and then helped her sit up. She put a hand to her head and gingerly felt around the lump with the tips of her fingers.

"This is not done swelling, I think," she said.

"What did she hit you with?"

"I'm not sure. I only had a glimpse of her, but I would not be surprised if one of the guns in Ramsey's case is missing."

"Let's get you out of the mudroom and into the kitchen." He helped her up, but once she was on her feet, she shrugged him off and moved to the kitchen table unassisted. She did accept the chair he pulled out for her. "You think she's left the house?" he said. "Are you sure of that? I can look around."

"She was dressed for outside. I saw that much. When I got here and found the kitchen empty and no coffee made, I figured she had been planning her escape since Dr. Pitman arrived. She seized the opportunity when he asked her for a cup of coffee." Calico rubbed the bridge of her nose as she considered the order of events. "She must have gone to her room, dressed, and then gone downstairs when I moved out of the doorway. I went down shortly afterward. I was thinking it through when I heard the back door open. I figured I could stop her, so I followed. She was still in the mudroom, and that's when she clubbed me."

Shaking her head, Calico sighed deeply. "God, that I could be so careless. I have had less trouble from men twice her size."

"True, but then you drugged some of

them." He merely grinned at the sour look she gave him.

"You don't seem concerned that she's gone," said Calico.

"It had not occurred to me that I should be. Aren't you Calico Nash?"

She was silent a moment, taking that in. Her senses were not so boggled that she couldn't recognize the compliment. "What a lovely thing to say."

Quill took her hand, squeezed it. "Whether or not Beatrice has figured out that you're Calico Nash, I don't know where she imagines she can go that she can't be found, and if she has realized who you are, then she must know she has very little freedom left."

"She could have killed me."

"It wasn't for lack of trying. The infection that festered in your wound was a good attempt."

Calico remembered the brown stain on the bandage. Beatrice had assured her it would help. "All those teas she insisted that I drink . . ." Her short laugh was humorless. "I might have died if she had ever served me one that I liked or stayed around to watch me drink entire pots of the stuff. I wonder if I have ever misjudged anyone as I misjudged her."

"You're in good company. I asked her to help you with exercises for your arm."

"And she did. She also took the time to encourage Ann's newfound interest in Boone Abbot. And then she came to my room with steamed towels and informed me that I had made a mistake in introducing the pair. She said Ramsey would not approve, that Boone is a painful reminder of his brother's accident and death."

"She said that? That Boone is a reminder?"

"She did. She said that Ramsey would not allow him to return to work in the mines for that reason."

"I happen to know that Ramsey has offered Boone a position in his office on several occasions. Boone turns him down. Boone Abbot is happy where he is. He likes the horses and his wages are good because Ramsey supplements them through an arrangement with the livery owner."

"Why would Beatrice make it out to be different than it is?"

"Maybe we've been thinking about this wrong. Ramsey has said he wants his daughter to leave Stonechurch and experience the larger world. What if it is really Beatrice who wants to keep her close? So close that she sees even someone like Boone as a threat to her. All her words to the contrary, she never accepted you. Hell, she tried to kill you."

"I don't know. Ramsey has kept Ann on a short leash. She was never allowed to attend the local school. She is not permitted to visit the mines. She doesn't ride. She does not —" Calico stopped because Quill was regarding her with a raised eyebrow. "Oh. I see. The Beatrice effect."

"She has more influence than either of us has suspected. That's probably true for Ramsey and Ann as well. Can you imagine Ramsey Stonechurch admitting that his sister-in-law has manipulated him? Not only recently, but for years. Where Ann is concerned, he was an easy mark. He loves his daughter, he wants what is best for her, and it would not be hard for Beatrice — for anyone — to use that against him."

Calico slowly shook her head. "Poor Ann. Isolated. Protected. It is little wonder she doesn't want to leave. Promise me we will not do that to our children. I could not bear to see them caged by so much love and good intention."

Quill stared at her. It was hard to know exactly how to respond to that. Finally, he said, "But you are generally not opposed to loving them."

"Of course not."

"And just to be clear, you are not opposed to having them."

"Of course not."

"Good to know."

"Really, Quill, I was the one who Beatrice cracked on the head."

"Uh-huh." He rubbed behind his ear. "But sometimes . . ."

Calico smiled. "It's the same for me." She started to rise, felt a wave of nausea, and dropped back into the chair. "But not at this moment."

Quill reached out to steady her. "Dizzy?"

"A little."

"Stay there. Beatrice is not leaving town. There is no train until late morning. I am going to get Dr. Pitman and send him down. I will sit with Ramsey. I don't want to disturb Ann yet."

Calico reached for Quill's hand and laid hers over it. "One of us has to tell her what's happening."

"I understand, but right now you need attention and I need to dress. I will bring your clothes to you as soon as Pitman tells me you are able to —" He stopped because it was clear from the look she gave him that there was no point in putting any conditions on her leaving the house. "Right," he said. "I will bring your clothes."

She squeezed his hand. "Just to be clear," she said quietly. "I love you whether or not you give me my way, but I think you will find I am easier to love if you do."

Quill regarded her with wry amusement. He was on the point of telling her what he thought of that when Dr. Pitman called down to them. "I'll go," he said. "I won't be long."

The doctor was standing in the hallway when Quill arrived. Pitman gestured to Quill to hurry and then disappeared into the bedroom.

"Has he come around?" asked Quill as he approached the bed. Before Dr. Pitman could answer, Quill saw movement behind Ramsey's eyelids. A moment later, he opened his eyes. "And so he has."

Dr. Pitman put out his hand and waved it slowly above Ramsey's face to see if his eyes would track. They did. "Mr. Stonechurch?"

Ramsey slowly turned his head. His eyes were rheumy, his gaze still vaguely unfocused. His lips moved, but no sound emerged.

"His color has improved," said Quill, and by that he meant that Ramsey's cheeks were no longer unnaturally flushed. "Does that mean he is finding it easier to breathe?"

Pitman nodded. He wrung out a compress

and carefully wiped the watery discharge from Ramsey's eyes and wet his lips. "I called you as soon as I saw he was conscious. Where is Miss Nash?"

"Still in the kitchen. I need you to attend her." He explained what had transpired since Calico left. "I'll stay with Mr. Stonechurch until you return."

Without a word, Pitman picked up his leather satchel and left.

"Obliging, isn't he?" Quill said to Ramsey. "And he saved your life. Keep that in mind when he starts ordering you around. He's earned the right."

Ramsey tried to say something again and had to settle for giving Quill a sour look.

"Noted," said Quill. "Do you want some water?" When Ramsey nodded, Quill soaked a clean compress in water and put it against Ramsey's lips. "Suck on that. You can't have more until Pitman says you can. I know. It's miserable." He held the compress to Ramsey's mouth until he indicated he'd had enough, and then he put it aside. "Did you hear what I told Pitman about what happened downstairs?" Ramsey's nod was slight but noticeable. "Do you understand what it means?"

Quill waited, but Ramsey did not respond. It was not possible to know what his silence meant, but Quill's best guess was that Ramsey was as reluctant as Dr. Pitman to believe that Beatrice was culpable.

"As best I can piece this together without a confession from your sister-in-law, Beatrice has been slowly, methodically poisoning you. She disguised her intent by using small amounts at first, only enough to give you discomfort and set a pattern of mild ailments that could have any number of causes. Headaches. Stomach distress. Fatigue. You rarely complained, but when you did, you took those complaints to Beatrice and unwittingly gave her further opportunity to poison you."

Quill observed a slight widening of Ramsey's eyes and stillness in the rest of his body. "So that is how it was," he said. "She had the means to end your life at any time."

Ramsey's eyes darted past Quill to the door. He lifted a hand and placed it against his throat. "Ann? She's all right? Safe?"

"She's the one who found you in your study and roused the rest of us. She refused to leave your side until we insisted that she rest so she could have a turn sitting with you later. I'll get her in a moment."

Ramsey's features contorted slightly as a stomach cramp seized him. He sucked in a breath and drew up his knees. His hands briefly curled into fists. When it passed, he swore softly. The clarity of the cursing pointed strongly toward his recovery. "God-damn Pitman," he muttered. "What did he give me?"

"A purgative. I watched him force it down your throat and I still don't know how he did it. You were not cooperative."

Ramsey grunted. He carefully unfolded his body in anticipation that another cramp would eventually pull him taut again.

Quill waited for him to settle. He said, "What did Beatrice offer you earlier? Tea? Wine? Was she still with you in the study when you collapsed?"

Ramsey said nothing.

Quill allowed the silence to linger, hoping it would prompt Ramsey to speak up. It did not. He said, "I suppose you have your reasons for wanting to protect her, or at least not think the very worst of her, but she tried to kill you, Ramsey, and without the intervention of your daughter and Dr. Pitman, she would have succeeded."

Ramsey's mouth twisted as his stomach contracted again. It required considerable effort on his part to speak, but he forced the words out. "I want to see Ann."

In spite of his frustration, Quill merely shrugged. He was gone from the room before Ramsey's grimace had faded.

Ann did not call out to Quill when he knocked. He had not thought she could actually fall asleep, but it seemed that she had. He knocked more loudly the second time. When she still did not answer, he opened the door just enough to put his head inside. Her bedcovers were turned back and she was not under them. That prompted Quill to step inside.

Ann's room was larger than the guest bedrooms, but it shared dressing and bathing areas with the bedroom on the other side. Quill, because he had made it his business early on to learn the layout of the house, knew that neighboring bedroom belonged to Beatrice, and that the arrangement harkened back to the days when the common area had been a nursery and then a sitting room. Until now, he had never considered how the configuration contributed to Beatrice's attachment to Ann and the influence Beatrice had over her.

Concerned, but not yet alarmed, Quill called out before he entered the bathing and dressing rooms. They were empty. He did not announce himself as he moved through to Beatrice's bedroom. Ann was not there.

Quill stopped at the foot of Beatrice's bed and stared at it, trying to make sense of something he was seeing and not quite understanding. The bedcovers were turned back but not disturbed in any other way. Beatrice had not been sleeping when Ann had gone to get her to bring her to the study. Quill returned to Ann's room. He had seen that the bedcovers were turned down, but he had only been concerned that she was not in bed. He had not fully comprehended then that she had not slept in her bed either.

He cast his mind back to what she told him earlier. *I was restless, couldn't sleep.* That seemed to confirm his observation. Had she and Beatrice been talking late into the night? Calico had mentioned there was discussion about Boone Abbot. It was conceivable that the conversation could have still been going on, especially if Ann was excited and Beatrice did not want to discourage her. Ann seemed to suggest she had found her father because she had gone downstairs in search of something that would help her sleep.

Could he believe her?

Quill recalled the panic in her voice when she asked, *If this is because of something he ate, will he recover?*

"Christ, Ann," he said, shoveling his fingers through his hair. "What the hell did she persuade you to do?"

Calico was impatient and doing precious little to hide it. She prepared Pitman a cup of coffee to demonstrate that she had her wits, but when he insisted on a medical assessment, she snapped, "You can tap my skull and examine my eyes and hit my knee with that little hammer of yours as long as you understand it does not make a bit of difference what you say about any of it. As soon as Quill gets down here with my clothes, I am leaving."

"I never thought it would be otherwise. In fact, he warned me that would be the case. I am here because it is important to him."

She sighed. "It is. He cannot help himself." She pointed to the lump on her skull that he needed to look at. "Well, have at it."

Pitman took his time making a thorough examination. When he was done, he closed his medical bag and said, "Good luck."

Calico regarded him suspiciously. "That's all? Good luck?"

He shrugged. "Just saving my breath since what I have to say doesn't matter."

"To me," she said. "It doesn't matter to me. What are you going to tell Quill?"

"Oh, well, I am going to tell him to stay close to you. I cannot predict which way you will fall, but he should be prepared."

"I think you are being overly cautious."

"See?" he asked, holding up a hand. "Waste of breath." He picked up his bag and headed for the stairs.

Calico made a face behind his back.

"I saw that," he called out.

"You did not," she said, but there was part of her that was not entirely sure.

When Quill returned to Ramsey's room, Pitman was sitting in the chair at his patient's bedside. "That did not take long," he said. "She didn't argue with you?"

"I didn't argue with her."

Quill nodded. It was a good strategy. "And? What do you think?"

"She has a concussion. She should rest but not sleep. And no, I did not tell her that. I said I would tell you to stay close."

"Already my intention." Quill glanced at Ramsey. He was lying on his back again, but his head was turned and his eyes were alert. He was following their conversation. Quill said, "Would you excuse us, Doctor? There is a matter I need to discuss privately with Mr. Stonechurch. It won't take long. You can wait in the hallway. Just close the door."

Pitman did not immediately comply. He

looked to his patient first. When Ramsey nodded, he got up and left.

Quill waited for the door to close. "Ann," he said. "It was Ann who visited you in your study, not Beatrice. She offered you something to eat, something she thought would temper your mood, perhaps make you amenable to what she had to say. Did she have a chance to tell you that Calico introduced her to Boone Abbot before you collapsed?"

"Ann has nothing to do with this."

Quill ignored him. "I think Beatrice encouraged Ann to go to you, and I think Beatrice suggested that she take something with her. What was it? Toast and elderberry jam? A sliver of elderberry pie?"

Ramsey's features remain unchanged.

"Whatever it was, Ann took it away when you keeled over. She was genuinely frightened by your collapse, but I think there was some small part of her that suspected the cause, and I believe that would have frightened her almost as much."

Ramsey breathed deeply, closed his eyes as he coughed. "Where is she? Why isn't Ann here?"

"She's gone," Quill said bluntly.

Ramsey's eyes flew open. He struggled to sit up, but Quill put a hand on his shoulder and did not let him rise. Ramsey had no choice but to lie down. "Find her. She will be with Beatrice."

"Yes, I think you're right."

Ramsey nodded faintly. Tears stung his eyes. He blinked but did not try to hide them. "Why?" he asked quietly. "Why would Beatrice use my daughter so cruelly? Can she really hate me so much?"

It was not a question Quill was meant to answer and he remained silent.

"No matter what she's done," said Ramsey, "I believe she loves Ann. I have to believe that. I have to. You understand?"

"I do."

"The threats? The attempts to shoot me? That was Beatrice?"

"I believe that if it wasn't by her hand, then she had a hand in it."

As soon as he heard himself say it, Quill felt a thread of tension pull his shoulders taut. His head came up and he stared away from the bed and in the direction of the window. He was not looking at anything in particular, but he was seeing things as he had not seen them before.

Without a word of his intent to Ramsey, he turned and strode to the door. Pitman was waiting in the hallway. Quill waved him in. "Stay with him. The cook and housekeeper will be arriving soon along with several others. Someone is sure to volunteer to sit with Mr. Stonechurch and relieve you. Don't accept the offer."

The doctor's mouth snapped shut so hard that his spectacles bounced and slid down the slope of his nose.

Quill strode out, satisfied Pitman understood. When he reached his room, he changed quickly and strapped on his gun, but before he put on his jacket, he rummaged through the uppermost drawer in his wardrobe. He found what he wanted beneath a stack of handkerchiefs. He palmed the badge and attached it to his vest without looking down.

It felt right. It was time.

Quill shrugged into his jacket then his coat. He checked his pockets for gloves. On the way out the door, he grabbed the Stetson he had only rarely worn since coming to Stonechurch and put it on.

He made quick work of gathering Calico's clothes, weapons, and cartridges. Without a doubt, the only impediment to her leaving the house was the fact that she was not dressed for it, and that included her guns.

"Finally," Calico said when he dropped her belongings on the kitchen table. "Where is my Colt?"

"Under the coat."

She found it. "Loaded?"

"Mm-hmm. I left the rifle and the derringer behind."

She nodded, removed her robe, and reached for her drawers. "Are you going to just stand there?"

"Yes."

"No." She motioned him to the stairwell. "Go there or I am going into the mudroom."

He sighed, shook his head. Once he was in the stairwell and out of sight, he said, "Do not expect this accommodation when we're married."

She smiled. "Consider me warned." She yanked up the hem of her shift and shoved her long legs into the drawers.

"You realize that was a proposal, don't you?"

"You realize I accepted, don't you?"

"Huh. That was not nearly as hard as I thought it would be."

Calico rid herself of her shift and pulled a heavy cotton chemise over her head. "Oh, you will have to make a better one later. Even someone like me wants a pretty proposal."

Quill did not ask what "someone like me" meant. He said, "Ann is gone."

That riveted Calico. She was half in and

half out of her shirt, her fingers frozen on the buttons. "Don't you think that's the first thing you should have told me?"

"We would not be any farther ahead than we are now. And we need to think, not react."

Although he could not see her, Calico nodded anyway. "Tell me everything."

He did, recounting his conversation with Ramsey, his search for Ann, and finally the conclusion he had reached that had prompted his abrupt departure from Ramsey's room.

"It's all connected," he said. "The shootings, the problems in the Number 1 mine, Ramsey's suspicions that the men are organizing, and Beatrice's very personal attempt tonight to kill him." He stepped into the kitchen when Calico called to him and was brought up short by the sight of her. She did not merely take his breath away; she made his heart trip over itself.

She was wearing the clothes he had chosen for her, the same ones she had been wearing when she arrived in Stonechurch. She'd told him then that she had dressed in that fashion because she was feeling ornery, but that was not the case now. Now she looked fierce, and he suspected she was feeling exactly the same way. Her buckskin trousers hung straight and loose until they disappeared inside her boots. She wore a white shirt similar to his and a dark brown leather vest that hid the small curves of her breasts. She was buttoning her jacket when she glanced up and caught him staring.

"What?" she asked.

He simply shook his head. "Nothing."

She shrugged and finished buttoning her jacket. She deftly plaited her hair and held the tail against the crown of her head while she slipped on her hat. When she reached for her scuffed and weather-beaten leather duster, she only grabbed a handful of air.

Quill held up the duster. "Turn around. I want to put it on you."

Calico hesitated, genuinely nonplussed by the gesture. "No one's ever —" She stopped, gave him her back, and let him be the gentleman he was. Standing there in her man's shirt and trousers, a Colt at her hip, wearing a vest that disguised any hint of her long curves and a Stetson that hid what she thought of as her one true feminine glory, Calico felt utterly female as Quill helped her with her coat.

When she turned around again, he was waiting for her. He tipped her chin, kissed her lightly once, then again. "You will be careful. You will let me catch you in all the

ways that I might need to." When she nodded slowly, he added, "You understand I
mean that more than in the literal sense."

"Yes." She slipped her hands inside his
duster, laid her palms against his chest. The
faint smile that tugged the corners of her
mouth upward faded when she felt the press
of an oddly familiar but unexpected object
under the left side of his jacket. A vertical
crease appeared between her eyebrows. Her
eyes did not stray from Quill's as she tapped
the slight bulge with her fingertips. "What
is this?"

"You know."

And as soon he as said it, she thought that
it was probably true. "I want to see." When
Quill merely shrugged, Calico opened two
buttons on his jacket and parted the material so she could see his vest. The badge's
simplicity made a powerful statement. She
had seen some badges carved from coins,
but Quill's was not like that. Silver in color,
round in shape, a single five-pointed star
filled the open center. Stamped in an arc
above the star were the words U.S. MAR-
SHAL, and on the rim below it was the small
stamp of another star. "Was there a reason
you did not want to tell me?"

"Not a good reason. I was taken with the
idea that you thought I was a bounty

hunter." He closed his jacket. "And your opinion of the marshals was not what one would call respectful."

"You're right. Not a good reason." She patted the badge through his jacket one more time. "Does Ramsey know he's being protected by a federal marshal?"

"No. And I don't think 'protected' applies here."

"Quill. I know I've called him the pharaoh now and again, but no one could have suspected Ramses required a taster for his food. This was not predictable. Beatrice Stonechurch falls outside my experience and yours." Calico could see that he was not prepared to forgive himself so easily. She took a step back and surreptitiously used the table to steady herself when she felt a wave of nausea uncurl in her stomach. "Were you assigned here? Is that how you came to Stonechurch?"

"I have no specific territory. I was tapped for the marshal service because I served in the Army and had a lawyer's background. I still don't know who brought my name to their attention. I was just settling down on my ranch when they came to me, and I was not easily convinced."

"But you agreed."

"Eventually. They needed someone to lead

510

a posse through territory scattered with renegades. I was familiar with the mountains and the renegades. There was some thought that I was in a position to negotiate a truce."

"Did you?" The question was a delaying tactic. Calico felt pressure building behind her eyes. Not wanting to call attention to it, she kept her hands where they were.

"I did. We were after Samuel Miller, not Indian hostiles. They did not like him much either."

"Cutlip Miller. No one likes him. So you're the one who brought him in."

"Not alone. I had men with me."

"Sure. The posse." Her tone could not have been more dismissive. "And Stone-church?"

"You were right. I was asked to take it on."

"Asked?"

"This is not my job, Calico. It's a diversion. I am a rancher."

"Mm-hmm."

"I own a spread."

"Uh-huh."

"I swear in as a marshal when it suits me."

"Sure."

Quill adopted the strategy of least resistance and stopped talking. He placed his hands firmly on her shoulders and nudged her just enough to encourage her to turn around, then he pointed to the mudroom and the door beyond it.

Calico drew a steadying breath and led the way. A silver dollar moon cast enough light to create shadows behind them. The area immediately around the porch was trampled with footprints. They had to walk out a piece to find ones that suggested Beatrice had gone in a particular direction.

"I never saw Ann," said Calico as they rounded the house to the front. "I barely saw Beatrice."

Quill pointed out a pair of small footprints facing another, equally small, pair. The prints were surrounded by circles of disturbed snow, indicative of the women's gowns sweeping the surface. "It looks as if Ann met Beatrice here. She must have left by the front door. We could not have heard her from Ramsey's room."

Calico stared at the prints. "I wonder if they had a conversation here. I can't shake the feeling that in the end Ann did not go without a great deal of convincing. To leave her father . . ." Calico shook her head. "It's hard for me to conceive that she would do that."

"Because you would not have."

"You're right. I would not have." She paused. "I didn't."

Quill started walking, careful to stay out of the tracks they were following. "There's no stumbling, no dragging. It appears that if Ann were reluctant, she still went willingly. I think Beatrice has been grooming Ann to play a role in her scheme since Leo Stonechurch's accident. When Leo died, Beatrice set things in motion. This has been a long time coming. Ann is the one who served her father the food that caused his collapse. She is innocent; she only thinks she is guilty."

"It is probably easier for her to take the blame herself than to look too closely at someone she loves. What she did had no malicious intent, but who can say what Beatrice has made her believe? She is scared. I don't like to think about her so scared." On her own, Ann might go anywhere, but Beatrice's presence changed things, made the route she would take with her niece more deliberate. Calico stopped suddenly and tugged on Quill's sleeve to bring him up short.

"I think I know where Beatrice will go," she said.

"Horses?" he asked, directing his chin toward the livery.

"No. She might take a mount if she were alone, but Ann doesn't ride. At this late hour, Beatrice will not ask for a rig, plus Ann's recent acquaintance with Boone Abbot makes that especially risky." Calico raised her hand, pointed to the far end of town, and then lifted her arm a fraction higher, indicating the shadowed adit carved into the face of the mountain. "She will be hiding in one of the mine tunnels. If you're right about her connection to the problems in Number 1, my guess is that's where she's gone. She will have friends there."

Quill considered it, nodded slowly. "She could walk to any of the entrances. It makes sense. But she cannot hope to hide in the tunnels for the long term; she must have some escape route in mind."

"Why? People who do not expect to get caught hardly ever do. That's been true in my experience. What drives them out is desperation, not an alternative plan."

"Desperation," said Quill, "makes them reckless."

"And unpredictable."

Quill said what they both were thinking. "More dangerous for us."

Calico nodded. "What you said earlier about thinking and not reacting? Let's do that."

"Yes," he said. "Let's do that."

Ann Street was deserted. Few of the shops

had lamps burning in the apartments above them. The saloons were closed, but a trio of miners crowded the bench in front of one. As Quill and Calico passed, one of the miners was elbowed to the boardwalk. He grunted softly but did not try to rise.

"That was Jim Shepard on his bucket," said Quill. "Hard couple of days. I would stay down, too." When Calico asked what he meant, he told her about the dynamite in storage that had not been turned. "George Kittredge had his entire crew working. Volunteers only, but I don't think there was anyone who did not come forward." He was aware that Calico's steps had slowed. They had just passed Mrs. Birden's dress shop, but whatever had distracted her, it was not something in the window. "What is it?"

"I heard this story," she said slowly. "Not precisely this story, but one like it." She stopped in her tracks. "Beatrice told me. Sticks of unexploded dynamite lodged in one of Number 3's tunnels caused her husband's accident. It was only today — yesterday now — that she told me about it. It came up because of Boone Abbot. He's the one who found the dynamite. Beatrice says the sticks weep nitroglycerin. No, she says they sweat it. She was particular about that. A man's invention, she called it. I suppose she's right."

"She is, but then that observation is coming from a woman whose preferred method of killing is poison."

"I'm aware." Calico picked up the pace again. She took inventory of her symptoms and realized the bracing air was helping. There was no longer any sense of pressure behind her eyes. She felt focused and alert. The one troubling leftover from her encounter with Beatrice was the intermittent surge of dizziness that made her stomach curdle. "I would say that women prefer subtler methods, but I am carrying a gun."

"True." He looked over at her. Moonshine put a pale blue cast on her features when she raised her face. "Are you all right?"

"I am."

"You would tell me if you needed to stop, rest, toss your dinner."

"I would."

"Liar."

Calico shrugged. "Why do you ask?"

"Still trying to see if I can surprise the truth out of you."

That made her grin, and there was faint evidence of it yet when they reached the entrance to the Number 3 mine. "How many men work at night?"

"Only five or six. They cluster in a single tunnel in each of the mines, especially at night. It improves the yield of the ore and reduces risk because they are looking out for each other."

Calico looked around. A couple of lanterns lighted both sides of the entrance, but the area all around was deserted. "Shouldn't there be someone posted here?"

"Yes, at least that's what I've been told." Quill also cast his eyes right and left. He took down one of the lanterns. "I think we should go to the other mine entrances before we walk blindly into this one."

Calico agreed. Thinking, she reminded herself. Not reacting. They took the path to Number 2. There was a gradual uphill grade over the course of almost half a mile. They set a pace that covered the ground quickly. At Number 2 they were indeed met by a miner sitting on a chair outside the adit. Calico hung back in the shadows while Quill questioned the man. Calico heard nothing in the miner's voice to suggest that he knew anything more than he was saying. When Quill returned, they began a switch-back descent to Number 1. The route took them close to town again.

Calico pointed out the dark, yawning mouth of another adit. There were no lanterns to mark the entrance of this shaft, nor anyone posted nearby.

Quill shook his head. "That's not Number 1. That opening leads to storage chambers. The dynamite is in there along with other equipment they don't want to expose to the weather. That's where I was earlier with George Kittredge. It looks as if everyone's finally stopped working."

He told her to look down and off to her left. "You see that wide, dark seam running along the side of the mountain?"

"Yes, but I don't hear water."

"Seam, not stream. It's a crevice, a rift. I don't know the proper term. I do know it's something like one hundred twenty feet deep, so if you have to go that way alone, make sure you use the footbridge." They continued on toward Number 1. "Didn't Ramsey bring you down here?"

"I only saw Number 1, but we came from another direction. We had a rig and we did not ride this far."

"The bridge would not support a rig. I don't think it would support a horse. Supplies are moved around the mountain from the train station, not across the rift."

They stopped before they reached Number 1 because they could see lanterns at the entrance and a miner perched on a nearby boulder smoking a cigarette. Quill said, "I don't think Beatrice came here, or even came this way. Her husband was injured in Number 3, and the lack of a man at the entrance back there seems telling."

"But Number 1 is where they are having trouble. If she has something to do with that, then I think that's where she would have friends. We should go in, and you should at least talk to the miner standing guard."

"All right. We've come this far."

They walked side by side until the path widened closer to the entrance. That was when Calico stopped and let Quill go on. She stepped into a moon shadow created by a large mound of snow that had been shoveled away from the adit, and she listened to the exchange.

Ann Stonechurch huddled inside her coat. The floor of the tunnel was hard and cold. She could not sit on it any longer. No matter how she tried to separate herself from the ground, icy fingers worked their way through her coat, her gown, her shift, and finally, her drawers. She wished she had worn half a dozen petticoats. She wished she were wearing her cloak with the ermine trim and deep pockets. She wished she had thought to bring . . . no, what she wished was that she had never been persuaded to leave her room.

Ann knew she belonged at home, not here. No matter what had happened, or would happen, her place was at her father's side. She was filled with remorse for every wrong choice she had made.

She started to rise, pushing herself up with the rough tunnel wall at her back.

"Sit."

Ann had been told to sit down before, but this time she ignored the snarled order and got to her feet. "It's too cold to sit." Her teeth began to chatter.

"Stop that."

"I c-can't help it-t-t."

"You want to be warmer? Go on down the tunnel. The deeper you go, the warmer it gets."

Ann thought they were already deep inside the mountain. She judged they had walked three hundred yards and her companion had extinguished lamps as they passed them. Without a lantern, the route to the outside was black as pitch. "You would let me do that?"

"Sure. Why not? Oh, you think there might be a way out. No. There's not. There's no way out but the way we came in."

Ann wrapped her arms around herself. She shivered again and averted her eyes from the man guarding her. It helped calm her to pretend that he was not watching her with what she thought of as unusual interest. He had already made a comment about her hair, something about it being as dark and thick as his sister's. It was not long after that that she unwound her blue woolen scarf from around her neck and wrapped it over her hair. He did not comment, but she intercepted his sly, secretive smile before she was finished. She had read about smiles like that, and seeing it in fact, not fiction, filled her with dread as cold as the floor under her.

His narrow smile was not merely cunning, not only wicked. In Ann's mind, it defined evil.

"Where is my aunt?" she asked. "She said she would not be long."

"Now I've been here same as you. What makes you think I would know the answer to that?"

Ann shrugged, shook her head.

"I asked you a question," the man said. "I answer yours. You answer mine. Or didn't anyone teach you that?"

"I saw Aunt Beatrice speaking to you. I thought she might have told you more than she told me."

"See? That was not so hard."

Ann watched him out of the corner of her eye as he leaned back against the wall and rotated his shoulders to scratch an itch he could not reach. He sighed and moaned as he moved.

"Found the sweet spot," he said. He hunched, rubbed between his shoulder blades. "Ah. And again." When he was done, he straightened and took a step toward her.

Ann could not help herself. She flinched. He seemed satisfied with that because he stopped, turned slightly, and rested a shoulder against the tunnel wall. He ignored her and examined his nails. He did not look up again until he removed a small knife from the pocket in his coat. This time Ann did not react. She stared at it without interest, in fact, without expression of any kind, and maintained those schooled features even when he chuckled.

She turned her head when he began to pick at his nails with the knife. "I would like to walk d-down a ways," she said. "Where it's war-warmer."

"Suit yourself."

She had not expected him to let her go so easily. It convinced her that he was telling the truth about there being no outlet. It did not matter to her as much as it probably should have. What she wanted more than warmth was to be away from him.

He was a large man, uncomfortably so. He occupied too much space, took up too much air. He spoke rather more softly than she thought he would, but his voice was deep and had a ragged edge that made every word sound as if he were growling it out. He had a thick neck and dark, shaggy hair. His beard was short, wiry, and his mustache did not hide his upper lip but outlined it. He had wide shoulders and a broad chest. His hands were as big as mallets when he curled them into fists. To Ann, they were blunt, heavy instruments of violence. She could not think of them in any other fashion.

Ann was already moving into the circle of light from a lantern some thirty yards from where she had been when she heard him call after her.

"Don't get lost, Miss Stonechurch. It'd be a real shame if I had to come looking for you."

Ann looked back over her shoulder, but he was not in view. She shivered. Once again, it was not because she was cold.

Quill held up his lantern as he approached

the miner sitting on the boulder. The tip of the man's cigarette glowed brightly as he took a last, deep drag. He ground it out on the rock and then flicked it away.

"Mr. Cavanaugh, right?" asked Quill, setting the lantern on the ground to leave his hands free.

"Ah. You remembered." He grinned briefly. "I have to say that depending on how you look at it, it's either too early or too late for you to be here on a casual matter. No one who can't sleep comes out here."

"I'm surprised to see you. I passed Jim Shepard outside the saloon. He looked as if the work finally caught up with him. I guess you finished."

Cavanaugh shook his head. "Not completely, but Mr. Kittredge called a halt not long after you left. He thought we were getting too tired to be as careful as we needed to be. I drew the short straw when they asked for someone to sit out here. I don't drink, and the wife's mad at me for volunteering to help out with Hercules, so this is not a bad place to be." He removed his hat, reshaped it, and set it more tightly over his head. "And I still don't know what brings you here."

"Mr. Stonechurch sent me."

"I figured that."

"I don't have leave to share the family's personal matters, but I can tell you that this involves Ann Stonechurch and one of the Abbot boys."

Cavanaugh's coarse black eyebrows lifted. "A tryst, is it?"

"I did not say that."

"And I'll not be repeating it. You think they might have come this way?"

"I don't know; I'm looking everywhere."

"Well, I haven't seen them. Haven't seen Mrs. Stonechurch either, 'cept for the other day when she came by with crullers for us. That was real nice of her."

Quill nodded. "Strange that you'd bring up Mrs. Stonechurch when I never mentioned her."

By the time David Cavanaugh registered his mistake, he was staring down the barrel of Quill McKenna's Colt.

CHAPTER SIXTEEN

Calico stepped out of the moon shadow as soon as she heard Cavanaugh raise Beatrice's name. She did not draw her gun. Quill's was already out, and she wanted to conserve the strength in her arm for as long as she could.

Cavanaugh had his hands up in a gesture of surprise and wariness, not surrender. He jerked his chin toward Quill's gun. "Hey. You've got no call to point that at me."

"We'll see." Quill watched Cavanaugh's eyes dart past him and widen slightly. That was how he knew Calico was approaching because she made no sound. Once she was abreast of him, he said, "I guess you heard."

"I did."

As soon as Calico spoke, Cavanaugh's jaw slackened. He stared at her, recovering just enough to set his jaw again and whistle softly.

"There's something you want to say?" she asked.

"Only that I didn't believe it when I heard. Not for a moment. Calico Nash, as I live and breathe."

Quill said, "Living and breathing is something we will be discussing. Where are they?"

Cavanaugh slowly lowered his hands. He set them on the boulder on either side of him. "Now who would 'they' be exactly? Miss Stonechurch and one of the Abbots, or Miss Stonechurch and her aunt?"

Calico glanced toward the mouth of the mine. The lanterns hanging outside the entrance made it difficult for her to see deeply into the tunnel. She and Quill, on the other hand, were standing in a pool of light, visible to anyone who might suddenly appear in the shaft. She picked up the lantern at Quill's feet and moved it to where she had been standing. It helped a little to have it out of the way. She could not extinguish all lanterns, not when they would likely need them.

"He's stalling," she said, returning to Quill's side. "He expects someone to come. If he can't help, you might as well kill him."

Quill asked Cavanaugh, "Is she right? Should I kill you?"

Cavanaugh threw out his hands as if they

could ward off a bullet. He watched Quill's thumb settle on the hammer and begin to draw it back. "Wait! Wait. Miss Stonechurch isn't here. She's never been here."

"I don't believe you."

"I swear!" He gesticulated wildly. "I swear it's true. The only Abbot boy I saw around was Joshua. You saw him, too. He left when Mr. Kittredge dismissed us. The last I knew he was going to have a drink with —"

"Make him shut up," said Calico. "He knows you aren't interested in any of the Abbots."

Cavanaugh looked from Quill to Calico and then to the gun in Quill's hand. "Tell me what I need to say."

The fact that Cavanaugh had not shouted a warning or raised the alarm in some other fashion, led Quill to believe that there was no one close by. Then again, firing at Cavanaugh would certainly bring miners out of the tunnel. Calico knew that, too. David Cavanaugh was the only one not thinking clearly.

Quill tilted his head toward the adit. "Is Mrs. Stonechurch in there?"

Cavanaugh raised his shoulders in a helpless shrug. "I don't —"

"Try again. I know you don't want to give her up, but you are not helping yourself. We know about the problems in this mine, and we know the role she's had in encouraging you men to participate. Apparently, crullers are a powerful incentive."

Cavanaugh snorted.

"Or perhaps," Quill said, "it is the memory of Leo Stonechurch that prompts some of you to stand by her, and others who want a larger share of the profits. All understand-able, but your motivation doesn't matter any longer. Beatrice Stonechurch involved her niece in her scheming, and that is unac-ceptable."

"I don't know anything about that. About any of it."

Calico sighed heavily. "It is no good reasoning with a man insensible to it. He might as well be as drunk as Jim Shepard."

"You're right." Quill raised his gun a frac-tion and sighted the space between David Cavanaugh's eyebrows. He addressed the miner. "Get down off that rock." He watched Cavanaugh closely. His target remained the same no matter how the man moved. Without a hint of his intention, he reversed the Colt in his hand and brought the butt down hard on the miner's head. Cavanaugh's slouch hat did not cushion the blow enough to make a difference in the outcome. The man's head snapped sideways, his knees buckled, and he collapsed on the ground. On the way down, his skull bounced off the rock.

Quill looked down at him, shook his head, and holstered his weapon. He hunkered beside Cavanaugh, slipped his arms under the miner's shoulders, and then he dragged Cavanaugh out of sight behind the rock. Satisfied with his work, he said, "He'll be out for a while."

"He did not seem to understand you were not going to shoot him. I think he would have been better prepared to put up a fight if he had realized that."

Quill came around the rock carrying a pickaxe. He hefted it once. "Just as well then that he could not reach this."

"Perhaps you should keep that."

"I intend to. Get the lanterns. We're going in." He waited for Calico to come back. "I could be wrong, of course, but I don't think he knows anything about Ann's whereabouts or about Beatrice involving her."

"My impression, too. But I think Beatrice is in there, same as you, rallying her supporters."

"Hiding out, more likely. Who will stand with her if they know what she's done? Sabotage and organizing are a far cry from attempting murder."

Calico followed him into the mouth of the tunnel. "I wish we had found Ann first. Not knowing where she is gives Beatrice leverage."

"No more talking," he whispered. "These tunnels carry sound like canyons."

Calico nodded her understanding. They tread carefully and lightly, and when they reached a fork in the main tunnel, they stopped and listened. Voices drifted faintly toward them from the left, and they took that route, pausing periodically to gauge what might be going on. It was difficult to pick individual words let alone a complete sentence, but they were successful in understanding tone and volume, and it seemed clear there was disagreement brewing among the participants.

They never once caught any feminine echoes.

At various points along the route there were small chambers cut into the rock. These were places where equipment had been stored as the tunnel was being dug. They represented stopping points along the route while the ore was being extracted before the decision was made to follow the vein deeper.

It was at one of these side chambers that Quill and Calico stopped and set their lanterns inside. They were closer to the conversation now, and they wanted to avoid someone noticing the swinging arc of light that accompanied them as they walked. The tunnel was dimly lit at intervals with hanging lanterns, but their eyes adjusted to the change and they moved with almost as much confidence as they had earlier.

It was only when they were within twenty feet of another side chamber that they finally heard Beatrice's voice. She spoke softly but still managed to cut through the disagreement around her.

"I do not understand your hesitation. You agreed you would help me. I made this happen for you. Stonechurch Mining is under my direction now. My brother-in-law will have no more say in any part of the operation, and my niece will follow my lead, just as you have done . . . until now."

Someone said, "It's like I said before, Mrs. Stonechurch, if you're in charge, I don't understand why you want to blow Number 3. It made some sense when we all wanted to get the pharaoh's attention, bring him to his knees, but you're telling us that's been done. By his daughter, no less."

"My husband died there," said Beatrice. "Oh, I know most of you understand how it was. I certainly have not forgotten. You saw him brought out the same as I did, but I am telling you that he died in that collapse. He was never right in his mind after that. Pain changes you, and protracted, persistent pain changes you the most. His legs withered, but so did his soul. It would have been better if Number 3 had been his tomb. That's what I want now. The symbolic gesture. I want his tomb sealed."

There was silence following this announcement. Calico and Quill exchanged glances, both of them easily convinced that Leo Stonechurch was not the only one changed by protracted, persistent pain. Beatrice Stonechurch had lost her soul as well.

"Look," said another man. In moments it was clear that he was speaking to the other men, not responding to Beatrice. "I say you do what you promised the lady. You live up to your agreements. Seems like at one time or another handshakes were exchanged, and that's a man's bond. A woman's got a right to expect that."

Every hair on the back of Calico's neck stood at attention. She took a step forward and walked right into the arm that Quill threw out to stop her. His steel bar of an arm frustrated her, but she understood the necessity of it. She relaxed, inched backward, and he removed it. When she looked over at him, his concentration was fierce. Without a doubt, he had recognized the voice also. It belonged to tall, skinny, stubble-faced Chick Tatters.

Quill returned Calico's stare. They shrugged in unison, drew their weapons, set their eyes ahead, and matched steps as they went forward.

Ann walked as far as she dared. It was not noticeably warmer, but putting distance between her and the man serving as her guard made her feel better. She thought she would have been more comfortable in the company of the other man, but her aunt did not ask her opinion, and this man, whose name Ann could not remember, was the one who volunteered to stay behind.

Ann could also not recall having seen him before, but then that meant almost nothing. She had never noticed Boone Abbot either, and he had been someone worth noticing. This broad, bearded stranger, once seen, would have been someone to avoid. She was not worldly, but she did have instincts that made her alert to danger, and the man responsible for watching over her was dangerous.

She stiffened when she heard footsteps

echoing. There were few choices available to her, and she had made so many poor ones lately that she did not trust herself to make the right one now. She could hurry ahead and hope that he would simply tire of the pursuit. There was also the possibility of slipping into one of the rooms off to the side and hoping he would pass. That offered the best chance for escape. If he passed her by, she could sneak out behind him and exit the way she came in.

She could also make a stand. How likely was it, she wondered, that she could convince him she was unafraid?

The steps drew closer. Ann Stonechurch backtracked to the last side room that she had passed and ducked inside. Lantern light in the tunnel barely reached the opening. She put her hands out and blindly felt her way along the walls to the darkest recess of the room. She was not prepared to run into anything on the floor so when she stubbed her foot against something hard and it barely moved, she came close to somersaulting over the object.

Ann held her breath and waited to hear if there was any change in the pace of the man's approach. She thought her collision might have made some noise but she could not be sure. When it had happened, all she had heard was the hammering of her own heart.

She bent and assessed the shape and size of what she had bumped. Just a wooden crate, she realized. The room was probably full of them. She had stumbled into one of the storage areas. That was all right, then. If there were enough crates, she might find some she could hide behind. The lid of the crate was slightly askew. She started to move it into position and stopped when she was filled with a sense of foreboding.

Her breathing quickened and she was aware of tightness in her chest. Some invisible pressure exerted itself against her heart. It thudded dully. The darkness disoriented her and her palms began to sweat inside her leather gloves. She tugged at her scarf, pushing it off her hair, and loosening it at her throat. It did not help her breathe any easier.

Ann tore off her gloves, laid them on the lid, and wiped her clammy hands on the sleeves of her coat. Pressing her lips together, she breathed carefully through her nose. It was something she had seen her aunt do when she was distressed. The thought continued to niggle that some part of what Beatrice did was for demonstration purposes only. Not everything about her aunt's behavior was true or real, and that understanding was only now being borne home.

Ann felt along the top of the crate to find her gloves. The unsecured lid slipped again and this time Ann did not immediately slide it back into place. She had the idea of a weapon in mind when she slipped one hand under the lid to identify what was inside the crate. She ran her fingertips along the top and felt the uneven surface. The way the contents were arranged reminded her of corduroy fabric, a vertical rib, a wale, and then another vertical rib. She recognized the cylindrical nature of what she was touching but not the object itself. To make that connection, she curled her hand around one of the paper-wrapped cylinders and separated it from the others.

It struck her as passing strange that she was unfamiliar with every aspect of what she held — the length, the diameter, the weight — and yet she had no difficulty recognizing it for what it was. What she knew about dynamite was limited to what she had heard, or overheard, her father say when he was conferring with men who worked for him, men like Frank Fordham or George Kittredge. Her father sometimes called it Hercules, and she had even caught a hint of him discussing it with Quill Mc-

Kenna. She wished she had paid more attention or asked questions. Mr. McKenna might have been willing to tell her more; her father certainly would not have.

Ann understood that what she held was relatively safe if handled carefully. She had no intention of handling it in any other way, but because of the tunnel collapse that had precipitated her uncle's death, she also knew that the stick did not necessarily have to have a lighted fuse to explode. Under certain conditions, dynamite was unstable. The problem for her was that she knew nothing about those conditions.

Ann put on her gloves and took four sticks out of the box. She chose that number simply because she could easily hold two in each hand. She replaced the lid, picked up the sticks, and continued on her blind search for a hiding place.

The rhythmic thud of footfalls in the tunnel grew closer.

Beatrice Stonechurch was the first to see the intruders. Her startled response made every man in the semicircle turn. They stood momentarily frozen, in part because of the guns pointed at them, in part because of who was holding them. Even Chick Tatters, who had encountered the pair before, was taken back by the star Quill McKenna flashed on his vest and the sight of Calico Nash in men's clothing.

Beatrice Stonechurch recovered first and pushed her way through a gap in the semicircle. She adopted a challenging posture, chin thrust forward, spine stiff, shoulders braced, and at the end of her raised arms she held a gun in a steady double grip.

"Jesus," Calico said softly, looking at Beatrice's weapon. "Is that what you clobbered me with? You were lucky it did not go off in your hand, which makes me wonder if it's even loaded."

"It's loaded. I know."

Calico shook her head and spoke in conversational tones to Quill. "I told you there was probably a gun missing from the pharaoh's collection." At her reference to Ramsey Stonechurch as the pharaoh, two of the men relaxed enough to snicker. It only required Calico's withering look to set them back on their heels.

Quill nodded in response to Calico's statement while his attention remained on Beatrice's grip and gun. He let his jacket and duster fall back into place so his badge was no longer visible. He was confident they had all seen it, but he had made it visible primarily for the benefit of Chick Tatters, the only man strapped with a gun. He hoped it would draw Chick's fire and keep him from targeting Calico first.

"Lord, Mrs. Stonechurch," said Quill, "that looks like Ramsey's Dance Brothers and Park .44 caliber revolver. I don't think you could have found a gun with a longer barrel in his case. I suppose a rifle did not suit you. You know that weapon's some twenty years old? A rare piece, too. It probably hasn't been fired since the end of the war."

"I know precisely what I have here. It belonged to my father. He gave it to my husband, and Leo put it in the case. That's how Ramsey acquired it. One more thing he allows everyone to believe belongs to him."

"Like Stonechurch Mining," said Quill.

"Yes. Like Stonechurch Mining."

Quill made no further comment about the revolver. It was a heavy weapon and the long barrel made it unwieldy. Calico, despite her injury, was in better condition to hold her Colt steady than Beatrice was to manage her six-shooter. The best evidence he had of the state of the woman's nerves was that she was not yet aware that her arms were already a fraction lower than they had been less than a minute ago.

"We are done here," said Quill. "We heard the arguments for and against. Excepting for Chick Tatters, these men are no longer so confident in your leadership." His eyes swept all five men and settled on Tatters. "Looks like the others agree, Chick. What about you?"

Under Quill's implacable stare, Chick shrank back a couple of inches.

Quill smiled, shook his head. "Up front. Where I can see you. That's better. How about you unstrap that belt you have on under your coat and put it on the floor? You're familiar with the routine. We've been through it before."

"No," said Calico. "That was Amos Bennett's gun belt we asked for. Remember? I put Chick down with a pitcher of water and my pocket piece."

"That's right. Well, Chick, I'm sure you've been asked to unstrap before. For instance, when you were a guest in the Reidsville jail. Nice and easy. Give him some room, men, just in case I have to shoot. I don't like thinking I would miss my mark, but it happens. Not often, but still." He smiled amiably as the two men on either side of Chick gave him plenty of elbowroom. Out of the corner of his eye he saw Beatrice's hands twitch. Without looking directly at her, he said. "Have a care, Mrs. Stonechurch. You move like that again and there is only one way my future wife is going to respond."

Calico said, "I still want a pretty proposal."

Quill grinned. "Working on it. How are you coming there, Chick? You are a little too slow in my estimation. There. That's better. On the ground. You stay where you are." Quill jerked his chin at the miner on Chick's left. "You." He paused and took better account of the man. "Joshua Abbot, isn't it? Now there is a damn shame." He shook his head. "Take the Remington out of the holster and push it over this way." There was no hesitation on Joshua's part, and when it was done, Quill tossed the pickaxe in his left hand behind him and picked up Chick's Remington. "I'm not as good with my left hand as I am with my right, but I'd guess you would say that it's relative."

"They would not say that," said Calico. "No one would say that." She offered the miners an apologetic smile. "What he means is that he is very, very good with his right hand. On the sinistral side? I'm figuring he is only competent." Her eyes darted to Chick Tatters as his eyes swiveled to the gun in Beatrice's hands. "Chick, I swear to God I can hear you thinking you can take Mrs.

Stonechurch's weapon and make a stand. This is what happens when you don't have Whit making plans for you. Where is he?"

Chick opened his mouth to speak and closed it when Beatrice told him to. He shrugged helplessly at Calico.

"Mrs. Stonechurch?" Calico's regard was candid. "Where is Ann?" Beatrice said nothing, but Calico noticed that she bent her elbows slightly and brought the revolver closer to her midriff. With her arms against her body, she was better able to support the weight of the gun, but she also had unwittingly changed the angle of the barrel so her aim was high. Calico almost wished she would fire; the recoil would knock her on her bustle and the confrontation would really be at an end.

"Ann," repeated Calico. "What have you done with her?"

Quill addressed the miners. "Calico is surprising me with her patience right now. I cannot begin to guess how long it will last. Where is Ann?"

Their eyes shifted left and right, but in the end, they shook their heads in unison. Chick stared straight ahead and offered no response at all. That was telling in its own right because Chick Tatters was a twitchy kind of fellow.

Quill's eyes bore into Chick's and he swore under his breath. "My God," he said to Calico. "They're together. She's left Ann and Whit together."

It was all Calico could do to keep her feet planted when she saw the truth of it on Beatrice's face. "Can you have any comprehension of what you have done? I want to believe you do not. That you could know who he is, what he's done, it's inconceivable to me that you would leave her with him. Please tell he is not alone with her. There are others, aren't there? Men who know her; men who would protect her."

Beatrice's head snapped back. The venom in Calico's voice was as poisonous as any tea she had ever brewed. "That man," she said, her eyes sliding sideways toward Chick. "The one you call Tatters. His name is Rocky Castro."

Quill snorted as he looked to Chick for confirmation. "Rocky? That's the best you could do?"

Chick shrugged. "Simon Peter. Like in the Bible."

"What's Whit calling himself now?"

Chick had to think about it. "Marcus White."

Quill remembered seeing the names of both men on the lists he looked over for

Ramsey and Frank Fordham. They had meant nothing, which was how Whit would have wanted it. He said to Beatrice, "Marcus White is Nick Whitfield." When he saw that Beatrice merely looked confused, he said to Calico, "I don't know what to believe anymore."

Calico drew Beatrice's attention back to her. "How did you know who I am? I know you did."

When Beatrice flattened her lips, Quill said, "It's better if you simply tell her what she wants to know. It must be important. Think of Ann. The danger to her is very real. Chick knows."

Chick said, "That little girl is in some kind of mess, Mrs. Stonechurch. I don't hold with what Whit does with his women, but there's no pulling in the reins when he's got his ears back."

Beatrice's hands began to shake and the revolver wobbled. "What is he talking about?"

"Answer me first," said Calico.

"There was a letter," Beatrice said. "It was addressed to you. To Katherine Nash. I picked it up at the station with all the other post. I read it and I kept it. It was from Joe Pepper in Falls Hollow. You can probably guess what he wanted you to know."

Calico could. "It was about Nick Whit-field's escape."

"It was about *someone's* escape. Except for using your ridiculous alias in the greet-ing, Mr. Pepper was cryptic. What was clear to me was that he wanted to put you on your guard."

"But you would have searched the papers for the story afterwards, so you knew he was writing about Whit. Don't bother to deny it. I am not inclined to parse your lies now. Where is Ann?"

Beatrice hesitated, although no one there could say whether it was fear for her niece that closed her throat or some desperate idea that she could still save herself.

Oddly enough, it was Chick Tatters who broke the tense silence. "Jesus, lady, tell them. You don't, they'll shoot you, and I'll tell them. Hell, I'll tell them anyway. That girl is —"

Beatrice made a quarter turn and fired at Chick. The spin lifted the revolver's barrel higher than it had been. Calico and Quill both saw it even if Chick did not. He threw himself facedown on the ground. The gun's recoil did precisely what Calico thought it would. Beatrice dropped her weapon as she stumbled backward. No man stepped in to stop the inevitable fall. Her bustle provided all the cushioning she needed and more than anyone thought she deserved. Calico holstered her Colt and picked up Beatrice's gun. There were two cartridges remaining in the chamber. She took them out, pocketed them, and placed the revolver on the ground.

"Chick?" Quill stepped forward and nudged Chick's outstretched palm. "You have something to say? Could be it'll keep you from hanging. No guarantees. That won't be up to me."

Chick's knobby chin dug into the dirt floor as he nodded. He lifted his head. "She's back at the storage tunnel. I would have stayed with her, let Whit come here, but he volunteered first and I didn't wanna spend another minute around the dynamite."

Beatrice started to pick herself up off the ground, but Calico put a boot into her shoulder and shoved her back.

"You see, Mrs. Stonechurch," Calico said. "Stomping on you this way is the sort of thing that Quill would never do. He's real mannerly. Me? I figure woman to woman, it's the proper response." Calico turned to Quill. She wobbled ever so slightly as she stepped away from Beatrice. Bile rose in her throat when her stomach turned over. She observed that Quill was alert to her distress and grateful to him for not extending a hand to assist her. She drew abreast of him. "Talk to them. I'm heading out."

Quill nodded and let her go. He ignored Beatrice and Chick and addressed the miners. "I am going to tell you what I told David Cavanaugh, who, by the way, is either still lying unconscious at the entrance or looking for a route out of Stonechurch. We know about the sabotage. We know how you slowed production in this mine. We know that Mrs. Stonechurch has promised better wages, a higher percentage of the profits, and I find no fault with you looking out for yourselves and your family's welfare, but coupling your caboose to Mrs. Stonechurch's train was probably not the wisest decision. She cares nothing about your interests. She cares only about her own, and if you still harbor any doubt about that, bear in mind that she left her niece in a tunnel where the only thing more volatile than the dynamite is the man she put in charge."

Quill pointed to Chick and then to Beatrice but continued to speak to the miners. "You're my deputies now. Consider yourselves sworn in. You're not my first choice, but you happen to be the only choice. Bring these two out, keep them close, and I will speak up on your behalf when the time comes. Do anything else — anything at all — and I will find you, and I will arrest you. Chick. Tell them what Calico will do."

"She'll kill you."

Quill nodded. He put his gun away and lowered the Remington in his left hand. "Is Whit carrying?" he asked Chick.

"You'll speak up for me, too, right?"

"You killed lawmen, Chick. I take that personal. Still, better if you just chance it and answer my question now."

Chick nodded. "He's always been partial to a Remington. He's got himself a new one."

"All right." Quill did not trouble himself to ask if everyone understood, nor did he answer Beatrice Stonechurch when she called out to him. He walked away, pausing once to take the pickaxe, and then he was gone.

Ann crouched behind a pyramid of crates. There was barely enough room for her to squeeze in, but she was oddly comforted when she settled sideways into the small space. It occurred to her that she was truly caught between a rock and a hard place, and something about that notion made her want to giggle. She pressed her lips together instead and kept them that way until the urge passed. It did not take long. The approaching footsteps froze all of her responses. That was just as well. She thought she would have begun crying when he called her name.

"Are you hiding from me?" asked Whit. His voice was a soft growl that carried deep into the tunnel. He liked the way it filled the space. "I told you not to go far." He stopped, listened. "I swear I can hear you breathing."

Ann knew he was lying. She wasn't breathing.

"Where did you go? Your aunt is here. She's come back with her friends. She's not happy that I let you out of my sight. I explained how it was, but that didn't satisfy her. Is she always so bossy?"

His voice was so close now that in Ann's mind he was standing outside the room where she was hiding. She was not far wrong, she realized, because a moment later she had a fleeting glimpse of light and shadow across the entrance. It was gone quickly as he moved on, plunging her back into darkness.

He called out to her again and continued talking. It seemed to Ann that he liked the sound of his voice, and she was grateful for that because it helped her keep his location in perspective. She understood that at some point, probably sooner than later, he would realize he had passed her, and he would turn around.

Ann could not wait any longer. She inched out of her hiding place and found her way back to the entrance to the room, this time without stubbing her foot on the crate. She hesitated on the threshold but not for long. Her guardian had not extinguished every lantern that he passed, and she could see light up ahead.

She ran toward it.

Quill caught up to Calico outside the mine. She was bent over at the waist, her hands braced on her knees. She was staring at the ground and did not look up until he was beside her.

"Were you sick?" he asked.

"No. Just thought I would be." She straightened slowly. Her cheeks puffed as she blew out a breath. "I did not want it to happen in front of them."

"Where is Cavanaugh?"

"Where you left him. Out cold. We should go."

"Can you? I can go alone." He told her

about deputizing the miners and leaving them to watch over Chick and Mrs. Stonechurch. "I know. Foxes in charge of the henhouse, but short of shooting them all, it seemed to be the most expedient solution. They'll be coming out directly."

"All the more reason for me to go with you. I don't think Beatrice is safe around me. I want to give her my headache." She picked up the lantern. "Did you tell her that Ramsey is not dead?"

"No." He fell in step beside her. "I figured I'd let her find that out later. I didn't have the sense that she would take news like that in stride."

"True." Calico kept her head up, her eyes straight ahead. It helped to keep the nausea at bay.

"Whit has a gun. A Remington, Chick says."

"I thought as much when I saw Chick was carrying. He will want a piece of you and all of me. I'm trying to decide how we can use that to our advantage. I want to get him as far away from Ann as possible."

"You're thinking he'll use her for cover?"

"I would, leastways I would if I were a depraved individual in the likeness of Nick Whitfield."

"So divide and conquer?"

"Yes."

They came to the rise overlooking the footbridge and paused. There was a hint of dawn in the eastern sky and the bridge was more than an indistinct silhouette. Calico could see it was every bit the ramshackle affair that Quill had told her it was.

Quill said, "It's not too late, Calico. You can cross there and get back into town. Let me deal with Whit."

Calico said nothing. She did not even look at him.

"All right," he said. "Forget I said it."

"Forgotten." She extinguished the lantern and set it down. "There's enough light now to continue, I think."

He nodded. The lantern would merely announce their presence. The mouth of the tunnel was still dark. If Chick had told the truth, then Whit and Ann were deep inside. "Can I at least go first?"

"If you like." It was the fact that he had two guns and the pickaxe that decided her, and she told him so.

He held up the axe. "Think you can swing this if you need to?"

"I think I can do anything if I need to."

"Of course you can." And he believed it. He handed it over and led the way down the hill.

Ann heard footsteps pounding after her, but she could not tell if they were real or only real in her imagination. There was nothing to be gained by looking back; she could not cover ground any faster and she was afraid the sight of him on her heels would paralyze her.

She raced from lantern point to lantern point until she was met by darkness. She had reached the place where the lanterns were extinguished. The route to the mouth of the tunnel seemed impenetrable. Ann had no choice but to proceed with caution. She had no sense of the distance she had traveled when she finally saw the vague outline of the adit ahead of her. Moonlight was fading with the approach of dawn, and the graduated blue-gray colors of the sky illuminated the opening.

Her heart seized when she heard him shout. She knew she had not imagined his voice because when he called out a name, it wasn't hers. He yelled for someone whose name she did not recognize. There was a pause after that, and she thought he must have heard himself because when he yelled again, it was for her.

She ran on. She could no longer feel the ground under her feet. In her mind, she was flying.

Ann was still flying when she emerged from the tunnel and slammed headlong into Quill McKenna. He had no time to brace himself against her rocketing body. Her diminutive stature and finely boned frame made little difference. She brought enough force to their encounter to knock him over. He managed to toss Chick's Remington to Calico before he hit the ground. He landed flat on his back with Ann Stonechurch sprawled indelicately on top of him.

"How about that," said Calico. "I sure am glad I let you go first." She set down the axe and grabbed Ann by the collar of her coat. The young woman did not show any signs of wanting to release Quill, and he was being rather more gentle with her than their circumstances called for. She tugged hard and peeled Ann away. "Are you all right? Did he hurt you?"

Ann shook her head. "He's coming," she said between labored breaths. "He's coming!"

Calico heard Whit's angry bellow coming from the tunnel. Quill heard it, too. He scrambled to his feet and put Ann behind him. He took the Remington back and drew his Colt. Calico also drew her weapon.

Nick Whitfield charged out of the tunnel, lantern swinging wildly. Calico and Quill gave him a wide berth and let him run. He was like a mad bull. They were not certain he noticed them. It was the absence of his quarry that seemed to bring him up short. He ground to a halt and slowly turned, and indeed, it was Ann he searched for. He nodded, satisfied, when he glimpsed her peeking out from behind Quill's shoulder.

"I would just as soon shoot you as look at you," said Quill. "What you do next will determine which it will be. Take off your gun belt."

Whit was breathing hard. He indicated the lantern in his hand. "All right if I put this down?"

Quill nodded.

Whit's eyes darted to Calico. "That all right with you, too?"

"I'd just rather shoot you, but yes, do what Marshal McKenna says."

"Marshal?" He turned his attention back to Quill. "Since when?"

Quill used the barrel of the Colt to point to the ground. "Set it there."

Shrugging, Whit started to comply but then did two things simultaneously. He threw himself sideways and tossed the lantern at Quill. Calico fired. Her shot was just wide of the mark, and Whit rolled out of the way so that her second shot slammed into the ground near his head. At the same time, Quill threw up an arm to deflect the lantern. The barrel of the Remington broke the globe. He and Ann were showered by shattered glass, oil, and then fire.

Calico saw that Whit was on his feet, but she holstered her Colt and let him go when he started to run. Sheer frustration made her heave the pickaxe at his retreating back. She did not wait to see where it landed. She stripped off her duster instead and threw it over Quill and Ann as they rolled on the ground. It did not take long to smother the flames, and neither Quill nor Ann sustained any burns, although the smell of burnt wool and leather made them check themselves twice over.

Calico let Quill fend for himself and helped Ann to her feet and patted her down for hot spots. She stopped abruptly when she felt Ann's bulging pockets. "Holy Mother of God," she said softly. "Ann? Is this what I think it is?"

Ann's face crumpled as tears flooded her eyes and dripped past her dark lashes. To her credit, she did not shy away. Her voice, when she finally had the wherewithal to answer, was hardly more than a whisper. "Do you think it is dynamite?"

"I do."

Ann sucked in a shuddering breath and nodded. "I forgot about it."

Quill stepped closer to the pair. "Someone tell me I did not hear what I just heard." When neither woman spoke, he swore feelingly. "Calico. Back away from her. Ann. Don't move. Think of it this way — since you and I haven't already blown ourselves to kingdom come, the chances are very good that you are in possession of sticks that have not been compromised." He waved Calico away. Not surprisingly, she did not go eagerly, and she did not go far.

Quill took up Calico's place in front of Ann. "I am going to unbutton your coat. Do you understand?"

She nodded and bravely said, "I c-can do that."

"I know, but allow me."

Uncertain, Ann looked at Calico.

"Let him," said Calico. "He's a preacher's boy. Sometimes he just needs to do good works."

"All right."

Quill smiled. That short exchange was all he needed to unfasten Ann's coat. He was removing it from her shoulders before she realized it was open. He carried the coat closer to the entrance and laid it on the ground. Over Calico's protests, he emptied the pockets and examined the sticks. There were no crystals on the sticks or in the pockets. Keeping his back turned, he slipped two of the sticks inside his jacket, and when he returned to Ann, he gave her his coat and helped her into it. It swallowed her whole.

"How did you get the sticks?" Calico asked Ann. "Did Whit make you take them?"

"No. Whit? Is that his name? That does not seem familiar, but I couldn't remember."

"Maybe he told you it was Marcus White, but he's Nick Whitfield."

"Oh. Yes, you're right. I heard both. But no, he did not force them on me. He let me wander down the tunnel. I think it was only so he could chase and trap me. I hid, and that's when I found them. There is a room filled with them, or at least I suppose that's what was in the crates. I took four sticks. I don't know why I did that. It was an impulse. I was afraid and I thought they might be useful. I swear I forgot I had them."

She blinked back tears as she looked from Calico to Quill and back again. "Tell me what's happened to my father. I shouldn't have left him. Aunt Beatrice said . . . no, it doesn't matter. I should not have left him."

Calico pulled Quill's coat more tightly around Ann. The gesture was both a hug and a shake. "Your father is going to recover. He was conscious when Quill and I left the house. He spoke to Quill. We know some — not all — of what happened. No one blames you. Ann? Look at me. None of this is your fault."

"But I gave him the —"

Quill said, "We know. Listen to Miss Nash. You are not responsible."

Unconvinced but hopeful, Ann nodded.

Calico stepped back and looked over at Quill. "I missed Whit. Twice."

"I won't tell anyone."

Ann said, "He tripped when you threw the pickaxe. I saw him go down as Mr. McKenna was tackling me. I think you might have hit him with it."

Calico's expression was a mirror of Ann's earlier one: unconvinced but hopeful. "He was heading toward the footbridge," she told Quill.

"Go on," he said. "I'll catch up. Find cover, Calico. Don't try to take him in out in the open." As she hurried away, he asked Ann, "Are there more lanterns in there?"

"Yes. But you have to go a ways before you'll come to one that is lit."

"Can you go back in there and bring one to me? You'll have to come in the general direction of the footbridge. I'll meet you." He could see she was scared, and he did not wait for her answer. She would either do it or she wouldn't. He left her shivering inside his coat and went after Calico.

Quill had no difficulty finding her. She was tucked behind the concrete block that supported an old water cannon. The monitor had not been used since gold mining days, but no one thought it was worth the time or effort to remove. Quill had reason to be glad that it was left in place because Calico was reasonably safe as long as she kept her head down.

Whit was crouched on the near side of the footbridge, partially hidden by rocks and a large mound of ice and snow that had been cleared from the bridge. His cover was almost as impenetrable as the support block Calico was using.

Quill did not have a clear shot. Crouching, he sprinted toward Calico. Whit fired once. The shot kicked up bits of rock half a yard in front of Quill.

"Waste of a cartridge," Quill said as he

squeezed in beside Calico. "He wasn't close."

"His shot was forward." She added dryly, "Maybe he thought you were faster."

"Amusing. Why hasn't he crossed the bridge? I didn't hear you fire at him."

"He's been hiding there all along. I saw him before he saw me. He didn't have a chance to fire before I got this far. I can't figure him. It's getting lighter out. He is going to be visible from the other side when the miners start reporting to work."

"You think they're going to show? I have to believe there are folks who already heard shots. Maybe they're curious, but they are also keeping their distance."

Calico inched her head above the block and cannon. "He's still there. I can just make out the top of his hat against the snow." She dropped back. "In his place, I would have made a run for it into town. Better opportunities to hide there."

"He might be injured. Ann could be right, and you really did hit him with the pickaxe. It would explain why he didn't get very far. Depending where you hit him and how the axe struck, he could be in a bad way."

"I would really like to believe that."

"How's your arm?"

"Holding up. I should have been able to

hit him with at least one of my shots. I pulled to the right both times."

"Maybe, but I appreciate you stopping to help put out the fire. I'm sure Ann does, too. I did not expect that move from him." Quill edged sideways to take a peek at Whit's location. He caught him poking his head above the rocks and snow and looking in their direction. "He's trying to figure out what we're doing."

"So am I."

Quill said, "Do you suppose he's afraid to cross the bridge?"

"What?"

Quill shrugged. "I don't know. I'm just wondering if he might be scared to go across."

"I'll be darned. That never occurred to me. The bridge can hold him, can't it?"

"Sure, but maybe he doesn't realize it. Or maybe he's afraid of the deep drop under it. Some of the miners take the long way around to avoid the bridge."

"If you're right, he's stuck there until the snow melts."

"I don't know about you, but I am not in favor of waiting for the spring thaw. Maybe we can get him to go for the bridge."

"And you can pick him off."

"Maybe, but we have to get him to go for

it first." Still crouching, he inched around to look back at the way he'd come. "And there she is. Good girl."

Calico followed his gaze and saw Ann picking her way across the rough, rutted ground to reach them. "Quill! Tell her to get back and take cover."

He was already waving Ann to move out of the open when Calico spoke. Ann found relative safety behind rubble and rock.

"I thought you told her to stay put," said Calico. "What is she doing? And why does she have the lantern? It only calls attention to her."

"She's safe, and she's not coming any closer. I'm going to her." Before Calico could try to stop him, he was up and running. Whit fired at him, missed, and Calico returned fire that put Whit back in his hidey-hole. Quill was a little winded but unharmed when he reached Ann. "I did not expect you to walk out in the open that way. Calico wants a piece of me almost as much as Whit."

"I didn't know," Ann said helplessly.

"Hey. It's all right." He took the lantern. "Whit's behind that pile of snow and rock. He knows you're around, so you keep your head down no matter what happens. No matter what. Understand?"

Ann nodded.

"Good." Quill leaned in, kissed her lightly on the forehead, and said, "Lucky Boone Abbot." Then he was gone.

"What was the purpose of that?" asked Calico when Quill got back.

Quill set the lantern between them. He reached inside his jacket and produced two sticks of dynamite. "This was the purpose of that. I took these from Ann's pockets, but I needed a way to light them. Since neither of us carries matches, it had to be the lantern. Ann got it for me."

"She went back in there?" Calico shook her head, smiling faintly. "Ann Stonechurch has spine. I think even she will know that now." She pointed to the dynamite. "I take it you have a plan for that."

"I do."

"We're going to blow the bridge?"

"No. We're going to blow his cover."

Calico grinned. "Even better."

"You want to throw? I think we're going to discover that you did well with the axe."

"All right." She opened the lantern so Quill could light the fuse.

"We don't want the fuse to go out so you'll have to let it get a good burn before you pitch the stick. Aim closer to the rock, not the snow mound. If he sees it coming,

565

he should run. If he doesn't see it coming, it should punch enough rock to make him run. Ready?"

Calico looked over the water cannon to judge distance and the best target for her throw. When she dropped back down, she nodded. "Ready."

Quill lit the fuse, gave her the stick, and removed his gun as he looked around the side of the block. It was hard not to hold his breath as he waited for her to throw. He could have sworn he heard her whisper, "Fire in the hole," and then he saw the stick somersaulting through the air, covering the distance in an elegant arc, the tip of the fuse like a firefly against the dim, dawning sky.

Calico's aim was true, but she had held the stick a little too long, and it exploded just before it reached its target. Whit popped up from behind the snow mound like a prairie gopher, but he was not ready to run yet. Quill quickly lit the second stick and gave it to Calico. "Again," he said. "But don't hold it as long."

Calico counted to three, stood up, and let it fly. There was no doubt it was going to reach its target. Whit must have realized it, too, because he was up again and hobbling as fast as he could to the bridge. Rock and snow exploded in his wake. Quill had to wait for the blizzard of debris to settle to get a clear shot, and he waited another moment to gauge the rhythm of Whit's ungainly gait, and finally he waited to ease out a breath and steady his hand.

He fired.

Nick Whitfield flopped sideways over the rail of the bridge and hung there like wet laundry.

EPILOGUE

From her comfortable corner position on the parlor sofa, Calico stared at the fire while Quill added logs. He stayed there until the flames licked greedily at the new wood, and then he returned to the sofa. In the short time he had been gone, she had decided to treat the sofa as if it were a chaise and was now stretched languidly across the gold damask cushion.

"Head or feet?" he asked as his eyes grazed the length of her. "I have absolutely no preference. Either end has appeal."

That made her smile. "Then feet, please, and if you will remove my shoes, I will love you past forever."

"Done."

Calico drew her feet up and let him do the rest. Watching him deftly unfasten the tiny buttons on her black kid boots without benefit of a buttonhook was a sight to behold. She actually sighed. "You are very good at that."

He glanced sideways at her, one eyebrow arched in a significant manner. "I am motivated. The idea of being loved past forever is persuasive." Quill turned his attention back to his task, slipped the buttons free on her right shoe, and removed it. The dull thud it made when he dropped it on the rug did not drown out Calico's soft moan of pleasure. He gave her foot a gentle squeeze, patted it, and then directed his attention to the other shoe.

"Boone Abbot's gone?" asked Calico.

"I showed him out before I came here. Ann went to her room. I suspect that right now she is leaning out her window and Mr. Abbot is standing below it with stars in his eyes. I promised myself I would not intrude."

"How tolerant of you."

"She is not my daughter, and it is not, thank God, Romeo and Juliet being staged out there. Ramsey did himself proud by not holding Joshua Abbot's participation in the sabotage against Boone. No Montagues and Capulets here." He removed the second shoe and dropped it beside the first. "Stockings? On or off?"

"Off."

Quill reached under Calico's skirt and

petticoats, unfastened her suspenders, and began rolling the stockings one at a time over her knees and down her calves. When he looked over at her, he saw she had dropped her head back and closed her eyes. He added the stockings to the shoes and garters and began to consider what else she might allow him to put there.

"Feet, please."

Chuckling, he applied his thumbs to her right foot. She arched her neck and shivered. "Feels good, does it?"

"Mm." She opened one eye and looked at him. "Did you hear from Ramsey today? You never said."

"There was a telegram. He only confirmed that he would be returning tomorrow."

"With or without Beatrice?"

"He didn't say."

Calico closed her eye. "I think that's telling, don't you?"

"I was trying not to speculate, which is why I didn't say anything earlier."

"But you do think it's telling."

Quill gave her foot a good squeeze. She yelped, laughed, and tried to get her foot out of his grip but did not try very hard. When she settled back again, he relaxed his hold and continued the massage. "I think it means he found the asylum as satisfactory as he could hope for and that he will be leaving her behind as planned."

Calico nodded. "I wonder if she can comprehend the tolerance that Ramsey's shown her? The only reason she is not facing trial is because he would not have any part of it." She fell silent, thoughtful, and finally said, "Maybe that is for the best. I hope it is. I want something good for Ann. I think she is making peace with her father's decision to commit Beatrice."

"Ann had a part in that whether she realizes it or not. I would never say as much to her, but when Ramsey refused to ask her to testify against her aunt, there was really nothing left for him to do. Can you imagine Beatrice Stonechurch living the remainder of her life outside of a cell or a locked ward? There would be no peace for Ramsey or Ann. No peace for this town."

"I know. I've thought of that, too. She believed everyone betrayed her and her husband's memory. She turned on every miner who fell in with her."

"She baited them with promises and kept them hooked with the memory of her husband. Cavanaugh. Joshua Abbot. And to learn that two of the men in the circle that night were Mr. Birden and Mr. Neeley-Brown? I had to admire the net she cast and how she passed information to them through their wives."

"She was . . . *is* . . . cunning. And deeply sad. Her grief, that bottomless, abiding grief, allowed her to justify unspeakable things."

Quill abandoned Calico's right foot and took up the left. He was rewarded by her heartfelt sigh. "Do you ever wonder if she murdered her husband?"

Calico's head snapped up. She stared at him. "You, too?"

He nodded. "It was what we overheard her say about blowing up the Number 3 mine, that it should have been her husband's tomb. It started me thinking that given what he suffered, it would have been understandable if she wished he had died there. He might have thought the same thing. He might have encouraged her."

"And he might not have. I would not be too quick to look for a reason to excuse her behavior."

"Not excuse. Understand."

"That's fair," she said. "It's odd, but if she admitted to poisoning Leonard Stonechurch, I'm not certain I would believe her. I suspect she did it, but to hear her say it would make me doubt. Her hate for Ramsey is so abiding that I can imagine her confessing simply to wound him. And it would. Profoundly."

"He's always thought it should have been him in the tunnel."

"So did she." Calico slipped an embroidered pillow behind the small of her back as she sat up straight. "I never suspected that she was the one who shot at Ramsey when you were gone from Stonechurch. I thought she would have persuaded one of the miners to do it."

"I thought the same until she spoke so confidently about that antique revolver being loaded. If she had killed Ramsey then, it would have been by accident, not design. She had no idea how to handle that gun. She was still trying to scare him away. What is hard to believe is that she ever thought that would work."

"I think it was for Ann's sake that she tried that tack."

"I don't know. Ann's accidents? That was Beatrice. She was present both times. She used Ann to scare Ramsey. It worked, but she couldn't anticipate that he would hire protection. Beatrice supported Ann's desire to stay in Stonechurch because it gave her leverage. Hell, it was probably Beatrice who suggested that Ann advance her education right here. And finally, she left Ann in Whit's care. Nothing she did was for Ann's sake."

Calico said nothing. It was as they had talked about earlier. Beatrice's desperation explained things but did not excuse them. "Quill?"

"Hmm?"

"Do you have regrets about Nick Whitfield? It's been a week. You haven't said a word." Calico felt the pressure of his fingers on her foot ease and then disappear altogether. He shrugged. She said, "That is no answer."

"No, but I thought it would be telling."

She smiled a shade ruefully. "You do wish you had been able to take him alive, don't you? I wondered. I thought it was probably true, but when you didn't say anything, I didn't trust myself to know."

"You have good instincts about me. You can trust them."

"There are things I would rather hear from you, whether I think I know them or not. It's important."

"All right, then, yes, I regret the way it ended, but not because I think I did anything wrong or even that I could have done anything differently. I shot to wound him because I wanted him to face a judge and a jury and eventually a noose. That would have been justice for the deputies he murdered, for the women he hurt, for Mrs. Fry and her girls, for the attempt on your life. Throwing himself off that footbridge when we were ready to apprehend him was just cowardly. Frankly? It pissed me off."

Calico remembered the moment clearly enough: Whit slumped over the rail, blood blossoming darkly near his shoulder where Quill had shot him, and his right foot dangling awkwardly inches above the bridge as if he could not bear to put weight on it again. Calico supposed the pickaxe had been responsible for that injury, but she would never know with certainty. When Whit had raised his head and turned it in their direction, she thought at first it was to watch their approach, but then his eyes slid past her, past Quill, and focused on something behind them. Calico had looked over her shoulder and followed the direction of his gaze.

Ann was no longer behind her rocky cover. She was standing in the open, and Whit's focus was entirely on her.

Calico had said nothing to Quill about what she had seen or thought in those last moments before Whit somersaulted over the rail, so she told him now, along with the conclusion she had drawn from what Whit had done.

"I don't think he was trying to get away from us, not precisely. I think he wanted to be with her more. Not Ann. His sister. When we were at Mrs. Fry's, Chick and Amos talked about the photograph of her that he carried around. Even they thought his affection for her was unnatural. I think Ann looked like her, at least superficially. The dark hair, the small frame. Her youth. That's what he liked. It's why I had to wear a black wig when I met him. And remember that Ann told us later that he called out another name when he was chasing her? I think Nick Whitfield was more deeply disturbed at his core than Beatrice Stonechurch. He was malevolent. She was dying inside."

After a while, Quill said, "You're probably right about all of it." He resumed massaging her foot. "And you know what?"

"What?" she asked, tempering her smile because she knew what was coming.

"It still pisses me off that he got away."

Calico's response was more philosophical. "And I like to think his fall put him one hundred twenty feet closer to the gates of hell."

He gave her foot a swift squeeze with both hands as he looked sideways and offered up a somewhat sheepish grin. "I should have said something to you about it sooner."

"As long as you know it." She wiggled her toes when he found a ticklish spot. "Do you think it's too late for us to elope?"

"Elope? I thought you wanted a proper wedding."

"I want a pretty proposal. The wedding ceremony scares me. You know, the judge who is coming to Stonechurch for Chick's trial and to oversee the transfer of Beatrice's share of the mining operation to Ann could just as easily marry us. There would be no fussing."

"I was not aware there was fussing."

"That's because you have not been allowed to accompany Ann and me to the dress shops. That is Ann's doing, not mine, because if I had my way, I would make you suffer."

"Oh, I know you would. Why don't you tell me about it? I promise I will suffer."

"You are good to me, Quill." Calico shared the awful details of being poked and pinched and pinned by not one dressmaker, but two. Ann, rather lawyer-like, had successfully argued that neither dressmaker was culpable for the choices made by their husbands, and that the nature of the competition between Mrs. Birden and Mrs. Neeley-Brown demanded that both women be involved in fashioning the gown. Calico found it was better to stand back while all three of the women pored over pattern books and discussed fabrics.

"And I am not allowed to tell you what was finally decided because they said it would be unlucky."

"Do I look disappointed? I am trying to look disappointed."

She snorted. "They measured and marked and hemmed and hawed. I am certain the Union and Central Pacific came to compromise more easily than these rivals."

"Yes, but the railroads were merely joining a nation. How hard could that have been compared to choosing between velvet or striped silk? With laying track, you have your narrow and your standard gauges to consider, but with a gown, there is the stiffness of the flounces, the tightness of the bodice, the placement of the darts, the ribbons, the lace, the netting. It is —"

Laughing, she dug her toes into his thigh. "Do you have any idea what you're talking about?"

"No, but then I am confident that neither do you."

"True."

"About the wedding, do you suppose you can screw your courage to the sticking place and meet me in church?"

"If it's important to you, I can."

"It's important to me." He paused, shrugged, and said, "And no one is more surprised to hear it than I am."

Calico's heart swelled, and she realized that she was dangerously close to tears. She gave him a watery smile when he regarded her oddly. Fanning one hand in front of her face, she blinked rapidly and whispered, "I am so in love with you, Quill McKenna."

He smiled then, and when Calico glowed in response, even he felt as if he'd swallowed the sun. He held out his hand to her. "Come here."

She did, taking his hand and allowing him to pull her close. She shifted until she found her niche in the curve of his shoulder. He laid his lips against her temple, kissed her, and then moved his lips to her fiery hair and kissed her again.

"I've been thinking about that pretty proposal," he said. "I have most of it worked out."

"You do?"

"Hmm."

"If you need someone to practice it on," she said quietly, "I would not object to listening."

"You understand it's a work in progress."

She nodded.

"I haven't decided about kneeling. It seems —"

"I swear to God, Quill, I am going to get my gun."

He chuckled, squeezed her shoulders. "And there you are, the woman who threatens me, challenges me, makes me laugh. Often all at once. I do not know how *not* to love you. You are clever, courageous. You humble me, and you lift me up. How can I not want you to be with me? I will take you in marriage if you will have me, but I will never leave you if you will not. You are as infuriating as you are interesting. You are never dull. I want to stand with you, and I want you to stand with me. You are my forever, Calico Nash."

She turned her head, studied his face. Her eyes were luminous and the breath she took softly shuddered through her. "Is there a question, Quill? I think there is supposed to be a question."

"I'm coming to that. But first, the caveat."

She regarded him suspiciously. "Caveat?"

"Warning. Admonition. Caution."

"I know what caveat means. I want to hear it."

"It's this: You will not always get your way."

"I will mostly get my way."

"Maybe."

"I like my chances." She lifted her head and kissed him on the mouth. "The question?"

"Will you do me the very great honor of becoming my wife?"

Calico smiled. "Yes." She kissed him again. "Yes. You only had to ask. But I shall cherish all of it. Always."

She stood then and took him by the hand and led him upstairs. It was there in their bed, in his arms, and in her heart, that she got her way by letting him have his.

ABOUT THE AUTHOR

Jo Goodman a *USA Today* bestselling author who has written multiple series, Including the Hamilton Family series and the Thorne Brothers series. Jo lives In West Virginia.